Sails of Black and Blood

The Revenge of Captain Vessia

Leslie Allen

For more information, address: leslie.allen.writing@outlook.com

First printing October 2024

Edited and Proofread by Cat Rector, Lilian Zenzi, and Carly Hayward
Cover Art by Helen Simmonds
Cover Text Design by Alexa Robin
Map Design by Leslie Allen with Wonderdraft
Interior Formatting and Design by Cat Rector

ISBN 978-1-0688150-0-3 (paperback)
ISBN 978-1-0688150-1-0 (ebook)

www.leslieallen.com

CONTENT WARNINGS

This book includes individual scenes that are graphic and may be harmful to some readers. Please proceed with caution.

Death
Violence
Needles
Deadnaming and purposeful misgendering
Public hanging
Sexual content
Starvation
Descriptions of underfed people
Emotional abuse
Parental abuse
Drowning
Forced Confinement
Grief and depression around loss of loved ones
Firearm use
Recreational alcohol, smoking, and drug use
Dark spaces
Blood, gore, and decapitation of various limbs
Descriptive scenes of biting and blood drinking, including in sexual scenarios
Poverty
Stabbing
Fire, burns, and burning buildings
Food restriction in the form of a vampire drinking rationed blood

PREFACE

To get right to the heart of it, this is not a lighthearted book. This is a book of blood and violence and living in an intolerant society, and the realities of fighting against it. This book is drawn from my own experience and traumas of being a trans woman, yet inspired by pirate history; and asking questions of how a vampire would act within that history.

Despite the dark themes of this book, I hope you find the experiences of which I've drawn, the history I've studied, and the themes of hope despite everything, enthralling.

For your convenience, there is a glossary of naval terms in the aft-end of the book.

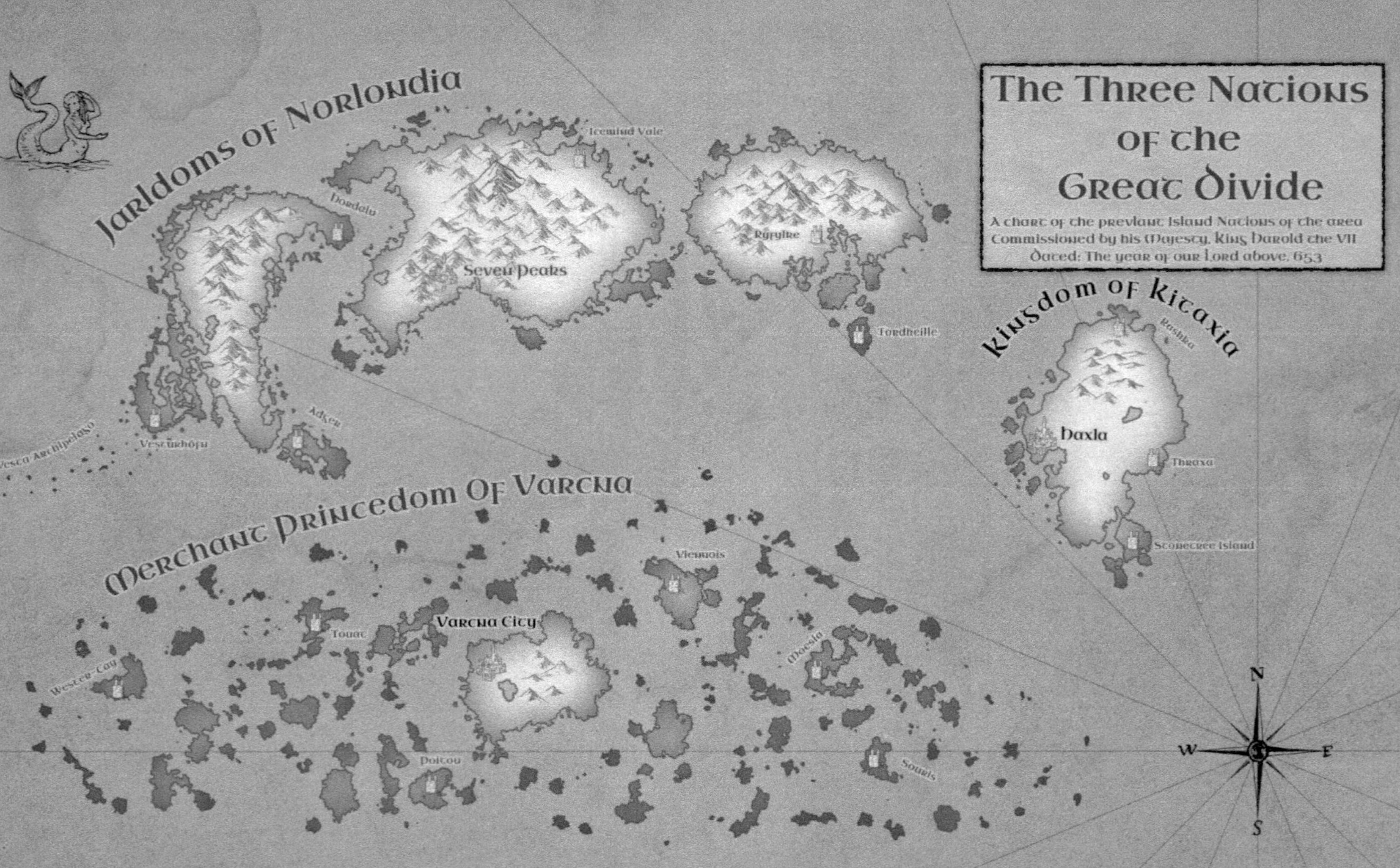

The Three Nations
of the
Great Divide
A chart of the prevlant Island Nations of the area
Commissioned by his Majesty, King Harold the VII
Dated: The year of our Lord above, 653
Jarldoms of Norlondia
Icemind Vale
Dordalu
Seven Peaks
Ryrylke
Fordheille
Adken
Vestukhofu
Vesca-Archipelago
Merchant Princedom Of Varcna
Kingdom of Kitaxia
Rashka
Daxla
Thraxa
Sconetree Island
Viennois
Varcna City
Touac
Maesia
Wester Cay
Poitou
Souris
N
W
E
S

I had to dig you out of the grave, despite an entire society piling dirt on you.

But finally, I can give you this gift.

To the girl who needed this book a lifetime ago.

CHAPTER ONE

"Captain Claire Vessia. For the crimes of murder in the highest degree, piracy, high crimes against his majesty the king, and assaulting a naval vessel, you are hereby sentenced to death. You will proceed hence in one week's time to the gallows, where you will hang by the neck until dead. Do you have anything to say before his majesty's court and god above?"

I looked up from the chains shackling my wrists.

Despite wishing that he'd look at me and see the fear and misery I was feeling, to give me any passing consideration past thinking I was a nail that needed hammering, the judge's wrinkled gaze didn't shift from those damn papers on his desk.

Dread gnawed in the pit of my stomach as I opened my mouth to speak, to plead, to do anything, but the shock of his words announcing my sentence cut into my limbs, making them feel heavier than cannonballs.

They were going to hang me.

Imagining a rope around my neck, the jeering crowds, and a pitiless executioner robbed me of breath, a tightness in my lungs making me gasp for air, unable to speak.

The judge adjusted his powdered wig, finally glancing up from his papers to peer over his jewelled spectacles in my direction. There was no pity I could see in his eyes. "No? Nothing to say?"

I thought my trial would be where I'd be vindicated, that they'd all see it was just a misunderstanding, and that I was innocent.

Anything but *condemn* me.

Think Claire. Think. There has to be a way out of this.

I racked my brain for anything I could say that would spare me the gallows. The drive to run was burning in my bones, a useless feeling, as all four of my limbs were chained to the pulpit. Heavy footsteps of guardsmen getting closer from their positions echoed from behind me in the silent courtroom.

No one here would save me. The only people here were me, the judge, the two guards who'd brought me in from the cells below, and my public defender. They didn't even let my mother —or worse yet— *my husband* in to see this.

The only person whose job it was to defend me had done an all-round shit job at it.

My lawyer stood off to my side, yawning. His indifference to my sentence would've made me feel nauseous if I wasn't so scared.

"No. I have nothing to say."

It took a few seconds to realize it was me who spoke. How could I possibly sound so calm at a time like this?

They were going to *hang* me.

The judge nodded, his eyes again on his papers. "Very well. Take her away." He swished his hand dismissively as if I were a spec of dust.

The same part of my shocked mind that drove me to deny my last right to speak must've also been driving my limbs as the guards appeared at my side, unlocking me from the pulpit, chaining my limbs instead to each other. They pulled at my bindings, and I couldn't find it in myself to resist them with any more than with a half-hearted tug. Whether that was due to the miscarriage of justice happening to me or the badly bandaged gash along my stomach was anyone's guess.

I limped after them, wincing through my teeth, and noticed that the sound of misplaced justice sounded a lot like the clinking of chains.

I didn't deserve to die, I wasn't even a pirate!

Well. I was *barely* a pirate.

I didn't get a vote when my captain and his officers decided they were going to raise the black. I didn't get a say otherwise when the ship's officers voted in favour. I didn't get to voice my concerns when we jumped merchantmen with our piddly 2-pounder cannon. I was just a midshipman; *I didn't get a choice.*

How the hells we even got that lucky to take four ships before we were caught was past me.

It had been idiotic, stupid, ill-thought-out, and several other words that I thought were smart sounding and disapproving. Or at least that's what I *thought* I remembered saying when I'd explained it all to my lawyer.

If I'd actually been captain... I'd have done it differently. I'd have done it right.

Despite it all, the Kingdom of Kitaxia suffered no threats to its maritime trade. The navy was sent after us.

Barely two months of flying the black, and the navy had us scuppered.

In the resulting shipwreck, all but four of us drowned, and it was a close thing for me as well.

When they pulled the survivors from the water, we were no better than half-drowned rats, and the naval officers decided the others weren't worth keeping alive.

They were shot and tossed back into the sea.

When it was my turn to taste lead, they couldn't bring themselves to shoot a poor defenceless *woman*. Trust a Kitaxian to be sexist about executions, so help me Gods.

They clapped me in irons and dragged me back to Haxla, the capital of Kitaxia. On our way there some bright naval officer on board thought they'd get a promotion if they told the authorities that *I* was the captain of the pirate vessel. The last survivor, the terror from the sea, mastermind of it all.

And so the stage was set.

The navy had sunk the pirate vessel, captured its captain, and glory, glory to the king and all that bullshit.

I would hang because some Kitaxian navy officer wanted a promotion.

I had been looking forward to my trial, getting to prove my innocence, curse out the captain's name, and then get on the first ship out of Haxla. The judge however, seemed disinclined to believe anything my public defender had to say. From how the lawyer had listened to me, I doubted he believed me either.

Now here I was, being marched back down to the dungeons with only a few days left in this miserable existence.

I held back burning tears as they dragged me into a cell I'd now long since been acquainted with, the memory of the transition from the courthouse to the dungeons lost to panicked reflection.

The shackles around my feet were undone, along with the one around my left wrist, but my right was chained to the wall. I offered no resistance to them, even if I was more present minded to fight them, I doubt I had the physical strength to manage much.

The fire was gone out of me now, if it was ever there to begin with.

The guards nodded at their work and left me in the cell, clanging the barred door closed behind them. After a few stomps of their boots against the hard stone floor, they disappeared into the darkness beyond the bars of the cell, leaving me alone in the black void of the dungeon once more.

Only the barest hint of moonlight shining through a crack in the wall illuminated the damp stone walls, the sound of dripping moisture, and iron-forged bars that separated me from hundreds of empty cells.

In Kitaxia, you were never a prisoner for long. The gallows waited for no one.

Once I was sure they were gone, I let out a shaky breath, feeling a clutched knot of sobs rising in my chest, an ache beneath my breast.

I was going to die.

The panic seeped into my core, and I clawed at my breast, wishing I could reach in and scoop it out of me. Despite tears and angry scratches finding no purchase in my chilled skin, I crawled over to what passed for my bed, a smattering of straw in a corner. I tried to scramble together some warmth and comfort.

I concentrated on where the steel manacle cut into my cold

calloused skin. Cold and pain meant I was alive. And if I was still alive, just maybe, I could find a way out of the gallows.

How many days did the judge say? Seven days?

Actually, it was six now. It was sunset when they led me out of the courthouse.

I cursed every swear I knew, banging my fist onto the merciless stone floor from where I lay, while broken sobs choked out of my throat. I contemplated my last days in teary horror. Sitting in this damp cell, starving, near frozen to death, all before they dragged what would probably look more corpse than woman to the gallows.

They hadn't exactly been feeding me, after all. I'd had nothing but spoonfuls of water, breadcrumbs, the smallest amount I'd need to keep breathing. The medical wrappings around my abdomen, an ugly wound I got during the shipwreck, was almost certainly infected. I didn't dare look at the blackened skin attempting to heal around blood and salt-soaked shrapnel underneath. My breathing had been raspy for days, and I didn't even want to begin imagining the levels of sanitation in this bleak cell.

Every day over the past three weeks was a surprise to wake up to. I fully expected to just... not wake up one morning.

I wondered what I'd die from first? The gallows? Starvation? Infection? Or would some random guard take pity on me and do me in himself? The possibilities seemed endless. The monotony of how I questioned my end made my panic slowly die in my gut with my sobs beginning to silence as I took a shuddered breath. Pushing myself onto my back with a wince, I tried my best to find a comfortable position laying my forearm on my brow.

A cold and merciless realization settled into the void the panic had left, letting calm wash over me, despite the tears sliding down my face into my matted hair.

I'll have to die with my head held high. That's the only way I win.

I thought… I could manage that. If they were going to kill me, at least I could die well with my chin in the air. Maybe I could flip them off with my last breaths?

I started to morbidly chuckle at the idea when an unfamiliar sound echoed through the silent dungeon. Not the usual thunderous boots of the guards, or the cart bringing meals or taking out a dead cellmate, but a sure and quiet *click-clack* along the cobblestone.

Strange.

I rolled over on the straw, looking through the bars of my cell towards the hallway, to see a flickering of orange firelight bouncing off the stone walls, growing in intensity as it got closer.

Their smell wafted down the hall, reaching me long before I saw them. A near strangling smell in comparison to the filth surrounding me, something rosy and floral. Quiet and sure steps carried them around the corner and I could finally see her through the bars, making her way towards me along the damp hallway with an expression that reminded me more of a hunting hawk in flight than a person.

The moment I saw her, I almost wanted to mug her. Her outfit screamed wealth and power. She wore a heavy well-made cloak on her head and shoulders to keep off the damp and cold; I couldn't help but stare jealousy. It protected a dress that was probably the most expensive thing I'd ever seen, hugging her figure tightly around the waist in that cinching fashion highborn women used to make their curves all the more pronounced.

If I wasn't dying, I would've swooned.

Her hair colour was difficult to tell, both from the light and the cloak's hood. If I'd have to guess, auburn or brown, but for all I could've known in the lack of light, it might've been red. It was tied back in her hood's shadow in some fancy braid, but a few strands dangled to frame her face.

I'd been too busy longing for either the warmth of her body or the comfort of her cloak to save me from freezing to death to notice she was looking directly at me. Her blood red lips were fixed in a practised neutrality, but she allowed the faintest of smiles to escape them.

There was something about her ice-blue eyes, locked on me as they were, they devoured the torch's light; looking in them lit some instinctual fear that settled deep into my bones, a lighthouse warning me of dangerous shoals ahead.

She stopped a few paces outside of my cell, her eyes raking me up and down, taking an awkwardly tense moment to stare at me through the bars, maybe looking for a sign of weakness.

I sat up from the straw, crossing my legs and clasping my hands, leaning forward onto my thighs. I didn't want to admit that I was gathering strength to stand, that even just sitting up was asking a lot of my body. But the more she stared, the worse I felt. My limbs shivered, my stomach wound ached something fierce, and Gods, the things I would do for a *bite* of bread.

And here was this noble looking woman who was looking at me like a dessert.

Whatever she saw in me, I began to think that she must've liked it, as her mouth loosened ever so slightly into a tiny smirk.

"You? You're the pirate captain?" she said in some ridiculous accent I had never heard before. Heck, maybe all nobles sounded like that, it wasn't like I would know.

I gave her my best sly grin, hoping that it masked how awful I felt. "That's what they tell me."

Her smile grew.

"You're not what I expected." She replied, tapping a finger against her bottom lip. "Or maybe exactly what I expected." She added quietly, her head tipping slightly to the side in contemplation.

I shrugged a shoulder dismissively, finally dragging myself to my feet with a wince, the clinking of my chains echoing throughout the cell. Now I could look her in the eye.

I would have towered over her, if I could manage to stand straighter; she was a good head shorter than me. The unnatural fear I felt at her gaze didn't lessen with my height over her.

Squinting my eyes at her through the cell bars, I tried to examine why this minuscule woman held such an aura of dread. She was dainty, *tiny* even, yet her gaze left me feeling like I was looking into the eyes of the goddess of death herself; leaving me with nothing but a feeling that I should either be reverent, or terrified.

I elected to be neither.

I scratched at my forearms to avoid grasping at my bandages. "I'm not sure what to make of that, Miss. Nor am I sure I should care." My voice was as raspy as I felt, and I cursed internally at my dry throat.

She laughed at my answer, which confused me. I didn't think I was being that funny.

"Oh, I like you captain," she murmured with a smile.

Her bemusement, the odd feeling of threat I got from her, the farce of a trial, on top of my starvation and pain... I wouldn't exactly say I was at my diplomatic best. Seeing her standing there with a pretty smile with obvious excess made me furious.

Here I was dying, and here she was to lord it over me and laugh at the condemned girl.

I took a deep breath, exaggerating the rise and fall of my shoulders before I let her have it. "I can't eat or drink your appreciation of my character, Miss. So maybe you can get to the damn point of why a highborn lady such as yourself is here in the first place, gawking at the half-dead woman in the cell."

The smirk disappeared from her face and her eyes hardened; I felt my stomach drop in fear. Those impossible eyes drilled into my skull, the light of the torch flickering in them. She was silent another full minute, considering me. I crossed my arms as much as I could around the chain attached to my wrist, in hopes I was striking some image of stubbornness.

Not that I wanted to think about my image. My dark hair was still salt-caked from the sea. My tattered blood-stained shirt and pants were the only things left of my clothes, still the very same I had been pulled from the wreck in. They hadn't even left me my boots and coat, the bastards. I had barely any feeling left in my bare feet, and I made a point of standing on the straw to separate my skin from the cold cobblestone.

The things I'd do for her cloak. Maybe a drink too...

"You said you couldn't eat my 'appreciation of your character'. Food and drink. That's all you want?" She asked out of nowhere, shattering the silence between us with a voice like a silk-covered cannon-shot. I'd found myself believing for a moment that she'd turned into a statue, maybe some hunger-stricken dream, but now found myself blinking back surprise at her words that seemed to read my mind.

"Unless you got a ship out of here in that fancy dress of yours, I'd be content with not starving to death for starters. Although a warm cloak sounds..." I waved a hand towards her dress, but she only raised a single eyebrow as she slowly shook her head.

I wasn't getting the cloak.

"Food and drink. No more. In return, I ask for one thing." She leaned in towards the bars, grasping one of them to speak through the gap in between, like she only had a few moments to ask whatever she wanted of me. "Just a tiny, little, thing." Her voice sank to a needy whisper as my suspicion grew. Nothing in Kitaxia was ever given out of the kindness of their hearts. Gifts were given with malice here.

"Don't know what I have to give that you people haven't already taken," I muttered, staring into her icy eyes with a hardened look of my own, yet her smile sharpened. It looked… unnatural. Her teeth were unblemished pearls of white, yet her smile looked... hollow.

"Blood," she whispered.

I raised my own eyebrow. I must have misheard, or maybe my hearing was going from my injuries. "Pardon?"

Instead of answering, she pulled out a thin glass vial from some hidden pocket in her dress.

"Just a small vial of blood," she said, her smile turning mischievous.

Oh good. So, I didn't mishear. All she wanted was my *blood*.

I tried to imagine why a Kitaxian highborn would want such a thing. Why specifically *my* blood? There was a horde of oppressed poor just outside the lower city she could've taken advantage of. I knew,because I'd lived there myself a decade ago. I couldn't think of any reason other than 'something she can't get from elsewhere for gods knew what'.

But if I was being honest with myself, if I was going to die, dying with a full belly for a few drops of blood didn't sound like too bad a deal.

I began to consider her offer seriously, my mouth watering at the mere thought of eating. It'd been almost two months since I'd been scooped out of the sea, and just as long since had a proper meal, and all my thoughts turned to my favourite foods as I licked my lips in anticipation. It seemed my decision was already made.

I shrugged my shoulders in defeat, my chain clinking against the stone floor. "Done." As if I could've said anything else; I knew who had the power here. She'd have gotten it from me one way or another, at least this way I was getting something out of it.

I hoped.

"You'll forgive me if we don't shake on it, I'm uh, a little tied up at the moment." I raised my wrist twisting the manacle back and forth in her vision. She chuckled as she unlocked the door with a key she pulled from some hidden pocket.

"I won't hold it against you Captain," she said, her tone suddenly sounding like a new lover being sweet to me.

As soon as she was through the door, she pulled out a needle of some fashion, clasped the vial to the end of it and stood just out of reach with an isolated glare.

"Now captain. You wouldn't dare take advantage of a lady's honour and try anything would you?"

I could've sworn her eyes glowed as she said those words; as soon as she said them, my head felt like it was filled with soaked sponges. I was woozy, vision fading at the edges; it felt like I was drifting off to sleep, swaying on my feet.

"No. Of course not my lady…" someone whispered in a slurred voice. *My voice.* Wait. Had I just said that?

"Good. Now hold still, this will only pinch a bit."

Her voice sounded like sweetened honey. Music to my ears. I couldn't bear to move a muscle even if the noose was around my neck right now.

A spit of pain at my inner elbow followed a breath later; I tried to raise my gaze to look at her. My head was so heavy, and her grip was surprisingly strong on my wrist. Didn't I *want* her to do this?

"That's it. Now hold pressure there for a few minutes." She said quietly as she took my other hand in hers, shifting it to the puncture she had made, her breathing laboured more than mine.

She stepped away. My vision focused and my thoughts cleared, but felt like I'd been drugged. I tried to shake my head free of this slurry-filled feeling. "What… What did you do to me?"

She stepped out of my cell, already locking the door behind her. She stopped for a half second to give me a parting glance, before her eyes shifted back to the vial of my blood in her hand a breath later.

"Nothing untoward, I promise captain. Your food and beverage will be here for you upon the morrow. Provided this is to my... *satisfaction*... I may have another bargain for you tomorrow evening. Till then, goodnight."

I almost wanted to shout after her to explain what exactly she'd done to me, but she'd turned away, taking the light with her to leave me to wither alone in the darkness once more.

The sound of her steps disappeared as soon as she turned the corner, the light of her torch winking out in a sudden dash of darkness.

Was she real?

Had I dreamed her into existence? I didn't even know her name.

CHAPTER TWO

"The Crown announces the confession and appointed execution of Captain Claire Vessia, for crimes of high seas piracy. Public hanging shall occur on the 14th day of Hitika, at morning's zenith. To be presided over by Brother Cantun, Church of the King Undying."

— Poster on a church noticeboard in the Upper city of Haxla

My eyes fluttered open and I stretched as much as I could on my straw, trying to wiggle soreness out of the multitude of cramped muscles making themselves known. Sleeping in my cell was a hellish enterprise, but at least it passed the time.

Dawn light filtered through the tiny crack of a window, illuminating a few droplets of blood in the centre of my cell, and to my surprise, evidence that the lady had made good on our deal. Some dry bread, salted jerky, and a flagon of ale sat innocently on folded cloth by the door like a gift from the Gods.

The moment I recognized it, my stomach gurgled in a sharp stab of pain and I all but launched myself at it. I probably should've made it last. Who knew when I'd get more food?

But I was dead in six days. What was there to save for?

The bread was dry and tough to chew through, the ale was watered down, and the jerky was more salt than jerky. It all sat in my stomach like I'd swallowed a stone, but it was the first real food I'd had in weeks. After not a crumb of bread had escaped me, jerky devoured whole, and the flagon licked clean of every droplet... I was the most content since the day I was thrown into this cell. For me, it might as well have been a feast for a king.

My wrist was scratched bloody from the manacle, I was starting to lose feeling around the wound in my ribs, I was covered in month old filth, I didn't even want to imagine what the rest of me looked like, but for the first time in what felt like ages I had something to be happy about. I had a full stomach.

I leaned against the wall on my straw, my hands pillowing my head, legs stretched out and a foot tapping as I hummed one of the shanties I knew, and thought that maybe, just maybe, dying might be easy.

An hour later, like clockwork, one of the guards showed up for their morning rounds. He quickly saw the flagon from my ale, placed without a care back on the floor where it'd miraculously appeared this morning.

And I immediately cursed myself for not hiding it.

"What the fuck?" He snapped. "Where did you get that, pirate bitch?"

Whatever arrangement I'd made with that highborn lady, she *apparently* hadn't informed the guards. It seemed the Gods had other plans about my happiness this morning.

"Don't know what you're talking about, shit for brains." I replied.

Turning my gaze away from him to the wall, not knowing quite what was driving me to push my luck. Maybe the judge's sentence robbed me of a self-preservation instinct.

The guard sputtered, having obviously heard me. Why couldn't I just keep my mouth shut? I was in for it now.

"What did you say?" he demanded, a surprised fury in his voice.

"I said 'I don't know what you're talking about, shit for brains'" I replied once more, in an exasperated tone.

He opened the door to my cell with a roar, crossing the space towards where I sat against the wall. His gloves reached down to dig into my hair, a cry escaping me as I was pulled to my feet to face him. He stared at me from inches away, his face spitting fury.

"What are you trying to pull? How'd you get out?" He demanded. I stayed silent as his shouts burst spittle onto my face, my hand clutching at my bandaged side, wishing I was just a bit stronger.

The door was open, it was *right there*, and he was alone. Gods, the *keys* were even on his belt.

I tried to reach with my free hand...

"Fine. I'll have to beat it out of you then." He let me go, and my grasp missed. He'd stepped away just enough, letting me drop to my knees.

He reached down to grab the offending flagon off of the floor. He raised it in the air, and I tensed myself for what was to come, trying to raise my hands to protect myself.

I caught the wooden mug in the face, instantly dazed. He shouted some demand that I didn't even hear through the ringing in my ears, as I tried to blink away the stars exploding in my vision. I'd been punched in the face a few times in my life, but none of those times felt like this. My half-dead body didn't know what to do with this level of physical abuse.

I didn't even notice the second hit. On the third, the mug broke as it clawed across my face, clattering to the floor at the same time I did.

I could barely register anything beyond the stars in my vision, the stinging of my face, and the fading of my consciousness, but I held on. Bloodied wetness trailed down my cheek onto the floor beneath me, my breathing coming in quick pained gasps.

I groaned, reaching for my face with my eyes clamped shut, a moment before his boot connected with my ribs, tearing my hastily made stitches, briefly lifting me off the floor with its force. I let out a loud screech as any breath still in my lungs rapidly exhaled out, leaving me gasping and reaching out for anything to clamp onto to anchor my body.

"What the fuck is going on here? Jenkins?"

A new voice shouted into the din of my gasping breaths.

My hands were wrapped around my stomach feebly, trying to will my pain away. The guard above me twisted his head towards the bars of the cell, spotting another man with greying hair staring in mute horror at us.

The asshole that had been familiarizing his boot with my stomach stopped dead and I writhed away from him as much as I could. "She had a flagon in here, she'd gotten loose somehow, so I was going to—"

"Kill her? Over somebody giving her food and ale?" The older guard suggested, disappointment bleeding into his voice.

"Well—" The first one sputtered.

"Well nothing Jenkins! Get the fuck out of there. *Someone* gave her that flagon. If it wasn't you, and it wasn't me, and you know it wasn't Roberts, he sleeps through his shifts. So who was it? Who. Was. It?" The older guard repeated his question through his teeth, emphasizing each word, nearly seething.

I thought I noticed Jenkins posture stiffen through my hazy vision. "O-oh." Jenkins muttered. The older guard shook his head as Jenkins stepped away, leaving me to grasp at my face and stomach, curling into a ball of twisted misery on the stone floor, thankful for its coolness for once.

"Exactly. I fucking told you. Once they're on death row, don't fucking touch them. Better yet, don't even go near them."

Jenkins closed the cell door, mumbling in worry as he did it. "Right. Sorry," he muttered, leaving me to barely register that the apology wasn't to me, but to the older guard.

"Come on then. Leave her," the older one ordered, as both trotted away without giving me a second thought.

My heart was beating hard, and if I wasn't hurting before, I sure as hell was now.

I sucked in air to my abused lungs, thankful the attack was over, but wishing I could fold into myself even more than I already was, breathing through my clenched jaw. Between the trauma of my ribs and the dizziness of my head, I tried to count what little blessing I had.

It could've been worse. *Far worse.* Pain meant I was still alive.

For the moment.

The lady who had taken my blood, despite having not told the guards about the food, apparently had enough of a reputation to frighten them into not killing me then and there. That in and of itself was terrifying, but I wasn't exactly in a place to do anything about it, let alone use it to my advantage. Right now, I was focused on breathing.

But... I did have something else now. Something I could use. I reached out to grasp it, lying there ever so innocently in the middle of my cell, like it was divinely placed by the Gods themselves.

A piece of broken handle from the flagon that could be made into... *something*. A weapon? A lock pick? At the very least... maybe it might save me from the noose.

The rest of the day passed quietly as I nursed my wounds and tended to my newfound tool. I wasn't brave enough to remove my bandages, so instead tore off a pant leg and wrapped it as tightly as I could manage around my midriff to staunch the additional seepage. It still hurt like hell, blood soaking the fabric slowly, but there wasn't anything else to be done.

I sat and tried to breathe through my pain, stubbornly clinging to life as the sun set and darkness once more overtook my cell.

And eventually, in the blackest hour of the night, the lady returned. Much like she'd left, appearing around the corner of the hallway as if manifesting from the darkness itself.

A torch in her hand illuminated a different dress, similar in style, a different shade of some dark colour, and again, that dark thick fur cloak that I couldn't stop wishing I could wrap around me. It felt like years since I'd touched anything soft, and I longed to stroke my fingers through that fur and hold it close.

She stood once again before my cell, in nearly the exact same spot and pose she had the previous night.

I tried to hide my improvised weapon in my shackle as much as I could, but her sharp eyes had spotted it right away.

"Really captain?" she tutted. "What do you mean to do, stake me? How laughable." She gave her head the smallest of disapproving shakes, tapping a slender finger against her bottom lip. "How perceptive and resourceful you seem to be."

I stood, but it was slow going, trying to hide the pain of how much effort it took to meet her eyes, where an undeniable hunger shone. Her gaze was different tonight. Now she looked me over less like I was dessert and more like I was the main course.

I didn't want to answer her. I couldn't. My hand wandered to the blood-soaked wrappings around my midsection. It felt like the Veiled Lady, the patron Goddess of death itself, was standing over my shoulder even now. I had no patience for whatever game this noblewoman wanted to play.

What had happened this morning was something that I wouldn't forget, and I couldn't deny the reality of my situation. Everything would be over soon.

They're going to hang me.

And yet this lady, somehow without even being in the room, was the reason that guard had stopped. She had power, influence, hells maybe even the ear of the king.

"Your face. You've been wounded," she observed, not seeming to notice the silence I was treating her with, eyes locked with severe focus on the dried blood on the side of my face. The longer I drew this out, I figured the better my chances were of getting to ask her what I wanted.

"One of the guards?" she asked, puzzling through a thought, as if she didn't know. Her expression switched from curiosity, to anger, contemplation and then to… *hunger,* in a span of seconds.

Only after another minute of silence, did she wrench her eyes from the dried blood on my face, wandering almost leisurely all over me hungrily and noticed I wasn't answering her. "You seem to be… a bit more… antagonistic towards me, captain. Was the food and drink not satisfactory?"

A breath passed as she looked me up and down curiously. It was now or never.

"What, do you want?" I crossed my arms over my manacle, doing my best to look and sound determined.

Her eyes suddenly latched onto my face, silently judging.

What did she see? A broken woman doomed to die? A pirate captain who murdered her countrymen? Just some poor girl down on her luck? Whatever she saw in my face, it made her smile.

"Do you know, you can tell so much about a person from their blood?" she asked quietly, seemingly out of nowhere.

I barely smothered the urge to roll my eyes in time.

Somehow it wasn't surprising that she decided to say something batshit weird instead of answering my very basic question. She did want my blood after all. I rolled my eyes, wishing I could just lie down and sleep through this monologue. Maybe I'd die from it instead of the gallows.

"You're brave, but not foolish. Uneducated, but smart. Unlearned, but observant. Your blood hails from Norlondia, but you were raised here in Kitaxia. And all those years at sea... You're as independent as they come. All that, I learned from your blood."

Her eyes closed as she ranted, her words seemed to be caught up for a moment in the *idea* of me. I didn't know what to say as she rambled on... but how in the hells did she know any of that?

There was no way to prove any of what she said. Was I brave, or smart? Observant? Independent, sure. I had to be to survive the Haxla slums in my youth and during my career at sea. According to her I was from Norlondia? That was news to me, not that my adoptive mothers would take issue with it. I was orphaned, and didn't know who my birth parents were.

But maybe there was something here I could push to get what I wanted.

"I take it that my little vial was satisfactory?" I asked, hoping that whatever fantasy she'd cooked up about me in her mind, it was enough to make her want more.

I bit my lip, praying to the Gods that my gamble was correct.

She smiled as she tipped her head slightly in admission. "I admit it was. Very satisfactory, in fact. I would very much like another. Name your price. Another round of food and drink, perhaps?"

I dug my nails into the palms of my hands. Finally, the question I was hoping she'd ask.

I felt my stomach lurch, as I gazed into those devouring eyes. The torchlight flickering across her proud face.

She was expecting me to beg for food and drink, and I would not.

I was done begging.

Feeling the remnants of the guard's assault, my battered body, and I knew that the only thing that was awaiting me after my last few horrid days in this cell, was death.

I wouldn't accept that.

"I want my freedom. Or you give me a quick and painless death right here, right now."

Her gaze narrowed, whether in disappointment or excitement I couldn't say. I glared back with every bit of fury I could muster. If she was looking for any weakness, any give, she wasn't going to find it.

"That is my price." I nearly spat at her feet.

She regarded me for another long awkward minute. She seemed a fan of these long silences, letting me stew in whatever she was thinking. The drip of far-off moisture and my own haggard breathing were the only audible noises in the dungeon.

Despite the quiet, she was silent and still as a statue. Again. Strangely enough, she almost looked like she *wasn't* breathing. No rise and fall of her shoulders, no sound in the cells save the subtle rattling of my chains.

I didn't budge despite the growing fear and anxiety building in my gut. I wouldn't deny that a meal a day sounded nice, Gods above and below knew I needed it. But it was nothing but a stopgap, for I only had a few more nights in this life. If she wanted my blood, it was a finite resource. She'd have to pay something I thought it was worth. And if she wasn't willing to give me either of those things...

She could take it from my corpse after the hangman was done and *choke* on it.

"Alright," she said quietly through that odd smile of hers, her voice slow-moving lava flowing into the silence between us. "Here's my final offer, since your price is so steep."

I expected her to walk away, to deny my price outright, and just order the guards to pin me down while she got her blood regardless. Not *bargain*.

I nodded, looking at her with suspicion, motioning with my chained hand for her to continue.

"Three vials. Every night till you go off to your execution. If by then, through some miracle of god you're still alive, I'll free you from the noose's consequences."

It felt like the floor had dropped out from me then and there. I tried not to let my expression shift into complete shock as my world tilted around her offer. There was a very obvious trick happening here. Some form of trap, her wording so stupidly specific. How could it *not* be?

The noose's only consequence was death. And freedom from that… That meant life.

And life meant possible, eventual, *freedom.* It had to. All for, what, eighteen little vials of blood? I thought I could handle that... Maybe. Just maybe... She was offering me a chance. The smallest chance. If I lived through her blood tax, I'd be *free.*

I couldn't say no. Even if the odds were not in my favour, I sent a silent prayer to the Goddess of Fortune.

I breathed in through my teeth, and felt my choice settle into my gut with full conviction.

"Done," I replied.

Her white, pristine, hollow looking smile widened to be as bright as the morning sun.

"I'll ask that you prove your sincerity, captain. Toss your little stake away and I will consider our bargain struck," she muttered with haughty prose, pointing a long delicate finger towards my shackle, where I'd hidden my improvised weapon.

I pulled my day's long effort out of the space between my shackle and my skin, holding it tightly. Honestly, I didn't know what I planned to do with it. Hold her captive? Assault a guard? My chances were slim at either but I had spent my entire day sharpening the little handle on my cuff to a dangerous point, and dammit I wanted to use it.

She wasn't moving, her eyes not wavering from the stick in my hand. For a moment, I could've sworn there was a smidgen of fear in her. But the reality of the situation loomed over me. I let out a deeply held breath as I tried to let the stress flow out of my body.

I tossed my little stake through the bars towards her feet, where she kicked it out of reach with finality. She looked up at me, flashing that damn unnatural smile.

"Good choice captain," she whispered.

She collected her due much like she had the previous night. Said a few words that left me half-awake and pliable somehow, and got her wretched tithe before I could free myself of it.

But unlike the previous night, I very quickly realized the consequences of the deal I had struck. One vial was a trifle. Three vials was probably fine to someone in good health. But to me? I'd been starved for days despite my 'feast' this morning, and was injured to boot. I immediately started feeling woozy after she had finished her collection.

"It wasn't part of our deal, but food and drink will be here for you once again each morning. You'll need it to replenish your fluids. Goodnight, captain."

Before I could even reply to her with how dizzy I felt after my bleeding, just like before, she disappeared into the darkness, leaving me to doze into a dreamless sleep on my straw.

I awoke the next morning to more stale bread and ale awaiting me in exactly the same spot as the previous morning.

The guards didn't show up for the usual morning rounds. Or their afternoon ones. It seemed by either the deal I'd struck or through fear of the lady, whoever she was, I was to be left on my own for now.

The days very quickly started to pass by in brief flickers of time that I could barely commit to memory. When I wasn't eating and drinking, I was sleeping, or getting blood taken from me.

My body was rebelling at the loss of its most precious fluid over my last days, leaving me near mad from it. With only so many nights to go, I could barely stay conscious. My heart felt like the loudest thing in existence, its slow beat the only thing I could concentrate on as I laid pathetically in my cell. She only had a few words for me after each collection.

On the second night before my execution, I was somehow lucid enough to ask her name.

"Oh, I'm no one of import, I like to imagine. A noble wife of Kitaxia. Nothing more." She stated as she put a stopper on her final vial of the evening, and left it at that.

She would never answer to anything other than 'my Lady', if she responded at all. Most nights, she wouldn't even bother to speak, just taking her cursed tribute and then leaving me to the darkness once again.

I couldn't even rise from my straw to eat, only barely managing to choke down the ale, before finally, the night before my appointed hanging, she came to me one final time.

Hands on hips, looking for a moment like a disappointed mother, she regarded me with an amused smile as I stubbornly refused to die. "Still alive. I'm actually impressed, captain. You cling to life with such… *ferocity*," she said, almost with amazed inevitability that I still breathed. "This has been a very profitable arrangement. Providing you are still breathing after this final tax, you shall have your appointed reward."

I barely stayed conscious enough to even amount a token resistance to her needle once again. The pain was too great, my entire body feeling either feeling numb, or inflamed with searing ache. As the blood drained from my body, she sighed happily.

"Annnnd… there. Done. You've paid your dues in full."

I chuckled darkly from where I laid in a heap on the floor, trying to lift my manacle towards her, my hands barely able to lift the steel from the straw of my bedding, let alone get up on my feet to make my escape. I hoped she'd be able to carry me. I was in no shape to walk. Even now, my vision blurred, her face looking more like a smudge on a canvas than a person.

I reached for her, my dark deliverance. "Now... get me out of here..."

She laughed in reply, making no rush to move. She instead slotted her torch into one of the slots in the wall, and lowered herself to my bedside. I felt her hands grip my shoulders, and I must've been weaker and lighter than I thought, because with no noticeable effort, she dragged me to sit against the wall, my limbs useless dead weight on the floor.

What was happening?

"Oh, captain. That wasn't the agreement," she whispered, her hand gripped my chin, pulling my face up with ease. Her smile grew ever more vicious as she tipped a vial of something into my mouth.

The liquid had a coppery metallic taste, but morphed into something delicious, a sick twist to the most tasteful wine I had ever had. I gulped it down instantly without a second thought, desperate for some tincture to alleviate my pain.

"Now... Sleep..." Her honeyed words seeped into my ear as she leaned down towards my neck, her mouth opening wide, her breath somehow cold on my skin.

I could not resist her order, and blissful rest claimed me.

CHAPTER THREE

"The transition of human to Vampyri is not a pleasant one. My subject's bodies seem to burn through every spare resource they have in a vain attempt to fight off the virus. Muscle tissue, organ health, every bit of liquid in the body… Everything is thrown at the virus in an attempt to fight it off. What results in nine times out of ten, the body is simply overwhelmed, the soul passing on to the Veiled Lady. But the ones whose will is unbowed…Well, living isn't the right word. 'Surviving' through the transition is a much more appropriate descriptor."

— ***From the journals of Valerie Du Bois, Scholar lord of Draculesti***

The morning of my execution, I awoke in more pain than I had ever felt in my life. From the moment I opened my eyes, my screams bounced off stone walls and rattled the bars of my cell, echoing throughout the empty dungeon.

That fucking bitch.

The guards, the same from before, the grizzled one and the other who beat me half to death, stood outside my cell as I twisted in my bonds. I felt uncontrollable, wild. My skin felt burned, blood boiling inside me. I could just barely understand, let alone register their conversation through the burning red haze of my vision, the aches across every inch of my skin, every muscle writhing inside me.

"Drove this one crazy. Surprised she lived through Lady Ameritia," the old veteran said.

Lady Ameritia.

Impossible. There was no way it could be her.

The fucking Crown Princess of Kitaxia herself. Heir to the throne. Bleeding me like some medical patient this entire time?

Her name felt like it was being engraved on the back of my skull, the visage of her face and her vile blue eyes a brand burning into my mind's eye.

"She kills most of them. Slow-like," he continued, ignorant of the horror on the other guard's face. "The rest are usually half dead by the time they reach the gallows. First time I've seen anything like this."

I cared not for what they had to say, their judgements, or these pitiful looks from fools of men. All I could focus on was Ameritia bleeding me like a pig, and these men were in my way.

I threw myself against the bars of my cell, reaching as far as I could towards them, clawing through the bars separating us, fury and pain propelling me into wild and unnatural contractions as I growled at them, my throat raw.

Lady Ameritia. Realising that I wasn't the first sucker to fall for her ploy only made my uncontrollable and pained rage feel brighter, more furious, more *violent.* She poisoned me with that tincture, just to make me live long enough to see the noose.

While my focus was on the guards, I didn't even realize that another guard had snuck into my cell and had unbound me from the wall. It was the bindings I felt suddenly clamping around my ankles that alerted me to their presence. Twisting towards the unexpected assailant with a wild roar only resulted in tripping on the chain's short length, and slamming into the cell floor.

Pain and panic made me try to crawl away, but guards poured into my cell and swarmed me. In moments, I was being dragged out of my cell, bound fast by every limb, manacles clasped around my body as I squirmed. Now held fast by chain, all I knew was fury and pain. Fury at Ameritia, her vials, her lies, the guards, my captain, Kitaxia.

All of them.

"Fucking hells Jenkins. You should've gagged her!" the old one bellowed beside me over my screams, dragging me forward by pulling on my bonds. Jenkins on my other side twisted away as I tried to kick him, but he held my bindings fast.

"Fuck that, have you seen her teeth? I swear she sharpened them," Jenkins replied to his superior, giving me the inspiration to chomp at him. A sick laugh escaped my throat as he visibly recoiled, and no attempt at gagging me was made. Not that I could form coherent words, there was too much pain oozing through every muscle. I was confused that I wasn't dead, no one should be able to experience this much pain and live.

It felt like I was being raked through hot coals. Everything *burned.*

Chains pulled at every joint as the guards dragged me through the darkness. They brought me step by agonizing step out of the dungeon and into the upper levels.

Where once in the light of day, and the pain ratcheted up to new heights.

My blood boiled still, searing pain skittering all over my skin. Both from inside my body and now strangely, from the *light* of the morning as well. My skin felt like it was sizzling as sunlight reached my skin. And Gods, had it always been so bright? It was overwhelming. Blinding. The sun on my open skin hurt so badly I thought I was going to vomit.

But the sun, painful as it was, illuminated something far more disturbing. A crowd had gathered for my hanging, more people in one spot than I had ever seen crowding Haxla's main square. They cheered as I was towed through them to the gallows, each seemingly throwing something foul in my direction. A piece of rotten fruit, a used dishrag, but most commonly with their poor aim, rocks that dinged off the guard's armor more than they hit me.

The townsfolk had begun a chant as I was dragged up the worn steps of the gallows and towards the rope, ominously hanging like a waiting promise. My eyes locked onto it, terror piercing the pain enough that I tossed and turned in my bonds, tugging left and right away from the sight of my doom, trying to find any way out.

But struggle was pointless, the end inevitable, the chains too thick, and my body too weak. The rope was lowered over my head almost comically slowly, no matter the tossing of my head. The executioner was even kind enough to draw my hair through the loop as he fastened the thick rope around my neck. A priest mounted the wooden stairs to join us on the wooden platform above the crowd.

I tried to wiggle my neck free of the rope, the chains around my waist and wrists denying me the ability to reach up and free myself, just as the priest began to speak to the jeering crowd.

"We gather here today—" the priest began, and *finally* I was able to get stuttered words out through the pain.

"Get. It. Over. With," I demanded, writhing in my bonds. I wanted to run, to fight, to do *anything* but submit to my doom. But this was all I could do. This last spit of defiance.

I would not go to the afterlife with the blessing of their god.

This, I thought through my grinding teeth, my seething pain, would have to be my small victory. My last laugh.

The priest gave me a single parting glance, before nodding at the executioner behind me, his silent pity speaking volumes among the crowd of jeers.

But that second of pity wasn't enough to prepare, to shout one final curse towards this hellish country before the floor dropped underneath me.

The shock of the rope breaking my fall against my neck was almost welcome, even though it felt like it should've broken my neck. It was an inevitability. But still, I would not let myself go quietly.

I choked, kicked, and fought at my bonds... But between the rope and gravity, there was nothing I could do. I almost wanted to laugh, if I hadn't been choking. That even now, here at the end, the burn of the rope against my neck was nothing compared to the burn of every muscle in my body.

But I needed *air*, and the rope's crush against my windpipe left me choking for breath that wouldn't come.

The crowd's shouts began to fade, the light began to dim.

Slowly, *slowly*, ever too slowly, death came for me.

And it was nothing like I expected.

The fire tearing through my body quieted and gave way to cold. My heartbeat, drumming with panic and pain, slowed. The air in my lungs grew cool and stale.

I swung from the gallows, all my momentum gone as my body stilled, blackness taking my vision. My muscles finally gave in and relaxed one final time.

No avenging angels came from the Kitaxian god to grant me their eternal punishment or reward. Nor was I claimed by the Veiled Lady to be taken to the waters below the world. Nothing claimed my soul that morning.

A stillness becalmed my awareness, a moment in the void of nothingness. For the first time in weeks, I felt no pain, no suffering, no sharp bite of *anything* plaguing my body. I floated in an empty expanse of black, with no thoughts, no dreams, no *nothing*.

Forever frozen in a silent swing, back and forth, back and forth, in a world of darkness.

Bit by bit… The sound of waves grew in my ears.

I opened my eyes and heard the sounds of the ocean, the busywork of a ship, and feeling the most intense hunger I had ever suffered. All the fire and pain I'd felt just moments before was now hyper-focused in my throat and jaw.

But the noose—

I reached up to grasp at my throat to remove the noose... and found it missing. A quick grasping around my body revealed my chains were gone as well. I took a moment to breathe in thanks, but my hunger was hard to think past. It burned in my throat, my mind, my gut, and most intensely... In my teeth. My entire jaw *ached* with it, a tightness in my body that felt like a hot poker was being shoved in my gums.

It took active effort, but I shifted my focus to the sensations and sounds around me. Or to be more specific, the tight cloth blanket I was stuck in.

The *sailcloth* tightly sewn around my body.

Oh Gods... *A burial at sea.*

For the briefest of seconds, I supposed I should've been thankful. Better that than putting my corpse in an iron gibbet. If I got out now— "I don't know why her highness wanted a filthy murderin' pirate to have a burial at sea," a voice walking towards me muttered.

"But I suppose we're far enough out. Ready?"

Oh. *Shit.* No no no no—

"Heave ho then. Hup!"

Despite my clawing outwards against the stubborn fabric, it was too late. They hadn't noticed my movement.

I felt the board I had been set on slide sideways as I fell several feet from the deck, the whoosh of air sweeping past rapidly before the unmistakable smack of water met my body.

Fuck.

I sucked in a quick breath as I immediately began sinking, water soaking through the cloth in an instant.

I pushed outwards, trying to find some hole to push out of, tearing at it as best as I could, but sailcloth was tough to begin with. It had to be to avoid tearing in bad winds, and underwater? It might as well have been made of steel.

I could feel myself sinking deeper, the blackness of the sea overwhelming my vision more and more by the second. With a lack of anything sharp on my person, I opened my mouth and bit into the cloth and was surprised as my teeth tore through it easily.

I pushed my hands into the hole I had made, tearing it wider, and shot through the salty water into the wake of whatever ship I had been thrown from.

Breaking the surface to breathe in the open air. And found myself... not short of breath at all. That was strange. I was under near abouts twenty feet... My lungs should've been burning.

Pushing the thought away to address the fact that my only escape from the waves was rapidly sailing away, I turned to look at the ship.

"HEY!!!" I yelled, waving wildly from where I bobbed in the waves. The aft lookout spotted me, pointing. Shouts ran up around the deck, making me let out a sigh of relief. It might be back into a cell, but at least I wouldn't drown. I began swimming towards the ship, expecting a line to be thrown.

But instead of throwing a line, there was a glint of steel lining up in the moonlight over the aft railing.

Muskets.

I dove beneath the waves just as splashes of shot exploded into the water around me. I stayed below as long as I dared, hoping they'd thought that I had drowned after all.

As I stayed longer under the waves, I found once again that my lungs didn't burn with the need for fresh air, and momentarily curious, I let myself ask the question.

Just how long can I hold my breath?

I stayed below the waves, letting them wash above me as the hull of the massive ship sailed away. Two minutes. Then three. Five. *Ten.* With gnawing worry in my gut, I rose to the surface once more.

I didn't gasp for breath as I broke the surface.

In fact, after a moment of concentrating on my lungs, it was obvious *I* wasn't breathing at all.

I racked through my memory, remembering my hanging... and the night before. The vial of liquid Ameritia had fed me before I passed out. What did she *do* to me? Some potion to… kill me temporarily? A deep sleep like death?

I bobbed in the waves, trying to push those worries aside to deal with the unbearable hunger, struggling to keep it smothered in my consciousness so I could *think.* Gods, it felt like there was an iron clamp on my head and a hot coal in my stomach.

The topmast of the ship that had carried me out here was the only part of it still poking over the horizon, and I couldn't catch it for the life of me. No one could swim that fast.

My only escape was long gone.

I'd somehow cheated death, despite being hanged, but now… I was adrift on the open sea.

And that was a death sentence.

I cast my eyes about the horizon, but there was nothing but more waves, nothing to do but float and pray I didn't starve or freeze, since *apparently* I wouldn't drown.

Without anything to distract me, I finally gave in and let myself feel the hunger in its entirety. Its intensity nearly made me gasp with how much it *hurt.* My whole body, every muscle and bone, ached with the need to eat... *something.* It was worst in my throat and teeth, a sharp need I felt in every fibre of my being, undeniable as I floated in the waves.

How could I be so hungry? How long had it been since I ate? How was I *alive?*

I didn't have an answer for any of my questions, and over the next few hours nothing came to me to explain further. How had I survived the gallows? Why wasn't I breathing? What was this inhuman hunger? Nothing made sense.

Eventually, the water began to rough up, and I looked up from my thoughts to the horizon knowing what would be there.

Dark clouds so thick you could mistake them for mountains.

A storm.

There wasn't much I could do about it. There was no shelter to swim for.

Before long, rain pattered my skin as the tips of waves crested with spray.

All the while the hunger grew harder to ignore, a burning need in the pit of my stomach. With nothing to hold onto, I loosened my limbs out into a starfish pose, and just focused on floating. Whether I liked it or not, the storm would take me where it wanted.

Hopefully somewhere where there was land.

I don't know how long I floated there in the rain. There was still no land to be seen. I became bored, surprised at my lack of exhaustion. I wasn't physically tired from keeping myself afloat for so long. Mentally however, I was exhausted. Pushing the awareness of my maddening hunger down into the bowels of my subconscious was testing my patience.

But when day finally broke, something changed.

The dawning sun, despite its beauty and expected welcome, its rays of light bursting in between the storm-clouds in dramatic fashion, overwhelmed my senses. The pain of the gallows returned in force, a sizzling on my skin, a searing of flesh that felt and almost *looked* like my skin was steaming in the sun.

It wasn't insurmountable without gritting my teeth, but Gods, it was dreadfully unpleasant. My skin felt hot, like I'd had my face pressed to a fire, the flames licking my skin for hours squeezed into a passing second. Worse still, it somehow amplified that hunger, making it all the harder to ignore.

I dove under the waves and felt some immediate relief. Thinking it was done and dealt with, I resurfaced only for it to return, making it abundantly clear that the light really was the source of that pain and discomfort.

Without anywhere to hide, I did the unthinkable. I let myself sink.

I hovered just below the surface, closed my eyes, and somehow felt myself drifting to sleep, cradled in the ocean's embrace.

Only for nightmares of the dungeon, Ameritia, and the noose to jolt me awake.

Blinked back into consciousness with alarm at what felt like a moment later, hands clamped onto my shirt, dragging me from the ocean.

I startled, reaching over my head to dislodge whatever had me, but the grip was firm, pulling me out of the waves.

"Thank the Gods above and below! You're alive!" A man's voice exclaimed, and I looked over my shoulder at the most welcome sight I could've possibly seen.

A fisherman, in an oilskin greatcoat with a thick brown beard, pulling me into his little fishing scow.

I clamped onto his arms, and helped him heave me onto the boat. I never wanted to kiss a man so desperately in my life.

Not that I'd ever kiss a man again.

I floundered into the tiny deck, the fisherman's hand on my back, as he knelt down beside me. "Are you alright? Miss? Miss? Speak to me please."

It was impossible. That I should be picked up by some kind hearted soul in the middle of Gods knew where, looking at me with concern and worry. Plucked out of a doomed fate floating on the ocean's forever more.

I couldn't help but throw my soaking arms around his neck in a sob.

"Thank you." I managed to get out, tears burning in my eyes.

His broad shoulders were shaking with laughter, his heart was hammering in his chest, and I could almost feel his blood pulsing beneath me—

How can I hear his heart?

He patted my back, ending his laugh on an awkward note as he felt me tense in his arms. "You gave me the fright of a lifetime miss. Pulling you up out of my nets like a prize catch."

The feeling of *need* at hearing his heart, a little dull rhythmic beat that couldn't be anything else. It settled in my gut, stirring a rumble of hunger that left me feeling anxious and irritable.

I tried to relax my body, remembered to *breathe*, and sucked in a ragged sigh of relief, only for the smell of him to hit me.

Salt and sea, warmth, blood, and sweat. He smelled... *delicious.* My mouth watered as I finally let him go to sit down on the deck of his small boat, my arms hanging loosely on my knees as I breathed through my teeth. I tried to make sense of the wild fire aching in every muscle, the sharp agonizing pain in my teeth and throat, the hunger making this man have a gravity I couldn't resist.

I forced myself to turn away from him to examine his boat, which was barely big enough for three people when empty, but a good half of it was filled with what looked to be a sizable catch. It forced me to nearly snuggle up beside him. But all in all, the little scow looked to be well made.

The fisherman however... Once my eyes were back on him, I couldn't look at anything else.

"Harold," the fisherman said, introducing himself a moment before pulling off his coat to put it around my shoulders. I pulled it tightly against me, desperate for its comforting embrace. It was the softest thing I'd touched in *months*, and it was still flush with his warmth. Despite the fact it was raining, and it looked to be the only coat he had, it nearly brought me to tears.

"I don't have any more water, but we're just an hour from shore. I'll take you to my wife, and we'll get a roaring fire going and warm you up." His eyes were kind and brown, like his beard, his hair tucked underneath a weathered cap. I couldn't stop my gaze wandering to his throat. The pulsing in his neck was... *distracting.*

He caught me staring as he began to set the boat in motion once again, letting loose the single sail. "What happened Miss? Can you say?"

I nodded, pulling his coat tighter. "There was... a shipwreck. I've been swimming for hours." The lie came easy, and was believable enough.

He nodded in understanding, turning the tiller with expert precision. "You're lucky the storm didn't shift this way then. Don't worry, we'll get you warmed up soon. You must be freezing."

I pushed the hunger down *again* to mentally check my body and found... I wasn't actually cold. The jacket wrapped around my shoulders was warmer than me, and its heat was fading fast.

I didn't feel... much of anything… No feeling of warmth in my core, no breath to hold in my hands to breathe warm moisture into my freezing fingers. I felt nothing.

Besides hunger.

I knew that I *should* be freezing. The ocean was the *ocean*. People died of hypothermia in minutes, yet I had been in there for hours! I put a hand to my wrist and felt... nothing. Neutrality. Soft skin under my fingers and nothing more.

Not even a heartbeat.

Was I... *dead*?

That single thought stirred the quiet song of recollected memory as we picked up speed to sail over the waves.

"I met a traveller from the eastern continent once," Mother June had once whispered quietly into my ear. *"Do you know, my darling, where that is? It's past the eastern shores of Kitaxia, across the Vibari sea."* She had been trying to get me to sleep for the hundredth time that night. I had been maybe six, or seven. It was so hard to sleep on an empty stomach in those early days.

"The land he called home was called 'Draculesti'. Such a strange name. You should've heard his accent. He told me a story of an undead monster his people knew. Their kind had ruled their country for centuries."

I had asked her what 'undead' meant with my blanket huddled around me as I had snuggled into Mum. The ghost of that same feeling hitting me again as I pulled Harold's coat tighter around me.

"It means, not quite alive, not quite dead. Something in between."
I remembered that had alarmed me. How could you die, but not be
dead? I had seen plenty of my friends die in Haxla's gutters by then.
Far too many. I knew death, even at that young age. I liked the idea of
them not being dead, no matter the circumstances for how.

"How do they do it? Become undead, and not die?" I'd asked, and
she wordlessly poked the fire outside our ramshackle tent for a quiet
moment before she had answered. I remembered that unsettled me, that
quiet pause, like she couldn't believe what she was about to say.

*"The traveller said they drank blood. They had pointed teeth to do
just that."*

I needed to see my face. *Now.*

"Do you have a mirror?" I looked up at Harold with hope and terror
from where I sat on the deck, my shoulder rubbing up against his.

He nodded with a smile, pointing at his pack laying against the
deck on the other side of me. There were only so many pockets, and
I found a small silver pocket watch where a mirror was set into its
inside cover.

It clicked open satisfyingly, and was undoubtedly a beautiful
piece, and I couldn't help but marvel at it for a moment before…

Before I saw my face in that tiny mirror, and my stomach dropped
in terror as raindrops dripped onto the mirror's well polished surface.

I wanted to blame the rock of the boat for how much the watch
shook in my hand, but I knew better.

The sea had washed the grime and filth of the dungeon away.
But... the woman that looked back at me I hardly recognized. My
skin was deathly pale, making me look like a shadowed corpse of my
old self. No longer was my skin suntanned from years of working on
sailing ships. My dark, raven coloured hair, that had looked plain and
thin before, now had a thickness to it that I couldn't deny, despite it
being soaked.

Any scar I had from my internment was gone. In fact, most of the
identifying marks on my face were gone, for there wasn't a freckle in
sight. I could no longer feel the wounds I got from the wreck in my

ribs either, or really, any injury at all.

But most noticeably striking… were my eyes.

Oh Gods, my eyes.

The sun of the morning broke through the rain-clouds for all but a second, and I saw the same danger I remembered seeing in the eyes of Ameritia, however now with a crueller difference. Their colour.

"What did they call those undead creatures who drank blood?" I had asked Mother June as I was finally falling asleep in my memory.

"Vampyri," she had replied with quiet hesitance.

My eyes were not the green I had seen in the mirror my whole life. These eyes were blood red. As the rain pitter-pattered against the coat wrapped around my shoulders, my saviour sat quietly beside me, probably in wonder at this strange woman he pulled from the sea.

I knew what I needed to do, the last piece of the puzzle to show me, without a doubt, what I had become.

I opened my mouth.

In a mix of muted horror and morbid curiosity, I instinctively flexed the muscles in my jaw that had been aching ever since I was tossed into the sea.

There, just there, extending down into view over my canines, were lengthy fangs, prominent and perfectly shaped as if I was born with them.

I looked up from the mirror into the concerned face of Harold. I could no longer push the hunger away from the forefront of my mind. It was all-consuming. There was nothing in my thoughts but my growing horror of what I was, what my body needed, and what I couldn't stop myself from doing.

"I'm so, so sorry," I said, throwing the coat off my shoulders to the deck.

Harold's face twisted from concern to fear as I crawled over him. He let go of the tiller to push me away, only to find I was immovable as stone. I grabbed his beard, wrenching his face to the side, and he cried out in pain.

The sight of his pulsing neck was all I needed to know what to do. I let the hunger override any feeling of control.

I bit down into his neck, my fangs digging into his throat viciously as blood spilled into my mouth.

I wanted to gag at what I was doing, until the taste hit my senses. It wasn't of copper and iron, but of... *everything*.

Unimaginable flavours, life and memory... I groaned into his neck with relief. It was *delicious*.

I drowned in the sensation, swallowing every drop I could in a pleasurable haze. The feeling of absolute satisfaction, my body overriding every thought with perfect clarity that yes, *this*, is what I needed.

And I needed *more*.

And really, there was so much you could know about a person from their blood.

Harold was a hard worker. He loved his wife. He loved the sea and the home they had built together. I tasted it. Devoured it.

And I could *see* it, as if it were happening in front of me in my mind's eye.

I could see they were trying for a child, that he loved that fact so, so much.

I reeled back into the present moment in shock, my mind suddenly cleared from the taste of Harold's memories and feelings as his heart beat one final time.

No. No no no no no.

I tried to put a stop to my murderous instincts as the blood flow slowed from his neck, pressing my hands against his throat to stop the bleeding, while mentally pushing against the hunger still burning brightly in the pit of my stomach, simmering in my throat.

I cried, grief and guilt tearing at my insides, painting me as deeply as Harold's blood all over my hands, my chest, *everywhere*. "No, Harold! No!"

But my eyes kept wandering not to his deadened eyes staring out over the sea one final time, but to the rivulets of blood seeping from in between my fingers.

I was still hungry.

CHAPTER FOUR

"Oaths to the Gods are never to be made lightly. But if you're going to pick a Goddess to swear to, don't be an idiot and make an oath to the Sea. The Sea never forgets what you promised her."

— Captain of the Queen of Sardis, Tarrick Yondu

Guilt tore at my unbeating heart, Harold's pocket watch swinging in between my knees. Rage burned in the back of my throat at Ameritia for turning me into... *this.*

Harold's boat lay on the sandy shore not too far from where I sat. I'd pulled Harold's body onto the sandy bar, and had dug him a shallow grave.

He would be yet one more sailor lost to sea, his wife forever wondering what had happened to him, like so many widows before.

My rescuer. And I'd killed him.

Vampyri.

Monster.

Oh, what wretched bargains you keep, Princess of Kitaxia.

The hunger had lessened now. It was much easier to settle it in the back of my mind. My jaw no longer ached with searing pain, more like a dull throb, and I had a horrifying feeling that if I had just a *bit* more blood, I could probably settle my feeling of desperate hunger to be negligible.

But for how long?

What other cursed new rules governed my existence?

I breathed in deep, and let it out with the next crash of waves.

Between feelings of anger, guilt, fury, betrayal, and brokenness... I didn't know what to do.

Behind me there was a deep mountainous jungle. Before me was the sea. I had no idea where I was, or *what* I was.

Did I deserve any of what had happened to me? Dragged across the sea to be executed for crimes I didn't have a choice in commiting, tricked into becoming some monster of undeath by the future queen of the ruling superpower of the region, and *then* thrown into the fucking sea?

I snorted. Of course not.

But nonetheless, it'd happened. I was what I was.

A monster.

I traced my finger across the blood still dripping from my mouth, licking it dry. Even the salt of the sea could not dilute its delicious taste.

Well. I'm not going to just sit here and die.

I didn't even know if I *could.*

But if I couldn't die... What was the point of living? What could I live *for?*

I stood from the sand, giving one last glance at the mound of dirt that was Harold's grave, before looking out to the sea.

One more soul laid to waste at Kitaxia's feet. At *Ameritia*'s feet. I knew that I shared some of the blame for Harold's death. My hands were still literally covered in his blood. I tossed the pocket watch onto the sand covering his grave.

Kitaxia. They're the root cause.

Them and *Ameritia.*

And suddenly, all that rage and fear, became pointed at one goal, and I knew what I was going to do.

"I swear, to the Gods above and below, that I will not rest until I burn it all to the ground." I clenched my fist, holding it out towards the ocean. "I will ruin you, and take every single little thing I can from you, Ameritia. I will repay your kindness with the death you've stolen from me a thousand times over."

Far, far away, almost out of sight, lightning arched across the sky and over the water, a flash of brilliance against the distant storm still raging. The thunder barely a whisper of noise by the time it reached my ears.

"I promise you. I will have my revenge. Against you, your country, your navy, *everyone* who let this tragedy happen. Not just my death, not just Harolds, but all the lives lost your genocidal country is responsible for. Mark my words well, for you will know the name Claire Vessia."

They had made me a monster. I would show them just what a monster really looked like.

CHAPTER FIVE

"Sailing is an art. There's countless things a good ship captain needs to consider to make a ship efficiently cut across the ocean. Wind speed and velocity, ocean currents, waveforms and height, heading, the seasonal shifts. But what a good captain needs most of all, is luck."

—Captain of the Queen of Sardis, Tarrick Yondu

Five Years Later:

I loved this moment.

All my worries, my little pains, my hunger... All of it washing away as our ship pulled out of the fog, the great wide ocean opening up before us, the sea pushing the deck back and forth in a gentle sway underneath my boots.

The sounds of waves breaking on the bow while a hundred hushed voices worked in tandem over the rigging, the snap of the sails in the wind, and the creaking of rope and wood. The smell of sea salt mixing in with the brisk air, the wind flushing my thick hair out behind me while I hung off the starboard railing, held up over the waves only by my hand grasping the rope above me.

I let this perfect moment sink into my skin, this feeling of limitless possibility before us, satisfaction deep in my bones, and I smiled from ear to ear.

Sailing, to me at least, was magical in its own way.

But all moments came to an end sooner or later. This one was disappearing with the fog as it lifted its shroud from around our ship. As the sun's rays burned away the mist, I winced as its revealing light reminded me I was unwelcome in its embrace.

I lifted myself back over the railing onto the deck, gaze locked on the masts poking out of the horizon that marked our target several leagues ahead. *A ship.* Pinching my wide-brimmed hat lower over my brow to shield me from the sun's rays, I licked my lips in anticipation, readjusting my thick spectacles to stop the light from overwhelming my eyes.

It looked like the focus of a seascape painting while the sun mercilessly glistened over the waves all around it. A beautiful depiction of a ship rising over the sea to some far-off destination.

Shame we were about to ruin it. Or we would, if we weren't going so damn *fast.*

"Haul in the royals, gallants, and tops! You want us to overshoot them? Bleed off our speed!" I shouted to the hands in the rigging above me, as I tucked my arms into my greatcoat to hide my fingers within its shade, making my voice doing the heavy lifting of promising violence to slackers.

Our target was slow. A naval transport ship at full sail, meaning it must be full to the brim with goodies, or its crew didn't know how to sail. Either way, it made it an attractive target.

And if it *was* heavy with cargo, well, wasn't it such a shame that our hold was barely half full. If all went to plan, we would be correcting that grievance.

Even then, if there wasn't cargo worth relieving them of, there were likely *other* treasures aboard catering more to *my* tastes.

My feeling was of growing excitement, despite the crew's anxiousness. There was always the possibility some of them might not live through the day. I would do my best to keep them safe, but that was the risk that came along with this life at sea.

I tried not to let my excitement bleed through to the anxious crew too much, the crew needed an iron face for leadership, not some madwoman looking giddy about bloodshed.

I turned away from the bow and marched across the weather deck of our frigate, a forty-two-gun monster with three square-rigged masts, a copper-bottom hull, and two 36-pounder chase cannons mounted in the bow. She was built by the Kitaxian navy as a ship-of-the-line, and ever since we'd stolen her, we'd given her the love only a crew of rebels, anarchists, and pirates could.

By painting over the blues and gold stripes of the Kitaxian navy on her hull in favour of grey and matted colours, like a ghost ship appearing out of the fog, seemingly risen from the deep, doing our best to make her look like her namesake.

Wraith.

All that stolen naval might, dozens of cannon strong, now bearing down on this middling military transport ahead of us that had maybe six guns *total.*

But just because she was lightly armed didn't mean they wouldn't fight back. I knew as well as anyone what a well-motivated crew could do with just a few pistols and shot. Hells, it was how we'd stolen the *Wraith* in the first place.

Despite the hopeful yet nervous mood of everyone I passed, I was grumbling as we inched closer and closer to the other ship. From what I could see, its crew was visibly alarmed at our heavy warship appearing directly behind them, the worst place that a *possible* enemy ship could be.

But their fears were slightly waylaid by looking up to our flag, flying nobly from the rigging, designating us as one of *them.*

For we were a wolf in sheep's clothing.

"Mr. Clun!" I cried out as I walked up the stairs to the quarterdeck where the *Wraith's* quartermaster, Markus Clun, stood beside the helm waiting for my command. "Let them know we're all friends here." You could likely hear the smile in my voice, despite the sun burning away the fog with its bright light sizzling on my skin, darkening my mood.

Markus, a barrel-chested man who looked like he should've been a prince rather than a pirate, all blonde hair and pretty blue eyes, grinned that perfect smile of his as he turned to carry my order to the man at the aft of the ship with the flag box.

A slew of brightly coloured communications flags rose into the sky beside the Kitaxian naval flag flying above.

Military ship Executor - safe passage - secure.

Translated: *Here to guard you on your passage.*

Even from here, a league away, I could see the glint of their spy glasses. If they suspected us, it didn't matter. The moment we'd come out of the fog they were done for. Now it was just a matter of how many lives would end today and how long it would take for them to come to terms with the inevitable.

But for now, the longer our disguise held up, the better.

Joining Markus beside the helm, the traditional spot for ship masters, I watched our sailors duck out of each other's way making quiet and brisk preparations.

Loading cannon, placing muskets and spare shot, stacking nail bombs ready to be thrown. And marching in their midst, his eyes supervising the men and women preparing for combat, was Rodger Castille, our master-at-arms. His responsibility was preparing and leading the boarders who would be taking their ship, but he was marching towards the quarter deck with purpose, holding the spyglass I'd asked for.

He held it out wordlessly, and I nodded in thanks, lowering my spectacles to bring it to my eye. The sun usually hurt my vision, but the remnants of the fog were enough for me to muscle through it. Long enough for a moment spent in contemplation at our prey, its crew moving slowly. Calmly. Without alarm.

"Thoughts?" I asked as Markus and Rodger's gazes shifted back and forth from the crew that was our responsibility and our intended target.

"It looks as though they bought it. Again," Rodger muttered, shaking his head as he leaned against the railing from where he stood halfway up the quarterdeck stairs. Rodger was very much an unserious man, but his gaze was professional, his judgement sound. Skin as dark as his hair, and he stroked his moustache with a free hand as he looked towards the opposing ship. His words made me want to crack a smile, as my gaze confirmed his observations.

They had indeed bought it. Despite reports of Kitaxian navy ships disappearing in this section of sea for weeks now, they must've thought we were here to escort them *because* of that threat.

And not that we *were* the threat.

Did they ever learn?

"Get us ready for approach then. Ready muskets in the tops. If they try anything I want shots on them before it happens." I slotted the spyglass closed, pocketing it before putting my spectacles back on, a small relief against the sun.

Rodger nodded, tapping two fingers against his brow. "Aye ma'am," he said with a mischievous smile before turning on his heel and marching down the command deck stairs.

I stared after his retreating back for just a moment. It'd been years, but it still shook me a touch whenever they called me 'ma'am'. Captain, sure. They *had* to call me that. But ma'am implied something more important than the elected title I held.

Respect.

With a breathless huff, I once more gazed at our prey over the water wondering what they'd do. By the immutable laws of piracy, they only had three options.

Run, fight, or surrender.

If they were smart, they'd surrender. We had more fighters, we were better armed, *definitely* more experienced, and we had more cannon. They got to live, we got our cargo, and no one would be harmed. Everybody wins.

If they ran, it wasn't a question of if they'd escape. We *would* catch them. We had the wind-gage, had a better sail configuration, and then once we caught them, we'd fight them anyway. And the wholesale slaughter we were capable of was legendary.

That was how it *worked*. That was how piracy *functioned*. Surrender your goods. *Or else.*

I hoped they would surrender for their sake, because otherwise...

My hunger growled in my gut at the thought of a fight, and I couldn't hold back a smile at the possibility.

Because if they fought, I got a proper meal.

Regardless of whether they chose to fight it out or not, it was rapidly approaching the time to see what we were in for.

"Ready up lads and lasses!" I shouted as I paced around the helmsman, Markus purposely avoiding tracking me with his eyes. I *liked* to pace. It passed time and let me feel like I was doing something productive.

Lowering my hand to rest on the pommel of my sword, I debated the final timing as my crew made last minute preparations to close the distance. Everyone was hustling in earnest now, the guise of low voices rising in volume as the critical moment approached.

There was a trick to raising the black. The act of throwing off the disguise at the perfect moment to let the prey know exactly how fucked they were. It had to be timed *just right*. Too early, and they have precious seconds to sober up through the shock of fear, find their courage, and fight or run.

Too late, and in their panic, they'll do something utterly stupid. Like fight or run.

If we timed it perfectly, they'd have all but a moment to imagine the worst as the two ships closed, and realize a decision has to be made *right* now, and surrender.

At the end of the day though, the choice wasn't up to me.

I watched as the *Wraith*'s hull inched ever closer to them, our ship nearly twice the size of theirs. Close enough that I could see the confusion beginning to develop on the faces of their crew as to *why* we were getting so close.

It was now or never.

"Raise the black!" I shouted, drawing my sword from its sheath to raise it overhead.

A unified shout echoed from every sailor onboard the *Wraith*, as the Kitaxian naval flag was lowered, and my personal standard was raised in a rush.

I *loved* my flag. It summed up the promise of my legend quite nicely. Two skeletal hands reaching from the lower corners on a black background, one holding a heart in offering, the other a dagger stabbing through it, dripping blood. And above and below where knife met heart, fanged teeth enclosing around it all.

The teeth were Markus's idea. I didn't quite like it, but people were terrified of the stories surrounding the *legendary Captain Claire Vessia, Bane of Kitaxia, terror of the sea, drinker of blood.*

Even though *obviously* those were just rumours.

I watched in real time as the realisation developed on their faces, processing the fact that it was *me* coming for them. The horror and terror as they looked at the black flag rising into the bright sky, twisting their faces into desperate fear just as we came into shouting distance. The *Wraith* was all but fifty feet behind them. I could see it before they could even think the decision through. The surrender was coming.

But a gruff sounding shout sounded from *their* quarterdeck, and I got a first look at the enemy captain.

A tall looking officer standing ramrod straight in perfect uniform, not looking at me, but his panicking crew.

I let out a delighted laugh, the hunger stirring in my gut as my mouth watered. I could barely hide my excitement; with one command everything had changed. This would be a *fight*. One command from the enemy captain lay the ultimate wild card of the seaborne arrangement that was piracy.

I could have the best timing, an unbeatable ship, a hardened crew, but up against a competent shipmaster who had his crew's respect and thought he had a chance of winning? He'd fight every time.

"Heave to lads and lasses! We're earning this one!" I yelled, screaming over the din. "Chasers! Fire!" Pointing my sword towards their piddly two-pounders, I heard my command repeated and echoed down into the hold, where Charlotte, our chief gunner was running the gun-crew. Not three seconds after I shouted the order, the massive cannonades in the prow barked, a loud silencing roar that rang ears across both ships.

Two giant twenty-six-pound iron balls punched into the side of the enemy ship at the perfect angle, taking out the side-railing holding their cannons, eliminating the worst threat to us in a single shot, before continuing to sail onwards, taking out anything in their path.

Railings exploded, limbs separated from men, and screams of the quickly dying were lost in the crack of gun fire.

"Hooks and muskets!" I ordered, and our crewmen responded in kind, throwing steel forked points onto their railing and rigging to drag their ship alongside. A moment later our snipers opened up from halfway up our mainmast, giving covering fire for our boarders.

Slowly they were dragged to their doom.

As our two ships became tangled up in each other, it quickly became apparent just how outclassed they were. Despite their loyalty to their shipmaster, men were throwing down their arms as we boarded them. Only a few were putting up determined resistance.

I paced up and down our quarterdeck, my hand tightening around my own blade, wishing more than anything I could be down in the melee. Steel in my hand freeing blood from veins, fighting to protect my fellow crew, I imagined I looked like some predator circling its prey.

But I was Captain. My job was to *command.*

Even though there wasn't much to command at this point. We'd pushed them back, and our cannon fire had decimated their only real defence. None of them had time to get small arms ready, so most of them were defending with what they had on hand. Fishing spears, hidden daggers, a pistol here and there.

Namely, not much.

I looked over to their captain, not more than a few dozen feet away on the opposing quarterdeck. He was looking at me through the side of his eyes, and I could almost smell his fear. With a grim smile, I motioned with the point of my blade towards where his men were screaming and dying en masse.

Pointed out the melee as if to say '*Do you really want to drag this out?*'

I watched his shoulders slump and knew it was over. He said something over his shoulder to another officer on the quarterdeck, and a moment later their flag was lowered, striking their colours.

A cheer went up among my crew, as every man aboard their vessel threw down their weapons. Everyone knew the universal sign for surrender. To strike after one has struck their colours was tantamount to spitting in the face of thousands of years of sailing tradition.

We were *pirates.* We knew better. Just because they'd surrendered didn't mean they wouldn't take the opportunity to kill us first chance they got.

"Captain! The ship is ours!" Rodger shouted from the opposing ship. He was the first of our crew to mount their quarterdeck, and currently raising his sword to the enemy captain's throat.

"Very well, Mr. Castille!" I shouted in reply over the cheers. "Take them into custody. Bring the captain and first officer to their quarters, search the rest of their hold for hideaways, and begin sectioning off the volunteers and guilty," I continued, sheathing my blade before I turned to Markus, still standing quietly beside me.

"Get us settled and ready to receive their cargo. From how slow they were running it's sizable. Get Maude and Jacine ready for the wounded," I ordered. He nodded, running off to pass along my orders. "Let's be about it, people!" I shouted, dismounting the quarterdeck stairs.

I hopped the railing and stomped across one of the boarding platforms to get my first up close view of their ship and crew.

Just like every other time, the differences between the makeup of the *Wraith* and this Kitaxian naval ship was stark. Their crew looked to be in worn clothes, no better than rags, while their men in officer uniforms looked pristine, well made, and free of filth. The men they led working for a pittance of wages, practically slaves, while their aristocratic officers lived large.

And as always, there were no women aboard their ship. Kitaxian religion demanded women serve at home as mothers and housewives. It'd been that way ever since the latest round of purges some twelve years back.

Which meant they had a *particular* fondness for vilifying me.

My crew were already separating the captured sailors into groups, but that was for later. I watched for a few moments, my crew busying themselves around the deck, moving cargo about, shuffling prisoners here and there, cautiously stalking the holds for hideaways and ambushes.

But duty, and my hunger, eventually led my feet towards their captain's door.

Stepping inside, again I was alarmed at the difference between the basic subsistence of the crew outside it, and the ostentatious taste of the officer who commanded this vessel. Fine china, silverware, silk sheets on his bunk, every expense catered to the man standing there like the greatest offence on board his vessel was *me*.

How the captain had commanded the loyalty of his crew into dying for him was something I thought best left to philosophers.

"Captain Vessia, I presume?" the man who'd been my opponent this day said to me as if I was coming over for tea. His words making me bite back a dark laugh. As if I could be anyone else.

I rubbed a thumb over my lips, briefly in wonder about if this would go down any differently than any other time. He stood behind his desk with his hands clasped behind his back, his uniform spotless, while his second in command stood at his side. Both of them had been disarmed and currently had pistols pointed at them by Rodger and another crewmate.

"The very same," I said with a smile, hooking my thumbs in my sword belt. With a nod of my head towards the door, I ordered Rodger and the crewmate out. Rodger gave me a shit-eating grin and a wink on the way out, nearly making me roll my eyes. Smarmy bastard.

Once the door closed, leaving me alone with my prisoners, I paced the room, leaving the captain and his underling to stew in the fear I heard in their hearts, tracing my fingers over their fine things. It wasn't that I didn't have fine furnishings in my cabin over on the *Wraith*—I'd stolen more than enough for my tastes over the years—but this felt like far too much. *Gaudy* almost. Not that it was surprising. This wasn't my first time dealing with Kitaxian naval captains. It wasn't even my fifth, or my eightieth.

I'd simply lost count.

"What happens now?" the captain asked, as I looked at some abstract painting that was likely worth more than my entire ship. His voice was steady despite the erratic beating of his heart. He was good at putting out a brave front, I'd give him that.

"I ask you a few questions, you most likely deny giving me the answers." I shrugged. "And then I kill you. Painfully." I twisted on my heel, turning to them with as warm a smile as I could manage, letting my hands rest on the pommel of my sword in obvious threat. They said nothing, so I volunteered the next step in this 'conversation.'

"I'm sure you've heard all sorts of stories about me. Care to name a few?"

The captain coughed, presumably to hide some sort of reaction, but the second in command gulped before he volunteered his thoughts.

"They say you're..." He couldn't finish the sentence.

"Go on." I motioned, urging him to complete the sentence as I strode forward one slow agonizing step at a time, each step as loud as a tidal wave.

"That you're... a monster. You kill most of the crew only leaving a few survivors to tell the tale. You maim and chop up the worst offenders and—" The second in command stuttered out, quickly silencing himself in horror of his own imagination.

I nodded with an apologetic smile, neither confirming nor denying the stories, watching their struggle to maintain their poise in the threat of growing fear. It was always so fascinating, what got passed around as my legend, the truth hidden in-between the lies and tall tales.

"Here's my final offer of mercy," I said politely as I sauntered forward. "If you tell me what I want to know, I will make your deaths as quick and painless as possible. If you don't, then it'll hurt. Simple as that." I raised my arms as if to welcome them into a hug.

"Don't tell her a damn thing," the captain ordered, his face stern and serious, making the second in command look from him to me and back before he tried to mimic his bravery.

Or mimic his foolishness. I would get what I wanted no matter what they did.

But this game was old now, and my patience was wearing thin.

I drew my sword, charging forward, crossing the remaining distance separating us in a blink of an eye, stabbing my blade through the second in command's throat. To their human eyes, it must've looked like I'd teleported.

"Oh, lord above," the captain mewled out as his underling's throat erupted into a fountain of blood, staining his naval coat burgundy. I couldn't help moaning out a longing sigh as he fell to his knees grasping at his mess of a throat.

Lifting a single finger, I dabbed at the river of red before he fell to the deck, bringing it to my mouth to lick clean.

Delicious.

The barest tastes of terror, bravery, and resignation.

"You killed him! He was disarmed! Why? Why did you do that?" The captain all but screamed at me, backing away in terror. I didn't deign him with a reply, instead giving him my absolute focus as I lowered my spectacles down my nose.

"*Where is the royal correspondence?*" I flexed my powers of compulsion in my demand, staring into his eyes, and felt him begin to wilt under the force of my question.

But he was too panicked, too oppositional. He knew I would kill him any moment now anyway. "I'm not telling you a damn thing!" He puckered up tighter than a clam, and I let my shoulders slump in frustration. It was worth a shot. It just meant I had to resort to more… *Messy* methods.

I strode across the space he'd retreated in a few quick strides, forcing him to back into the wall. With nowhere to go, I easily grabbed him by the scruff of the hair, wrenching aside his head, and ripped into his throat with my teeth.

His screams were a delight to hear, before I registered his taste on my tongue, instantly wishing I'd drank from the second in command instead. He'd been much tastier this… mess of a man.

The captain tasted insufferably of steam. A factory owner's son, his entire boyhood spent among the blast furnaces. His fondest memories were of his father's office, emulating him in every way. But these memories were useless to me, and so I shoved them away, hunting through the tastes of his blood for the answer to my question.

The royal correspondence. Where?

His blood offered the desired memory as I devoured his life, regretful of the taste of soot that would stick in the back of my throat for a day.

A fuzzy recollection of a palace servant, instructing him to make his best time to Seven Peaks, with a very shiny and official looking sealed letterbox, and of course that it wasn't to be opened. He'd taken great care to entrust to the servant that once it was hidden in his locked cabinet, it wouldn't be moved until it reached its intended destination.

Too bad it'll never get there.

I dropped the captain's now lifeless corpse to the floor, my hand hanging in the air, and my sword hanging lightly at my side as I hesitated for just a moment, letting myself relax.

Just after a feeding was the only time I ever felt my hunger completely fade away, and so I let myself feel completely at ease, reaching out like freedom from my hunger was *just* within my grasp. To me, there was *nothing* in this world more satisfying than these moments.

Which meant that of course, in the midst of bliss, the door slammed open behind me. I lifted a pistol out of my belt and near shot Markus dead, pulling my finger off the trigger at the last second.

"Claire," he said with a smile.

I paused for all of a second before clicking the flintlock closed. "Nearly shot your damn head off Markus," I muttered, slotting my pistol back into my belt. "What is it?"

He paused in an assessment of the bodies that littered the floor of the cabin, dabbing at his chin. "Missed a spot," he said quietly.

Oh for fucks sake.

Rolling my eyes, I raised a finger to my own chin, mirroring where he'd indicated, and yes, there was a trail of blood that had escaped me in the pleasure of the moment.

Sloppy.

"Thanks," I said awkwardly, attempting to lick my lips and wipe away the mess that I couldn't reach with my thumb.

"We got everyone present and accounted for, Rodger is going through the trials," Markus reported. "We've also gone through the manifest… But unfortunately, not a whole lot in the hold is useful to us. It's mostly building supplies for one of their new colony forts."

Fuck. I'd been counting on at least *something* more useful than timber and stone. My nose wrinkled at the thought of more Kitaxian supply forts in Norlondia.

"At this rate, there'll be more Kitaxians in Norlondia than Norns," I grumbled as I left Markus standing in the doorway, going to the cabinet the captain's memory had indicated. "Well then, let's see if it was worth it."

While goods were always worth taking from holds, the *true* target of this entire raid took all but a minute to find as Markus wandered over to watch me in quiet wonder.

A false back of a cabinet, where once a little panel was pressed in such a way...

There, just like in the memory. A lock covering a little door set into the hull. I sheathed my sword, instead pulling free one of my throwing knives, shoved it into the keyhole, and snapped the metal with ease, spilling its contents into light once more. *Vampyri* strength and speed did have its uses.

And inside the captain's little improvised safe sat a fine letterbox, with yet another ostentatious lock altogether more ceremonial than functional.

The letterbox was labelled with the royal seal of House August, a great lion clutching a crown and a blade. It was a symbol of Kitaxia's ruling family, and I wanted nothing more than to wipe that seal off the face of the planet.

We stepped over the bodies to take our little prize to the desk, Markus following at my elbow as I set the little innocent letterbox on its surface. We shared a quick glance before he nodded, a hopeful smile on his face. I snapped the lock, opening it with trepidation to where a smattering of letters sat there as innocently as a nail bomb.

Markus let out a defeated sigh, probably expecting something more scandalous or shiny, but I tore into the envelopes with excitement, skimming details of letters and contracts between some of the most powerful people in the Great Divide.

"Most of these are from the King to Jarl Viken," I stated, skimming a few of the names. Hakkon August, the King of Kitaxia, and Isolde Viken, the Jarl of Seven Peaks, had been exchanging letters for months now, haggling over something only labelled in their agreements as 'The Arrangement'. Rumours and betting rings had run rampant among the crew over what it could possibly be. Suggestions went to everything from Kitaxia annexing Norlondia one Jarldom at a time, to colony rights, to a permanent alliance between the two.

I was intent on finding out exactly what it was, in hopes of finding a new way to put the screws into the royal family.

For that I needed information. And the *best* information came from ships just like the one we now stood on. Military transport ships. The ones carrying the royal family's *mail*.

"Anything interesting in this one?" Markus's eyes had begun to wander as I read, poking through the cabin's things, pocketing a small trifle here and there.

"Eight more stipulations about mineral rights, shipbuilding prospects, ugh. Nothing useful yet. Hang on, a personal note here," I murmured while I finally read something more interesting than the math between empires.

And then my eyes widened as I read what the King of Kitaxia had proposed.

"Markus, get everything we can off this ship, and then get everyone in my quarters in an hour. This is it!" I said with quiet shock at Markus. Clenching the letter with an excited joy, hand shaking with wild nervous energy, I almost wanted to shove it under his nose. "Markus, this is *everything* we've been fighting for."

CHAPTER SIX

"The Kingdom of Kitaxia's ruling family has been kept deliberately small this generation, King Hakkon seeming to care more for religious reform than fostering a large family to guarantee his dynasty. Why he's so obsessed about fostering this 'cult of the King Undying' is still a mystery to me. Rest assured, I intend to find out."

— Lord Hartfeld, Varcnan Ambassador to the Kingdom of Kitaxia, in a letter to Varcna City

I opened the doors to my quarters in a huff, before slamming them closed behind me to seal out the noise of crew busywork and bright sunlight, finally leaving me alone to feel relief in the quiet darkness.

My hat, heavy coat, and spectacles did wonders for dealing with the sun, but it still felt like standing in a boiling pot as I wandered about the decks in the light of day.

I crossed the spacious room in a few strides, past the dinner table that was rarely used—currently covered in maps and charts—and circled around to the chair behind my spacious desk that had piles of letters, documenting my obsession of years.

My revenge on Kitaxia, and more importantly, Lady Ameritia.

The letter in my hand burned its implications in my mind. *Finally,* after so many years… There could be no better opportunity than this.

I removed my spectacles, putting them beside an oil lamp on my desk, and threw my hat onto the corner of my chair. Removing the letter from my jacket, almost unable to believe its contents, I placed it with care beside my spectacles and began removing the weight of captaincy from my shoulders. A few seconds of practised unbuckling removed my sword, throwing knives, and pistol, hanging the belts that held them over the opposite corner of my overly sized chair, and I sighed as I stretched protesting muscles into relaxation at the lack of weight.

A moment readjusting the thick black curtains that shielded my quarters from the accursed sun, before walking to the right-hand corner of my quarters, where the cubby-bunk of my bed lay, the sheets a tangled mess.

Shimmying out of my coat—but not before retrieving a flask from its innermost pockets—I tossed it onto my blankets not caring that it would make them smell of gunpowder for the foreseeable future. It wasn't like I was spending any immediate time there anyway.

I avoided sleep as often as I could.

Sleep was where the *noose* would be waiting.

I shuddered at the memory that always robbed me of a proper night's rest, popping open the flask to take a sip, the second in command's blood dripping onto my tongue.

The briefest bite of memory, just enough to distract me from mine, the taste of a summer field with a childhood sweetheart sighing into my muscles as I turned towards my private washroom.

Setting the flask on the counter, I splashed some water from the washbasin onto my face, and raised my gaze to look at my reflection in the small mirror bolted to the hull.

Not a single wrinkle, not a thread of grey in my hair. Nothing. Not a single change in five years.

Still the same wild raven coloured hair, now much better kept with spiralling braids along one side. A narrow-pointed face with dramatic slashes for eyebrows. Pale skin that looked just barely healthy, betraying no blemish or shade. Full lips that almost looked painted, only for me to realize they were still damp with blood.

As I licked my lips, I noted the only difference between now and five years ago was that my eyes had returned to their normal green, the same colour as forest leaves. It took nearly a month of living this life to learn that the shade of my irises reflected how hungry I was.

Thankfully, being a pirate held *multiple* avenues for keeping my hunger at bay, but none of them went without their own challenges.

It was always there, my hunger. Even now, it began to stir weakly in the back of my mind, just minutes after feeding. Always urging silently for *more*.

But for now, it was easily ignorable, and would be for a few days yet. Even if my gaze lingered over the shape of the flask just below my mirror.

Hunger or no, I could push that flask out of my mind easy enough. It wasn't what was on the forefront of my thoughts, for every train of thought sifting through my mind was locked on that *letter.* I shifted away from the mirror, flask in hand, and back into my cabin. The creaking of wood and the dull vibrations of water against the hull a comfort of familiarity as I returned to my desk to stare at the envelope, sitting with all the gravity of the tides.

I almost wanted to disbelieve it. It couldn't be real. But yet, seemingly inevitable like the swell of an ocean wave, here it was.

I pinched it in my fingers, as if it were made of the most fragile of glass, and reread it yet again:

To Isolde, Jarlessa of Clan Viken, ruler of Seven Peaks,

I ask that you welcome my grandson, Nicholas, in the greatest of hospitality, so that he may perform the duties expected of him as we have previously discussed surrounding the Arrangement. He shall be leaving Haxla in a week's time on my fastest ship, the Blackhawk, and escorted by two naval sloops to ward off the pirates that have become a larger menace in recent times, as you are well aware.

I expect his arrival in Seven Peaks should be upon the twelfth of Hautena, give or take a day.

No matter his request, do not indulge in his fantasies. He is there to do his duty. Nothing more.

Yours in equality and in the light of the one true god,
King Hakkon

The letter trembled in my hand as I nursed my anger and fury against her. Against *Lady Ameritia.*

King Hakkon had only *one* child. The Crown Princess, *Ameritia.*

The same Ameritia who had taken my blood. Turned me. Lied to me, and then put the noose around my neck anyway.

Which meant her *son* would be sailing right under my nose.

Fucking *Ameritia*.

Even just *confirming* that it'd been her that turned me was years of putting palace informants on my payroll. Then even *more* years waiting for the opportunity for her to sail to one of Kitaxia's neighbours on some diplomatic mission, where I could wait in ambush.

But the bitch never left the palace. Not once in all the years worth of records and mail I'd stolen, nor among the informants I'd paid, nor in the requests of diplomats I'd bribed, had there been a single message or rumour even *hinting* that she left the castle.

Years I'd been waiting, ever so patiently, to strike.

And now, if the letter was to be believed...

In ten days, her own son would be on his way to Seven Peaks.

I smothered a cackle as my anger at her twisted into sick glee, imagining the look on her face when she learned that her precious son and heir had been taken. Full of nervous energy, a bounce in my leg, fingers tapping against my desk, I rose from my chair and paced the room.

I walked in a slow circle, looking for anything to distract the twists of my thoughts from just sitting here in the dark, imagining my enemy's demise like some villain. My eyes wandered to my weapon racks, the charting cabinets, and the remnants of some meal that Gracie had brought up to entertain the crew's idea that I was human.

I'd tried a few bites, and it was... *fine*. Gracie was determined to find a meal that I enjoyed as much as blood, and I didn't have the heart to dissuade her.

These days, barely anything compared to blood.

Which reminded me of the flask, sitting in my pocket.

Lifting it to my lips, I was pulled out of my thoughts mid-stride by a solid sounding even-spaced knock that I recognised as Markus ringing out against my door.

"Come in." I ordered, screwing the top back on my flask with a sigh.

The door opened, near blinding me with light from outdoors, making me wince momentarily in pain, holding back a seething curse.

The doors were thankfully closed quickly—my officers knew better by now—and I blinked away the splotches of white that'd formed in my eyes only to see Markus and Rodger standing there blinking as if they were as blind as me.

It took me a moment to realize they *were*. I hadn't lit *any* candles.

My eyes could see in the dark just fine. Humans however...

"One minute gentlemen," I murmured quietly before striding to my desk, grabbing the match box, and beginning to light one candle after the other. The little sticks of wax were seemingly endless around my quarters. On shelves, tables, windowsills, even on a stool here and there.

Slowly, a calm and comforting orange light covered the room.

Markus and Rodger squinted in the dark, but nodded, their steps surer now that the shadows were held at bay, giving rough salutes before I returned to my desk. I flopped into the great chair that held my weapons and hat on its upper reaches, and felt the immediate relaxation of familiarity. This chair… This beautiful perfect chair. It was one of the few comforts I went out of my way to *specifically* steal when I'd become captain.

"The others should be here soon ma'am," Markus intoned as he sat in his usual spot in one of the chairs opposite my desk. "Winters is dealing with a few more injured on their part than we expected, and Jacine is making sure their hull is sound before we send them on their way. Charlotte..."

"Is being Charlotte?" I summarized pouring my flask into an empty goblet on my desk, as Rodger snorted as he leaned against the charting cabinet.

Markus diplomatically shrugged.

"They're being Charlotte," he admitted, a tone of long settled defeat in his voice.

I shook my head, sipping at my goblet of blood, the last vestiges of warmth almost completely gone. Downing the rest of it, I wanted to chase it with an ale.

Just because ale *usually* didn't compare to blood didn't mean it wasn't comforting to have a glass of *something* in hand to pass the time as we waited.

With nothing to occupy my focus, I instead examined Markus and Rodger, hunger *already* snipping in the back of my mind to look towards their throats, listen to their beating hearts.

Markus Clun was a perfect specimen of masculinity. Or at least what I supposed one was expected to be. My experience in attraction to men was a singular part of my past I did my best to forget. But he was well built with blonde wavy hair, piercing blue eyes, and a commanding demeanor. He also had a… *vulnerability* to him. It was what made him such a good quartermaster. He *listened.* He'd made nearly every woman on board swoon, along with the men who were of that particular inclination, but he'd never returned a single hint of affection shown towards him in any of the years I'd known him.

When I'd asked him about it once, he simply stated he cared not for attraction at all.

Rodger Castille on the other hand, was his polar opposite. Even with his arms crossed, looking like he had not a care in the world, he was all lanky limbs and charm. Short ruffled black hair only a few shades darker than his skin, a thick moustache to match that twitched when he smiled, and an attitude that disarmed most opponents. A former guardsman, he'd taught me everything I knew about swordplay, and never stopped flirting the entire time. He only stopped once I began to beat him at his own game.

But all that suave character fell apart when it came to his relationships. The moment he began drinking he had a hard time remembering his exes from his current fixations, and so half of the ship, and half again the port we called home, all had some form of relationship history with Rodger, women and men both.

The doors slammed open once more without warning, and this time I could not hold back a small screech as Charlotte strode in looking like they were imitating a tropical bird, all colour flat in your face. Gracie followed them in, chanting "Sorry! Sorry!" while moving to swiftly close the doors behind them so I could see again.

Sucking in a breath through my teeth as I rubbed at my eyes, I cast a murderous glance towards Charlotte, with their shaved head, men's military dress jacket (with their accurate rank of gunnery chief stitched on the sleeves) and an ill-matching lengthy skirt that was completely impractical. They looked completely out of place on board a warship. If Rodger was a hurricane of sexuality, Charlotte was a typhoon of gender.

They would only answer to being called 'they' or 'them', and anyone who so much as formed the first syllable of 'she' or 'her' quickly earned a glare that could've been lifted from the Goddess of Death herself. And that was if they *liked you.* Otherwise, it was a punch in the mouth.

A Kitaxian who, like so many others, were press-ganged into service in the navy. Since they joined up with us, they'd come into their own aboard the *Wraith.* I saw them as freedom personified, as much as their chaos-loving attitude tried the patience of most of the crew, no one could deny that they were the best at what they did. The *Wraith*'s guns were some of the quickest and most accurate on the entire Great Divide.

They gave me no words of greeting but did give me a sly wink as they hopped onto their usual spot, the corner of the dining table.

Gracie Cavendish, the ship's cook, was trailing in behind them. A shorter woman but somehow still long in limb, she always had a ready smile and an ear to listen, and her judgment was an excellent measurement of the crew's mood. Her wild flurry of frizzy brown hair almost took up twice the room her body did despite it being tied up, and as usual, she looked to be covered in flour. Her biggest passion in this world was cooking after all, and her expression was twisted into a perpetual frown of worry.

"Charlotte!" Gracie yelled, looking more like a thundercloud than a person. "Say you're sorry and knock next time!" Gracie stammered, her fists clenched at her sides like she was holding off on smacking Charlotte over the back of the head like an infuriated mother. Charlotte shrugged in reply, ignoring the cook.

"It's fine Gracie. Really," I stated with a wave of my hand. "Besides—" A quiet knock before I flung my hand back to my eyes as the door admitted one last flash of light and the final members of the *Wraith*'s officers.

Doctor Maude Winters stepped inside, and I did my best to still my breathing, because she *reeked* of blood. Her tall refined and proud stature betrayed her high-end upbringing in Varcna City, where she trained with the Surgeon's college before grief for her husband had driven her to sign on as a ship's doctor to get away from home. She stood by the door, pushing a single displaced blonde hair back into place before crossing her hands behind her back. She quietly nodded to the rest of us, not moving from the door. More out of courtesy to me I imagine, considering her smell.

Jacine, the ship's carpenter, walked past Maude to take the other seat beside Markus in front of my desk, her quiet strides sure but silent.

Like Charlotte, Jacine had a difficult issue with gender, but hers was more... oppositional. Looking at her now, you'd never know she was born a man. Some medical concoction that Maude and her partner back in port had cooked up let her go through something they had called a 'second puberty' that feminized her features.

Ever since she'd started taking it regularly four years ago, she was the happiest I'd ever seen her.

She had been so quiet once, constantly hiding her nose in a book and her eyes behind her lengthy brown hair, but now she was much more vocal, more vivid with life. I watched those bright hazel eyes and knew she was listening. Always listening.

As everyone found their spots, all eyes turned to me.

One by one, I gazed into the faces of every person in the room, knowing in my heart that I trusted each and every one of them. We had each other's backs. We'd been through everything together. Mutiny, battle, injury, and together our combined wanted posters must've been half a league long. They'd helped me carve a bloody path across the three nations of the Great Divide, and I knew without a shadow of a doubt they weren't just good people.

They were *my* people.

My crew. My friends. My *family*.

But what I was about to put forward was going to test every bit of loyalty we'd built up over the years.

"I hold in my hand," I began, as all other conversation in the room halted. "A letter from Hakkon to Isolde."

This brought out a snicker from Charlotte. "What is it now? The size of the boat he's willing to give for her to pop out his next kid?"

Everyone else tried to hide their grins and snickers, Charlotte's snide remark bringing a bit of levity to the room, as they always did. Even I felt a corner of my mouth swinging upward. But they weren't exactly wrong, a provision in one of the pages was actually about ship keel lengths.

"As interesting as that would be, what *is* happening," I said, interrupting the chuckles around the room. "Is that Hakkon is sending his grandson to Seven Peaks."

All smiles in the room were wiped away in a single breath, the silence now absolute. They all immediately grasped onto what was at stake. What I was about to propose.

"In ten days, the royal yacht will be coming up the straits escorted by two naval sloops… Carrying a prince." Now I really couldn't hide the smile from my lips. I threw the letter onto my desk towards Markus and Jacine.

"You can't mean..." Gracie said from where she stood by Charlotte, her voice and heart both trembling. The hunger in my throat *loved* that combination of noise, but this was sweet, innocent, *Gracie*. And her concern was delicious to hear, adding to my excitement of the moment..

I raised my arms as I imagined the very scenario I described. "Oh, but I do. I mean to take the yacht, and capture the royal bastard."

No one spoke, no sound was made. Hearts stilled and fluttered in panic. Excitement. *Fear.* Jacine reached forward quietly to grab the letter, then after giving it a quick glance, passed it around for everyone to read.

"Now before you start questioning me on *why*—" I said, raising my hands exasperatedly as everyone turned their worried gazes towards me from the letter being passed around. "—we've been chipping away at the armour of Kitaxia, over and over and over again. We've bled them enough to fill this hold full of bodies four times over, not to mention our own losses over the years. But have we actually *hurt* them? Have we?"

No one could answer that, their silence affirming my words as they stared towards me in a mixture of horror and fear of what I proposed to do. I pushed on.

"Of course we bloody well haven't. All we've done is kill poor people, working shitty jobs, stealing rich peoples shit. The merchants, the aristocrats, the royals..." I said the last word with venom in my voice. "They never get hurt by us, not really. Except..."

I picked up the letter that had been put back onto my desk, the coup-de-grace of my argument. "Now we *finally* have an opportunity to strike *directly* at the fucking royal family of Kitaxia. I will not let this chance to actually hurt the people that deserve it slide out of my grasp."

I stared at their muted faces, seeing the deliberations processing through their minds.

It was a huge ask. The fleet would inevitably be there to protect the prince's ship. He'd be well guarded. I would be risking—no, *spending*—the lives of everyone on board our ship with one battle. Who knew how many of us would die just so we could capture one measly little royal?

But.

It was the culmination of the last five years of my life. *Our* lives. Five fucking years of moulding myself, this crew, and this ship into a devastating weapon. It's what we were made for.

Markus was the first to break the officers' silent deliberations, "For what? What would we do with a royal brat? Ransom him? No one would pay. Why should we risk ourselves for no gain? It's only going to cost us lives and supplies," he said with his practised neutrality, quiet murmurs of agreement echoing with him. I wasn't surprised by Markus's argument; his job was to question everything I did. But I bristled at how many voices agreed with him.

"If we do this, they will hunt us," Maude said softly from where she stood by the door. "More than ever before. Why invite that terror?"

More murmurs.

"And there's not even a guarantee we'll win," Charlotte stated, reaching over to grab the letter out of my hand to reexamine it before explaining their argument, "The yacht with the brat won't be armed, but two naval sloops? We'd outmatch their weapons, but not as much as I'd like. It'd be a tough fight."

The murmurs were now a chorus, the feeling of control, of assuredness, slipping through my fingers like fine beach sand.

"I can't say I agree either, why—"

Why why why why—my thoughts screamed before the dam I kept in place to hold back my fury broke.

Slowly rising to my feet, my fists clenched around the edge of my desk, a hairbreadth away from tossing the damn thing out the fucking window. "Because they *owe it* to me," I seethed through gritted teeth, the depths of a growl in my throat.

The silence was suddenly so thick that it could've been cut by a blade.

It was only once I heard the *fear* in their hearts that I realised I was scaring them.

They might be my family, my *friends*… but they knew what I was capable of. What I'd *done*. I desperately didn't want to hurt them, I *loved* them, and if anything happened to them…

I breathed heavily, in and out, finally letting the desk go, and pushing my hair away from my eyes to grasp my forehead. Pushing that fury down into the pit of my stomach.

"I would do anything. *Anything*. For each one of you. I cannot describe how important you all are to me. But please," I whispered. "I need to do this. I can't *not* take this chance."

A single bloody tear dropped down my cheek, leaving a trail of red as it dropped from my chin to the floor.

Tears of blood. One more fact of this cursed life.

I turned away from them, to stare out a crack in my curtains at the glistening sea beyond.

"If you won't agree to this, then I'll release you to port. But this is happening. It *must,* " I ordered.

I was the captain. My word was law. But that didn't mean they were without options. A vote would have to be called for something like this. The crew would get their say.

I'd been hoping my officers would've agreed with me. I *thought* they'd agree with me.

But if the choice was between my revenge and them... My *family*...

It may cost me my soul, but I would do *anything*. Spend any cost to see Ameritia's head hanging from the bowsprit.

I would move mountains to save them, *protect* them from any harm.

But I couldn't let this opportunity slip through my fingers… I had to try. If I stopped now, what had the last five years been for? We all knew the risks. They'd known the whole time what I would do. If not the details, then the grand picture. I could protect them in this battle, I knew I could… But there was always risk. Why was this battle any different?

I didn't move, my eyes locked on the much too bright waters through the crack in my curtains. A breathy sigh was released, as some unseen communication passed between all of my officers. A few steps rang out against the deck, as my door opened and I could tell by their heartbeats everyone save Markus had left.

I wiped away the single tear, leaving a bloody smudge on my cheek.

"It still creeps me the hells out when you do that," Markus said with a smirk in his voice, making me look over my shoulder at him questioningly. "What, tell you no? Five years you've been the captain. You haven't led us wrong yet."

CHAPTER SEVEN

"Pirates sure are an equal lot. Shares split evenly across the crew?
Almost makes you wish they'd swoop outta nowhere here so you could
join em'. Know what I mean?"

"Yeah, I hear ya. If only it wasn't for the fact everyone in the world
would want ya dead."

— Reginauld Taylor and Simmons Barrington, sailors aboard the Queen
of Sardis

"Anyone who brings me the head of Captain Vessia shall have their
longship's weight in gold."

— Jarl Duncan Ryfylke to the Captains Assembly of Norlondia

It took until sundown to empty the transport of anything we deemed valuable, but like Markus had said, there wasn't much.

A few crates of sundries, woodcutting supplies, metal scrap, a few barrels of gunpowder. The most valuable items were the *art* in the captain's cabin, and that was more valuable to us as kindling than as decoration. Useless. We couldn't sell pieces that valuable, too high profile.

But now the cargo was stowed, it was time to deal with the crew. That required a bit of... *theatrics.*

Despite the crowding of the decks on both ships, the silence permeating the night was absolute. I walked out of my quarters, knowing that with each step I took there would likely be another curse at my name in the stories told of this day.

Once more, I wore the very things that made me stand out as captain. Anything to sell the story that little bit more.

Spectacles on the bridge of my nose, despite not needing them as the moon hung in the sky. My greatcoat's tail chased after my calves as I walked across the deck. A wide-brim hat sitting neatly on woven braids trailing down one side of my neck, the other side of my hair wild and free.

And most importantly, the belts holding my weapons. My sword, my pistol, a few throwing knives.

I felt like a walking promise of violence. The very spirit of piratical vengeance. For that was my role to play in this theatre of carnage. All across the Great Divide this was the image that sailors imagined when they thought of the great and terrible pirate *Claire Vessia.*

The bodies of my crew parted like waves across the prow, making way for me as I stomped across the boarding platform to the other vessel. Once across, the purpose of this evening's exercise became clear.

Set outside the crowd of onlookers, Rodger and a few others all stood silently with pistols and blades at the ready, surrounding two groups of the opposing crew sitting down on the deck. One, much larger than the other, had fifty or so men. An ill-at-ease feeling of worry bleeding off them like mist, their hearts sounded a loud staccato of fear in my ear, every gaze locked onto me to watch what was about to unfold.

The other, a much smaller group that was separated from the rest, *reeked* of terror. They made the other captives seem downright chipper.

This small group of four huddled in front of Rodger's pistol, and what happened to those men would be the story the rest would tell. The same story they'd all heard a hundred times before.

They'd heard it in taverns, in harbours, and in markets. The same story that made my flag the legendary promise that it was throughout the three nations.

I walked past Rodger and the guarding circle of our sailors, Rodger nodding at my silent question. These four men were the *condemned.* As usual, all were wearing officers' uniforms, probably what was left of the remaining leaders of their ship, save for the second in command and the captain.

I always reserved those for *me.*

These ones were just an extra treat.

Standing over them with one hand on my hip, the other resting on the pommel of my blade, I couldn't help but consider the pathetic and defiant glares they stared up at me with. All it took was one glance towards them, and those glares turned into reverence. *Hope* even. Now they looked up at me like I was the River Maiden herself, the Goddess of Transitions, off to ferry them off to their final judgment. Because that was *exactly* what I was.

Judgement.

"I'll make this quick, as we have somewhere to be," I stated with barely restrained impatience, beginning to pace around the circle of huddled uniforms. "You have been voted by your crew to be the worst offenders of humanity on board. By a judgment of your crewmates, you have been found guilty of murder, assault, violence, and numerous other charges too vile to mention. As captain, it's my duty to see their judgments *executed.*"

I couldn't help smiling as I said the last word. The feeling of self-satisfaction at the twist of irony was fuel for my soul.

"But I am merciful," I clarified. "I shall give each of you one, and *only* one, chance to save your wretched lives."

I turned to the nearest sailor of my crew, who held out a sword at the ready. I drew it cleanly, the sound of its draw sharp against the night, and tossed it to the deck in the midst of our condemned captives.

"You will duel me," I ordered, my demand as inviolable as iron. "If you win, you get to live."

It was as simple as that. I stepped just outside their little circle of four, waiting for the first man to stand and pick up the sword. I ran my thumb affectionately over the pommel of my blade, waiting.

After a few moments, as expected, the gazes of a few hundred men and women staring at them motivated one of them to reach for the blade with shaky hands.

He stood up from the deck, and our crew guarding them stepped away.

Standing just a few paces away, I waited to see what he would do, my thumb still flicking over the pommel of my blade to mask my growing impatience. Every second we wasted here was one more second we weren't going after the prince.

I motioned him forward with my free hand, and watched him take a few tentative steps toward me before breaking into a wild dash, screaming some Gods awful battle cry.

His footwork was awful. He'd probably not used a blade since his schooling to be a naval officer. Either that or he bought his commission outright. Regardless, it was plain he would be no threat.

With barely a huff, I didn't even bother drawing my blade. Instead, it was easy to dodge his sudden wild swing, ducking under his horrid follow up, before grabbing his wrist to twist his blade to his own neck and...

With just barely a nick, forcing him to slit his own throat.

His eyes widened in surprise, coughing up a mouthful of blood as he dropped the blade into my waiting hand.

I stilled my breath, trying not to smell the previous fluid dripping down his neck as I longed *desperately* to lick the blade clean. I had to stop myself, the excitement building in my chest at just a tiny little taste… Instead lifting the blade to my face as if to examine it for marks, watching the blood drip down its steel, ever so deliciously… So… *inviting*.

But every sailor under my command was watching. And despite the desperate need I felt in my gut to run my tongue along the sword, the fact that I was a *Vampyri* was still a secret to most of my crew.

Rumours swirled of course… Being under the command of a notorious pirate was one thing. Being under the command of a notorious pirate who most of an entire city had seen hanged was another. To my crew, it was plausible enough to explain that I'd escaped, made some deal, or even faked my death. That was the story that was told time and time again in taverns.

But being under the command of a woman who *had* been hanged, *died*, and now *drank blood*?

It was a step too far. People were already terrified of just the *concept* of me. Our recruits would evaporate overnight if the real truth got out, half our crew disappearing the next time we made port. Only my officers knew the full extent of what I was.

A monster.

Monster that I was, I still couldn't lick the stupid fucking sword in front of so many people. I tossed the blade between the men once again, their fellow's blood still dripping from it.

I turned to grab the man I'd defeated, his hands grasping weakly at his throat as he died, and dragged him to the railing. I tossed him overboard with the ease of a sack of potatoes. The splash of water that sealed his doom shattered the noise of hundreds of hearts watching my every move.

"Who's next?" I demanded, turning back to face the condemned, my hands on my hips.

In moments, the next two died much the same. Untrained, angry, desperate. A stab through the heart, a cut across the face, resulting in two more souls admitted to the sea without remorse.

The last one however, had been planning his moves from the beginning.

As I was tossing his last fellow into the sea, he'd taken the dropped blade and charged me from behind. No one on my crew warned me, nor did they feel they needed to. They'd seen this play out hundreds of times by now.

I dropped the body into the sea, dodging to the right to sidestep his wild stab, jumping up over his down-thrust to kick at the railing, back flipping over his upward third swipe.

He knew what he was doing.

But I was a *Vampyri*.

Now that I had distance on him, I drew my blade as he tried to rush me once more, and in a single block and deflection, separated his hand from his wrist.

The man screamed, clutching his bleeding stump of an arm and didn't even notice my blade cutting towards his throat to silence him.

His screams cut off into a choking gurgle, and with a single grasp of his collar, I threw him over the side to join his fellows in the sea.

"Mr. Castille!" I yelled out, turning to leave the stunned looks of the fifty or so of their sailors we were leaving behind on their vessel, their stares torn between me shouting orders and the man's hand still bleeding onto the deck. "Get our people back aboard, and let us get underway. We're done here."

The *Wraith* exploded into noise and busywork as I stepped back aboard, a song breaking out among the sailors climbing the masts as I supervised. It would take us the rest of the evening to disentangle the *Wraith* from our prize.

Eventually the other crew realized that we were leaving them to their devices, and began to do the same on their own vessel, albeit much more slowly.

The head had been cut off from the snake choking them. They had to figure out who was in command now, where to go, how to function without the overbearing fist of Kitaxian officers over their heads.

Where they went from here, we rightfully didn't care. We'd taken everything of value from their ship, only leaving them enough supplies to get to a port somewhere. If they didn't figure it out, they'd die.

Some of them had volunteered to join us, out of the fire and into the pan, rapidly adjusting to their new lot in life.

We didn't take *everyone* who wanted to join us. Ours was a ship of war and constant battle. We were hunted throughout the Great Divide. We had one single port to call home, and its location was a secret we all held dear.

We simply *couldn't* take those who weren't really prepared for what that might entail. Never to be accepted into society ever again. Never to see their homes or family again. Never to know the peace of the 'good life'.

To be a sailor of the *Wraith*, meant freedom from society. Society, in turn, wanted nothing more than for us to be marched to the gallows. We only took those that we needed. Mates, cooks, carpenters, anyone with a proper or rare skill set. Today we picked up a fore-masts mate and a gunner's apprentice.

Back aboard our ship, my gaze was raised to the sails being set with a critical eye, watching the new arrivals for any sign they were

Kitaxian spies. Within a few hours, without a second glance at the vessel still withering in indecision behind us, we were off.

For we had a prince to catch.

We sailed the *Wraith* like we stole it, (which to be fair, years ago we had) and made our arrival to the spot of our planned ambush with barely an afternoon to spare.

Ten wretched days of sailing like madmen into the frozen and rough waters of Norlondia, just past the sea border with Kitaxia. The prince was due to arrive this very evening on his way to Seven Peaks, providing his schedule according to the letter was on time and he'd not been delayed.

With thankfully overcast skies, I paced the ship, holding my coat tightly around my shoulders as snow fell on the decks around me, wafting in on the chilled breeze from Norlondia's cold shore. Ice caked the deck, some of the crew clearing it away with pickaxes. Icicles dripping from the lines above, ready to skewer some poor unfortunate soul that walked under them at the wrong time, the more experienced hands of the crew keeping a weathered eye skyward just in case. Nearly every member of the crew shivering in heavy coats as we made ready our ambush.

The island of Tordheille, just off shore, was mediocrely sized. It possessed a small forest, dominated by a snow-capped mountain rising up out of the sea, with a small settlement and tiny harbour on the far side of it. An old Jarldom that had long since been absorbed into one of the larger fourteen through conquest or diplomacy.

Norlondia was still "a land where might made right", and its Jarls bickered, warred, and raided each other with reckless abandon. Its lack of unity made easy pickings for Kitaxia, taking advantage through colonial forts for 'trade and outreach'. More and more were popping up on the icy shores every year.

I gazed out at the blinking lights of the small settlement,

wondering what life was like in their longhalls. The Norns had a tradition of hollowing out mountains, building great forge cities where craftsmen made amazing gold trinkets along with unstoppable weapons of war. Even my sword, lightly bouncing against my hip as I walked along the deck, was made in one such longhall.

Life wasn't perfect in the Jarldoms, for not everywhere in Norlondia was blessed with plentiful ore, deep cavernous holds, or rich farming fields from their volcanoes. This island settlement was a prime example.

Its land was nothing but ice and snow, blasted with frigid winds from the North-East, and despite winter not being for another month, its harbour was choked with ice.

How and why those people lived out there on that ice-cursed island, I couldn't say. I could hazard a guess about some idiotic idea of being stronger than a season, but I knew not the land of my birth. I was raised by Kitaxia, and I shuddered as I imagined growing up with that traditional Norn outlook.

"Cold fucking night for it, Claire."

I turned on my heel to see Rodger, having just escaped the warmth of the decks below from the nearby crew ladder, shivering in the cold as he joined me at the railing to look over the waves at the nearby settlement.

"Is it?" I asked with a smile, brushing away the snow on the railing with my bare hands so he could have a spot beside me to lean against.

I was *always* cold. My skin was cool to the touch, incapable of producing warmth. Although, even though I couldn't feel cold anymore, the icy winds of Norlondia certainly tried to make me.

Rodger's mustache ruffled back and forth. "Don't rub it in my face, I'm sick of this shit. It goes right through the hold." He shuddered as he placed his elbows on the railing beside me, holding his arms tightly against him, rubbing warmth into his biceps. "Needed some air though. Just got out of *another* argument with Maude about this venture with the prince. She's still not the biggest fan," he murmured through his chattering teeth.

I nodded, turning my gaze back to the island.

"Be thankful we don't live over there then. I could just kick all your asses and then you'd have to do what I said, no questions asked." I thumbed over the railing at the Norn settlement, and Rodger only rolled his eyes at me as he grumbled under his breath.

In Norn society, anyone could challenge anyone for anything they had. Jarl Isolde had done just that. She had won the throne to Seven Peaks in a *holmgang*, an honour duel in the Norn tongue. And now she was trying to hold it against all comers, while at the same time trying to unify all of Norlondia under her banner.

If King Hakkon was sending his grandson to her in some scheme, maybe they *were* fostering an alliance with Kitaxia that would finally give her enough diplomatic weight to make her the first *High* Jarl of all Norlondia.

I smiled, realizing that if all went to plan tonight, we could be undoing two different schemes at empire.

Silently, we listened to the creak of wood and rope around us, the crunching of ice on the waves, and the quiet curses of the crew making preparations for the battle with half frozen fingers.

"Do you think it'll be worth it?" Rodger asked, his breath a soft cloud into the air.

"What? The prince? Of course." I waved off his concern. "It has to be."

He tipped his head back and forth, like he didn't *really* agree, reaching a gloved hand to carefully touch his moustache. He winced when he realised the damn thing had frozen.

"Just because the crew agreed with you, doesn't mean you'll get what you want," he said, his words reeking of wisdom I didn't want to entertain. "He could die in the attack, we could *fail* to catch him. It's a long shot and you know it. You're too smart for that."

The decision to ambush the prince's ship was relatively an easy one to sell to the crew now that *most* of my officers were convinced. The *Wraith* was, after all, a democracy. As captain, I provided *general* direction, but on major things like this ambush… That required a full vote of the crew.

And they didn't need much imagination to think of what we'd

do with a prince.

Most of them were just like me, looking for revenge against a family that had harmed most of them in one way or another. While our crew was made up of sailors from all over, Kitaxian ships were our favoured prey, and as a result almost all of our crew had defected from those very ships. They had just as much a bone to pick with the royal family as I did.

Religious purges, class warfare, sexist laws, all of it making Kitaxia a state controlled by the whims of the rich and powerful, its citizens suffering under the King's iron fist that enforced its rules.

So, using our… *liberty* to kidnap the man second in the line of succession certainly seemed an amazing opportunity for payback. The vote passed nearly unanimously.

Huffing out a steamless breath into the cold, I hugged my elbows as I looked up into the sky, seeing the beginnings of a small cloud of flurries.

As much as I wanted to admit otherwise, Rodger was right. There could be a million different ways this heist went wrong, and a million more ways that the crew died in the attempt. Could I stomach failure? I could still call it off. Go back to looking for another opportunity to spite Ameritia that wouldn't put everyone in my command in the crosshairs of the entire royal navy.

But then what was the *point*?

The hunger swirling in the back of my mind wanted to give no consideration other than my fangs in the prince's neck. Throw everything away, a deep wonder of what royal blood must taste like. The very idea made a corner of my mouth lift into a smile. That vengeance could be *so close* after so long.

"I have to try Rodger. What else is all this for otherwise?" I said quietly, my eyes glancing skyward at the pink sky, the sun slinking into the waves behind us.

He shrugged his shoulders. "Riches. Fame. Freedom from tyranny. We have a good life, leaching from the rich and giving to our poor. Why risk everything we've worked for?"

The answer came to me immediately, sinking into my skin like the frigid wind cutting through the air. "Because I want more. I always want more. It's not enough for me to just live large, picking at Kitaxia's stinking flesh." My fingers dug into my elbows, fury in the pit of my stomach. "I want to be there, looking in Ameritia's eyes when I slide the knife against her throat. I want to show our people that an honest life is possible without nobles pressing their boots into our necks."

Rodger huffed a silent laugh into the cold air before he spoke. "Well then. I hope enough of us are still alive by then to help push her head against the blade."

CHAPTER EIGHT

"Idiot. Have you ever tried to command a naval squadron in the thick of battle? Let me paint a picture for you. It. Is. Chaos. Smoke from the cannons covers the sea like mist, the wind hardly ever co-operates, and the noise. The noise! You try shouting over the din of cannon and muskets firing, the shouts of two hundred sailors, and the explosions of wood and steel. Any Captain can manage a ship at sea. Only the most battle-hardened souls can command."

— Randall Givens, Lord Admiral of the Royal Kitaxian Navy, in an address to the Lord Steward of the King's Council

❝Bring us to half speed, and be ready for battle!" I sounded out the order, watching the ship begin to bustle with its usual efficiency despite the cold.

Right on time. An hour after sunset, they slinked out of the horizon, their masts barely noticeable against the fading grey of snow and fog in the dimming light. The idiots had already lit lanterns to help them see through the worsening weather.

I leaned off the quarterdeck rigging, eyeing the ships with my telescope.

They were like little ducks in a row.

A navy sloop fore and behind, the royal yacht in the middle. They weren't hugging close, but it was a relatively tight formation. "Dash the lanterns," I murmured to Markus, and he quietly passed the order down the line.

It would buy us a little time, using the weather to camouflage our ambush. The *Wraith* was painted a molted driftwood grey, its sheets as white as snow. In the fog and frost we were all but invisible without the distinguishing light of the lanterns.

Creeping forward towards them like a reaper in the dark, sooner or later I would have to call it. They were fast movers, and we were closing the distance rapidly. This was the moment. The moment I decided if our cushy life of plucking prizes across the sea was over, and if we were actually going to *do* something to royally piss off the Kingdom of Kitaxia.

Even then, it would be a tough battle. We would have to punch out the sloops as quickly as possible, and *then*, immobilize the yacht. The *Wraith* was manoeuvrable, but couldn't match those lighter frames for speed. If they ran, we wouldn't be able to catch them. If the sloops got a lucky hit or immobilized us, then they would circle and doom us.

But I had two devastating advantages. Surprise and firepower. I needed to pull out the rug from underneath them in one fell swoop with such ferocity that they couldn't fight back.

With perfect timing, the fog and snow began to worsen, leaching out of the waves to surround everything. Trodhielle, the *Wraith*, the approaching convoy, everything disappeared into a sea of grey.

"You must be blessed by the Veiled Lady," Markus murmured from beside me on the quarterdeck. The comparison made me smile deviously. His invocation of the Goddess of Death, Mysteries, and the Unknown was also the Goddess of Mists, strangely enough.

"If she favours me, she's had a particularly odd way of showing it through my life," I whispered, the fog silencing the crew's mutterings enough that only the slosh of ice-caked water against the hull was audible. The silence comforted me, but I could feel Markus's anxiety bleeding off him like a cloud of worry.

"What do you think? Charlotte's sure they can pull this off?" I asked, a hint of disbelief in my voice, but he nodded. The plan I had devised the moment I saw our opponent's formation was crucially in the hands of our genderless cannoneer more than mine.

"They practised it in the last hour for as much as they could. Swore they'd get it in about fifteen seconds," Markus mumbled, making me grimace. I wasn't sure we had *ten* seconds for what I had planned, but we were out of time.

The Kitaxians had to be close now. I could hear something out over the waves, and as the minutes passed, it slowly began to solidify into shouts and commands. Close enough now that I could hear their screeching over the sea. Not long now...

"All quiet!" I shouted. The crew were immediately deathly silent, waiting for the beginning of battle. The silent anticipation of ambush. My fingers dug into the quarterdeck railing, as I fought the urge to pace, listening intently. I needed to do *something*.

"Give me the helm." I grabbed the helmsman's shoulder, pulling him aside. He barely stepped away in time to avoid falling to the deck by the force of my grasp. I grasped the great wheel, feeling its heft. Rarely did I ever take the helm myself. Usually when exact manoeuvring and timing was needed, or if I just needed something to do with my hands.

This would be a little bit of both.

Another minute passed, the screeching of the Kitaxians on the other side of the fog sounding louder with each passing moment. Every single one of the *Wraith*'s crew's hearts were hammering in their chests, audible as if a great drum to me.

Any moment now...

The bowsprit of the lead vessel speared through the fog directly in front of us.

Ready or not, it was time.

"Let fly!" I screamed, moving the helm to shift us to the starboard, the lead ship passing us on the left side. A cheer went out among the crew as our gunports opened wide on the port side, my flag rising above my head from the beam.

The shadowy figures taking rapid shape aboard the sloop erupted into a panic, but it was too late for them. The sight of them scrambling for anything that would save them was a delight, a giddy anticipation at this beginning of the end.

"FIRE!" I screamed over the din, pointing fire and fury at the lead vessel as twenty-one 18-pounder cannons ripped into the tiny vessel.

At this range, with such a heavy broadside, it didn't stand a chance. A sloop was a fast vessel, made for epic manoeuvres and flanking fire, not for taking the brunt of a ship-of-the-line's broadside from point blank range, sandwiched between us and the shallows of the coast. As soon as we were clear of the mess we had made of the sloop—more than a few holes below their waterline and a list already developing—I started counting in my head. I turned the helm back port to swing around the sinking vessel to line up with the bow-spirit of the yacht behind it, steering the *Wraith* towards it head-on.

Charlotte, if you manage this...

The first chaser cracked, a thud in the air I could feel in the vibrations of the hull through my boots, the air cackling with sound. Our huge cannons in the bow were by far our biggest armament, the weight of fire devastating. It was that firepower that I was gambling it all on. The shot punched a hole clear through the mainsail of the yacht, but no crunch of wood met my ears.

A miss.

Shit.

Just one last chance. The second cannon fired, punching a second hole through their sail, followed by a satisfying crunch of an explosion of splinters. The groan of a collapsing mainsail echoed through all of our ears, as it thankfully started to fall to our starboard.

A textbook demasting. But the first one I'd ever heard of being done from a chaser cannon head-on before. The crew cheered wildly as I spun the helm a few degrees port once more, weaving us like a thread through the little squadron.

Arguably, the hard part was over, but we still had one final enemy, the last escorting sloop coming up behind the yacht. And only about ten more seconds to get a broadside into it before we'd overtake the ship. We were moving *fast*.

If they got past us, they'd likely scoop up the prince and be on their way before we could bring the *Wraith* back around. Charlotte had to get our gun crews over to the starboard side.

Four more seconds. We passed the Yacht just as the portholes opened on our starboard side. Two seconds. The sloop would be past us in an instant at these speeds.

One.

"FIRE!" I screamed.

Charlotte had made good on their promise. Fifteen seconds for the crew to fire from port, to fore, and to starboard. As the cannons barked, I remarked silently to myself with a smile, that I had the best damn gunnery chief in the whole Great Divide.

The sloop didn't even get a shot off as our cannonballs bit into their hull, as men, metal, and wood scattered into several pieces.

It was done. A few of them got off half-mad musket shots in retaliation, but at this speed, even my best snipers wouldn't have hit their targets.

We flew past them as water boiled into the holes our cannons had made.

A cheer went out among every soul on board the *Wraith*, with half of the crew chanting my name.

We had them. A perfectly executed ambush. It could've gone wrong a half million different ways, but we had done it. Only my crew would have accomplished something so laughable as taking on three faster ships, only firing off three salvos, and not taking a single salvo in return.

We'd *won.*

I passed off the helm back to the helmsman who was staring at me as if I was the Goddess of War herself. I stepped to the command rail to give the command everyone had been waiting for.

"Bring them in lads! We have a prince to loot!" I shouted to their cheers.

CHAPTER NINE

*"Just got one of those weird flyers from the monks prowling the street.
'Announcing his Royal Highness, Prince Nicholas!' Ha! Wonder where
that fuck has been, no one's seen him nearly five years.
Who gives a shit."*

*"Well, the church folk certainly seem to want us to give a shit. You
seen this? They're mandatin' prayers for his health.
Is he sick or somin'?"*

— Overheard conversation outside a poorhouse in the lower city of Haxla

By the time we came about—no small thing in a sailing ship—most of the fog and snow had cleared away, as if to only specifically bless our singular battle. Enough time had passed that the ugly hulks of the sloops were properly sunk, settled on the bottom of the shallows, with the survivors of their crews swimming in a panic towards the nearby shore.

In the frozen waters of Norlondia, they'd be dead in minutes. Even if they got to shore by some miracle, they'd still most likely freeze to death. We leered and laughed at them, the few expressions I could see gawking in terror as my flag flew free for all of them to see.

The smart ones who'd stayed on what floating pieces of debris they could find… *Might* live. And if they did, they would know. They would carry my story to Lady Ameritia.

She would know who had taken her son and bested her pathetic navy.

We spied the yacht soon after, attempting to limp away down the coast towards the nearby settlement, but they would never make it. It was only a two-masted vessel, and with its mainmast not only gone, but now slowing them down as it pulled their vessel perpetually port, with its beam and sails dragging in the sea, it was slow going. It had barely gone a few ship lengths ahead, its sailors desperately trying to cut away the blasted thing.

The moment they saw the grey hulk of the *Wraith* slipping out of the remnants of the mist, chaos exploded on their deck. We pulled up alongside them, hooking the tiny thing and pulling it close, and dropped down en masse.

Usually, I stayed back from boardings. A captain's place was to command after all, but this was an exception. The excitement I felt in my hunt was electric, my nerves seemingly alive, my boots hitting their deck with a satisfying thud as I examined the yacht's crew.

A few men that were better armed than the rest—royal guards presumably—had galvanized the sailors into a ready defence, their uniforms pristine against the rest of the sailor's rags. My musket snipers were lining up shots at their little barricade from the *Wraith*'s railing above us. The taste of fear in their hearts, so tempting that I couldn't help licking my lips before I gave them their final warning.

"I will say this once, and only once. Surrender the prince, and you'll all live to die another day." I drew my sword to make my point, letting it rest cleanly at my side, a ready promise.

Several eyes followed my blade's point, their gazes lifted to my face as I tipped up my hat with it, just so they could see my spectacles and know *exactly* who I was. "Where. Is. The. Prince?" I put as much venom in my voice as I could.

A shout from one of the royal guards gave away his charge, and I levelled my blade to wait for him patiently, letting my thoughts empty for nothing save the fight.

Block, parry, sidestep, lunge, execute.

Three seconds and it was over. His throat slit, his body continuing its momentum to slide past me into the waiting arms of my crew behind me, who immediately began pilfering his pockets.

"Bad choice. I wouldn't recommend repeating his mistake," I said quietly, daring anyone else forward. There were four more royal guards, each pacing out their steps, but the yacht's crew seemed to be waiting to see if I'd kill them first.

"If anyone besides them moves, kill them all," I ordered, pointing at the four guardsmen with the tip of my sword. Cocked rifles sounded all around me as I stepped forward into the space of no man's land separating my crew and the yacht's defenders. I let myself feel a long familiar, yet still altogether foreign feeling...

Of my dead heart beating.

The guardsmen attacked with a synchronous precision. *Ba-dum.* I side stepped three of their lunges, deflecting the fourth into the throat of one of the others. *Ba-dum.* The follow-through swing was wide, making me fall backwards under it as I sliced open the attacker's stomach, before righting myself to block the other two's downward thrusts on the length of my blade. *Ba-dum.* The last two were wary, pacing out away from me, clearly aware I was just as good as the stories stated. Their lunges became careful. *Ba-dum.* Which was their mistake as I went on the attack. Forcing myself through one's defence as his attempted deflection wasn't strong enough to parry my stroke. His surprise as I pierced his heart with my sword was only surpassed by his last fellow trying to strike *through him* at me in a last-ditch surprise attack. *Ba-dum.* I pushed myself over the fellow I had just stabbed, using my sword as a leaver over him as the guard who thought to take advantage suddenly found himself tumbling into his corpse as they both fell into a heap. I landed neatly, spinning to slice at the back of his neck as he fell, hearing the satisfying noise of him gurgling on his own blood. *Baaaaaaa-duuuuuuum.*

I let out a quiet breath, suddenly feeling ravenously hungry as I always did after making my heart beat. I rarely used it, for that very reason. It made me faster, stronger, and *unstoppable.* But after… I needed to *feed.*

Despite having gorged myself only ten days ago, the hunger now awoke in the back of my mind with a vengeance. Making me imagine my fangs in the neck of the prince, cutting open every Kitaxian sailor before me, a sick smile on my face as I looked at the four guardsmen bleeding into the frost covered deck. Breathing heavily, *aching* with a need to lean down and lick up their spilled blood from the deck.

Control. I needed to control myself.

I clenched my jaw, forcing myself to look away from the blood steaming into the cold air. "Now. Last chance," I demanded, leveling my blade towards the remaining crew of the yacht, who started tossing their weapons to the deck.

I could barely restrain a chuckle. "Better."

The ship was ours.

A few 'volunteers' from our captives told me an interesting story.

No one else had seen the prince during the voyage. Not even before the convoy set sail. The door to the prince's room was locked before anyone else was allowed aboard, even the crew. The room itself was a strange thing. Expertly carved wood covered what was a very sneakily hidden siege room. Behind that wood paneling, sat an iron forged wall locked up tight.

If the guardsmen were using it properly, shot and muskets would have no effect on the damn thing. We would need to starve them out, or attempt to shoot it open with cannon or powder. And if we'd blew it to the high heavens, there was a good chance we'd also kill the prince.

And the only man who had the key was the captain. Who was nowhere to be seen.

But piracy provided all sorts of opportunities for a mistreated crew, and our volunteers' list of grievances was enough for one to lead me down into the cargo hold to drag the captain, a man named Dietrich, out of a barrel he'd been hiding in.

The barrel trick wasn't the first time I had dragged cowards out of unsuspecting places, but it might have been the first time a man had nearly drowned in wine as a result. He was half drunk and barely making any sense. Even my compulsion had no hold on him, ranting and raving about pirates and vile women.

He was as useless as salt water was to me, so despite the fact that by right I should've bled him dry, I instead had him tossed overboard, taking the only useful thing he had.

The key to the prince's room.

Now that we had the key...

My breath quickened. *Finally*, my revenge was at hand.

Markus had followed me every step of the way. The reveal of the prince's room, chasing down Dietrich and the key, silent as the grave the entire time. The rest of the crew was pilfering the yacht for what valuables they could find, while we made our way to the prince's room from the cargo hold.

"You alright, Claire?" Markus asked as he followed at my elbow, four armed crewmen walking in escort behind us just in case the prince had one last trick up his sleeve.

I considered his question. Between the hunger and the nervous energy I could feel in every limb, I wasn't sure if I was. "I'm… something. I don't know yet. But let's get him aboard and then we can figure out our next moves."

I didn't know that I had a better answer for him. I felt… like a spool of knotted rigging. Anxious, excited, terrified, estatic.

Worst of all, *hungry.*

Markus nodded at my explanation, looking contemplative, but followed silently.

We stood before the door, and I hesitated. I thumbed the key in hand, wondering what I would do... *after.*

Would I raid Kitaxia forever more? Continue pirating? Retire with the prince in custody?

Maude's words from my cabin suddenly haunted my mind.

If we do this, they will hunt us. More than ever before. Why invite that terror?

Did I really need this?

"Whatever is behind that door, we're here for you," Markus said quietly, as the weight of his hand settled onto my shoulder.

I stared at him, looking at first his hand, and then into his eyes with quiet appreciation.

Markus and I never quite saw eye to eye on many things; it's what made him a good quartermaster. His ability to not lose sight of the realities was never clouded by the fact that I, being a *Vampyri*, routinely did the impossible.

And now, here he was, at the point of no return for a raid he didn't even think was a good idea.

But he was here for me. My friend. My brother.

I reached up to pat his hand a few times in silent thanks, breathing deeply as I stepped towards the door. What could *possibly* be on the other side? The only thing I was sure about was the fact that no matter what happened from here on out, we would be the ones who'd finally taken something *back* from Kitaxia.

I would taste the prince's horror at seeing my face, relishing in his despair once he knew whose grasp he'd fallen into. Maybe I would do what Lady Ameritia had done to me, bleed the man dry as a bone, and yet keep him alive.

Maybe I might even turn him, if I could ever figure out how she had turned me, then starve him just to see what would happen.

Or I could just murder the fucker, I thought with a smile.

The possibilities were endless. And they all began with that door.

I entered the key, turning the lock and heard a plethora of mechanisms shift as the tumblers turned in the iron wall.

The door shifted, suddenly free on its hinges. I pulled on the handle, hearing it screech from unfamiliarity with motion.

My eyes adjusted to the barely lit room in an instant, only to see four women sitting in the centre of a well-furnished bedroom in a panicked huddle.

Their hands clasped around each other in a pious circle, two of them murmuring in prayer. I gazed at them briefly for weapons, and upon not finding any pointed in my direction, stepped into the sizable room, gazing quickly around, and saw no one else.

No one else.

My gaze flickered back to reassess the women as they stared at me in mute horror, despite the lack of a threat they presented. I drew my sword, the sound of the metal escaping free of its sheath made one of them yip in fear as I perked my ears.

There were no other heartbeats. Just the four panicked... *No...* One of them was steadier than the rest. The redhead glaring at me with malice in her eyes.

For the briefest moment I forgot about the prince. Who was this woman with furious eyes staring at me with such hatred? Why was her gaze so focused? Was she not afraid?

"Where is he?" I demanded of them, shaking my head free of her gaze, still searching for what I knew wasn't here. My heart didn't want to believe it. After all that pain and effort and suffering and bloodshed, he wasn't even *here?*

None of them answered my demands as my anxiety warred in my chest.

Their stony silence only made my frustration grow, I began poking my blade into piles of dresses, clothes, the beds, anything that might hide a body.

He really isn't here.

The growl that escaped my throat made every heart in the room pick up in pace, and my hunger stirred underneath my anger, urging me to tear the room and everyone in it asunder.

"Where. Is. He?" I demanded to no one in particular as I flipped the large bed with ease, finding the deck underneath it bare. I had circled the room around the women multiple times, finally coming to a pause before a dresser with a large mirror over it.

My visage was marred with a spattering of blood from my deckside duel, and my own reflection stared back at me with fire and fury. My eyes, peeking out over the tops of my spectacles, were green as they always were, but ringed in deep red.

Breathe. I needed to breathe.

I took a deep breath, pushed my spectacles back up my nose, and tried to calm the monstrosity of my hunger, anger, and disappointment, turning towards the four women on the floor as breath slowly exhaled from my lungs.

"Where did he go?" I asked, trying to make my voice as calm as possible as I did so. This was the exact type of situation that required tact, not bloodshed.

Or it *would*, but none of them answered me.

I wanted to be diplomatic. To be considerate and get them to *see*. These women were just as much victims of Kitaxia as we were.

But as I watched them blubber in their tears and shaky hands, anyone could see that they were too caught up in their own fear and terror to actually think past saving their own skins.

I didn't have the time, *or* the patience. I was too hungry.

I hated that it would come to this, but I *would* find him. I grabbed the back collar of one of the women, her shriek of fear as she was pulled away from her comrades, loud and terrified. Pushing her against the wall, I levelled my sword to her throat. The press of sharp edge against her neck stilled her thrashing in an instant, sobs dying in her throat as the room instantly quieted.

I turned my gaze to the other women on the floor, all grasping each other anew in fear and loathing, their terror mixing with their hatred of me. Even Markus and the sailors standing by the door were tense.

"Where?" I demanded.

A single word, filled with so much meaning. I stared at each of their faces, the red-haired woman visibly gulping, but holding her silence. Each woman in turn looked at her, something unsaid between them. There was something there. Some inkling of knowledge or deference.

But the silence continued, none of them answering me.

"Fine. I only need one of you alive anyway," I stated, turning my gaze towards the woman under my blade. The least I could do is look her in the eye as she died. I reached for her hair to steady her head, a solid clean cut for a quick death, and—

"Stop! Stop, *please.*"

Pausing a second away from tensing my muscles to *cut*, the woman's throat actively bleeding just from the struggle against my sword, I bit my lip in an aching *need* to run my tongue along that trail of red.

"*Please.*"

Somehow, that pleading tone connected with my struggle against my hunger.

Slowly, I turned away from my victim, and saw the red-haired woman now standing tall, her fists clenched at her sides, her gaze locked on my boots.

"It's... me. I'm the one you're after," she whispered.

I tilted my head in confusion, unsure of what she meant at first. But now that I examined her in detail...

No... Impossible.

I looked at her again with a renewed eye. A proud jaw, perfect nose, and eyes that were that colour of green only women of her complexion could have.

But she had a thinness of frame, a shallow, underdeveloped chest, an almost starved complexion with hollow collarbones…

And now that I could *see* it, I wanted to laugh.

All these years imagining Ameritia in that cell, I could never remember her hair colour. But now, it was clear as day to me. *Red.* Take this woman's eyes, shift the cheeks and jaw around... and there it was.

She was the spitting image of Ameritia.

The realization hit me with the force of a hurricane. Ameritia's son was standing right in front of me.

"Nicholas?" I stated, my jaw wide open in astonished surprise, Markus's eyes bulged along with the crewmen with him.

She winced as if slapped, but didn't back down. Only now did she look me in the eyes as she lined her voice with the most potent venom.

"You may call me *Moira*, or nothing at all," She stated with all the authority of a queen.

At that, I *did* laugh, lowering my sword. My laughter did nothing to lessen the tension in the room. Only once I let go of my hostage, all but forgotten, did Markus and my sailors let out a relieved breath.

This woman was like Jacine.

Born the wrong gender, and from the looks of it, had managed some small success in changing it. Suddenly the King's letter made *so* much more sense. Such women were accepted in Norlandia... Not even remotely tolerated in Kitaxia.

They were *vilified* in Kitaxia.

All of this left me in a bit of a predicament. Considering I was here to *kidnap* them.

"Very well, *Moira*. You will call me *Captain Vessia,* or nothing at all," I replied, unsure if I should be pleased or infuriated with this development.

I could've sworn every heartbeat in the room stilled for a moment, the other girls broke into a mess of tears and sobs anew as they realized just who they were looking at.

"The stories... They're true. You're... supposed to be dead," Moira intoned in silent wonder, her eyes widening and watering enough to give the green a beautiful shine.

Every time. It never gets old hearing that.

The stories of my execution and escape from the waves had made my rise to infamy all but certain.

"Eh. Death's overrated. Decided it wasn't for me," I said almost jokingly, beginning to saunter around her in a slow circle, a vulture orbiting over a dying animal, debating what to do with the other women that I couldn't care less about.

Moira on the other hand... I needed time to debate this revelation. What it meant for my revenge. How I could maximise this opportunity.

Time I didn't have. The longer we stayed here attached to the yacht, the more vulnerable we'd be.

"Take her away," My order was crisp, stark, and absolute. As sure as the tide.

The screeched protests of Moira's companions were enough to spite a touch of guilt in the pit of my stomach, but were silenced by the click of my sailor's pistols being cocked.

Markus quietly stepped forward, manacles in hand with a victorious grin on his face, reaching for Moira's delicate looking wrists. She offered no resistance, but held her head high, chin pointed to Markus as if he was just another servant offering her a platter of some fine delicacy she disapproved of.

"Show her the hospitality of the *Wraith*." I paused, for a moment debating between the brig and something more… Presentable. "In my cabin if you'd please, gently" I ordered, deciding on the latter.

My voice stern, yet somber as Moira looked at the irons clasped around her wrists with a face full of wonder. Like she was *excited* to see what happened next. It was shattered the moment Markus tugged on the chains, pulling her gruffly towards the door, and she was led out of the room. I watched her be escorted down the gangway with all the poise of an empress.

"Well. That's... Surprising," I stated to no one in particular, the women in the room with me still cowering in tears.

I don't know how long I stood in that doorway listening to Moira's maids crying, watching Markus and our captive ascend up the ladders to the weather deck above. I didn't know what I expected this moment, the culmination of my revenge against Lady Ameritia, to feel like.

I had won yet another impossible victory. Captured a prince-*cess* Stolen Ameritia's child from right under her nose.

But all I felt was... *nothing.* Amusement at best, hollow *emptiness* at worst.

With a sudden angry huff, I tore off towards the captain's cabin, determined to find something worthwhile for my troubles, maybe some poor neck to bury my fangs in to wipe the taste of ashes in my mouth.

CHAPTER TEN

"Emergency order to Admiral Yanshu. Your orders are as follows: Make best speed for an intercept course of the Blackhawk. It is enroute to Seven Peaks with an escort. We do not expect escort to be sufficient. Expect pirate activity."

— Randall Givens, Lord Admiral of the Royal Kitaxian Navy

The door to my cabin slammed open under the force of my boot, and a terrified voice within let out the tiniest hiccup of fear.

I kicked the door close, covering my cabin in blessed darkness with a huff of excitement at my *guest*.

My mood wasn't really in the place for entertainment, but I had to decide to do *something* with her. Throwing what I'd looted from Dietrich's cabin onto my desk, I finally looked my *main* prize in the eye, easily enough in the dark with my enhanced vision.

Moira had been chained to a chair in front of my desk, her wrists all but immobile against the wood. She lurched outwards, head turning back and forth trying to find who had walked in, but with no source of light, she couldn't see me in the pitch black of my cabin. Her eyes wandered the space where she *thought* I was, whipping back and forth in growing fear and alarm.

I stilled my breathing, taking a moment where she couldn't see to lean in and examine her in detail.

A deep burgundy dress, narrow hips, hollow neck. A mane of red hair that looked like she'd just started growing it out. She almost looked like she hadn't eaten a thing in months.

Grinding my teeth against each other, both to simmer the hunger back ever so slightly, and to keep my focus on her, I—

"I know you're there," She stated quietly, eyes still gazing back and forth in the dark. She probably thought her voice was steady and controlled, but I could *hear* the panic in her heart.

But as delicious as I thought that fear would sound... All I felt was sadness. This wasn't the gloating prince standing on a pile of purge victims I expected. This was a *princess* for starters.

I didn't know what to expect of her yet.

With an audible sigh, I opened a drawer to reach for a match, lighting it.

An explosion of soft orange light flickered into reality, startling Moira as she realized I wasn't just in the room, but *right in front of her.*

There was still my sizable desk in between us, but I didn't think she imagined for a moment that it would shield her from me from killing her.

Did I even want to kill her?

I paused in the midst of lighting a third and fourth candle. Silence, save the silent creak of the *Wraith* rocking along with the waves underneath us, the busy footsteps of the crew above us, and Moira's little quick breaths of fear.

I... I wasn't sure.

It took me until this exact moment to realise that I'd never thought I'd get this far in my revenge.

I continued lighting candles.

Once enough were lit that we could see each other clearly, I also opened the curtains along my aft-windows, letting in some of the moonlight as well. The horizon along Trodheille's shore was black, a twinkling of light from some campfire the survivors of the battle had made. It looked like little stars in the dark, and beyond that the horizon. A pale shade of a half-moon reflected in icy but calm seas.

Once the scene was set, I took off my hat, spectacles, weapons, and overcoat, hanging them off the back of my oversized chair, and settling into it. It elicited a relieved sigh as I finally looked my prey in the eye.

Her gaze had been locked on me the entire time, and now she looked... *confused* might have been the right word.

"Are you... not going to kill me?"

I raised my thumb to my lips, rubbing them back and forth,

pinching my cheek in consideration.

"Not sure," I stated, tracing my own jaw with my fingers to settle the ache in my teeth.

"I should," I admitted with a slight shrug before continuing. "Torture you at the very least. Maybe send you back to your mother, maimed and broken. In pieces would be the classic move."

I wrinkled my nose at the thought, it felt... *needlessly* cruel.

But Moira... Didn't stutter in fear. Her heart, if anything, *slowed.*

She tilted her head towards me, questioningly. "My mother?" She asked. "Not the King?"

I let out a small chuckle, motioning my hand vaguely in the direction of Kitaxia.

"I know who pulls the strings in your kingdom, little princess."

At that, for some bloody reason, she laughed. Not just the prim and proper chuckle I'd expect from a noble, but a boisterous laugh. A drunk-at-the-end-of-the-bar laugh, a funniest-joke-you-ever-told laugh, a I-can't-believe-that-just-happened laugh.

It was full bodied, and something about it made *me* want to see her laugh like that again.

"By heaven and hell," she murmured in between chuckles, tears still going down her cheeks. She couldn't wipe them away with her hands, so instead tried with her shoulder, smattering a few strands of orange hair against her freckled face.

"That's... that's just too funny," she breathed out through half breaths, sucking in air to make up for her laughter.

I narrowed my vision at her, unsure if I should be entertained or annoyed, drumming my fingers against my desk. "What, may I ask, is so funny?"

She shrugged in her bonds with a happy smile. "Refused to be recognized as a woman my whole life, sent off to Norlondia to marry some lady I've met maybe twice. Now here I am, about to almost certainly be killed by *you*, and you have no problem seeing me as a woman."

She started chuckling again, threatening to lose control of that laugh once more. "It's just. So fucking *funny*. The gender affirming executioner at the end of the line. Hilarious.”

I felt my mouth silently hang open in surprise, realizing in that moment that I *wouldn't* kill her, even as she laughed in the face of her supposed death.

Because Lady Ameritia hated her child. I'd probably be doing her a *favour* by killing her, and I refused to be her plaything.

But if I wasn't going to kill her….

What do I do with her?

Silence stretched between us once more, as Moira quietly writhed in her bindings, trying to find some comfortable position while still keeping an eye on me as I debated, drumming my fingers against my lips.

I could keep her captive. But a mouth to feed was expensive, and honestly, it didn't feel right to just throw her in a cell and chuck the key overboard. She'd likely just go mad over time.

I could take her back to port, put her in the care of someone there, but that was just another cage. And even then, I wasn't too sure about putting her smack dab in the middle of our best kept secret.

What would piss off Lady Ameritia the most, while also doing right by this woman?

And just like that, I had it. I knew what I was going to do with her.

“What if I told you...” I leaned forward on my desk, folding my hands together to set my chin on them. “That I wasn't going to kill you?”

Moira stilled, eyes narrowed while she considered my words. “Why?” Was all she asked after a moment. Points for looking gift horses in mouths, it made me think that she was smarter than my initial estimations.

I tilted my head, closing my eyes ever so slightly and raised my eyebrows. “Why indeed?” I murmured, more a purr of contentment as I imagined how this would all play out. “Do you care for your country, Moira?” I asked, smirking behind my folded hands.

I could nearly *smell* the suspicion bleeding out of her eyes. I felt like the spider, having caught a fly in its web, toying with my prey before I plunged the killing blow when least expected.

“As much as any noble child of Kitaxia I suppose.” She admitted.

That was a smart answer.

"Let me lay it out clearly then." I lowered my hands, leaning ever more forward. "I plan to keep you close. Mostly to screw with your mother. She and I have unfinished... *business.* " The look in her eyes told me she understood the gravity of what I was saying. I took the moment to roll out the charts I'd stolen from Dietrich's cabin on my desk, mostly to distract my hands while I laid out what I planned her fate to be.

"That leaves me with quite the conundrum where you're concerned. So, I'm leaving how you spend your days on board the *Wraith* up to you. I can throw you in the brig for the duration of your stay, an undisclosed amount of time, keeping things *very* simple between us." I noted the dates on the charts, cursing internally at them. Several years out of date.

"Or?" She volunteered, her voice hopeful.

I looked up from the charts with a devious grin.

"Or... Join my crew. Help us bring justice to Kitaxia."

The second in line to the throne turned rebellious pirate. The ultimate betrayal. I get my revenge on her mother, she gets to stick it to a parent and society who's never accepted her.

I win.

All I had to do was keep her on a tight leash. And from the looks of her, that'd be easy enough, if she-

"I'll do it."

I blinked in surprise, taken aback by her *again.* I was expecting her to deliberate, or straight up deny me. Not to *immediately* agree to my terms.

I looked her over, only to see the very picture of determination. The sound of a steady heart, clenched fists, serious gaze. It made me want to laugh in victory, or smile in appreciation.

But the game wasn't over yet.

"So ready to give up on Kitaxia? You haven't even considered what you're agreeing to," I said deliberately, turning through the pages of Dietrich's charts.

"Can you sail?" I asked.

"... No," She answered, immediately crestfallen.

Wrinkling my nose, I tossed the chart aside, onto the next one. "Read and write I assume?" She nodded. "Ropework?" A shake of her head.

She had to be useful for *something*. If I just tossed her onto the crew roster with no skill to speak of, they'd eat her alive. They wouldn't just accept a Gods damned *royal* out of the blue. I needed *something* to justify taking her on.

"Do you have *any* trade at all?" I complained exasperatedly, more to myself than her.

Her eyes lit up with fire as she refocused on me with that last question.

"I can smith!" she stated, as if she just won a contest of wills. At that I couldn't help but laugh, the very image of it impossible.

This waif was a blacksmith?

"You? You are dainty as a tart my dear." I rose from the charts, motioning towards her in disbelief. "You're telling me that you know how to forge?" I said, unable to hold back my amusement.

She was *tiny*. Imagining a hammer in her hands beating metal into shape was almost out of the question.

Her eyes sparkled with a challenge, her back straightening despite her bonds, pointing a finger from her manacles towards my sword where it still sat in its sheath hung over the top of my chair. "Four thousand degrees. Folded. Hammered. Tempered. Cross stock with a smithed handle, burnt oak for the grip. Pommel a wide grip. Four part assembly, but the guard is a bit more intricate than most." She said it all with a knowing smile, as if deigning the blade worthy of her notice.

I looked from her knowing gaze to the weapon I'd had at my side for half a decade. She knew my sword better than I did apparently.

And we *did* need a blacksmith.

This was beginning to work too well. Like the Fates had somehow decided that this was supposed to happen. Now it was me who felt suspicion bleed into my bones, feeling like the shoe was about to drop any moment.

"When do I start?" she asked, almost giddy.

With a bite of worry in my gut, I thought to teach her a little lesson in humility, and curb that enthusiasm. Ignoring her, I turned my full attention to the charts on my desk, leafing through them to examine my spoils in detail.

And most of them were *useless*.

A long silence stretched through the cabin as Moira's heart and breath quickened just a pace, making me smile in the low light of the candles.

"Uhm. Claire?"

Oh she *definitely* needed the lesson in humility if she thought she could use my *first* name off the bat. Most knew me as *Captain Vessia*, for her to know my *first* name meant she'd done some reading, yet she still thought herself free to call me Claire.

I flickered my eyes up to her in annoyance as she tugged on her manacles, making the point she was still immobile. Continuing to ignore her, I flipped through my charts.

"You're doing this on purpose now, aren't you?" She stated with an annoyed sigh.

It took everything I had to smother a grin. I tilted my head back and forth, still keeping my mouth closed, giving her no satisfactory answer.

"*Captain Vessia,*" she intoned with all the disrespect she could likely muster. Only then, did I lift my gaze from the charts.

There it is.

The feeling of vindication, at the princess of Kitaxia, looking up at me in supplication. Five years, all for this moment.

"Yes, crewman?" I answered with a raised eyebrow.

She pursed her lips and nodded.

"Point made," she sighed in defeat as she slouched into the chair.

Victory.

This revenge felt so much sweeter. Beaming with a joy I hadn't felt in months, I nearly wished I had some warm beverage to toast to it.

Instead, all I had was these infuriating charts...

"You'd think the royal yacht would have every luxury, charts included. But this..." I motioned to the papers I'd stolen from Dietrich's quarters. The very rooms the captain of that vessel looked like a party had just been interrupted moments earlier. "Just a mess of finer things,"

I continued, crumbling up a chart to focus on the next one.

"Just going to let me sit here through whatever monologue you got going on, eh?" Moira muttered, almost bored now that she was sure her life wasn't in danger. But her eyes focused on the charts, considering. "Do the finer things... Not impress you? I thought you were a pirate?" she asked with suspicion.

It made me snort out a light chuckle, standing up from my desk to motion around my cabin. I felt Moira's gaze follow me as I traced my hands along my curtains, my shelves of books, my weapons and charts. My cabin wasn't without its own ornamentation, but it was *tasteful*, and everything had a purpose. More a den of comfort than richness.

"Finer things you say... That's a misconception of how we work," I stated, pointing to the charts on my desk. "These, had they been up to date, would be worth ten times their weight in gold. Better knowledge of the sea is what makes a good captain a *great* captain in my estimation. Much better than any silver or gold trinket."

Her head tilted to the side, obviously thinking. "What do you mean, *misconception*?" she asked, with honest curiosity beginning to bleed into her voice.

I crossed my arms, my mood beginning to really lighten as I answered her with a smile. "Gold and silver are heavy. And only worth what any nation says it's worth. Now... something like... say, *silks*—" I began to pace as I talked, back and forth behind my desk. "—I *love* when I unbox a crate and spy the unmistakable colour of Ithakian silks. You know why?" I stopped and levelled my gaze on her fully.

A gaze of curiosity looked at me with seriousness. A hunger for knowledge. I *liked* that look.

She shook her head, motioned for me to continue with her manacled hand, a wry smile on her face.

"I can *use* them. I can decorate, make clothes, and store them for later. Fuck, I can use 'em as a scrub cloth if I need to." A memory jogged itself into my mind's eye of a desperate adventure off a tiny islet in Varcna. We were looking for potable water, our stocks had been dangerously low, and the port was too far. The memory made me smile, remembering Charlotte's look of relief after spotting the freshwater lagoon, their cry of 'CANNONBALL' as they dove in seconds later. "Have, in fact," I admitted, remembering using the silks to towel off after.

Her face twisted up in shock as she processed that I'd used some of the most expensive fabric in the world as a *scrub cloth*, before finally breaking into a quiet little giggle.

But I didn't stop there. "I can also trade them." I began my pacing once more. "A transferable good that I can use or sell. It gives me *options*. Now, if I open a crate of silver, it's just silver. It's not something I need like other materials are. Even then, I can't spend it. When you're not welcome in almost every port in the world..." I let the sentence trail off to see if she caught it.

"Who's even going to take your coin," she finished, and I put one more point in her favour. She was smart. "I understand now. Thank you," she said quietly, tapping a single finger against the arm of the chair in silent thought. "I wonder what else I've thought wrong about pirates."

I shrugged once again, leaning back down to my desk to flip through the remaining charts, looking for *anything* more recent. "Plenty, I imagine. The way I see it, in a world without gold, we'd be heroes," I muttered with slight disgust, not finding a single damn chart worth keeping. "Fighting the good fight against tyranny and hard rule, fighting for the people. But because the story is 'pirates are greedy sea-bound scum who are only in it for the money' we get painted by the worst possible brush."

She was staring at me once again in open-mouthed surprise, but I'd ruined my own good mood, thinking about how my crew and I were labelled by society. How any one of my people would be hanged the moment they stepped outside of my protection. It made me so fucking *angry.*

Adding to that fury, was the realization that the charts were absolutely useless.

"These are all ten years or more out of date. No more than half-drunk scribbles on charting paper." I crumbled up all the charts, ripping them into a giant messy ball of shredded paper, turning to throw them at the glass panes behind me, for a moment, my hunger pushing me to wish my windows would shatter like a stone through glass.

But then I stared past the glass in shock.

There, plain as day on the horizon through the panes, was a huge warship under full sail, glistening in the night like a miniaturized city. A three-decker at the head of several *more* large vessels rising up out of the horizon behind it.

The Gods dam High Seas Fleet of the Kitaxian Navy.

Either they'd been sent the moment the mail ship was overdue, or… It was a trap. Ameritia trying to eliminate me, by using the child she hated as bait.

I wouldn't put her past doing either.

"Oh," I managed to breath out before reflexes kicked into gear, propelling me to jump over my desk, reaching down to snap the manacles on Moira's wrists open with ease, grab her arm forcibly, and drag her to the door.

When she started to protest, I didn't relent, instead pulling her close enough to feel her breath on my lips, her face inches from mine.

"We have to go. *Now.* This is your last chance. Are you with us or against us?" I asked in a rush, unsure about the feeling stirring in my chest at those eyes being this close to mine.

A moment passed with her heart hammering in her chest. She'd agreed to join us, but now it was time to put action behind her words. Would it be the cage? Or helping us fight off the very people who'd come to save her?

She nodded.

"That's what I thought." I smiled as I pulled her out the door and onto the crowded weather deck, the sound of the *Wraith*'s deafening bell calling all sailors back aboard from the yacht.

I pulled Moira through the rough-and-tumble crowds, looking for the one soul I knew would be Moira's most steadfast ally. The one person who wouldn't toss her overboard at first opportunity for who she was.

But Moira lurched out of my grip, running to the rail to look over the side at the yacht, letting out a wail of a yell.

"Moira—" I stated in quiet worry, running back to get her, but she held firm, looking to start climbing over the side.

I was about to put her in irons once again if she couldn't be controlled, but then I saw her face.

Tears, openly weeping, at the sight of the dead guards on the deck of the yacht.

Ah.

I wrapped my arms around her, holding her back from jumping back aboard. "Moira. They're gone." I tried to whisper in her ear, but she wasn't having it. There was nothing for the dead. They weren't coming back.

"Claire... They were family! My family!" She cried, reaching over the railing.

Maybe I should've felt guilty. But they were in the way. If I let myself feel guilty about them, there were a few hundred souls I'd killed over the years waiting in line for me to feel guilty about first.

I shook my head, holding fast. "I'm sorry. I am. But they'd rather have died than give you up." I didn't think I was sorry, but it was the right thing to say.

She tried to punch at my grip pathetically, writhe out of my grip, but at the end of the day, I was *Vampyri.*

"Moira, we have to *go.* Or those ships bearing down on us will kill us all," I said quietly, undercut with emphasis, slowly pulling her away from the railing.

They'd kill us all, but they wouldn't kill me.

They'd bring me back to Lady Ameritia.

"... Or worse," I admitted, unsure of why I added that last bit.

Finally, she stilled, her head nodding. She took in a shuddering breath through her sobs, and I tentatively loosened my grip on her. She clenched her fists, set her jaw, staring at the deck. But she was following me.

And it was at that blessed moment that through the panicking sailors, I spotted the very person I was looking for. Jacine, running by at alarming speed, her arms full of a box of woodcutting supplies looted from the yacht that looked untouched by experienced hands.

I hoped she *probably* wouldn't gut the poor girl the first chance she got… Unlike almost anyone else on board.

"JACINE!" I shouted over the yelling of the crew. Jacine was one of the most deliberate people I knew. Nothing was done without meaning, and while we didn't talk as often as friends or family should, I considered us close.

She skirted to a stop, turning towards us in a rush. "Captain." She stated with a dip of the head, her eyes darting back and forth between me and Moira. "Who's the—" she stared at Moira for a moment, looking her up and down, gaze neutral with a touch of confusion. "—person?"

I motioned towards the carpenter for Moira. "This is Jacine. Our carpenter. I trust her with my life. Go with her, she'll get you settled." I watched both of their expressions do a double take, sizing each other up.

Moira nodded, finally a beat of panic stirring her heart as she looked up from her grief at the faces of the crew, maybe realizing what she had just done.

I turned to Jacine. "New recruit. We'll sort her out properly as soon as we escape this mess. Go," I ordered, taking off at a sprint towards the quarterdeck, leaving Moira in Jacine's capable hands for the moment.

Regardless of what I'd said, sailing ships did not start on a dime, and getting the *Wraith* underway was a complicated affair.

To get away from the fleet, we'd have to be damn lucky.

CHAPTER ELEVEN

— Captain of the Queen of Sardis, Tarrick Yondu

As Charlotte put it, 'they had us by the short hairs.'

For starters, we were entangled with the yacht, smushed between it and the coastline. With the wrecked naval sloops behind us and the shoreline on one side, the Kitaxian fleet was beelining towards our only exit, trying to cut us off.

While we were experts at sinking navy vessels, this was an entire war fleet, probably sent the moment they learned that the ship carrying the King's letter was a single *hour* overdue. Or even if it was a trap, they still had us nearly dead to rights.

But thankfully, we were *also* experts at running like hell while carrying as much loot from our kill that we could get our hands on before the authorities really showed up.

But this… this was pushing it for us. There was far more chance we would be surrounded in hours.

We had to make it to open water and pray that we were fast enough to clear the fleets intercept course, or in other words:

Run like hell.

"BATTEN THE MAINSTAYS, GET THE GALLENTS AND ROYALS OUT. TOPS TOO. GIVE ME EVERY SPIT OF WIND YOU CAN, DAMN IT!" I yelled to the crew amidst my cursing, and running down to help heave the lines myself.

In record time, despite the ice and snow, we'd broken free of the yacht, cleared the shore and the sloops, and were slowly picking up speed. But the fleet had mass and momentum.

We needed more speed. Frozen water clunked against the hull as the prow parted water and ice cakes before it, the winds trying to freeze us dead as we harnessed it with sail.

"HEAVE LADS, HEAVE!" I screamed, stretching those sails as far as they would go.

Finally, every sail that could be of use in the current angle of the wind was open. If I judged the distance and speeds correctly, we would *just* skirt by them.

The problem was that they'd have hours to chase us, run us down, and wait for us to make a single mistake. All the while they could rain chaser shot on us to hopefully catch a mast or something else dangerous while we tried to widen the distance on them. And that was nothing to say of the point if we ran into any other naval vessels from the *other* direction.

But lady luck seemed to be on our side this day, because the weather was pulling out all the stops for us on this journey.

A storm hovered on the horizon, and we sailed straight towards it with all haste.

Hours passed as the *Wraith* plowed through the waves, every member of the crew working through rain, sleet, and snow. Each shift pushing through their exhaustion managing rigging to keep us in the prime of the wind, the fleet closing in behind us with speed. The heavier ships were falling behind, but the lighter vessels, a squadron of sloops and frigates like ours, were still gaining even now.

I stood on the aft railing, rigging in my hand for balance as I stared at the shape of the monsters chasing us, the storm's rain beginning to shower us heavily, and the gentle rise and fall of the waves becoming more of an angry upheaval.

The swell of our great ship through the sea, my body held steady only by letting gravity have me ever so slightly to absorb the shock of the crash of waves with my knees. Swinging in the wind, the howl of that same wind through the sails, masts, and rope, sounding like a great forest in a hurricane. The great groans of the hull flexing against the forces of nature while water pounded the prow.

And there, the sudden feeling of a rush of heat from the water, the buzzing in the air, and—

A great crack of light slashed through the sky, and a millisecond later, a wall of sound echoed through the ship. The thunder rumbled overhead as the storm made its presence known to every soul on board.

I couldn't help but laugh in bright joy as the blizzard began to fall in earnest, coating every part of the ship and every person aboard in white.

Even in moments like these... ships chasing one another, with life-or-death stakes... I loved sailing with every fiber of my being. It all came down to who had the better crews, the better sailors, and the better *seamanship.*

And I was quite sure anyone would be hard pressed to find a love of the sea like mine.

Slowly but surely, the fleet faded away in the sleet, ice and snow pelting us as the night came on in full. Only the barest hint of their lanterns could be seen burning through the blizzard when we crested the tops of waves. But even those faded with time. However, that didn't mean they weren't there.

The moment I lost track of the last hint of light from their ships, I turned from the aft railing to shout towards the helmsman. "Shift us six degrees south!" I yelled over the howl of the wind. Hoping against hope that if we could keep up this pace, we might lose them in the turn, and somehow escape this mess. It would keep us in the storm for longer, we were essentially sailing *with* it south, but I couldn't see any other way out.

"Captain! Six degrees south!" the helmsman confirmed, twisting the great spoked wheel a few turns port.

Hours passed slugging the *Wraith* through miserable weather, the storm doing its best to sink us. Hours watching crewmen hurl their stomachs over the side, wincing against the icy wind. Hours feeling the great seesaw of the ship rise and fall, the crash of the waves every few seconds with such force that the hull shuddered with it.

I kept watch the whole night, despite my brain crying for sleep. *No. No sleep. I must avoid it as long as I can.*

But the considerations for why it must be *me* to keep watch through the storm were also more practical. The cold didn't bother me, nor did the snow, and I didn't need to give any of my officer's hypothermia. I even sent the helmsman below and took the wheel myself, barking out only the most essential orders to keep us in the wind.

The worst part was over. Now it was time to endure, and pray my gamble had paid off..

With nothing left to do but wait and keep the helm steady, I let my mind wander. Flowing with the rise and fall of the waves we crested, and kept finding my thoughts returning to Moira, the look of anguish and hope she had in so readily agreeing to join us.

Why? Was it really so bad to be a princess?

When the storm finally broke, the sun stabbing through the dreary clouds still spitting pitiful rain, the seas beginning to calm… I glanced behind us and saw no pursuer aft of us.

We'd made it.

Barely.

And all we had to show for it was a pretty redhead.

Not much later, with hours gone by and not a single Kitaxian sail in sight, the horizon looked clear enough that I finally felt that I could give away the helm as the last of the storm died off. My brain felt like mush, and I was *hungry*, but I still needed to check in with everyone. Make sure that everyone was safe.

That I hadn't spent lives for the sake of this stupid fucking venture.

As I stepped down off the quarterdeck leaving Rodger in command, and deeper still below the weather deck, I felt instantly more comfortable as the warmth of the hold settled into my skin.

Just because I was incapable of producing my own body heat and my skin was as cold as stone, didn't mean I didn't enjoy *warmth*. I *craved* it. It was... comforting. Relaxing. I was eternally cold, much to my annoyance, and I'd be damned if I didn't try my best to seek out some source of heat.

And right now, there was something warm I craved almost as much as blood.

I barged into the galley with a vengeance, where a good number of the crew were also warming up with ale and hot food, almost every table wanting to call me over for a conversation.

Despite the lack of anything to really show for it, the crew went out of their way to show admiration and respect for how everything played out. I felt like I didn't deserve it, as I put us in that horrid situation in the first place. All for a woman Kitaxia was essentially throwing away.

But… we *had* trashed a royal convoy, and escaped the High Seas Fleet with not a scratch. Taken a princess, and won the day.

It always surprised me, their faith in me.

But finally, I made my way to the galley's counter, where Gracie was cooking up a storm as usual, looking to be just finishing up breakfast.

"Your usual Claire?" she asked with a knowing smile, her cheeks near glowing with the heat of the kitchens. Seeing her, standing up on a short stool with warm and flushed cheeks… Hunger rolled in my gut, but I stifled it. One craving at a time.

I nodded, my mood already perking up at the sound of the boiling kettle behind her.

She reached for a china mug and poured a small packet of powder into it before sliding the kettle free of the cast-iron stove in its fireproofed housing. She added steaming water to the mug and gave it a thorough stir with a spoon before placing it in front of me.

I gently clasped my fingers around its handle, and felt heat bleed off it into my hand. Gently, I held it to my chest, and felt the warmth spread into my core. I let out a blissful sigh.

"...Thank you Gracie," I said quietly. The heat felt… I didn't have the words for it. Warmth was unfamiliar to me now as kindness was. I appreciated this feeling of comfort spreading in my chest.

She waved off my thanks. "Thank you for getting us out of that mess. I see we got one new face out of it. She seems nice," she said with a wink.

I gave her a disjointed look. Rumours among the crew had started *already* apparently. "Don't you start." I shook a finger at her with my free hand. I did *not* need an association of some sort of infatuation with the woman I was most likely going to end up killing.

She shrugged, but smiled deviously. "Don't know what you're talking about, captain." she said with all the nuance and subtly of a piece of the bulkhead.

I shook my head at our cook, unable to believe her sincerity for a second, before I took a sip of the swirling brown drink in my hand.

In this life, if there was anything that came close to the joy of the taste of blood to me, it was this.

Hot cocoa.

Liquefied chocolate. It had been in the kitchens of the ship when we'd stolen it, and I'd gotten a taste for it. Warmth, chocolate, comfort, it was like a hug in a cup. I'd gotten Gracie's sister back in port to put in a regular order to keep us supplied, and now there was a stash of it on board just for me.

I took another sip, and felt the warmth spread out from my core, and felt *almost* human again.

The hunger still burned in the back of my throat, my teeth ached, and my stomach rumbled, all unimpressed by the chocolatey deliciousness, but my mental strain was better for it.

"Have you seen our new arrival recently?" I asked her over the edge of my cup, taking another slurp as I said it.

Gracie nodded, her attention turning back to whatever stew they were turning with a spoon. "They're with Jacine in the surgery bay, last I saw."

That got my attention. "I'll go see them now. Thanks again," I murmured, turning to leave as she waved goodbye. If they'd gotten injured in the storm somehow...

The galley was literally just down the hall from the surgery bay, and I found myself in front of its doorway in half a minute. I knocked on the doorway, stepping through the privacy flap, and came into the middle of what looked like a patient consultation.

"Now you'll have to be a bit particular about your diet, but these should produce results—" Maude quickly silenced herself as I strode in. Moira sat on the counter with an excited, unfiltered joy on her face, along with a matching one plastered on Jacine's. Moira had changed out of that ridiculous dress, and now looked to be in a loaned set of Jacine's clothes.

I had no idea what I was stepping into, and everyone turned to look at me with similar surprise.

I sipped my hot cocoa.

"Captain," Maude said coolly to break the awkward silence.

"I can… come back later?" I suggested quietly, but Maude shook her head.

"You're here for your… medicine?" Maude replied with a raised eyebrow.

It wasn't my original purpose for coming here, not exactly, but I did actually need my shot for the day. I nodded. "And just checking in on things after… well everything that was." I motioned above me as if to the fleet still out on the waters. As much as I thought Moira would be safe in Jacine's care, it somehow surprised me to see her without a scratch.

Barely a day on board and no one thought to gut her yet.

Maude smiled, but turned to Moira. "The important bit is to take it every day. If you're uncomfortable about the dosage or any of the effects, let me—or once we're back to port—Isabella know. Or consult with Jacine. She obviously has had more experience."

Ah. Suddenly everything made sense. Jacine had apparently told Moira about whatever medicine Maude and her partner had cooked up.

Moira nodded enthusiastically. "I will," She said near reverently, her gaze unto Maude as if she was a Goddess.

Maude folded her arms in slight amusement. "Good. Now, beat it you two, although don't go too far. I imagine the captain will have words after," she said with a smile and a thumb hooked towards the door.

I couldn't help letting out a chuckle. "She knows me too well. Meet me in the galley, and I'll be there shortly."

Jacine and Moira nodded, leaving quietly, excited whispering between them as they stepped around me, heading to the galley. Enough that I raised an eyebrow at Maude. "Well. They're like peas in a pod already," I admitted to Maude's restrained laugh.

"More than you know," she mumbled, making me raise the other eyebrow.

Something in my heart wrinkled at her description. "That was... quick. I didn't know Jacine had it in her. Well, good for them then," I replied, hoping I was hiding the note of sourness in my voice.

Why? Why did I care?

Maude laughed even more.

"No, no, it's not like that," she said with a happy smile, waving me off as she stepped across her office. "Although who knows. I'm no expert. Anyway." She reached one of her locked cupboards, unlocking it with a key only she and I had, and pulled out a vial, passing it to me.

"Very curious to see what you make of this one," she said with a knowing smirk. I squinted suspiciously at her as I took the vial in hand.

A vial of blood.

Being stuck on a ship for weeks at sea as a *Vampyri* produced certain... *challenges.*

Before I was a captain, years ago when I had signed onto a ship just to do anything to get back to sea, I'd fed from abusers, bullies, and their like. Folks I thought *deserved* it. But it made my feedings infrequent and irregular, and I spent months trying to figure out just how little blood I could survive on. I pushed the limits of my control on the regular, and it caused more than a few close calls.

Including once when I fed from Maude herself.

Why she hadn't turned me in I considered one of the great mysteries of our friendship. By the very act of not killing her when I fed from her neck, she seemed to take that as a sign that she could *trust* me.

Maybe it was medical curiosity, maybe it was madness; it certainly was stupid on her part, but I wasn't going to look a gift doctor in the mouth.

It wasn't until I was captain, that me, Maude, and her partner

Isabella, worked to come up with a solution.

The answer was I needed at *least* a proper feeding once every three days. Or, about a vial a day, bare minimum.

But where to get such vast quantities of blood? That answer was much more obvious. We had about just about two hundred souls on board the *Wraith* at any given time.

So, under the guise of 'inoculations' where the crew donated a drawing of blood to 'fight ship-borne disease' we had my meals.

It wasn't *quite* enough to cover every day of the year, but the bloated feedings from enemy captains that didn't surrender to our flag more than made up for the difference. It wasn't a perfect system, blood started to taste *awful* around the five hour mark, but it worked to keep the crew out of danger from my hunger.

Thank the Gods.

But Maude's entertained and curious expression made me suspicious of the vial in my hand. I uncorked it, debated putting it in my hot cocoa but thought it'd more likely ruin it, and instead downed its bloody contents on its own.

It wasn't nearly enough to replenish what I had lost in pushing myself through the duel with the royal guards, but it was enough to take the angry edge off.

But then… its taste hit me. *Delectable* flavour.

Sadness. Loneliness. Self-hatred and parents that could never understand—and even wilfully, *purposefully*—misunderstood. Cold fury, frustration, and a broken heart all wrapped into one tiny little package. It tasted like a *mourning* song.

Without a doubt, some of the best blood I'd ever eaten. I nearly choked on a moan of pleasure as I devoured it and licked the lip of the vial clean, determined not to let a drop escape me.

It took only a moment to realize I had just tasted Moira's freshly taken blood.

"Claire!" Maude yelled into my ear, shaking my shoulder.

I shook my head, freeing myself of the daze of emotions from Moira's blood.

I'd been so caught up in the mess in just the faintest hint of memories that I'd couldn't help but wonder what a full… *tasting* might be like.

"Sorry," I mumbled apologetically to Maude, reaching up to remove her hand from my shoulder. "I'm fine." I handed her back the vial, and pushed my spectacles further up my nose to hide both my shame that I'd been so easily distracted by the hunger, and the red rim around my irises.

Maude knew all too well what that red in my eyes meant.

I could feel her glare, in the universal stance of disapproving mothers and doctors everywhere, with her hands on her hips, looking like she was about to smack me upside the head.

"Well. Fine then. If you're 'good' then you're up for your yearly donation to research," she ordered, turning away to begin gathering some tools. Her suggestion made me groan.

"You just topped me up though," I whined, but walked forward to shimmy up onto the exam table Moira had just vacated.

Maude's face was a stony mask, except for her eyes daring me to resist.

"Ugh. Fine," I pulled one arm out of the sleeve of my jacket, rolling up my burgundy undershirt, and offered her my arm.

We had been trying to examine what made my blood any different from human blood. Looking for any small hint to reverse what had been done to me.

Blood was delicious, my speed and strength were awe-inspiring, but I missed the sun. I missed eating more than a few bites of *actual* food, and not having to fight off the beast in my head urging me to rip and tear through my friends and lovers every waking minute.

I missed *life*.

So, *any* step we could make towards discovering a cure... was worth it.

But that involved donating my blood to the cause, which was yet one more thing taxing my hunger.

She quietly pushed a needle into my inner-arm, and I stiffened as I always did as I felt the bite of fear of familiarity. The memory of Lady Ameritia in the dungeon sticking me in just a similar fashion bled into my vision, and I tried to ground myself with the swaying of the ship.

I breathed deeply, slowly, trying to just get through it without looking at where the needle met my skin. I thought of the sea, of sailing, of my favourite sword forms, anything but the metal piercing my skin.

"Annnnd, done. You're my model patient," Maude said with a smile, as if reading my thoughts.

I grumbled, feeling the pinch at my arm, as she retrieved the needle. A moment later, she had her little vial, my blood no different from anyone else's in the cupboard, labelled innocently as *C.C. Vessia.*

I felt the swirl of my hunger in my throat looking at the next few vials I'd be feeding from over the next few days. Maude only took from a few crew at time, because usually around the three day mark, even with the icebox in the cabinet, the blood spoiled. It began to taste like rot, and held no sustenance for me.

Such was my curse. I was meant to feed from *people*. This was just a stopgap.

I was still not back to anywhere near 100% where my hunger was concerned. I'd have to play it carefully until tomorrow's top off.

"Thank you. See you tomorrow," I grumbled. Still for all intents and purposes *starving*. My stomach felt hollow, a crankiness seeping into my bones. It took active effort to not let my goodbye sound snappy.

She gave a gracious bow and a devious smirk as I pulled my coat back on, before I retrieved my hot cocoa, and left the office back towards the galley just down the hall.

Passing off my empty mug back to Gracie's counter, I then found Moira and Jacine huddled close together over matching flagons of ale. Moira's face twisted up in disgust, seeming to not agree with her drink.

I couldn't help but be struck by her.

Who was this princess of Kitaxia? Why did she taste so Gods damned *sad*? Yet as I looked at her, there was no sadness. None visible at least. Even with her face scrunched up in disgust at the ale in her hand, she looked... pleased? Excited? Maybe with a touch of worry in her eyes.

We did *kidnap* her after all. Maybe she was just excited at the opportunity we were giving her to live outside her gilded cage.

More alarming was the crews stares around her, aiming daggers at her from every corner. This was something I had considered, the general mood of the crew at seeing the princess walk among them, seemingly free, un-murdered.

Regardless of how curious I felt about her, it would have to be addressed sooner or later, or it'd boil over into something *much worse.*

Usually, a dagger in the dark of the hold, a body tossed overboard in the dead of night. It wouldn't be the first time. Everyone would know, but no one would talk. A ship was a small place, and there were few secrets on board.

Save mine.

I strode over, feeling multiple sets of eyes follow my movement across the galley as I sat down next to them, pushing Jacine down the bench. Grabbing the flagon of ale Moira had been avoiding, I stole a swig as Jacine laughed.

Moira's glare was worth the annoyed expression I got in return. Jacine's laughter died into a chuckle beside me, clapping a hand on my back even though I'd really only taken a small sip. Ale was refreshing, but it did absolutely nothing for me. I couldn't even get drunk anymore.

"It's an acquired taste. It's better back home," I offered the ale back to Moira with a teasing grin. She shook her head, pushing the ale towards me with two pointed fingers like she was parting curtains to peek at the nonsense outside her castle walls.

I swirled the tankard around in the air in front of her, tempting her with it. "I suggest you take it. We're low on water, and it's your liquid for the day. With how thin you are, you need to keep down whatever you can."

Her eyes hardened at my probing comment. I didn't know why she looked more skeleton than girl, but I found myself wishing she wasn't.

She took the flagon from my grip like she wanted to punch me more than do what I said, wincing as she took a swig. "Fuck," she mouthed.

Jacine elbowed me in the ribs. "If you're so worried ma'am, then why steal a sip from her in the first place?"

Jacine's comment caught me off guard.

Why? Why did I care?

I shrugged, clutching at my side as if Jacine had wounded me.

"Wanted something refreshing after Maude's needle," I replied. Both their faces paled as they nodded in understanding.

"Yeah, she just got us too. After all the crap we give her though…" Jacine said with a smile, "giving her a little blood is worth it. Gods, I can't thank her enough for that medicine she gives me," her face glowed, bright as the morning sun. It was infectious, and I couldn't help reaching over Jacine's shoulder to hug her close.

She'd changed so much over the years. When I'd first met Jacine, she looked more boy than woman, all gangly limbs, constantly wearing a scarf to hide their stubble, their hair unkempt. But after years of Isabella and Maude's medicine, she had slowly grown into her own. Transformed day by day to the shape of her desired gender, and she'd taken to it with grace and beauty.

She was the happiest I'd ever seen her.

"You shine now Jacine. I'm happy for you," I said with a smile. No one could doubt her gender anymore. She looked so at home with herself that I was nearly jealous of her understanding of every inch of her person.

Moira's eyes bugged out at my words, looking back and forth between us. "You... you're okay with this?" she whispered under her breath, as if such a thing was scandalous.

Jacine let out a huff, almost of disappointment. It didn't surprise me to hear her suspicion of our tolerance, considering where she was brought up.

By *who* she was brought up by.

"Long before all this, I knew someone like the pair of you." I admitted quietly, not volunteering any more than that. It was the kind thing to say, even though the pain of grief still hurt, even in undeath. Moira seemed about to burst into a million and one questions, but I cut that off to address why I was *really* here.

"Tell me something, Moira," I asked quietly, taking off my

spectacles and pocketing them, before leaning forward over the table to put my chin in my palm. Jacine stiffened beside me. Something in my tone, combined with the fact I rarely took off my spectacles, must've sparked a warning for someone who knew me well.

I wanted to get a good read on our newest recruit. Moira herself tensed, both hands clamping around her mug.

She looked beautiful, even without the fancy dress we found her in. But something lit a fire in her heart as she stared into my eyes, a bite of surprise and alarm making it pick up in pace a hundred-fold.

She was scared of me.

Good.

"Why'd you *want* to leave?" I asked. "Why join us, when you probably lived in the lap of luxury? Are you not the daughter of the woman putting the boot on our neck?"

The entire galley shushed. Conversations didn't die, but I was no one's fool. The crew were listening.

Moira took a moment, breathing in deeply before she answered. "Because," she said proudly, her tone steady as she spoke from some hidden depth I had not seen the face of yet. "I will never be a royal plaything ever again." Her liquid green eyes hardened, her hair seeming aflame in the light.

Well. That was surprising.

I couldn't blush, my skin was cold and my heart did not beat to pump blood to my cheeks. But I felt like I was.

"A toast then, to the royals of Kitaxia! Long may they suffer!" Jacine shouted, a hand cupped to her mouth to shout. Every person in the galley cheered. A hundred boots stomped the deck twice in unison.

Moira looked around, panic settling in her heart as it picked up the pace, but I stomped the deck with the rest of the crew, standing up from my seat to take a bow, I held aloft my hat for lack of my own drink.

"May they taste the ashes of their kingdom!" I shouted, and then two more stomps were made to the deck, every single soul in the room cheered, and then downed their cups.

"To the crew of the *Wraith*!" someone shouted next, and everyone laughed, another drink, the mood of the crew turning near jovial.

Moira didn't know it yet, but with a single sentence she'd won the crew over.

I knew next to nothing about this gangly, loose-limbs, half-starved redhead, but I knew I wanted to know *more*.

With a happy sigh, I felt the desire to sit back down and get a refill of hot cocoa, wishing I could just sit and relax with Jacine and Moira for the next several hours. But duty called.

"Alright you two. Jacine, you have something somewhere that needs doing, I'm sure. Moira, you're with me," I ordered. It was time to see if she could back up her claim of usefulness.

Jacine gave a quiet two-fingered salute before grabbing the empty tankards, heading back to the counter with them, and gave Moira a wink before she left.

Moira looked after her like a puppy being left alone for the first time by its mother.

"Come on. Up." I motioned with my hand in a come-hither. She finally turned to face me with a smattering of fear, and I could swear I saw her gulp.

But she stood up from the bench, and dutifully followed me towards the kitchen.

The kitchen on the *Wraith* was one of the more innovative fixations of the ship. A box of heavily fireproofed wood to protect the outer layer of the ship's frame from any chance of possibly escaping flames. The day we stole the ship from its former Kitaxian masters, I'd tried rolling a hot coal across the deck inside, and it did not burn.

And as an extension, a warship needed a smithy for all sorts of needs. So, as the only other profession needed on board that worked heavily with fire, it shared the other half of the kitchen.

Where Gracie was patiently peeling potatoes humming a song that could be heard over the galley counter where she worked.

I opened the door and showed Moira inside.

"Gracie. May I introduce your new bunkmate." I motioned to Moira behind me as Gracie's expression lit up like it was her birthday. "Moira, this is Gracie Cavendish. The forge is attached to the kitchens due to fire prevention, so you'll be sharing a workspace. When not doing your own work, I expect you to pick up and help her. Clear?"

Moira nodded, looking at Gracie's beaming expression with trepidation, while I glared at her.

"Clear?" I asked again with growing severity in my tone. She would get the habit eventually. But her earlier nervousness was gone. She's found her courage between the kitchen and here, letting whatever she was scared of disappear.

When she finally looked at me, there was some mirth in her eyes. "Yes, Captain," She said dipping into a curtsy with a lavish bow.

Gracie's mouth opened wide and sucked in a shocked breath at what was clearly meant to mock me. It was almost as hilarious as the actual curtsy. Where had the nerve-wrecked girl gone a minute ago?

"Don't be cute, Moira," I muttered, hopefully hiding the smile in the back of my voice. "That'll only get you in trouble faster." I was starting to think that she was testing me. Poking and prodding to get some reaction.

She rose from her curtsy to glance at her nails, set into long fingers. "Why Captain? Is it working?"

Gracie burst into laughter as I rolled my eyes. I had to give her that one. She had a sense of humour at least. "Gracie, for the love of the Gods above and below, get me a refill of hot cocoa before I throw her overboard." If I was going to deal with Moira pushing my buttons with jokes, I wanted something sweet to distract me from the temptation of draining her dry.

Gracie nodded, still sputtering giggles, grabbing the pouch of powder and the same mug I'd given her a little bit ago, and putting the kettle on the stove. "Coming right up ma'am. Gosh, I did say I like this one. And she's gonna work the forge! Well, she'll need to fatten up some muscle for that, she's as thin as a cookie!" Gracie exclaimed, making me wince as I regarded Moira's form. She wasn't wrong; Jacine's loaners were hanging off her like rags on a scarecrow.

Moira looked down at the clothes hanging off her with a frown, looked to be silently debating that exact concept, until she spied Gracie pouring the sweet concoction into my mug, eyes locked onto it with alarm.

I walked over to the forge half of the hot room, and motioned at the immaculate space before explaining a few things about the space.

"The only times the tools had been moved was when Jacine needed them for some project or other. So, if something's missing she'll know where. If anything's not to your liking, bring it up with Markus or Gracie." I sipped at the steaming beverage, letting out a brief sigh of relaxation at its chocolate-y flavour, before finally turning back to her. But she was still staring in shock at my mug. I didn't think she had heard a word I just said.

"What now?" I asked, impatience bleeding into my voice.

She shook her head, amazement crossing her face.

"I'm just losing my mind a bit over the fact that the great and terrible pirate Captain Claire Vessia, Bloody Queen of the seas, terror of the three nations and scourge of Kitaxia… *Drinks hot cocoa.*" At her last words, she stifled a choked laugh, making me look from her giggle at my expression to the steaming mug in my hand.

"You take that back," I barely choked out, beginning to laugh as I did. And then she was laughing, and Gracie too. She had a point. I was known as a monster across her kingdom, but here I was sipping something warm and cosy like a school girl. It was *funny.*

I felt relieved, because I hadn't laughed like that in weeks.

As our laughter died down, I finally motioned over the forge. "Well? Is it serviceable?" I wanted to know what she thought. About the space, about what she needed, about, well, *everything.*

She shrugged, the smile still on her lips, finally roaming her gaze around the forge. "I don't know," she replied. "Depends on what I'll be making I suppose. I've only done castle forging."

I set down my cocoa on the sizable workbench, rummaging around in the scrap metal pile, pulling out a copper plate I knew was there.

"Maintenance on these mostly." I handed it to her. "They line the outer hull, to protect the wood from salt degradation and barnacle formation. Better the upkeep, longer lifespan of the ship."

Moira held it this way and that, the light from the stoves sluggishly reflecting off its surface. "Simple enough. Flat copper sheet with rivet holes. Easy. What else?" she asked.

I motioned to examine everything around her, explaining as I went. "Everything. Nails, tools, needles, rivets, everything you can imagine that a ship could need. Occasionally weapon maintenance and forging. Ammo and shot in a pinch. We have a proper castle forge for you once we're home."

Her eyebrow raised, setting the copper sheet on the workbench beside my cocoa, which I just remembered existed, and reacquired.

"Home? The mythical Port Sable?" she asked, to which I smiled and nodded.

Port Sable was a legendary pirate port, told of in stories and myths since long before I rose the black. It was a useful myth to have.

Because no such port existed. We made it up. Better to have the Kitaxian navy searching for an island that didn't exist rather than a port whose authorities were heavily in my pocket.

"Our former blacksmith is there, Old Man Tom," I continued, ignoring the obvious question of where Port Sable was in her tone. "A cannonball took his leg some ten months back. This is how he stays a part of the crew."

She winced at the thought of such an injury. "Well, I look forward to meeting him. Which is something I never thought I'd say," she said quietly, picking up the copper plate again. The way she phrased it suddenly made me remember how her blood tasted. *Sad.* The smile on her face was still mischievous and teasing, but now I was begging to see the sadness just underneath.

"What do you mean?" I asked over the lip of my hot cocoa, taking a comforting sip as I leaned against one of the work benches.

She motioned to the wall that separated the forge from the kitchen, where the rest of the crew sat in the galley. "Everyone's been nice. *Kind.* Accepting. You're *pirates.* You shouldn't be *nice.* And now here I am honestly excited to meet another one. I must be losing my mind." Her tone made it sound as if she believed herself in a dream. "But now here I am, wanting to know more about all of you. What lies I've been fed by my parents. Hell, I don't even know if you *have* parents. Do you?" She asked, the sudden intensity of her gaze on me.

And of course, the first question she ever asked me was one of the most difficult to answer.

I took a deep breath, and tried not to crush the fine china mug in my hand as a million memories crashed through my skull in a tidal wave of trauma.

"I'm adopted," I admitted quietly, taking a sip from my hot cocoa. "I had two mothers who raised me. They were happy." I dipped a finger in the scalding hot cocoa, not caring that it burned. My hunger growled in my throat, and my teeth ached. I concentrated on the feeling of my hunger, not to let myself be pulled in by the ghost of memory, and all the horrors within.

I hated this life after death, but sometimes it felt like I deserved it. I looked up from my cocoa as I silently stirred the chocolate with the tip of my finger, looking her in the eyes. She must've known she'd overstepped with such a question with an expression of growing silent terror plastered on her face.

My tone betrayed no happy memory here.

"They were happy together," I continued. "But then the first purge happened." Moira's eyes closed in understanding. She was the daughter of the woman who'd ordered it, she would know. "They were two Kitaxian women who were married. When the first purge happened, they were among the first to be cast out. They found themselves in the slums, where they found little baby me, washed up on a riverbank."

I pulled out my burnt finger, sucking on the liquid that had accumulated around it, my skin healing in an instant. Pain was never very permanent for me, unless it was from the sun or my hunger.

"They raised me as their own, and we survived," I explained.

I took a deep breath once again, sighed, and watched her expression twist into further imagined pain. She knew this story wasn't over yet. She knew where it was going.

"Then the *second* purge happened," I breathed out, a quiet statement of fact, yet filled with so much horror. I felt it in the clench of my jaw, the rumble of my hunger, the strain of my muscles.

Yet I would say no more.

What was there to say? The Second Purge of Fire and Faith shook

Kitaxia to the core. It had been the deadliest of the three, because its greatest weapon was the slums *themselves*. The first purge had been an exile of undesirables to the slums. They became overcrowded and filth ridden nearly overnight. So, for the second purge, the slums fit to burst, they lit them on fire.

My mothers had taken me and tried to get out of the flames.

Mother June didn't make it.

"Claire, I'm so—"

"You do not get to say my name, Moira."

She tightened like a sail's slip line, a rope gone taught in a sudden gale, and I had to fight my hunger, wanting nothing more than to rip out her throat and drink her dry. She backed into a corner of the forge, sliding down to the floor.

"You've not earned that right," I hissed. "Nor have you earned the right to my life story. You've not earned a damned thing on this ship yet, Moira. And until you do, you may call me *Captain*, or nothing at all."

My order was absolute. I glared at her, watching her wither under my stare as our repeated words from my cabin hung in the room like toxic smoke. She'd sailed straight into the sea of one of my biggest traumas. How could she have known?

I inhaled, slowly, through my nose, trying to bleed stress out of my bones. Her hands were clasped over her mouth and nose, her knees up to her chest as she sat on the corner. She looked as if she was terrified if she made a single noise I would pounce.

I took another sip of hot cocoa.

"Tell you what," I said quietly, a half dead smile on my face as I started to walk for the door.

"You sign the Code tonight, and I'll tell you one more thing. Full truth. Signing that means you're one of us now. A *pirate*, not a princess."

I left Moira in the forge wondering silently at what exactly I'd just promised her, walking through the decks trying to get rid of the memory of her terror-filled face.

CHAPTER TWELVE

*"I don't care that you want to add daily prayer to the Church of
the King Undying, it's not that simple! Ship's Contracts are the
fundamental document of governance on a ship, it's the rules of which
the whole crew agree to. You can't just write in a 'new line of rules',
you imbecile. Otherwise, you're making an entire new document…
You're not leaving my office until I agree to this are you? Fine."*

— Randall Givens, Lord Admiral of the Royal Kitaxian Navy

After that mess of conversation with Moira, I made my way up to the weather deck feeling nearly ill. For some damn reason, that look of terror and guilt on her face as she slid down to the floor, back against the wall… haunted me. Hoping that fresh air would clear my head, I hid in the shade of the overhang of the deck that sat above the entryway to my quarters. I sometimes liked to stand here and watch my sailors work.

"Aren't you supposed to be sleeping?" Markus yawned above me, the morning light still brisk overhead. The temperature had warmed up dramatically, the icy water of the north a distant memory, storm clouds now nowhere to be seen.

I sighed into my cup, feeling my shoulders slump and filled with longing for what I imagined an actual day of rest to be. How nice it must be to sit in the warmth of the sun without it feeling like my skin was cooking off my bones.

"You know how it is, Markus. I get enough. I always do," I mumbled, just loud enough for him to hear over the sounds of the ship's busywork.

Which was a lie. I rarely slept, if at all. Between my nightmares of the noose, the deaths of several innocents at my hands when I was still figuring out this life, the dungeon, Lady Ameritia's vials, the shipwreck…

127

I got maybe two, three hours of sleep at the most if I was lucky. More often I tossed and turned and woke up in a cold sweat in minutes.

It would've killed a human, I was sure. I didn't tire, and my body healed even the most grievous of wounds. But the weight on my mind... My *soul*... Gods I was so tired. All the time. I craved sleep, but could never manage much.

"Fine. Aren't you supposed to be *attempting* sleep?" he replied sleepily above me, still rubbing an eye. My sleeplessness was near legendary around the crew, one of the larger betting rings was on when I would collapse from exhaustion.

I didn't answer, and Markus snorted once he realised I wasn't going to.

So, we both stood there looking at the morning on the *Wraith* develop as it usually did. People of all sorts, climbing up and down the rigging, shifting the sails just so. The gentle rock of calmer seas raising and lowering the deck beneath their feet. The crinkle and groan of the wind through rope and sail above us.

The calls, the jokes, the songs and shanties. *Laughter*.

Here, on the *Wraith*, people could be *free*.

I watched it all delightedly, beyond proud that I could provide this environment for the people I'd helped liberate. The people that I helped *protect*.

I briefly imagined a life where I could relax with them in the light of the sun. Joking and laughing without a care in the world. Living in hope of a brighter tomorrow.

But dead women didn't get dreams.

I looked above me at Markus leaning forward on the quarterdeck railing, almost looking divine with his sun-bleached hair, a smile on his face… And jealousy stirred in my gut. The feeling of *want*. Of *life*.

But life was something I could never have. I was *me* after all. The shadow in the blackness of the overhang, grimacing in the dark, sipping my hot cocoa. Where I'd be forever more.

"I worry about you, you know," Markus said above me, just loud enough for me to hear.

I stopped swirling the remnants of my drink in front of me and stared up once more at our quartermaster, his gaze up in the rigging.

Markus knew almost more about me than anyone on this ship. He was my first and closest friend in this life after death. As much as he disagreed with everything I said, he was without a doubt the person I trusted more than anyone else. But his care and concern for me... I thought it was misplaced at best.

I was an undead monster. I didn't need to be worried about. No one should worry about me, *period.*

"You shouldn't," I said back, taking another sip of my cocoa, feeling a warmth in my chest I disagreed with. I didn't feel like I deserved any of this. This ship, this crew... this family. He let out a frustrated sigh. "Claire… When am I going to convince you you're worth more than the destruction you carve through the seas?"

That made me want to laugh. I was *made* of destruction. I shrugged my shoulders, even though he couldn't see me down in the shadows below him. "Probably never. I am known for my stubbornness," I replied, amusement in my voice.

Now it was him breaking out into laughter. "Aye. That you are. That you are." He quieted a moment later, silently considering the wind whistling through his hair as I clamped my hat down onto my head, still hiding in the shade.

"Claire. You can't be serious about the brat," He said, changing the subject.

I raised my eyebrow, lifting the rim of my hat so I could see his face better. "Brat?" He obviously meant Moira, but she'd not been on the ship long enough to justify his disdain like this. I expected an attempt on her life, not for *name calling.*

He nodded, a sarcastic smirk developing in the corner of his cheek. "Oh, come on. A *rebel*-princess under your thumb? Tied to the woman who killed—" He silenced what he'd been about to say, and for good reason. No one among the crew needed to know I wasn't a member of the living. "I mean, come *on. A redhead?* Claire. She was *made* for you to bring aboard," Markus continued.

Again, if I could blush, I was sure I would've. I couldn't be more thankful that I was hiding in the dark out of eyesight. Markus was an expert at reading my moods.

I tipped my hat down to hide beneath its rim nonetheless as embarrassment boiled in my cheeks, which of course, made Markus laugh.

"Claire, she's at best a useless entitled royal. At worst, her loyalty is still to the crown. Stop thinking about your revenge, or with what's between your legs, and more with what's between your ears. We should just kill her and toss her overboard." He shook his head, looking out over the ocean. "Because you're so damn smitten with her, you can't see what needs to be done."

Me? *Smitten*? With Moira?

Of course not.

It'd been *two fucking days*.

I'd like to think I had some restraint about developing feelings for someone after more than two fucking days.

"I not hearing anything about her yet, Markus Clun, only what you may *think* I feel." I stated with as much severity as I could muster in my voice.

"It's obvious, isn't it?" he began. "What Kitaxian royal in their right Gods damned mind would want to join our crew? She obviously just wants to find the location of Port Sable, then jump ship at the earliest available opportunity, and give its location away."

I frowned and felt my insides twist into knots. She *did* ask about it...

I didn't comment on his evaluation of Moira, silently stewing in whether it was possible Lady Ameritia would use her own daughter as a plant just to get to *me*.

It certainly was... *possible.*

"It's not just up to you, or to me. We'll see what everyone else has to say," I said over the rim of my cocoa. There would be a vote among the officers whether to *formally* offer her a place on the ship.

"Fat chance in all the hells that everyone will agree, but sure Claire, sure..." His face scrunched up like a ball of paper as he looked up into the rigging. "You think she'll sign it?" he asked quietly.

I thought of all I had spoken with Moira over the past day about, her declaration in the galley, and the memory of how her blood tasted in my mouth.

But what settled in my memory of the few times I'd seen her, wasn't the sadness I tasted in her blood, but the *hope* I saw on her face. In the galley, in my quarters, in the surgery bay. Even when Markus put the shackles on her wrists. Despite everything, and the fact I probably scared her half to death, she was *happy* to be here.

I smiled as I finished the last of my cocoa before answering him. "I think… that we'll all be surprised by just how fast she signs the bloody thing."

A few minutes later, I bid Markus goodbye, and made my rounds across the ship once again. I checked in with everyone to see what loot everyone had gotten from the yacht, did my best to make sure everyone was still in good spirits despite our close call with the navy, and listened to the general mood of the crew about our newest member.

Surprisingly, it was going… *well.* I half expected the crew to want to tear Moira to shreds, but considering her gender… Everyone could see plain as day why she would want to be among us, save for a few like Markus, who suspected her to be some form of royal spy.

It put some of my worries to rest, but eventually, sleep *finally* decided it would come for me. Once my rounds were done, I found myself back in my quarters, shut off from the noise and bustle of the ship, staring at my bed with longing.

At this point I'd been awake for nearly four days straight. I couldn't put it off any longer. I *needed* rest.

I hung up my sword belt on the rack beside my bed, threw my coat and hat onto my chair, and shrugged out of most of my clothes.

I crawled into bed with a blissful sigh, feeling my barely used sheets and mattress nearly swallow me whole, smelling faintly of gunpowder, and was asleep in minutes.

Sleep lured me in with false promises, whispers of rest just *barely there* out of reach.

Because there in the darkness of my dreams, I only found Lady Ameritia's cackling laughter. Manacled wrists kept me in place while she stabbed me repeatedly with the handle of the tankard I'd made, bleeding me onto the stone floor beneath my feet.

And just before I died, she put a noose around my neck.

As soon as I felt the rope, I gasped awake in terror, clutching the air above me with a cry.

Every damn time.

I cursed every swear I knew, and then every swear I knew in every other damn language I could remember, rubbing at my exhausted eyes with a longing for rest that would never come.

Please... just let me forget. I don't want to remember.

Beg as I might, the Gods had never shown me mercy from my nightmares.

I threw off my covers with frustration, threw on my coat over my naked chest and grabbed some pants before walking over to the windows to peer into the light behind the ship's wake.

The sun was still high in the sky, its light searing onto my face, making me hiss in brief pain before I closed the curtains once more. It'd been all but an hour or two.

As usual.

With an aggravated sigh, I rubbed my fingers at my eyes, fighting the hunger in the base of my throat, the heavy exhaustion I felt on my shoulders, and slumped into my chair.

Five *fucking* years of nightmares, every single time my head hit pillow. Try as I might, I couldn't forget dying.

Well. I was awake now. Might as well be useful.

I set to work.

I spent the rest of the daylight hours charting our path across the ocean separating Kitaxia in the east, Norlondia in the north, and Varcna in the south. Port Sable, our home port, was technically in eastern Varcna, where its shores stretched across the southern part of the Great Divide in a smattering of near countless islands. The myth of the Great Divide was that there was an island for every single thousand and one Goddesses.

Kitaxia, the easternmost landmass of the Great Divide, was itself one great island, one of the largest in the sea. Norlondia, in comparison, was only made of three islands with narrow channels between them, and a few smaller satellites orbiting a messy and choppy coast.

I'd ordered a homeward bound heading for now. We did not have quite a full hold, but we needed supplies and rest. The crew wasn't overworked, their mood still chipper for now, but they were certainly a bit skittish.

But if something appetizing showed up on the way, we'd certainly take advantage. We *were* pirates after all.

Hours of charting our course, predicting possible encounters, rationing ledgers of supplies to make sure we had enough to get back home without starving to death… All before the sudden lack of pressure in the back of my mind with the ringing of the eighth bell, alerted me to sunset. A few moments later, Markus was knocking on my door. It was time.

I put some more clothes on, and welcomed everyone into my cabin.

All of the ship's officers piled in, taking their usual spots. All here to debate, a singular topic.

Moira.

"I call this meeting of the ship's counsel to order," I said loudly to the room, knocking my knuckles against my desk and trying not to squirm in my chair. "Let's be about it, folks. I'm in a foul mood and want to make it quick, Let's just put it straight to a vote. Unless any of you really want to have this argument?"

No voice was raised. Heads nodded.

"Very well. All in favour of adding Moira to the crew?"

By rule, I couldn't vote. Only in a tie.

I watched each officer, as they shifted eyes towards each other, a silent debate among each of them. I didn't doubt for a moment that they hadn't had their own discussions on it, but I thought I could count on a couple safe bets.

Jacine and Maude, for starters. Both of them raised their hands.

Gracie's vote of confidence was a surprise, but a welcome one.

I was hoping for at least one more.

But it never materialized. Moira had *only* three. Which meant…

"Against?" I stated, my voice purposefully neutral.

Charlotte, Markus, and Rodger all raised their hands.

I wasn't sure it was going to happen. I half expected all of them to throw her out. But now… It was up to me.

"Breaking the tie, I vote in favour of welcoming her to the crew," I put as much iron in my voice as I could, taking care to look as neutral as possible as I watched the others' reactions. Jacine, Maude, and Gracie all seemed rather pleased. Rodger shrugged more than anything else, but Charlotte and Markus seemed to *not* like how this had played out.

It was at that moment that it really hit me. That I would have the *Princess of Kitaxia* aboard. An equal member of the crew. The idea of her as a permanent fixture on board hadn't really settled in yet. I had Lady Ameritia's child *right here*, and was treating her like my own family.

What in the blazes was wrong with me? Was this really the right move?

The chance to hit Lady Ameritia was all but non-existent if she never left the damn castle. If I let Moira live... would I ever get another chance?

I sighed. It was out of my hands now. I nodded to Jacine who was standing with a happy smile by the door.

She opened the door to admit Moira, and I watched her gaze shift over every other officer gathered in a haphazard circle around my desk in a mixture of awe and terror. It brought a smile to my face.

This was a ritual we'd done countless times, for every new crewmember who signed on.

"Moira. Welcome," I said quietly from my chair, my hands folded in front of my mouth, much like when we had our first little 'interview'.

"You've met Jacine, Maude, and Gracie of course." They all nodded as I said their names. "But these are the rest of the officers to whom you also owe a bit of loyalty to." Moira, providing she signed onto the Code, would be theirs to command, just as much as she was mine.

Moira took in the faces of each officer present, doing her best to hide some fear in her heart.

I raised a hand towards Charlotte. "Our chief gunner, Charlotte. Refer to them as they and them. If you don't, it's on your head." Charlotte was sitting on their usual perch, on top of my mapping table, earning a hefty glare from me that they matched with a shite-eating-grin.

"Time to sign your life away," Charlotte sing-songed from the mapping table as Moira regarded them. Charlotte gave her a suggestive wink, and I tried to smother the sharp stab of jealousy that I told myself was anything but. Charlotte had only grown raunchier over the years. "Haven't fucked a redhead in awhile, wonder what she tastes—"

I slammed my hand onto the desk, making everyone jump. Jealousy or not, that was going too far.

"Charlotte," I muttered, a growl in my voice. They stared at me, still holding that grin, a challenge in their eyes.

I was about to order them to apologize, compel them if I had to, but Moira surprised everyone, by letting the comment slide off her like water.

She looked down her nose, holding herself like any proper lady should, and I swear to the Gods above and below, sneered at Charlotte, and in the most authoritative voice possible stated; "You wish."

Rodger chuckled as Charlotte's grin turned into a frown. "Alright, I'm starting to like her," he mumbled. It didn't surprise me that he would, as much as she had pushed my past earlier, she was settling in alarmingly quickly. But there was another reason I thought Rodger might grow to appreciate her.

I raised my hand towards him at my side. "I believe you might already be familiar with Mr. Castille, our master-at-arms."

Moira's eyes widened into shock as she looked Rodger over. She *had* to have recognised him, he was a former royal guard.

"I must've seen you somewhere at the palace. You have the aura of familiarity," Rodger said jokingly with a smirk, rubbing at his chin as he looked Moira over, obviously knowing exactly who she was.

"It's… good to see you again," Moira said as she nodded at him with respect, the ghost of a smile for someone from her old life. Her heart began to settle, each new face a bit more welcome.

"And finally, our Quartermaster, Markus Clun." I lifted my hand towards the man standing at my right-hand-side. Moira eyed him with a suspicious glance, and I could nearly feel the air tense around him.

"Alright, Gentlemen. Ladies." I eyed Charlotte as always. "Charlotte."

They winked.

"Bringing this meeting to order, you all know why we're here. Moira. This is the leadership of the ship. Providing you read, understand, and sign the code, you'll be answerable to them at all times. If you have a problem with any of the leadership…" I eyed Charlotte.

"Then you go to either Markus or me. Preferably Markus," I explained. She tilted her head questionably.

"Why Markus and not you?" Moira asked, unsure.

Her question annoyed me, hunger tightening all the muscles in my throat. I just wanted this to be *over already.* I flopped back into my chair, raising my arms in exasperation, my lack of sleep and the hunger making me feel snappy.

"My charming personality?" I replied. Maude snorted, but Rodger was feeling brave.

"It's because she's about as likely to bite off your head as much as listen to your complaint," he bravely volunteered.

I fixed him with a glare, letting my exhaustion and impatience bleed out of my face, but didn't say anything.

"It's true though. You can't fault me for truths," he said to defend himself, pointing finger-guns in my direction with a smile. Out of all the officers, Rodger probably got away with most these days.

I made a motion to push him away from me, rubbing my hand over my face before turning my attention back to Moira. "Regardless. If you sail with us, you must sign the ship's charter. It's the binding agreement we all agree to. Breaking any of its rules results in… unpleasant consequences."

She held silent for a breath at my words, before asking yet another question. "Like what?"

I turned to Markus. "Was the last one the quartering or the poison?"

I asked, making him wince. But it was Maude who spoke up.

"It was the poison." Her words were like ice. She would've known, she made the poison in question. I nodded, turning back to Moira.

"Last one was some greedy double-dipping idiot. He'd been keeping a logs of everything. Where we went, who we traded with, an exact list of our 'crimes'. Caught him trying to stowaway onto one of our prizes. Admitted he was going to sell the information." I explained it with hard eyes locked on her. "So we left him on a sandbar with nothing to drink but water tainted with Pythriean poison." I tapped an annoyed finger on my desk at the memory.

Moira stared, open mouthed horror at the words I had just said, and with good reason. Pythriean poison made your skin slowly fall off. But rather than letting myself imagine that horrorshow as Moira was clearly doing, I just slouched further into my chair, wishing I could sleep. "Is any of this… serious to you? Are you even… sane?" she mumbled out.

With a sigh, I pushed myself to sit straight once again, wishing I was wearing my jacket to cozy up into. The hunger shifting exhaustion into even more frustration. Frustration into impatience. Impatience into anger.

"Probably not. I don't think it's possible to be sane and sit in this chair," I replied. Everyone laughed at that, even Moira letting out a surprised but broken half laugh.

"But to the matter at hand, this is our great document." I opened the locked drawer in my desk that held the most important piece of paper on board, setting it gently in front of her, and then the following forty pages of names, marks, and other signatures of crew members come and gone. More than a fair share scratched out as they passed from battle-wounds, disease, or were released.

"Read through, twice, make sure you know what you're signing. If you decide not to, well. You're a unique case. But we'll make sure wherever we'd stuff you would be humane," I murmured quietly, watching her eyes go over it line by line, and then again from top to bottom. She was taking my advice. Good.

The rules were simple enough, although hidden in the complicated wording of legalise. Firstly, equal shares among everyone. Even the officers. We took no greater share than anyone else on board. Second, was outlawed practices, mostly about stealing and abuse. Third, was a stipulation about leadership. A vote for captain or any officer's slot could happen at any time, provided it was outside of combat. In the middle of a fight was no place for leadership debates. Fourth, was a stipulation on crew disagreements. They could be settled by duels, games, arbitration... But most of the crew settled on duels. Fifth, was executive punishments, mostly to be done by me, unless I had a conflict of interest.

Sixth, was... different. It stipulated that when we took enemy ships who attempted to run or fight, that the first officer and captain of those prizes would be reserved for me to do with as I wished. Otherwise, the enemy crew would vote and debate among themselves any other crewmember they wished to be 'tried for abuses'. We saw ourselves as an opportunity for prize crews to get even with the power structures that had ruled their lives.

And then there was the seventh and final rule...

"I'll be honest. This sounds a lot more favourable than any other contract I've ever seen, and I've seen more than most," she said quietly, nodding. "But I've never seen this last bit. 'Signature of this document entails service to the crew until death or release by the captain.' What does that mean?"

I smiled. "It means you agree to serve the ship, until death, or I discharge you." It wasn't as bad as it sounded, but I was enjoying the implications playing out across her face.

Her eyebrows rose, face twisting in thought. "You… what, get—"

I nodded.

"It's exactly how it sounds. Meaning either you're dead or I agree to let you go. Anything else is desertion," I explained with a vile smile, her eyes narrowing.

"How in the hells is that fair?" she exclaimed, and I shrugged, feeling myself slide back in my chair again. All the officers had heard me make this speech before.

"Simple," I explained, posing a question. "How many ports in the world can we dock at?" Understanding blossomed across her face as I continued, holding up a single finger. "Exactly. We have *one*. Just one. We cannot, *cannot*, let knowledge of the fact that we berth there escape, or the armies and navies of three nations will be all over that port in a heartbeat." I pointed the finger down into my desk, literally, making my point. "I will tell you that I have released many sailors who were tired of serving under me. But you know where they all retired to?"

She nodded, throwing up a hand in defeat. "Port Sable," she murmured, a sigh of defeat in her. Finally, I think she understood exactly what she was signing up for, and I had to give her credit, she was proving quicker than most.

"Exactly," I replied. "So, when you sign for this, you're stuck with us for life. Or you can be trusted enough to not spoil our secrets. And I can tell you that right now, the only people I'd trust enough with such a thing are standing in this room."

I looked to the face of every officer I had, knowing they had my back no matter what. They had followed me into hell time and time again, and I knew in my *bones* that I'd do anything in the world to provide for and protect them.

Moira was quiet for some time, re-reading the last segment of the Code three times now.

"Okay. I… *think,* I can live with that," she said quietly, picking up the pen. "But I don't see an inkwell, and why is this all in red ink?" she asked.

I smiled, grabbing a dagger from the belt I had swung around the top of my chair. "My dear, that isn't ink," I said as I leaned forward to grab her slim wrist.

CHAPTER THIRTEEN

*"Have you heard what happened to the Strident Venture? That ship
out of Wester-Cay?"*

"No, what happened? Don't tell me—"

"Mhm. Vessia got em'. Poor bastards."

"God above have mercy. What'd she do this time?"

*"Do you really wanna know? She left a single man
alive to tell the tale."*

"Shit. Wasn't… wasn't Jesson on that ship?"

*"He was. Now he's probably in pieces on the bottom
of the Great Divide."*

— *Overheard conversation outside a Upper City monastery in Haxla*

“Did you really have to cut my thumb like that? Like, *really*?
Signing in blood is so cliché," Moira mumbled around her thumb
in her mouth, a face full of pout that made my unbeating heart ache.

Markus's words about me being *smitten* haunted me, but I
refused to entertain the thought. Moira was at worst, my prisoner, at
best, another underling. The moment she signed the Code, she was
no longer the princess, but a rebel against the crown, and my victory
was complete.

I shrugged in the form of an answer as I gathered up the pages,
my eyes burning with the need for more sleep. I thought that signing
the Code in blood fit the ship's… *character*.

I looked at Moira's signature with a curious glance. She had signed with just her first name, which was unsurprising, but I'd still hoped I'd have the name *August* in the ship's code as a trophy. Still, a win was a win.

Thinking about it, I thought that maybe her last name was something she very much wanted to leave behind with her birthright. But what had caught my eye in the first place was how perfect her script was. I guess that was to be expected with a noble.

"You have beautiful handwriting," I said quietly, pushing the last paper in with the others, locking them into their hidden drawer in my desk.

Everyone else had started filing out of the room, while Markus was chatting with Charlotte and Jacine about something in the doorway, noise from the weather deck wafting in around them. Moira was still sitting across from me, nursing her thumb from my dagger, the smell of her blood biting the back of my throat and making my mouth water.

"Well," I said, putting words in the air less to get Moira's attention and more to distract myself from the imagined taste of her blood. "You'll be working under her directly." I nodded towards Jacine. "But you're thick as thieves already, so I doubt that'll be a problem. But sharing a space with Gracie will be a challenge in of itself. Don't be afraid to establish some boundaries. Again, if there's trouble, go to Markus. Jacine in a pinch. Last resort is me."

Moira nodded, licking her thumb, a small smear of blood on her tongue. I couldn't help but stare, my mouth hanging open as a different kind of hunger swelled in my gut.

Damn it.

"Will do, Captain," Moira said quietly, thankfully not noticing my stare, her own gaze still focused on keeping pressure on her thumb. "I admit. Everything happening here is a bit more… *democratic* than I imagined. Save the part of the code on duelling I suppose."

I rolled my shoulders, focusing on my muscle, the tension over bone, trying to push the image of blood on her tongue from my mind.

"No tyrants, no kings," I replied, raising my arms as if to show myself off in a grandiose manner. "I am queen of nothing at all, despite the titles they call me," I finished with a laugh.

Leaning forward to place her chin onto her hand, she fixed me with a curious look of a half smile. "What do you think of them? The titles?" she asked.

Unsure what she could possibly be getting at, I decided to entertain her.

"They're useful," I replied. "The grander my story is, the more ships that surrender when my flag flies. The more a crew is scared by my banner, the more likely it is that no one gets hurt."

Her eyes narrowed. "Don't you care that they make you out to be a monster?"

I felt my brief joy at our conversation turn sour once again. Moira had a talent for hitting me with words exactly where it hurt. My fingers clenched into my chair's arms, as I turned my head to look away from her, anger kicking hunger into a vile wave shuddering through my body.

Of course I cared.

"They made me into one first," I spat out with venom in my voice.

Out of the corner of my eye, I saw her face twist into shame and guilt, her mouth beginning to shape a word that she didn't get to finish before the shouts of "sail!" were screamed in through the open door from the weather deck, the noise of the crew mobilizing cutting off whatever she'd been about to say.

A single word that changed my mood from grouchy to elated in a heartbeat. The lookouts had spotted a sail on the horizon. The possibility of a *feeding*. My ears perked, I jumped up in my seat, turning to smile at Moira. I could barely restrain my fangs in my gums as the hunger roared in my dry throat, the sudden anticipation of a proper meal.

"And now you get to see the monster up close," I excitedly chirped, shooting from behind my desk to storm past Moira and out of my quarters, not caring where she went for now. She was no longer my direct responsibility, just one more crewmate on the payroll.

Climbing up the stairs up to the quarterdeck, I wished I'd at least grabbed my coat. The cool night air was *frigid*, the winds from the north still quite cool. Everyone else was in jackets and sweaters, and here I was in nothing but a shirt.

But I pushed my displeasure at the temperature and hunger aside. I could hold until I saw the shape of our prize. We were days ahead of the fleet, far enough south that we'd *probably* lost them, and now we were back into the trade lanes.

That meant *merchants*.

With our predators' days behind, and a prize to our fore, I felt confident enough about our chances. I hopped up into the aft rigging and eyed our prey through the telescope.

A Kitaxian merchant brig sailing without a care in the world, illuminated by the very last vestiges of dying sun. Had it been ten-minutes later we would've been lucky to spot her in the darkness of night. She was on a southerly course away from us, most likely from Norlondia, probably carrying fine tools from their forge cities. A hold full of tools that were not only useful, but *expensive*.

I called out for an intercept course, and the lanterns dashed. It was already past sundown, the last light of day disappearing into a black cloud filled night. Without lanterns to give away our position, we vanished.

It was doubtful they caught sight of us, but even then, if they had seen us, it'd only been at a great distance before the black of night cut off any further examination of our ship. I was led to believe that they hadn't, because they didn't dash their own lanterns. Their glow in calm seas like this shone like miniature lighthouses, guiding our way.

With such a bright target, and such perfect seas and a northerly wind, we made excellent time catching up with them.

Despite being a warship, we were lighter and better crewed than any heavy merchant brig I'd heard of. Over the night, we came closer and closer, their lanterns growing brighter and brighter until we could see their crew's moving shadows on their sails.

Merchant captains were not always smart enough to surrender. Fewer still changed course or tried any shenanigans to hide from a potential enemy. This captain apparently had no self preservation.

Which didn't surprise me. Some merchant captains thought that just because they were wealthier than their crew, they deserved to have their crew die for them like little soldiers.

They believed themselves invincible. That their money could make any and all problems disappear.

As much as I hated myself for it, I wished they would fight or run. I was *hungry.*

We chased them all through the night before we closed the distance, the windows on their captain's cabin glowing in their aft getting detailed enough to see framing. At this point I was pacing back and forth on the quarterdeck like a starved madwoman, fingers twitching as I watched their ship quietly bop along, all systems nominal.

The *Wraith* however, was a warship. It would only be a matter of time before we were noticed.

And the moment I thought it, finally, one of their crew heard the *Wraith* cutting through the seas behind them, the misplacement of water by our hull, the snap of our sails and rigging alerting them to *something* out on the waves.

One single soul, coming to the aft railing to peer over the side, and saw our massive prow slowly advancing out of the darkness like a ghost.

We were close enough now that I could see his face, clear as day with my vision, and almost felt a bite of pity as it twisted into terror.

I tried to imagine it from his perspective.

A great hulk of warship, completely dark save for the lights in the cracks of its lower decks. The entire ship painted a dark brooding grey, the same colour as driftwood and shipwrecks. People scurrying about the deck in the dark, shapes in the night.

For all he knew it could've been a ship crewed by demons.

He stood stock still while he took the sight of us in, before rubbing his eyes and looking again. And then a whole *new* wave of horror across his face when we didn't disappear like some folk tale.

We were *real.*

He screamed. And took off running towards the man on watch, and slowly, the ship came to alert but it was far too late. We were practically on top of them, less than a ship-length behind.

I gave the order. "Raise the black!"

The *Wraith* exploded into noise and light as lanterns were lit, torches flamed, and a roar went out from my crew with delight at our prize.

There was nothing quite like the feeling of grim satisfaction from seeing a ship we were about to pirate sink down an ugly spiral of confusion, into worry, fear, suspicion, and then to finally have that fear confirmed as their hearts plummeted in their stomachs.

I watched them scurry about their ship, likely pleading with their quartermaster and officers to surrender. The stories of what I did to crews who fought or tried to flee were near legendary.

Captain Claire Vessia. Scourge of Kitaxia, demon witch of the sea, she who revels in bloodshed, the best duellist on the Great Divide.

'Did she kill all the crew save one?' 'I heard if she finds out your Kitaxian, she cuts off an ear!' 'No, she boils you alive!'

I'd heard them all.

The sea slowly began to brighten with the coming morning as our ships inched closer and closer, and we watched with all the interest of a parlour show as their crew begged and pleaded with their master through our spyglasses.

But they found no bend to their captain's will, and they began to grab what few weapons they had.

I was getting a proper meal today, thank the Gods.

Smiling with glee, I paced the quarterdeck, shouting out orders. "Heave em' in! We're fighting for this one!" I shouted, to an answering cheer rising throughout the crew.

The bulks of the two ships grew closer, and I couldn't help but remark to Markus standing beside me at how sad this was. They had no cannon, from the looks of it barely any flintlocks, and about two dozen crew, if that. The hooked lines went out, dragging their hull closer with each heave, the merchant's defenders' shots missing horridly, if their rotted and rusted pistols fired at all.

Shot rang out from above, our snipers in the tops picking off defenders who dared look to have hostile intent, while our boarders swished over the rails and cut them down like they were wheat in the harvest.

They didn't even officially surrender, the defending crew just gave up entirely, despite their captain stomping around demanding they fight for him still.

"And that's that," Markus said beside me with a grim shrug. I couldn't help but agree. Seeing their pathetic attempt at a defence left a sour taste in my mouth. But one I was excited to drown out in blood.

"Ugly business. But they did fight," I said quietly.

Markus let out a deep sigh. "I know."

My hunger gnawed at my throat, and my teeth ached something fierce as those still alive were pushed into loose circles, the dead dropped over the side, and the captain sent to his quarters to await my 'interview.'

I licked my lips in needy anticipation.

Soon. I told myself. *Soon.*

Nearly lost in my hunger, I almost didn't notice the brief scuffle breaking out. Rodger, leading the captain away from his crew at gun point towards his quarters, along with two other crewmen in escort.

A blink and miss it moment.

The captain ducked, Rodger fired, the shot missing, going over the captain's head and going through the door to his quarters. The captain, taking a pistol out of the belt of one of the escorts, ran for the far railing, but the last escort lifted his own pistol to fire, and his aim was nearly perfect.

The captain screamed as the shot took him in the shoulder, just left of his spine, in the spot where the shoulder blade didn't cover. The sudden scent of blood and gunpowder in the air, both me and Markus couldn't believe what we were seeing.

The captain would be dead in minutes, that was for sure. But he whipped around, pointing the pistol, ready to kill the next person he set eyes on. And that person was Rodger.

Ba-dum. Drawing on the beating of my undead heart to push myself to inhuman limits was as easy as breathing. *Ba-dum.* If costly. *Ba-dum.* I imagined to human eyes, it looked like I'd disappeared.

Ba-dum. One second, I was standing on the *Wraith*'s quarterdeck with Markus, overlooking this farce of a prize. *Ba-dum.* Next, I was standing in front of Rodger, batting away the captain's stolen pistol with my sword.

Baaaaaa-dummmm. My heart began to silence, hunger *boiling.* In my gut, my jaw, my very *bones.* But I had to protect Rodger.

The captain stared at me with horror and terror, blinking in surprise as I appeared out of nowhere to him, his pistol momentarily knocked away, but not fired.

"I'd let you pray to your god, but you'd reach them long before your prayer will." I growled, raising my blade to his throat.

His heart hammered in his chest, heaving with every breath as the pistol shook in his hands, eyes searching mine for any hint of mercy. He was dead, and he knew it. His chest was bleeding heavily, but he probably hardly felt it with the shock.

But I still needed a meal. *Desperately* now and-

My thoughts were interrupted as he brought the pistol to his head, and fired.

What remained of him fell backwards, over the railing and into the sea.

Fuck.

There went half of my dinner.

Lowering my blade, I let out an annoyed sigh, turning around, slowly, with the dawning sun *just* beginning to simmer at my back. I struggled to hold back my rage and hunger with every muscle tensed to snap at the nearest person.

It was Rodger's horrified yet thankful face that stopped me.

"Get me their quartermaster. I'll be in the captain's cabin," I said through gritted teeth, my hand gripping the handle of my sword so strongly I thought it might snap. Rodger nodded, gulping as he did so, turning to shout orders at both of the crews.

Shutting out the noise of panicked sailors and enraged crew, I wrenched the door of the cabin off its hinges, the wood groaning as it splintered and snapped, making me spit a curse. Without a care, I tossed it to the deck, and stepped into the darkness to feel safe and welcome in the dark.

Here, out of the sun, I could wait for Rodger to bring me the condemned man I was owed. Then I would *feast*. There wouldn't be a drop left.

Patience. I needed to have patience. Soon.

Sheathing my blade, I wandered the cabin quietly, simmering, *waiting.* There wasn't much here to indicate personal taste. No awards or letters covered his desk, no photos of family, a bed that looked perfectly made. Just the regular minutiae of everyday captaining. Charts, sextants, pens and paper with navigation notes and delivery schedules.

The single personal touch in the entire room, was a cup of coffee, still steaming as its brown liquid slushed back and forth in time with the waves.

I tried to remember his face, but found the only image I could recall was of the blood trailing down his neck after he shot his—

I shook my head free of the memory. It was doing no one any good. My stomach *growled*. Hunger raked its claws on the inside of me, making me clutch at my throat, trying to rub relief into the muscles. What was taking them so long?

A brief knock at what remained of the door followed a few moments later, making me sigh in relief. *Finally.*

I stomped out of the cabin, awaiting my doomed man, but all I saw was Markus, Rodger, and Charlotte all looking… unsure.

"What's all this then?" I demanded, resting a hand on the pommel of my blade. I wanted to be tearing out a man's throat, not fucking *delegating* right now.

"They're not giving him up," Charlotte stated exasperatedly.

"*What*?" I replied.

"You'd think they'd never been pirated before," Markus joked, hands behind his back. "Put simply, you scared the shit out of them. Rather than give up a man they know you're going to kill, they're shutting up. Not saying a word."

I crossed my arms and awaited any word from Rodger, but he just shook his head, a grimace on his face.

"Did you *not* tell them what'll happen if they don't?" I asked, seething.

None of them answered me for a moment, and while they were stewing in what exactly to tell me, I looked over Markus's shoulder to see someone staring at me from the *Wraith*'s bow. Really, everyone was staring at us—the captured crew, the sailors of the *Wraith*—but this one stood out, her red hair flickering in the wind like a candle.

Moira, staring at me from the forecastle, her eyes damning, hands clutching the forecastle railing as if holding on a life-raft. Was she scared? Angry? I couldn't say. Her face was a rage of conflict that I didn't know well enough to decipher.

I wrapped my arms tightly around me, forcing my fangs back into their sockets, and glared right back at her.

"Don't you care that they made you out to be a monster?"

Her words rang in my ears, making me grind my teeth, her gaze seeming to taunt the exact thing that was annoying me right at the moment. I was *hungry.* I didn't have a choice. I *had* to be a monster.

Fuck her.

"Claire!" Charlotte cursed. "Did you hear what we said? Oh, for fucks sake. They're calling your bluff."

With a sigh, I shifted my focus to Rodger, his face grim. I was beginning to see he knew where this was headed.

"How many of them still live?" I asked, my voice suddenly steady. My hunger would be *well* sated soon.

"Crew of 28. Ten died in the fighting, seven injured. Most won't make it through the night according to Winters," He listed off before nodding over his shoulder to the small group of men sitting in a tight circle.

"Leaves eleven of 'em still in fighting form, ma'am," Rodger said with a sigh that betrayed his guilt.

I nodded, clicking my tongue against my teeth. "Fine. I'll handle it from here. Give me a blade." I held out my hand, and Rodger stared at my open palm for a moment like I was handing him a live scorpion.

"It's not your fault Rodger," I explained, trying to put some patience in my tone. Again, he sighed, placing his blade in my palm.

"Markus, see to their cargo. Charlotte, go give Maude a hand." I sucked in a breath, trying hard not to show how excited my hunger was making me. "Tell her today's going to be a reminder to the world."

Markus and Charlotte nodded, their faces now equally as grim as Rodgers. All of them stepped away to do their assigned tasks, Rodger heading to the railing of the ship to sit against it and watch, a mixture of hope and guilt on his face.

Which left me, with a couple hundred pairs of eyes watching my every move as I stepped forward to the small circle of captured men.

I held Rodger's sword loosely in one hand, the other resting on the pommel of my own, staring each man in the eyes, weighing the strength of them.

"My name is Claire Vessia, Captain of the *Wraith*," I shouted, loud enough that all could hear. "My terms are perfectly clear. From the moment my flag rises, you are to surrender, putting yourselves completely at my mercy. I will then take your goods, and leave you unharmed." I paced, each step slow and purposeful as I shifted my gaze around the damned men.

"To fight against me, is to violate that agreement. And this day, not only have you fought me, forfeiting your pathetic lives, you now deny me *again*, when your lives are at my mercy. I ask you to surrender one man, one *damned man*, who damn well *had power over you*, and instead you *refuse*."

I leaned down, clenching my fist at them, prompting them to join me.

But not a voice stirred, nothing made a sound save the sea.

With a sigh, I stood tall, and threw Rodger's blade at the nearest man's feet.

"Then if you will not help me, then you're *all* damned. I care not if your quartermaster still lives, I care not about *any of you*. Duel me for your lives," I ordered. "I will kill you all, one by fucking one."

Their hearts stuttered in their chest, all of their eyes drifting to the man who *must've* been their quartermaster. But none of them spoke.

The man nearest me shakily grabbed the sword off the deck, just as I raised my eyes to the *Wraith*'s forecastle... but Moira was gone.

I drank my fill of the man, not able to stomach any more. Lifting my teeth from his mess of a neck, I moaned in delight to the ceiling, the opposing captain's cabin now looking more like a morgue than a navigator's office.

Bodies, a few of them completely drained of blood, lay strewn about the room. Some with stab wounds, others with slashes, all felled by my sword.

One day, someone would beat me in a duel, but today was not that day.

I felt… *amazing*. Bloated. Stuffed. I could curl up and sleep in this pile of death if my sleep wasn't so Gods damned cursed. But it wasn't meant to be. I sat up from my latest victim, letting his head fall from my grip, reaching for his sleeve to wipe off the blood on my face. I'd eaten so sloppily.

My brain was fuzzy with memories and emotions that weren't mine. A mess of colours and faces I didn't recognize, a haze of lives I hadn't lived.

Picking myself up off the nameless body I'd been straddling with a groan, I made a quick trip to the captain's washroom to make sure I didn't leave any splotches of evidence on my face. Somehow, in my blood-drunk haze, I'd only managed to soak my shirt in blood, and that was enough to be blamed on the duels, or the fact a man had shot himself in the head in front of me.

It would have to do.

But once again, I hardly recognized the woman in the mirror. When had I gotten so used to violence? A man had killed himself rather than face me. Did I care?

When… did I *stop* caring? When did I let myself get so used to this violence? A shuddering breath escaped me as I looked at how I almost looked alive because of how stained with blood I was, my pale white skin a shade of pink from washed away blood.

I didn't know if I wanted the answer to that question.

A last-minute readjustment to my spectacles and hat, I kicked open the cabin doors, the bright noon sun stabbing downward with its accursed light, the heat skittering on my skin even under all my layers.

But ten duels I'd fought under its harsh rays, and ten duels I'd won.

And ten bodies I'd dragged to the cabin.

Now, there was just one left. The man I highly suspected of being the quartermaster.

I stepped across the deck, over the blood spatters and occasional pieces of limbs I'd cut off a couple of my victims in our fights, towards where only Rodger stood guard over him now. The rest of the crew were working, stripping their ships of *everything*. Not just the cargo, but every little piece of value. Rigging, tools, even the fabric off the beds.

Its crew was dead or dying. They wouldn't need it anymore.

All save one man.

I came to a stop before him and Rodger, both of them looking so pale it looked to be a coinflip between who would be sick first. Blood dripping down my boot, I tilted my head to look down at the man who, if he'd simply stepped forward, would've probably saved his comrades' lives.

"You're probably expecting to die next," I said, kicking away the blade that his last fellow had dropped. "But instead, you get to live. Lucky."

Neither of them seemed to register what I'd said. The quartermaster looked up at me in horror, Rodger's gaze locked at his boots.

"We're leaving you here. If you make it back to Haxla, do tell the Crown Princess I said hello," I leaned down to rustle the quartermaster's head, the hunger in the back of my mind sleepily reaching through the haze, a pathetic push to eat him as well.

Tossing the quartermaster aside, just like my mewling hunger, cackling with morbid delight as I stomped back towards the *Wraith*. Rodger followed at my heels, just as the quartermaster realized what his fate would be.

Left adrift on a ship he could not possibly sail alone, with no company save the bodies of his comrades. Eventually, he'd be rescued by some passerby; we were smack dab in the middle of the trade lanes and had left enough supplies in the hold for him to last a month.

I turned around to watch from the shadowed overhang entryway to my quarters, seeing the last of the cargo loaded aboard the *Wraith*, while the quartermaster broke into tears.

Wherever he went from here they'd pass the story on. Of the day they met Captain Claire Vessia, and what horrible torture she'd visited on the crew. How she dueled ten men and won. Was I a foul witch? A demoness? I snorted in wonder at what stories would be told this time.

I glanced upwards from my hidey-hole at the bright afternoon developing with a silent curse as the crew salvaged every last piece of worth from their ship, our boarders standing vigil at the railing to make sure the quartermaster didn't try to board us.

Feeling that my job had been done, and more exhausted from bloat rather than the tiredness of post-battle, I fell into my cabin with a huff, relieved to finally be out of the sun with a full stomach.

I felt myself drifting off to sleep in my chair, but I refused sleep's tempting embrace. That way laid madness and nightmares that I cared not to revisit so soon after my last round.

Besides, I hadn't needed to wait long for the knocks on my door.

Markus and Rodger stepped inside to make their relative reports. One to tell me what we gained today, the other to tell me what we lost.

I sat up and forced myself to listen, making minor notes as Markus tabled all the cargo we'd taken on, their weight and value, what we lacked, and issues of resupply. Then Rodger listed off the optics of what such a slaughter had done. The killing hadn't sat well with the crew and morale had taken a hit as a result. Even if I'd given the quartermaster an effective message to deliver to the world, we couldn't be sure a single survivor to tell the tale would, well, *survive* to actually justify everything we'd just done.

Let alone the scars my actions had caused for his *own* soul. Rodger wore his guilt like a shroud, and felt that my killings put just as much blood on his hands as I had on mine.

I took in both of their explanations, and was in the middle of doing my best to assuage Rodger of his guilt, when a knock sounded at the door.

We all exchanged glances, unsure. The entire crew should've known that we'd be deliberating the intake of crew and cargo from our prize.

"Enter," I said loudly enough for whoever was knocking to hear. The door opened to let Maude in, looking more concerned than I'd ever seen her before. For her to be here and not tending to her patients below from the brief battle meant either it was either serious or our injured weren't as bad as I thought. "Yes?" I asked quietly, rising from my chair.

"Captain..." Maude stated, her voice dripping with concern. "You may want to go down to the cargo hold." I raised my eyebrow at Rodger and Markus, but they both shrugged their shoulders, sharing a confused glance. No one knew what this was about.

"Why?" I asked, suspicion in my tone. Something must be *very* wrong. My mind went through a handful of disaster scenarios, but none of them were close to what Maude had to say.

Maude shook her head before answering, her hand opening the door wider as if to hurry me along. "It's Moira. She's... distraught."

Markus's sudden chuckle made me glare at him, making him spit out a defence. "What? She's *a princess*. Of course she's going to be 'distraught' at a little blood."

I was about to correct him, but Rodger beat me to it. "You would be too if you were her. Hells, anyone would be after seeing what Claire does to people." Rodger said quietly, a hand loosely pointed in my direction.

I stilled, trying my best to not show that his words had put a needle in my core.

Nothing but a monster, wasn't I?

Markus guffawed, making me glare at him with threat in my eyes even more. "So what? If she can't stomach it, then just chuck her in a hole and be done with her."

Rodger's sharp intake of breath matched the surprise I felt. I'd not known Markus to be hateful or malicious, and that was a hell of a jump for him.

With a sigh, I pushed away from my desk, glaring at each man, walking towards where Maude was still waiting in the doorway.

"Well, we're about ready to be on our way anyway. Our heading is unchanged, South-by-Southeast," I ordered. Rodger's complicated feelings over being saved, and then the following bloodshed was one thing to deal with, and now Markus's virulence towards Moira was also building up to something untenable. But I could only deal with one crisis at a time.

Rodger nodded, making way for the door, but Markus hung behind, eyeing me up, biting his lip with something to say.

"What?" I demanded, stopping on my way out the door. Using the moment to shrug back into my jacket, fingering my glasses onto my nose, and setting my hat into place.

Markus shook his head as he crossed his arms. "Don't give her special treatment, Claire," He chewed his lip in annoyance, some part of him seemed to hate the very prospect that Moira was aboard. Saw her as a threat.

I wanted to roll my eyes at him, but stood my ground.

"What else could we do with her Markus?" I muttered through a sigh. "Slit her throat and chuck her overboard? You need to get it in your head that maybe, just maybe, she has just as much a bone to pick with Kitaxia as we do."

He nodded, mouth twitching this way and that. "And *you* need to start thinking about what if she *doesn't*. What if her whole purpose here is just to fuck with you, Claire?" He all but wagged a nagging finger at me. "We're giving her a hell of an opportunity to hurt us, and I'm not sure I want to play this fast and loose with such a dangerous prize. Maybe you're right. Maybe she's genuine and hates her parents and will swear off the throne. I genuinely hope that's the case."

He stepped forward to put his hands on my shoulders and leaned even closer, almost whispering his point with fury. "Claire, I love you like my own sister... but what if I'm right? Because if I am, we're playing straight into Kitaxia's fucking hands." He held my gaze for a quiet moment, daring me to deny his accusation.

I didn't have proof one way or the other yet.

"I'll be careful Markus," I said quietly, reaching up to pluck his hands off my shoulders.

He nodded, his face twisting up like he'd smelled rotten planks beneath our feet. "You're an idiot. But you're our idiot."

I wanted to smack him. "Don't push your luck, Markus. *Please*," was all I stated as I separated from him and made my way out the door.

CHAPTER FOURTEEN

"'magine what it must be like to be on the crew of the Wraith. Does she feed 'em pieces of people for grub? Grog lined with blood?"

"I reckon anyone who sails with Vessia must have an iron will to witness such murderin' every damn day."
"And an iron stomach too! Ha!"

— Reginauld Taylor and Simmons Barrington, sailors aboard the Queen of Sardis

Thanking Maude for her patience, she led me quietly to the crew ladder to the lowest part of the *Wraith*, the bowels of the lower hold where the sounds of... *something* echoed from the depths below.

It sounded like the screeching of a banshee, echoing against the hull that replied to the abuse of sounds with its own repetitive dull thud of steady waves.

A sailing ship didn't exactly have quiet corners for alone time, save for the lower cargo hold. It was kept purposefully in perpetual darkness. No torches, lanterns, not even a *match* was allowed down there, just in case a single spark escaped notice, lighting up the ship's magazine.

I'd no idea how Moira had navigated herself to the furthest reach of the ship, but she'd managed it.

With her cries sounding from below, and Maude fixing me with a worried stare, I left her at the top of the hatch, promising her I'd take care of it, and to get back to her patients. What exactly I'd meant by 'taking care of it' was still a mystery to me, but it seemed to satisfy her without protest.

Landing with a thud at the bottom step, I could feel the ocean's pulse *right* beneath my feet, just two layers of paneled wood, some caulking, and a copper sheet separating my feet from the depths of the sea. I didn't know whether to be in fear of it, or amazed that we could have a little floating castle of human existence in such an inhospitable environment.

That was the *usual* thought I had when I was down here. Now I was mostly wondering what in all the hells was I doing.

Pacing through the darkness of the hold, looking for a Kitaxian princess who was, most likely, losing her mind over some spilt blood, and I didn't know if I wanted to comfort her, fuck her, slit her throat, or toss her overboard.

Maybe all four?

Regardless of how I felt, first I had to find her. My eyes had no problem adjusting—I'd been made for such darkness after all—so all I had to do was follow the sounds of her wails.

"Moira?" I called out, some distance away to warn her of my approach. I knew just how terrifying my sudden soundless appearance could be. My steps were quiet when I wasn't focused on making them stomp, and more than a few times I'd scared crew half to death without meaning to.

"Moira?" I called out again, chasing her teary cries to round what I was sure was the second last corner, around a barrel of salted beef.

"No!" she cried out, her voice echoing off the walls of the hull. "Leave me here, I don't want to talk to you!" Of course she didn't. I'd killed how many people in front of her? Fuck, I couldn't even remember.

But still I winced, the tear-filled hate in her voice apparent. Why her hatred bothered me, I couldn't say, but I felt a sudden determination to put things right.

"Too bad," I called back. "You have dozens of orders to fill at the smithy, and Gracie would be sad if you never showed your face there again."

Why am I here? Why do I care?

She sniffled in reply, choking back an ugly laugh through her tears.

I couldn't suppress a smile. "That's right, you're lucky it's me down here after you, and not her. She's not done stuffing you full till you're sick of potatoes." Humour wasn't my strong suit, but I didn't want to hear her cry anymore.

Her blood tasted like she'd shed enough tears over her life.

Another choked laugh, echoed through the hull, this one less forced.

Finally, I rounded the last corner, to where she was coiled on top of a pile of spooled rope in the dark with one of the ship's glowstones, hugging her knees tightly as tears fell down her cheeks, face flushed.

My heart broke a little for her.

"There you are," I whispered, taking slow steps towards her.

She snorted, raising her arms at her little fort of rope. "Here I am," She mumbled back.

I stopped just far enough away from her pile of rope to be respectful, crouching down to her eye level. She glared at me with all the accusation of a priest.

"You killed them," she stated, her voice dripping with distaste. "All of them. Just to take their stuff."

Here we go.

I nodded slowly. "I did," I said without emotion. "I could tell you that none of those men owned any of the cargo we're taking, and that those men had their own choices to make. But, I won't. It's me who puts them to the sword." I didn't consider myself much of a liar, nor did I think it'd do me good to lie. This was the life I lived and how I existed, and how I could protect my people.

She glared at me, as if daring me to admit guilt, to apologize, to demand her forgiveness.

She would not get it.

"So, yes. I killed them," I said the words evenly, plainly, and without guilt or shame. I may have gotten used to the violence, but it did me no favours to admit I was the monster she now saw me as.

The quiet stretched between us, the tension near audible.

"I can't believe for a moment... I thought you were better than Mother," she snapped, her heart stammering.

She couldn't have aimed a sharper arrow, seemingly to be divinely placed to stab me at the sorest of wounds.

"I am *not* Ameritia," I spat, anger and fury boiling in my chest as I clenched my fists at my side, my nails digging into my palms. Sucking in a breath, I forced my tone to even. "I've done horrible and rancid things. But every time I take one of their ships, I bleed a monster larger than any one person can contemplate. I fight *Empire*."

She was unfazed by my remarks, sniffling, yet so *angry* at me. Staring me in the eye to communicate something scathing, but I would not be bowed.

"You want to judge me for a handful of murders? Fine. But have a look in the fucking mirror first. Your mother, *Ameritia,* kills thousands, if not hundreds of thousands of her own people, with the stroke of a Gods damned *pen*. Starvation, purges, slums, enforced poverty…" I wanted to slap the hatred off her face. She looked ready to spit some biting remark, but I still wasn't done.

"Let alone the very few people in her dungeons she murders herself." I added.

Whatever she'd been about to say was silenced, her face twisting into guilt.

So, she knew then.

Then... did she know about me? Was I just one more of her mother's victims bled for her hunger? Just how *much* did she know?

And where did her true loyalties lie?

"For so many years," I murmured, leaning just a bit closer. "You've been living at the teet of the crown. But out here on the waves, I get to look my prey in the eye, face-to-face. It's bloody, messy, and I *have* to send a message. I don't get the *choice* of leniency. Not like Ameritia," I spat out my maker's name, unable to keep a level voice whenever I pictured her fucking face. "The promise of violence is what makes my victims surrender. All it would take is one rumour that Captain Vessia is 'going soft' and then we'd have to fight for every single *fucking* prize, and then the bloodshed would be worse."

I breathed in a tight breath, letting it out slowly to keep my rage in check.

"... So much worse," I admitted, unsure why I was spending so much effort on this damn girl.

She was quiet now, staring at me with fear in her heart.

"With a single ship, I'm labelled a pirate. Thief. *Monster.*

Meanwhile, Kitaxia, no… *Ameritia* with her whole navy, molests the entire three nations and gets called a fucking *queen*. Now tell me, how is that fair?" I clenched my fist, motioning with my other hand as if to say *'could you believe this shit?'*

Moira was silent for so long, her shiny green eyes still teary and searching, her heart hammering in her chest. Down here in the hold, the dull thud of waves rocked against the hull, giving the darkness around us a cavernous feeling.

Unable to keep this silent standoff, I stood slowly from my crouch, her eyes following mine. "You don't have to agree with my methods. You don't have to put a blade to your people's throat. *But* you did sign the Code. Like it or not, you're one of us now." I held out a hand towards her. "You can do one of three things. Help me by being a member of this ship and teach your family a lesson. Or be escorted to a cell. Or I can dump your body overboard." There was nothing I wanted more than to have her take my hand, but it was a vain hope.

She eyed my hand like I'd offered her a dead rat to eat.

I sucked in a deep breath through my teeth, and tried to think of something better to say. I wanted to tell her I had some noble cause, I wanted her to *believe* in me. I wanted this girl to like me, and I had no idea why.

And despite my grandstanding, all my high morals about being the better of two evils, she smacked my hand away.

"A murderer is a murderer," she muttered. "Mother might be for all intents and purposes *genocidal,* but while you're there calling yourself a 'hero' for measuring the blood you spilled as lesser than hers, you've never stopped to think that *no* blood should be spilled."

For all but a moment, I was surprised. But of *course* she denied me. I snorted, her naivety misplaced on board *this* ship. Every person aboard had lost someone, knew someone gone, at the hands of her mother's overbearing regal fist.

Because we dared fight back... *we* were the problem? How *dare* we resist?

"Go ahead. Laugh at me if you like, *Captain*." She turned away from me, showing nothing but her back as she leaned her head against the hull, the dull throb of waves pounding the side.

"Leave me alone. I'll get to my forge orders in a moment." Her voice deadened, quiet, sullen.

And just like that, she shut herself off to me.

I stood from where I had kneeled beside her, resting my hands around my elbows as I considered what she said.

She was a Gods damned naive idiot.

Maybe Markus was right. Maybe it was easier to just gut her and be done with it.

So why does this hurt?

I turned on my heel, marching back the way I came. Wondering that exact question with every step.

CHAPTER FIFTEEN

"My experiments into the differences between Vampyri and human physiology continue to provide interesting results. Humans prove to be hardy creatures by any measure of the animal kingdom, and in testing their pain tolerances, I've learned they can recover from the most grievous injuries given enough time and respite. Vampyri, on the other hand, only have to wait until the following evening for full recovery… In most cases."

— From the journals of Valerie Du Bois, Scholar lord of Draculesti

"They've struck their colours!"

A cheer went up from everyone on the weather deck as the tension instantly relaxed, the Kitaxian flag lowering from the brig's aft.

The universal sign for surrender.

I tried to hide my disappointment.

It'd been a month since I'd tried to drag Moira out from the cargo hold. Since then, we'd taken one more prize, a Varcnan council ship full of government letters, seals, merchant contracts, and to top it all off, several chests of taxes just begging to be taken. Despite what I had told Moira, coin was always welcome. Especially as the icing on the cake of a nearly full cargo hold.

And now we had this, another Kitaxian merchant skirting the edge of the trade lanes, one last treat before we made our final approach for home.

I leaned over the quarterdeck railing, eyeing the professionalism of the other crew. They were almost nonchalant about being pirated, already politely putting cargo on the weather deck as if it were just any other cargo transfer.

It'd usually be disturbing to see such unconcerned behaviour, but I was more grumbling about the fact I wouldn't be eating today.

"You always look so sad when they surrender. Do you love the fight that much?" Markus asked from where he stood beside me. I glanced towards him, trying to smother my grumbly mood.

I sighed, rocking back and forth on the quarterdeck railing, unsure if he was teasing me or not. "Just always wondering what's on the menu," I replied, seeing his eyes flashing with understanding.

"Ah. That explains it then," he said with a chuckle. I shrugged, looking back at the crews rapidly bringing the vessels together.

"Well, guess I'll go have another insufferable 'tea' or whatever it is with their captain. Ring the bell when we have their goods," I stated, pushing off from the railing.

"Aye ma'am," he said with a flourish, already turning to shout orders down the line.

I didn't make it four steps down to the weather deck before Moira collided with me with all the force of a cannonball.

"Captain, you, *please*—" She stammered for breath, latching onto my arms.

"Moira," I said quietly as she caught her breath, more than a few glances shifted towards us with brief interest. I reached up to detach her from my person, only for her to grab onto my wrists. "I suggest you take your hands off me—"

"You can't trust them. You can't," she blurted out, staring into my eyes with alarm.

I paused mid-retracting her arms in mild alarm, seeing the fear plain as day on her face, hearing it in her heart. "Moira?" Her name on my lips, a billion unasked questions in my voice.

She'd been all but standoffish towards me ever since our shared moment down in the hold. Doing the bare minimum of her work orders, not saying any more than two words to me. If she was trying to get kicked off the ship, she was doing a hell of a job at it.

So, for her to be *here*...

"He'll try something. I..." She clamped her mouth shut, eyes cast down towards our boots as I finally shook her off me. She was trying to warn me of something, without actively selling out her countrymen. She could *not* have it both ways.

"If you have something to say that pertains to the safety of the crew, say it," I stated plainly, growing impatience in my voice.

She looked back with panic, and I didn't know what to make of it. She closed her eyes, and finally figured out whatever was going on in her internal debate.

"The captain of that ship. I knew him. At the palace. He's a favourite of mothers. He's malicious, and doesn't suffer pirates lightly. He'll try something, I promise it. The whole crew is in danger." Her words were pointed, state of fact.

I looked at her with suspicion, but couldn't deny the actual fear I heard in her heart.

And any *favourite* of Ameritia's... well that'd be one more corpse I'd happily feed the depths of the sea.

"Rodger!" I called out over her shoulder, making Moira wince with the volume of my voice. Rodger appeared momentarily, trotting along with a musket. "You know this vessel?" I stated, shifting my head towards it, trying to confirm Moira's information.

His eyes widened in brief surprise, but he gazed over it with immediate concern and shook his head a moment later.

I debated, ready to throw Moira's concern out of hand, but then the captain walked out of his cabin and into view. All pompous attitude, a man with a styled beard and fine clothes, and who'd obviously never touched a rope on his ship in labour. His gaze towards the *Wraith* was full of disdain and disgust, there was no way in any of the nine burning realms a man with that expression would've surrendered willingly without a plan.

His heart was as steady as a rock.

Something felt... *very* wrong. I couldn't put my finger on it. Why did it suddenly feel like *I* was the one getting pirated? The demeanour of the captain, the nonchalant attitude of his crew, the relative slowness of their tasks...

Looking the ship over once more, turning my gaze to Rodger's confusion and Moira's worry... I'd be a fool not to act on a freely given warning.

"Rodger, have the boarders stand by at the gunports, ready to jump out at the barest hint of anything going wrong. If they so much as smell treachery, act. Get Charlotte's crew ready to throw a few cannonballs below their waterline as well." I turned my gaze one more to the captain, grimacing. "Something seems... off."

Rodger nodded with a sudden hardness, immediately turning to issue quiet orders to the crew, as Moira breathed out in relief.

"You know, I could really help out if someone gave me a sword—" she started to say as I rolled my eyes in reply. She'd attached herself to this argument for the past week. The only time she'd spoken to me was to ask for one.

And giving her a weapon was the last thing I wanted to do. I wasn't sure I could trust her. Not yet.

"I said you'll get one when you deserve one," I murmured, leaving her standing alone with worry as I made my way over the boarding plank to the Kitaxian vessel.

Their captain greeted me with a grimace, not bothering to shake my hand like some often did. Surrendering captains entreated me with all sorts of emotions, everything from spitting curses at my boots to awe inspired respect. I was a legend in the Three-Nations, and I'd earned every bit of those reactions, both good and bad.

But this particular captain was a new reaction altogether. Feigned indifference. Oh, he was without a doubt upset that he was being pirated, I could tell by that furrowed brow he was actively trying to suppress under a proud face. Probably livid as all hell that he was going to lose his goods, but he was actively trying to behave as if none of it mattered.

"Vessia?" He said my name like he was announcing the proper title of a bug he particularly disliked, his body still as a statue.

I nodded, a hand resting on my sword. "*Captain* Vessia," I emphasized with a glare. "You are?"

He grinned, for some bloody reason. "Count of Stonetree Island, Stephen Macberra," he said with a lavish unneeded bow. I stiffened in slight surprise. It wasn't often the nobility of Kitaxia captained their own merchant freighters, but the fact he was proving the exception to that rule left me wanting him to try *something* to excuse violence against him *very* badly.

To bleed a noble was an opportunity few and far between in my experience.

"May I interest you in a warm beverage of choice in my cabin?" he asked, interrupting the imaginings of just how he'd taste. I couldn't help but smirk at his choice of words.

"It'd be my pleasure," I replied with complete honesty.

The Count's cabin was lavish, if held to a simplistic taste, in that way rich people often decorated their spaces to indicate that they didn't see themselves as wealthy. Which annoyed me to no end, seeing so much space *wasted*, just because it fit some useless aesthetic.

"Please, sit." He motioned towards one of the seats opposite his own desk, a weird mirror of my own.

I debated for a moment shoving him out of his own seat to take it for myself in a display of power, but I was still willing to play at courtesy.

For now.

"Thank you," I replied, taking my seat. "Now, if you'd be so kind as to hand over your shipping manifest." My tone might have been polite, but my words were layered with intent and meaning, a ready promise of violence.

His eyes flickered in annoyance as he took his own seat.

"I would think Miss—"

"*Captain,*" I corrected him, my words severing whatever thought he'd been about to finish. "If you forget my title again, I'll feed you your own fingers. And that is my *only* warning," I nearly growled, my words thick with the implication of all I could do to him.

Yet his heart didn't jump in fear.

He stared at me with barely hidden disgust, as if I was a lizard that had crawled onto his shoe, without a spec of fear in his person.

I glared at him, focusing on every detail as I tried to parse what it was about this man that led him to believe himself immune to me.

Why? Why wasn't he afraid? Did he not know who I was?

His attitude, paired with Moira's warning, was ringing all sorts of alarm bells in my head.

"I will take that into advisement *Captain* Vessia," he replied with disdain, an ugly pitch in his tone for my title. "May I interest you in some wine?" he continued, snapping his fingers to summon a steward who'd been standing off to the side of the cabin. The man stepped forward, an expensive looking bottle in hand, pouring it gently into two silver goblets with practised ease.

I was hesitant to drink anything this man served, but he took his own cup and drank easily. "Wine isn't usually part of my palate, so I don't partake often, but thank you," I said quietly, taking my own to sip at the goblet in my hand. It was much too sweet, its viscosity reminding me more of flavoured juice than the blood I craved.

"Delicious," I lied, making him smile. I didn't care for whatever he thought, just whatever got me out of this room the fastest with what I needed.

He stood from his chair, turning his back to me, looking at the sunshine glistening on the waves through the window.

"It is such a delicate flavour, is it not?" he asked, swirling the goblet in his hand.

I shrugged, not sure what to make of these strange circumstances, wishing I could somehow skip wasting another second in his company. If I killed him and blamed it on the steward… Would anyone believe me?

I tried to hold in my sigh of annoyance, but I was done with this farce the moment I stepped into this room.

"If you'd be so kind Count, I'm afraid I must insist. The manifest," I demanded.

His gaze turned over his shoulder and towards me, a vile looking sneer as the line of his mouth twisted. "Very well Vessia, I'll get you what you deserve." He turned back towards me and his desk, noisily opening a drawer as if he was having difficulty with it.

It very nearly masked the sound of quiet footsteps behind me.

If I hadn't received Moira's warning, I wasn't sure I would've been listening for them.

This wasn't him surrendering, this wasn't him getting the damn manifest for me, this was a fucking *trap*.

With all the power and fury a Vampyri could muster, I threw

the foul tasting goblet of wine at the Count's head, watching it satisfyingly bounce off of his forehead with a wild gash. I began to push myself off the chair, reaching for my blade, only for a pair of hands to grab my shoulders to haul me back down.

While I struggled against my latest attacker, the Count began pulling himself up from the floor, clutching his bleeding head. The steward was rushing forward making a wild swing towards my head with the wine bottle, while the man from behind was attempting to hold me down to create a better target.

Easy enough to deal with. While the man holding me in place made it slightly off-balance, I deflected the swing of the wine bottle from the steward as easily as parting my curtains.

Enough was enough, it was time to end this ridiculous ambush.

I put all of my strength into standing up, dragging the man trying to hold me down over my chair as he clung to my shoulders. Pushing forward, my fist connected with the steward's face with as much force as I could muster, multiple bones shriveling under my knuckles like paper tissue.

He was dead before he hit the floor.

With the steward dealt with and the Count still nursing his head wound, there was only one left.

Prying the man's fingers off my shoulders, feeling him grunt with effort and pain as I bent them back, I finally got to face him as I turned around. Making sure not to let the Count out of sight as I felt the man's fingers break under my grip, little snaps one by one. The Count watched with growing horror through his blood soaked fingers trying to staunch the bleeding from his forehead.

Now that my assailant's hands were useless, mewling through tears over his broken hands, I turned my attention to grasp his throat, aiming to snap his pathetic neck while the Count looked on, knowing he'd be next.

But I didn't notice the *fourth* man creeping closer to my side until something sharp was shoved into my gut, and my world exploded into fire and pain.

Instinct flung the man I'd been grappling with away, panic driving me back from the two attackers to a corner of the room in a mad dash, putting a solid wall at my back to stop any more surprises, as I grasped at whatever had been stabbed into me with baited breath.

Wood. Just plain wood. Sticking out of my ribs, soaking my shirt in blood, a fouling intruder.

"Gods above and below..." I muttered in pained disbelief, reaching for it with shaky hands. Every instinct I had in me screamed to run, to get away, and to *flee*.

It *burned.* I'd been stabbed, gutted, whipped, chained, and *murdered.* But none of that compared to this, the most painful thing that had ever been done to me, bar none. My entire consciousness was seared to the point of where this thing stuck inside me. It felt like it was *made* of the sun, all that light focused into a small sliver of tree.

It even sizzled my flesh, a mist of smoke rising from where it met my ribs.

"You idiots!" The Count screamed at my assaulters. "You were supposed to stake her in the *heart*!" The last able-bodied-man looked from me, to his wounded comrade, and then Count in alarm. "And that's the only stake I have!" The Count continued to scream.

Ah. So not just *any* wood.

Good.

"That—" I breathed out, my fangs now fully extended "—was a very poor decision," I muttered as I grasped the stake.

They'd missed, but not by much.

Somehow the damn thing burned the skin around my fingers and the palm of my hand as I grasped it, the world narrowing in my vision as my hand seethed with *fire*. This tiny little thing, just a small sharpened stake of dark coloured wood, was somehow the bane of my existence.

Gods, did it hurt.

I screamed in fury and burning fever, as I felt it leave my chest much too slowly, searing everywhere it met flesh on its way out.

But finally, *finally*, it was out, and I could *think* again.

The pain, other than the thing sizzling in my hand, became so much more bearable without it stuck into my flesh. And my first clear thought free of that pain, was that I was going to tear these men to pieces with my bare hands.

With growing fury, I threw the damn thing with enough force to fly across the room right into the Count's eye. He let out one ugly scream as he died, his man turning to look in horror as he collapsed.

I was already halfway through the air before his glance turned back to me. I clawed out the throat of the man with the broken hands with a wild slash of my hand, a splash of blood exploding out of his neck as my fingers cut away tendon, muscle, and skin.

And then there was one. The man who'd staked me, making a slow retreat back the way he came.

He made a run for the door, but he didn't make it far enough. I clawed into his fack, digging my fangs into the back of his neck. With my weight on him, he collapsed to the deck, trying to crawl away.

But with my teeth in him, he had all but a few seconds until his heart gave out.

I fed gloriously, but still my stomach and hand still burned.

I lifted my fangs from my last victim, looking at his dead eyes locked on the door before turning to stare at the innocent stake sticking out of the Count's eye with fear and trepidation. Even now, all my instincts were telling me to get as far away from that thing as possible.

I groaned as I stood up from the body I'd drained, feeling blood flow in a tiny rivulet down my leg, making me wince with each step. I was no stranger to pain, but still, getting through the rest of the day was going to be an experience in misery.

Gathering the stake in a blood-soaked cloth to avoid skin contact, I kicked the door open to the weather deck where a mess of both crews stared at me in abject horror.

The picture of me standing there nearly made me burst into sick laughter. Covered in blood, clutching my side at a wound that would kill lesser men in a minute, red coloured eyes glaring at them all.

"KILL THEM ALL!" I screamed at the top of my lungs, the bloodstained stake still in my hand, gaping hole in my ribs.

Not a creature moved about the deck for five whole seconds, all eyes staring at the bleeding gouge in my chest, and the footsteps of blood leading into the darkness of the cabin behind me.

"Fuck this," I muttered, pulling free a pistol and shooting the closest man I didn't recognize.

The crack of flint against powder, a miniaturized explosion in my hand, and the man falling to the deck in a heap, killed instantly by the lead ball I shot into his head.

The decks of both ships exploded into chaos.

I threw my spent pistol to the deck, drawing my sword to meet an oncoming attack, getting an ugly deflection and counter into the unnamed man's guard.

By the time he'd fallen, the boarders I'd ordered prepared were screaming out from below, like an unchecked tide spewing from the crew hatch, hacking into the Kitaxians with aplomb.

It was over before it really began.

Clutching my wound, trying to staunch the bleeding, I staggered through the surge of bodies towards the gangplank back to the *Wraith*, wincing with every step. Even the thought of the blood-covered stake I'd put in my coat pocket terrified me on some primal level through my pain.

Someone shouted over the din and ringing of muskets. I wasn't sure I could've heard who said what, but before I could register it, Maude and Jacine were scooping their arms underneath me.

"No... the crew. Get the crew first," I mumbled through sharp intakes of pained breaths as they ushered me below.

"Claire, don't you worry your murderous little head," Maude replied with her stern voice. "Your forethought with the boarders saved most of everyone from that ambush. Most we got so far are a few unfortunate scratches. You got the worst of it."

I breathed out an uneasy sigh of relief as they tugged me down into the *Wraith*'s lower decks and into the surgeon's office.

Where Moira was pacing quietly. Why was she here?

"Made a mess of yourself properly this time, Captain," Maude tsked as they helped me hop onto the operating table, Jacine pulling my jacket off my shoulders, then taking my hat and spectacles. I handed my sword belt to Moira, who immediately gawked at the blade in her hand.

"Not my fault the fuckers attacked me with a damn stick," I muttered through my hurt as my shirt was pulled over my head.

"Oh god," Moira whispered quietly, covering her eyes with her hand, whipping around in a tight circle to face away, nearly dropping my blade.

I tried to smother a laugh at Moira's embarrassment as Jacine put my things on the counter, and returned to help Maude with whatever she requested. Maude fussed over the wound in my gut, putting pressure on my stomach, making me suck in a breath through clenched teeth.

"You've been shot as well," Maude murmured, making my eyebrows widen. I didn't... When the hells did someone get a shot off? They must've gotten me sometime between the first and third man, or maybe during the battle... Some lucky bastard in the melee?

As Maude poked and prodded at the wound under my breast, Jacine staring anxiously at her with readied anticipation, I looked towards our newest member of the crew in hopes of distracting myself from the fresh stabs of pain.

Moira, clutching my blade to her chest, slowly began to turn back around with her eyes glued to the floor, a warm blush in her freckled cheeks.

Ha. Adorable.

Slowly she raised her gaze to look at me, eyes not able to help wandering. I watched mostly out of the corner of my eye, trying to keep from looking down at what Maude was doing poking around in my guts. A moment passed as Moira's gaze turned from embarrassment to morbidity, eyes tracing the shape of my shoulder, and down to my ribs.

I couldn't see what had caused the change in her expression as Maude shifted one of my ribs just enough to make me wince again, close my eyes, and curse. "Fucks sake," I murmured, trying to block out the pain.

The room grew quiet besides the clink of medical tools. I could guess Maude was likely debating cutting me open to get the shot out.

It wouldn't be the first time. It was certainly likely and would also very much suck, as pain herbs had just about as much effect on me as alcohol. Meaning they simply *didn't*.

I kept my eyes shut, waiting for the moment when Maude told me to lie down.

But then… I felt a warm set of fingers tracing shapes… no, the scars on my back. "There's… so many…" Moira's quiet and sombre voice murmured from behind me.

It was such a contrast to the pain, a soft and gentle touch, that it made me twitch in a brief moment of relaxation.

I concentrated on it, the feeling of warmth spreading from her fingers as they wandered, downward around my lower back. It was… comforting.

I knew what she was seeing. Years of scars from duelling, fighting, off shots, opportune strikes, and one horrid day of the captain me and my crew had mutinied against, his viciousness with a steel whip.

I was dead. There was no question about that. My heart rarely beat, I was deathly cold, and I drank *blood* to survive. There were so many *rules* to this life, and one of the most important ones I'd learned over the years was how I *healed*.

Any wound I received during the night healed almost instantly. Any wound I received during the *day*... Those stayed there until nightfall, leaving ugly scars.

We couldn't control the time of day when we took ships. We had to strike as soon as possible, while the iron was hot. Lookouts couldn't see in the dark—Not as well as *I* could—which meant we usually saw our marks early in the morning. Nine times out of ten, we took their ships during the daytime.

And every wound, every cut, every mark that I received in the day protecting my crew that would've killed lesser men, *stayed* there, only to be healed over in the night.

I tried to count the wounds in my mind's eye as Moira's hand traced them. Knife in the ribs. Sword cut to the back. Shot five—*no* this would be the sixth time now. Shrapnel grenade that had caught me in the side, that one was the worst. All *fucking* day spent with Maude plucking little pieces of steel out of me before night fell and my wounds healed over.

I felt my breathing calm as her fingers rose goosebumps over my back, the searing pain in my stomach slowly becoming more forgotten.

Before I felt the tension of my entire body *twist* as something was wrenched out of my gut, making me yell.

"Fuck!" I screeched, opening my eyes, forcing my fangs to retract to look at Maude grinning happily with a tiny blood covered musket ball in a pair of giant tweezers.

"Got the shirt too. Excellent," she murmured, satisfied with herself.

"Captain?" Rodger's voice rang out from the other side of the privacy flap, a light knock on the doorframe.

"What is it now?" I demanded, the pure exhaustion I felt coming through my voice as Moira, Maude, and Jacine all exchanged glances.

"There's something in their hold you should see," he replied, a worried enough tone that I thought whatever they'd found, it was worth seeing.

Ugh.

For just a moment, I wished I could just be carted off to bed and sleep off this pain, that it could be someone else's problem for a day.

Gods I'm so tired.

I grumbled, sending a pleading look at Maude, the distant hope that she'd say I couldn't be moved. But of course, she shrugged and set about stitching me up.

I tried my best to tough it out as Maude's needle and thread wove through my skin, slowly sucking in breaths through my nose, out through my mouth, while Jacine began work on other patients as they were brought in.

She may have been the ship's carpenter, but that made her the second most qualified person on board to treat medical issues after Maude, and thankfully, she didn't complain.

Fuck, did that damn needle hurt though.

My jaw clicked from how hard it clenched, my fingers digging into the palms of my hands as I rested my forearms on Maude's shoulders as she dipped her needle into my skin, again and again, the hunger rolling in my gut at the warmth of her, *so close.*

I let out a shuddered breath, considering it, but Moira's hand landed softly on my shoulder.

My head twisted around to glare at her. One hand holding my sword, the other holding my shoulder, eyes full of empathy and pity. I huffed. Pity from a princess was nothing I wanted.

But the warmth from her hand… her fingers clenched around my blade…

I let out a hefty sigh, making Maude tsk. "Be still woman, do you want to be here longer?"

Closing my eyes, I concentrated on just bearing through the pain, and the warmth from Moira's hand.

Better that then the needle.

I lurched out of the surgeon's office, thanking Maude, who'd taken over from Jacine now that the worst of the injuries had been dealt with.

We were lucky. With nothing more than superficial wounds among my crew, I didn't want to think of what might've happened without Moira's warning.

Moira and Jacine followed me out, Jacine thankfully helping me back into my jacket without too much trouble, while I did my best to hide just how much everything hurt. It wouldn't be night for hours yet, and it couldn't come quick enough. This wound from the stake *still* felt like it was sizzling, and I was looking forward to healing it proper.

"Claire… What happened in there?" Jacine asked quietly, keeping her voice down as she and Moira followed in step behind me. I didn't answer immediately, pulling my jacket tighter around my frame as Moira handed me my blade. Only once I thought it looked like I was the invincible Captain Vessia once again, strapping my belt of weapons on, did I do my best to explain.

"Ambush. Tried to do me in with this." I pulled the stake out of my inner jacket pocket, still wrapped in its bloody cloth, handing it to Jacine. She took it gently from my hands, eyes morbid as she peeled back the still sticky cloth, Her brow furrowing ever more as she unwrapped it.

"What the fuck is this?" She murmured, holding the stake this way and that, while fear of the thing ate at my gut. Threat emanated from it like a miasma.

"No idea," I replied as we walked, fixing her with a look of surprise. "I thought *you* would know, you're the carpenter."

Jacine shrugged, tossing the stake back and forth between her hands, testing its weight. "It's not wood I've ever seen," she admitted. Whatever it was, she seemed fixated by the thing. She ran the bare skin of her calloused fingers over it like it had secrets to share if she—

It didn't burn her.

The thought came to me with an immediacy like a thunder bolt to the mast.

It's a weapon. Against Vampyri.

Jacine began to mumble as I stared at the stake in her hand with all the fear and loathing at the one person outside of the crew of the *Wraith* who knew what I was.

Lady Ameritia.

"I don't even know what kind of wood this is—"

"It's Black Scarwood," Moira said quietly, interrupting Jacine as her gaze locked on the stake in Jacine's hand, a mask of neutrality on her face.

Her heart was hammering in her chest.

"You know what this is?" I asked, pointing at the stake in Jacine's hand as she shook with surprise that someone knew more about a piece of wood than she did.

Moira nodded her head, motioning towards it. "There's a single tree of it in all of Kitaxia." She looked from me to Jacine and back. "In the palace gardens," she admitted.

That confirms it.

Either way, the wood in Jacine's hand seemed proof aplenty that the Count's ship was a trap designed especially for me. A poorly planned one, but a trap nonetheless.

I expected better from Ameritia.

"Jacine, toss it overboard," I ordered, not wanting to have such a weapon that could hurt me aboard my own ship.

"Will do ma'am. Just have to stow the rest of their wood kits and it'll be done," she said with a nod. I sighed with relief as she pocketed the stake and disappeared towards her goal, as me and Moira began a slow trek towards the hold of the other ship, the silence growing awkward between us.

If Moira knew what that wood was… Then she had to know what I was by now.

Did I admit it? She hated me. What was the point? What did I say to a girl who hated me?

Most of the time people who hated me were either dead, or soon about to be.

And why was she here now, not avoiding me like the plague like she'd been doing this past month? Why was she waiting in the surgery bay for me? Why that supportive hand on my shoulder?

A hundred, hundred questions wove through my mind, distracting me from pain and hunger as I watched her quietly keep step with me alongside, the weave of her red hair bouncing with each step as she pursed her lips.

I felt I needed to say *something*.

"You've been on board a month now. How are you settling in?" I asked.

Moira breathed out a huff of a laugh as we made it back across to the Count's ship and down its crew ladder. "Well enough," she replied. "Most of the crew are friendly, if a bit confused as to why I'm here. They can't seem to understand that just because I was rich, I wasn't happy. But—" She clammed up, a look on her face as if she just discovered she'd smelt something awful.

Probably realising that she was talking to *me*.

She gave me a hateful look, and I knew I wasn't getting any more out of her today.

A few quiet moments passed before Moira pressed her luck,

speaking again. "If today taught me anything, it's that I need a goddamn sword already."

I let out a chuckle at her complaint, after we dropped into the cavernous cargo hold of the other ship opened up before us, strangely unladen with much cargo.

"Do you even know how to use one?" I asked with a teasing tone to my voice.

She fixed me with a look that seemed to suggest that she wanted to skewer me with the blade she wanted so badly. "I know which end to stab a man with, Captain."

I shrugged with another chuckle, motioning her forward. "You get one when you earn one," I replied, the phrase long familiar.

Letting out a noise of complaint I'd imagine more from a teenager than a grown woman, Moira followed me through the hold.

But the cargo hold was… *strange*. It should've been packed to the brim with *some* kind of goods, yet there were only just enough crates of sundries and water stowage to justify a very short trip. Where was everything?

"Over here ma'am," Rodger's voice echoed from a quiet corner of the hold, a lantern in his hand along with a few other men.

"Alright, what's so bloody important—" the words died in my mouth as he stepped aside to show what lay in the corner of the hold, every eye attached to it in morbid wonder.

An iron forged coffin covered in chains and deadbolts every few inches, its thickness suggestive enough to throw off a cannonball, the lid open, waiting invitingly open for whoever would be trapped within its confines.

Now this… this is more Ameritia's style.

I shuddered, feeling like I'd dodged a fate worse than death.

Moira's heart was beating a league a minute, and for a second, I wondered if she thought this was *for her*. We stared at each other, while I imagined in horrified wonder about what they planned to do with me if they'd succeeded. Staked through the heart and trapped in an iron coffin.

Moira had to know what I was now. I could see the truth of it in her eyes, emerald forests tearing up with *guilt*, and *empathy*, and *pity*.

I did not need any of it, not for my revenge. Despite my heart lurching, wanting to reach for her, the memory of that damn hand on my shoulder…

I couldn't help but harden my heart and laugh.

"Well. I guess we really did piss off the Kitaxians," I said with a chuckle, as every eye turned to me in mute worry.

CHAPTER SIXTEEN

"On crew disagreements: Crew shall answer any challenge between each other with arbitration and judgment from the captain or quartermaster. They may also elect to settle the matter upon a duel or similar challenge, but only upon the permission of the captain and quartermaster."

"On duels: The challengers may provide a champion to fight in their place, if the champion is agreeable to the risk of injury, and the captain and quartermaster agree a substitution is needed. Any such duel is to be presided over by the Master at Arms, and judged by the captain unless they are involved in the dispute."

—Article Four, Sections three and four of the Ship's Code aboard the Wraith

Another sleepless day as we made our way home, I found myself prowling the weather deck as a warm day's winds blew harmlessly through our sails. My eyes burned with the need for sleep, but that was a long familiar sensation.

The sun was setting, giving the sky a bright pink glow as the rigging creaked like trees in the wind above my head.

I felt relief skittering out across my skin as the sun dipped over the edge of the world, watching the lanterns being lit one by one, the gentle rock of the *Wraith* under my boots.

Twilight. My favourite time of day. The promise of relief just moments away, blessed by a warm and comforting sky.

It'd been two months now since we'd raided Moira's convoy, yet weeks since the battle with the Count, and I was in a grouchier mood lately than I usually was, despite my lack of sleep and the ever-present hunger, because unlike every other wound I'd ever received since my turning, the stabbing from the stake healed slowly.

Ever so slowly.

An ugly pale scar stretched from the bottom of my left ribs to just below my breast, still aggressively sore, and although sealed, still ached. It was getting better by the day, but it was still annoying the ever-living hells out of me.

I'd gotten too used to healing overnight. To have to deal with a wound the same way *humans* did… was humbling.

Making my way along the decks, I eyed the very last whisper of sunlight setting below the horizon of the aft, and wasn't all that surprised to find Moira sitting with her legs threaded through the aftmost railings, leaning her head to rest over her arms on the railing itself, watching the last vestiges of the dying sun.

It was probably her favourite spot on the ship; several times I'd seen her with her legs dangling out over the ship's wake, watching the seas disappear behind us in silent wonder.

Months now since she had come aboard, and I had to admit that after the initial growing pains, she was adjusting to this life well.

In contrast to her first month where she'd barely worked, the day after we left the Count's ship sinking into the deep, she had worked herself ragged over the forge.

Gracie had to drag me down to the forge in a panic, where Moira's bloodied hands, arms shaking from the effort, had been working for nearly eleven hours straight, on little to no food.

I didn't know if the Count's ship had scared her to death, if she felt a sudden obligation to the crew for fighting off her would-be captor, or if she'd simply just had a crisis of faith.

But she needed help.

"You're no use to the crew working yourself to death," I'd said, worried over how hard she was pushing herself.

She ignored my words, not stopping her hammer from coming down onto hot metal on her small anvil for even a moment.

"Please," I had pleaded.

Only then did she stop. I didn't think I had ever asked anyone with 'please' since I had become captain so many years ago, but there I was. With intense focus, she had stared at the molten iron bending under her hammer in a trance.

"We need you to take care of yourself," I had said seriously, yet her eyes did not meet mine, she instead huffed out a breath of frustration.

"*I* need you to take care of yourself," I'd said, and finally, that broke the trance. She nodded. I took her bleeding hands gently, and guided her step-by-step to Maude waiting hands.

It took everything in me to not lick my fingers clean after I passed her off. It didn't feel right.

Since then, she was getting better. She was eating regularly, her hollow frame filling out as her shape took the most subtle of womanly curves, smiling more. Every time I saw her in the galley, she seemed to be laughing at some joke from Charlotte or Jacine.

Her trade was building muscle on her quickly, but she was still long and thin. I was beginning to think she always would be, since I had started watching her progress on board.

Not that I'd been keeping track of her or anything.

Watching her now here on the aft of the ship, I couldn't help but think her hair matched the red of the sunset. I grumbled as I joined her, leaning over the railing beside her.

Her eyebrows furrowed as she noticed me.

"Do you… ever sleep?" she asked, making me smirk. She'd finally noticed that habit.

Deliberately, I didn't answer the question, instead looking to change the topic. "We're finally on our way home. You've earned it."

She didn't break her gaze from the horizon. "I hardly did anything. I've made some nails and clamps for Jacine. Fixed a flintlock for Charlotte. Made more copper sheets than I could count," she mumbled into her folded arms.

"That's still something," I replied. "We would've gone without had you not been here."

Her silence spoke volumes. It just felt like I didn't have a codex to translate what that silence was saying. It left me without words to continue the conversation, and so we just stared at the sunset for another few awkward moments.

"Why *don't* you sleep?" She asked again, turning her head to rest sideways on her arms, gazing towards me.

The last vestiges of sun gave her face a pink glow, her hair looking aflame. It would've left me breathless had I been breathing. I sighed, turning away from her, trying to think of something else to change the subject to.

"You said you'd tell me. A full truth if I signed the Code. I've paid the price in loyalty." she said. I could hear the anticipation in her voice, like a shark that had clamped onto it's prey after a long chase.

I turned my head to glare back at her, but her face nestled into her arms wore a shadowy smirk.

I didn't have the heart to tell her that these last few weeks, thinking over her warning of the Count, I'd decided she'd paid that price hundreds of times over.

"You said—" she murmured quietly "—you owed me the truth. This is what I want. Why don't you sleep?"

Fuck.

No one knew exactly why I couldn't sleep, none of them did. It was a weakness, and so I couldn't admit it. So many of them knew little pieces of me, but none knew this, not even *Markus*. I turned from her smug gaze to look out over the water.

"I have nightmares," I admitted, unbelieving my own admission. "Every time I put my head to rest. I don't manage more than an hour or two of tortured sleep."

I didn't see her expression, but I heard the Gods damned *pity* in her voice.

"...That would drive most people mad, if not to their deaths," she replied.

It made a dark laugh eek out of my throat with no heart in it.

"As the stories say, I'm a dead woman walking anyway. And like I said. You have to be a bit mad to have my job."

The silence stretched as the darkness of the night began to grow from the East. I didn't dare look at her.

"What do you have nightmares about?" she asked.

I silently told myself not to look at her. If I did, I was sure I'd break. "Do I still have to tell you the truth?" I asked. If she said yes, I was terrified of what I might admit.

"...No. Only if you want." Her voice was… *careful.* Quiet.

I breathed out a sigh of relief, but I still felt she was owed an answer.

I gave her part of the truth. "I have nightmares about a time not long ago when I was… powerless. At someone else's mercy entirely." Another deep breath, steeling my soul for admitting such weakness. "Every time I close my eyes I am back there." I clenched the sleeves of my coat. "So, I don't sleep."

She was silent at my words, digesting what I had told her for a moment. "I'm sorry that you dream of such things," she said quietly, yet sincerely. "Thank you for telling me."

The last fading pink light of the sun wisped away like a leaf in the wind. We had stayed there for longer than I thought.

But I wasn't sure I wanted this moment to end. Not yet.

But a few breaths later, and she finally sighed, standing tall. One last glance over towards the horizon. "Come get a drink with me?" she asked, her eyes not leaving the sea.

I felt both of my eyebrows raise in surprise, suddenly thankful that I could hide behind the brim of my hat.

She *hated* me. Why was she asking me this?

I couldn't answer at first, cowering under the shade of my hat, wondering. But… Did it matter? She was offering me a way in.

I wasn't even sure if I *wanted* in.

But I wasn't one to say no to an adventure on stranger shores.

"Sure," I replied, pushing off the railing to follow after her.

We walked down towards the galley, just as the space was getting a bit snug with overcrowding. The day shift sitting down to enjoy their meals and drink after hours out in the sun, the night shift grabbing last minute food and drink before their workdays really started.

And everywhere, hunger rolled in my gut, the smell of sweat and breath and *warmth.*

My mouth watered.

We wove our way through the galley, more than a few pairs of eyes tracking our path towards where Charlotte and Maude were quietly conversing.

"Mind if we join you?" I asked. At their nods Moira, instead of taking the obvious empty seat, squeezed Maude in between her and Charlotte, leaving me the whole opposite bench to myself, much to Charlotte's annoyance.

"Come'on girl, she's not going to bite!" they muttered as they were pushed towards the bulkhead wall, Maude somehow looking undisturbed as I tried not to snort at the pun.

I wasn't going to look a gift horse in the mouth however, and stretched down the bench, putting my feet up to lay down it lengthwise. "I consider it captain's prerogative," I stated with a smile, as Charlotte mocked me in tone.

"'Captain's prerogative', fuck you." Charlotte flipped me an obscene gesture, mocking my words in a high-pitched imitation, making the whole table laugh.

"I'll... go get some food," Moira said awkwardly through her laughs. "Anything for you, Captain?" she asked, standing up almost immediately after she'd sat down.

"Ale for me. Nothing else," I answered with a smile, watching her nod and retreat quickly.

Maude and Charlotte exchanged looks as she stepped away, looking like they were in on an inside joke that I wasn't.

"What?" I asked, not liking the idea of the pair of them knowing something I didn't, drumming my fingers against the table as they smiled like thieves in the night.

"Nothing Claire, just—" Maude began to say before Charlotte interrupted her.

"Crew's taking bets on when you and her will fuck. If you want, I can cut you in on a deal, get you some good money for the day before we make port—" Charlotte stopped short as the glare I fixed them with only made their grin wider, before turning to Maude. "Told ya she was into it," they said with a wink.

Maude sighed as my glare got ever more murderous. "This doesn't prove anything, just that—"

"That *somebody* wants to fuck the newest broad on board. Ha!" Charlotte smacked the table with a loud bang, pointing at my face with glee when I didn't immediately deny them. "Holy fuck she does! She wants a taste of that royal d—"

Quick as a flash, I reached to grab Charlotte's collar, tugging them over the table, pressing their face downwards into the wood, my elbow was on their back.

"Charlotte," I said, as simply and evenly as if I were saying hello.

"Captain," they winced, hands up in surrender.

"I told you not to push it," Maude muttered, crossing her arms as the nearby crew all got quick laughs at our chief gunner.

"How about you shut the fuck up, eh? Seem like a good idea?" I suggested, feeling a bit like a disapproving mother.

"Got it, clear as glass Captain," Charlotte said with a pained chuckle.

"Good," I replied, and I let them go a moment later. Pulling myself off of them to lean back down the bench, watching them bite their lip as they picked themselves up.

They fell back into their seat, trying to make it look like they hadn't just gotten reminded not to bite the hand that fed them.

I didn't care. Or maybe I cared too much.

Fuck if I knew.

The crew could make bets about whatever they damn well pleased. Maybe… maybe I did have a thing for her. Time would tell one way or another. My eyes glanced at the crowd as Maude tsked, chiding Charlotte to be less direct in their teasing, while my eyes searched for a mane of red hair.

"What's your opinion of her?" I asked both of them as they readjusted in their seats once more.

Maude rolled her eyes, facepalming as she muttered about lost causes, but Charlotte looked delighted I was asking and fired off an answer. "She's timid. But she's angry. Gods is that girl angry. She just hides it well."

Charlotte's answer surprised me yet again, but I couldn't find myself disagreeing with them. I'd made the exact same observation when she was first tied up in my cabin.

"What you should both consider, is what happens when she stops being timid," Maude said with a sagely flourish, sounding more wiser than both of us put together.

Me and Charlotte exchanged glances, as I briefly wondered who would be on the suffering end of that volcanic eruption of royal repression.

"I wonder," I murmured quietly, stealing Charlotte's mug out from under them.

"Hey!" they stammered out, blindly reaching for it as I brought it to my lips. "Fuck off! Get your own!"

I laughed, handing it back to them. "I am, she's just taking forever—"

A loud exclamation echoed from the galley counter, making all of us turn our heads to a pile of bodies crowding around whatever was happening, blocking it from view.

"Oh, Gods above and below, what now?" I murmured in frustration, standing up from the bench as both Charlotte and Maude strained their necks to get a better view themselves.

I walked through the circle of sailors, who were by now chanting between them 'fight! fight! fight!' making space for me one by one as I forcefully pulled them out of my way. They were ready to fight *me* off at first, before stammering into panicked silence when they realized who exactly was pushing them.

I reached the edge of the circle, towards the supposed combatants, and saw the last thing I expected.

Moira toe-to-toe with Markus, faces inches from each other, spitting angry.

"You're a god damned idiot if you think—" Moira yelled before Markus snapped off a reply, "—more like the smartest man here! You're a spoiled royal *brat*, about as useful to this crew as a Varcnan groundhog!"

Moira seethed, lips pulled back over her teeth as she spat a reply, "You're an egotistical thick skulled boorish man with a grudge! Nothing more!"

They were seconds away from blows, Gracie standing still as a statue in a panic behind the counter, looking to be currently debating between freeze or... flight.

Oh, for the love of—

"ENOUGH!"

My shout was hard, authoritative, and undeniable.

Every voice in the room silenced, every pair of eyes turned in attention towards me.

All except for two.

"Captain, glad you're here. Maybe you can clear this up and get this traitor off our ship," Markus said with vindictive ease, not taking his eyes off of Moira. I felt furious and a bit betrayed that he could be this... *spiteful*.

"You can shut the fuck up Mr. Clun! You've got no evidence other than your own prejudice," Moira spat.

"Please, every boarding now you're cowering in the hold—" Markus began to reply, before Moira cut him off. "—Because no one will give me a damn sword!"

"I said ENOUGH." My shout vibrated the deck, and finally, both of them turning to look at me with their full attention, positively fuming with dislike of the other.

I rested my hand on the pommel of my blade, for all intents and purposes, my badge of office as I played the disappointed mother of the crew.

"Mr. Clun. Your displeasure of Miss Moira is well known, but unless you have a *specific* grievance, then I suggest you keep your displeasure *to yourself*. I would rather not have to lash my own *quartermaster* under Article Two."

My threat, and the Code, was crystal clear. If you suspected someone of treason, keep it to yourself unless you have evidence. In all my years of captain I'd only had *one* traitor. And I was a *very* harsh mistress when it came to when sailors betrayed the code.

"Do I make myself clear?" I demanded.

Markus's face twisted into a grimace, but he nodded. "Yes, Captain."

"Miss Moira." I turned my steely gaze towards Moira's even set determined eyes. I didn't want to have to make an example, but...

"Mr. Clun is out of line, but we can't have fights beginning in the middle of the galley. We have the Code for a reason. If you have cause, challenge him under Article Four."

She nodded, raising a single hand, and I tried not to roll my eyes.

"What is it?" I asked.

"I *would* challenge him, but no one will give me a sword," she replied matter-of-factly.

Now I had to roll my eyes, as did nearly every crewman around us. This was getting old, but it was true. Anyone else in her position would've been given a weapon by now.

There was hesitancy on my part simply because... I wasn't sure if I could trust her yet.

"The point of the matter is that you're... a *unique* case. And giving you a blade—" I began to explain, but she wasn't having it.

"Fine then. I challenge *you* for the right to have a fucking sword," she stated.

For the briefest of moments, I thought I'd misheard. In that single second, not a soul was breathing in that crowded galley. I heard a pin drop, the cry of a far-off seagull, and the tipping of some forgotten ale over the side of a table, spilling onto the floor.

But then everyone registered what she'd said.

The echo of gasps rippled throughout every soul in the room, and even I wasn't immune. I couldn't hold back my surprise as I lifted a hand to my face.

It was out of my hands now. Now it was in the Code's.

"A challenge has been issued," my hollowed voice announced, as the crew exploded into excited cheers.

I let my body switch into muscle memory, finding solace in disassociation. I wasn't allowed to have any feeling now, my duty was to the Code, not to some redhead I felt...

I didn't know what I felt about Moira.

And I had no choice but to accept her challenge.

Moira was fully within her rights, but it was a foolish move.

Among the crew it was seen as unfair. It just wasn't done. I'd never lost a duel, and was known as by far the best fighter on the entire ship, let alone the entire Gods damn seas.

But I did have the right to turn the challenge down, admit defeat and give her the damn sword.

But that wasn't all that was happening.

If I said no, I'd be showing *weakness*. Despite me being a bloodthirsty monster, all it took was one little sign of weakness, and the crew would vote me out of captaincy, or worse, *mutiny*.

And worse than that, if I declined, I'd be showing the crew that Moira was a *favourite*.

As Captain, if there was one thing I couldn't do, it was to have *favourites*. I was the end of the law on the *Wraith*, I was both justice, jury, and executioner. The crew had to be equal in every way before my purview, knowing that no matter the cause, my strength and authority was absolute.

If I declined, I was admitting to the crew at large that some were more important than others.

And that couldn't stand. So, I said the only thing I could.

"I accept."

Within minutes of my acceptance, the crew had the weather deck cleared, more lanterns lit, and bets placed. All obviously in my favour. The odds were so stacked against Moira that bets were called off because no one would bet against me. Bet in favour of the newbie? Who could barely stand without the wind blowing her away? Against the captain? The captain who had *never lost a duel?*

It was unthinkable.

Moira hadn't spared me a single glance since I'd accepted, even if I wanted her to. On one hand, I loved a good fight. On the other hand... I had to play the part.

We were led to a growing circle of nearly every sailor on board, where a wide-open space sat in the midst of the weather deck. Crew crowded the forecastle and quarterdeck, the outer railings, and even hung from the rigging.

I shucked out of my coat, passing it and my hat to Markus. He was still looking to gloat, and seemed to have a permanent smile stitched onto his face. I imagined he would be enjoying seeing Moira possibly cut into pieces.

But with the excitement of the crew, now I could *feel* the fight in my blood. I could nearly taste the electricity in the air, and knew that the clash of blades was *just* around the corner.

I drew my sword, slinging the scabbard and belt over my shoulder to add it to the pile in Markus's hands. I swung the blade lightly in my grip as if it were a walking stick, pacing around the circle of excited crewmen that was forming around us with a ready smile on my face.

Moira had been handed one of the naval sabres we kept in storage, its blade keen and ready, but unloved. She swung it wildly, seeming to test the weight.

"You know you can nominate someone to stand in your place, even as the challenger," I sing-songed at her with a smirk, unable to deny that I was going to enjoy this.

She ignored me, seemingly satisfied with her blade, turning towards me, holding it lightly at her side. I sighed, near prancing back to my side of the improvised duelling circle, gazing at the stars overhead, marvelling at their beauty for just a moment before turning back to my opponent.

"Alright. Mr. Castille! Let it be done," I shouted to the crowd, a wild cheer erupting.

Rodger stepped out of the crowd and into the middle of the improvised circle. As master-at-arms, he was the referee of the whole debacle. He loudly shouted, "Captain has given her blessing for this duel, and the time is now!" Like some arena announcer, his voice livened up the crew. "Miss Moira here, has challenged the captain."

He looked back and forth between us, as if this statement alone would make either one of us back down.

"Miss Moira has demanded the stakes upon her victory be an apology from Mr. Clun, the right to wear a blade, and join the fighters roll." Everyone's eyes turned to me, and where Markus was standing in the circle just over my shoulder.

"Captain Vessia, what do you demand?" Rodger asked as I twirled my sword in my hand, watching the point spin, rolling my shoulders back.

I could demand nearly anything I wanted out of Moira.

My imagination was *very* interested in all the predicaments I could put her in... but I decided to be fair. I was *captain* after all, and the punishment I could dole out with just my blade…

An even wider smile broke out over my face as I answered. "That Moira tells me a story," I said nonchalantly.

Laughter from every corner of the ship. No one would deny me. The Code ruled us all.

"Are you sure Captain?" Rodger asked, a raised eyebrow towards me. I answered with a shrug, resting my blade on my shoulder, as I motioned towards Moira with my free hand.

"She can't pay with much else," I replied. The laughter grew.

Rodger's mustache twitched from side to side. "...Very well. The Captain has demanded the stakes upon her victory will be... a story." He shook his head in disbelief. Whatever his feelings were on the power play happening before him, it was out of his control.

"Are these terms agreeable?" Rodger asked us both, to which I nodded, finally gripping my sword properly. I was curious to see how Moira performed.

Rodger turned from me to Moira. "Yes," she said quietly, her expression unchanged despite the ridiculous 'stakes' I'd put at her feet. Rodger's muscles tensed.

"To first blood then. Begin!" He waved his hand between us and stepped back rapidly.

I stepped forward, a slow saunter of an advance. A very casual stance, really, barely trying, as I cut haphazardly through the air to test her defences. But as she met my strike, I found that I'd underestimated her.

Because her parry was *perfect*.

I retreated from her counter, and what I saw in her stance

astounded me. Free hand behind her back, feet perfectly spaced, sword lightly but firmly in grasp, held at the perfect angle. It was fucking textbook.

She knows what she's doing.

But I had murdered plenty of men who knew what they were doing. I firmed up my stance, went for a three-hit combo. She blocked, parried, and dodged before replying in kind.

Cheers from the crew rang out as I quickly found myself in one of the toughest fights I could remember being in.

She was good. *Very* good.

Our blades turned into a rapid fire of blows, her parries productive, counters solid, thrusts timed extremely well, and swings sure as rain. But I could tell she was rusty. She hadn't held a blade in some time, certainly not since we picked her up months ago. And I had years of slaughter under my belt.

She was nonetheless giving me a certain challenge. I found myself laughing, enjoying every minute of the fight, as I struck again and again and again, but she remained just out of reach of the bite of my blade.

The crew were having the show of their lives, and the hooting and hollering were white noise to the symphony of our blades clashing. Moira's face was set into an iron mask, never budging from the stare into my eyes. Only the barest amount of enjoyment was playing out in the tiniest smirk of her mouth.

But she was tiring, and I *never* tired. Her blocks came just a breath later, her dodging becoming less and less clean. Her thrusts lacked the power they had upon the start of our duel.

I saw the desperation building in her eyes as she began to realise she would lose unless she tried something. And when she finally did, I almost didn't catch it.

A wild thrust where she tripped. I thought I had her—obviously the length of the duel had tired her footwork. I swung wide to catch her in the fall. But she dropped down under it, letting the dead weight of her body barely drop below my swing. If she had mistimed it, I would've taken her head clean off.

But she hadn't.

As soon as she had ducked under the blade, I knew I was fucked. She righted herself as she passed me, turning to lift her blade in a wild slash at my unprotected back. A very well put together trap.

Which meant it was time for some wild bullshit of my own.

Ba-dum. I lightly tossed my blade into the air as my heart began to beat. *Ba-dum.* It arced quietly just above my head, immediately coming back down. *Ba-dum.* Gravity pulled the blade enough to counter her wild strike just enough for me to sidestep it. *Ba-dum.* In my sidestep, I twirled, her wild cut having been forced into a thrust while my own sword thunked into the deck, where it quivered, handle to the sky. *Ba-dum.* I reached out, my hands wrapping around her neck and wrist, pushing her into the mast. *Baaaa-dummmmm.* I started to tighten my grip on her wrist, her fingers beginning to let go of the blade.

I had her. Or as my heart steadied out into silence once again, I *thought* I had her.

I wasn't expecting the knee to my ribs, right where the stake had gone, making me wince in gasped pain, right before her fist met my face.

Cursing, forced backwards, one hand grasping at my gut, but I was glad that I had a backup plan.

I stumbled backwards directly into where my sword stood up from the deck. Her swing was from on high, and I lurched my blade free from the deck to rest its point on her cheek quick as a flash, her blade still harmlessly in the air, too far to counter.

I pushed just hard enough to cut into her cheek, a single drop of blood welling up from the tip of my blade.

"THAT'S THE DUEL!" Rodger shouted from the edge of the crowd as the crew went absolutely insane.

Moira's breath was haggard as I released my sword from her cheek, tapping the bottom of her chin with the point so that she was forced to look at me down her face as her head was tipped upwards.

"Moira, you are as dangerous as you are delicious," I said quietly enough over the shouts of the crowd that only she could hear.

Her eyes glistened into something I couldn't place, as she visibly gulped. *Gods.* The temptation to bite into her throat was… intoxicating.

Let alone to do... *other* things to her.

Smitten. Gods damn it.

I sighed, finally letting my blade lower. Moira's hand rubbed at her neck, before she dabbed at the cut on her cheek, blood seeping through her fingers. Turning away from her, I took back my items from Markus, who was positively beaming, and sheathed my blade.

I gave Moira one last parting look, her eyes as green as grassy fields, still staring at me as though our duel hadn't ended, searching for something in my face I didn't know was there or not.

Not knowing what to say, I walked away from the cheering crowd, and left her standing there, her hand still on her face, as I went to my quarters. Once the doors had shut, and the shouts of the crew outside were muffled, I leaned my back against the doors, sliding down them to the floor.

For some reason that I couldn't fathom, the tears didn't surprise me.

CHAPTER SEVENTEEN

"I've been privately approached by her Royal Highness, Lady Ameritia, with a proposal that I find as intriguing as it is informative. As long as we are willing to stomach a small number of civilian deaths, we very much could see a substantial payout to certain members of the Merchant Republic of Varcna, along with the possible eradication of piracy once and for all in the eastern part of the country. I highly recommend you instruct me to reply in affirmation to Her Royal Highness at your earliest convenience. Opportunities like this don't land on our doorstep every day."

—Lord Hartfeld, Varcnan Ambassador to the Kingdom of Kitaxia, in a letter to Lord Gravin, Chancellor of the Merchant Navy of Varcna

"You're telling me that little *Souris harbour* is the legendary Port Sable?" Moira all but yelled in unbelievable fury, which made me *really* want to laugh while Maude sighed from where she was sitting on a barrel behind us, sewing something into a green coloured scarf.

It was, frankly, *ridiculous* when you first heard.

"Is it so unbelievable?" Maude asked quietly, not looking up from her work.

"Yes! Yes, it is!" Moira exclaimed. I twisted the helm just a few more degrees to dodge some shallows I knew were touchy at low tide. I couldn't sleep—of course—so I had taken the shift for the helm. Every once in a while, I felt the need to feel the *Wraith*'s every shift under my control, and it answered with soothing simplicity.

We pulled past Souris's harbour with some grumbling disbelief from Moira as we stood on the quarterdeck, the last beams of sun setting over the mountains.

Souris was a tiny sleepy harbour in eastern Varcna, the only major settlement of its island, and housed less than a thousand people. It was the very definition of the word *quaint*. People from all across easternern Varcna considered it nothing more than a rural backwater of a town, more akin to a hide-away resort, or a quiet fishing village.

For it to be a *legendary pirate port*? Well, that was impossible.

And it was that very impossibility that made it *home*.

"Technically, it's not Souris, but the next cove over to be exact," I explained.

Moira rolled her eyes at my words. "Don't you get technical with me, Captain," she all but pointed at me accusingly. I couldn't help the silent laughter in my shoulders at her disbelief.

"Its quaintness is exactly what makes it perfect." I raised an eyebrow at her over my shoulder. "Who would suspect?" I said over the din of the crew making ready most of the cargo ready for delivery to our warehouses.

Moira shifted on her hips, puckering her mouth in disbelief, looking at the sleepy port with her sword hanging off her belt, clinking against her thigh.

She deserved it after that duel.

I had presented it to her the day after with pride. There were maybe three in the entire crew who were better, if not equal to her. I didn't tell her that, but at her skill level, she probably knew it.

"Still..." she said quietly, looking over the port, the crowd at the docks waving. The town had nearly doubled in size since I'd first stumbled onto her shores so many years ago. We'd poured goods, sailors, and money into the sleepy little village, and now there were new and growing families among the crew, plus everyone who'd retired from the *Wraith* over the years.

"It's just hard to believe. It's so… *picturesque*," Moira said, making Maude snort and forcing me to bark out a laugh.

"You haven't seen the tavern the first night we're in port," I replied through my laughter, twisting the helm ever just so. "It'll be plenty rowdy tonight my dear, don't you worry your pretty little head."

I could feel Maude's stare into my back, and I deliberately avoided Moira's gaze as I shifted the helm a few degrees back starboard. Returning home always left me feeling a bit jovial. For just a little while, there were no enemy ships on the horizon, no revenge against Kitaxia. Just rest and recuperation.

My hunger very much wanted to disagree, but that was a problem for later.

"Bring her in lads! We're home!" I shouted as I made the last turn, affirmations relayed up and down the decks to my orders. Just as the last of the sails were hoisted and stowed, the *Wraith* swung into a sheltered little cove, covered by thick jungle trees. No one would know to look here, unless they *knew*.

The *Wraith* slowed, drifting into our berth, perfectly out of sight.

We couldn't let Souris be the 'actual' pirate port of Varcna, otherwise we'd be fighting off the navy every time we came home. Gracie's sister, the legendary Miss Cavendish—she absolutely refused to be called by her first name, Annabelle—and I had made great pains to hide a secondary port just up the shore from the main entrance to Souris, with enough camouflage to hide the entire ship, along with our warehouses.

That was where we stored our ill-gotten goods for Miss Cavendish to relabel and sell, her merchant captains taking our loot to sell across the Vibari sea in the east and across the Syntari sea in the west. She was our fence, our master merchant, and we'd made her—and by extension, Souris—rich.

It wasn't perfect, but a system we made work in a world determined to see us dead.

I waited, feeling the *Wraith* glide into place as she bled speed, running the helm perfectly starboard as I felt her shift underneath my feet. I let it run for just another half a breath before giving the final command. "Drop it lads! Weigh anchor!"

The hammer was dropped against the breaking pin, and the chain let loose. The splash of the water echoed as the giant steel hook shifted into the sea. The loss of forward momentum let us coast to a smooth stop as the drop of the chain smoothed out, the hidden dock bare inches away.

"We're home," I said quietly, bringing the helm back to rest, securing it with a tight lash of rope. My hands never forgot the knots, no matter how long it'd been since I was just another yard rat in the rigging.

Maude didn't move, content to finish whatever she was sewing, as I walked over to the railing to view my handiwork with quiet pride. Not five feet away from the dock. I nodded to myself in satisfaction.

Moira leaned over the railing with me, followed my gaze in wonder, looking at the mouth of our hidden port, waiting warehouses, and the slew of dockworkers standing at the ready to unload us. "Quite an operation here Captain," she admitted, clearly impressed.

Seeing her appreciation at our years of work, made me swell with pride. For some reason, I wanted her to be impressed by what we built here more than anyone else.

I swung an easy arm around her shoulder that she didn't immediately shrug out from under, as I guided her to the dropping gangplank.

"You haven't seen anything yet, my dear," I whispered into her ear with a promise of sights to see on my tongue.

I led Moira down the gangplank with a happy smile on my face, every single person around us on the weather deck lively with excitement. Whether they were new crew like Moira, seeing their new home for the first time with wonder in their eyes, or old hands who'd been here a hundred times or more. Finally, we were *all* home for the first time in months, and that was always a reason for a party.

Markus was the first officer I saw off the ship, giving final orders to the dockworkers. He only gave me a quiet nod, casting a snide look towards Moira at my side. In a moment, I knew he'd be rushing off to see his family. They'd moved from Wester-Cay last year, selling their little plot of land there for a tidy profit. The crew had all chipped in and built the house they now lived in happily together. He was close with his parents, and their hopeless attempts to set him up with a partner in hopes of grandchildren were something we shared laughs and drinks over nearly every time we made port.

I was about to lead Moira to the warehouse, when a blonde woman in deep green rushed past us, almost shoving us both off the gangplank and risking a dip into the water in her rush to get aboard the ship.

"Who the—" Moira began to ask, affronted, but I shook my head, leading her on. There was a line of crew behind us waiting to get off the ship who'd seen this time and time again, and no one had much patience for Moira learning how things worked.

"That would be Isabella, our resident port-bound doctor. Maude's partner. Call her a 'doctor' at your peril though," I said with a light laugh, a hand on the back of her waist, a light force pulling her down the gangplank with me.

Moira nodded in sudden understanding, staring up at the woman rapidly running up the quarterdeck stairs to swoop Maude happily into her arms.

It made me smile, seeing the two women laughing together in the bright sunset like this, considering when Isabella joined us forever and a day ago, they'd *despised* each other.

Maude was a traditionally trained surgeon, while Isabella was something akin to a forest witch. She was from the eastern continent, some settlement no one had ever heard of in the forever woods of the Everwilds.

Her hair shook wildly as she laughed in Maude's arms, planting a kiss on the smaller woman's forehead.

"They're *adorable,*" Moira mumbled beside me. I couldn't help but nod with her.

"They are," I said in agreement. "You should've seen the fights they had when they first met though. Legendary." Their argument over using a tree lichen for an emergency bandage was one of my favourites to recall over drinks.

Leaving them to follow us at their leisure, I steered Moira through to the warehouse, past an ever-growing trove of raided merchandise. Everything from tools to cannons, shot to building materials. Produce and pottery, silks and dresses of every kind, to lumber and whale oil. I was quite sure that if anything had ever been traded across the Great Divide, I had stolen at least one piece of it.

But one of our greatest accomplishments in the Port of Souris was now before us as we approached the back of the warehouse, built into the side of a mountain.

The hidden rail tunnel that led straight to the giant basement underneath Miss Cavendish's tavern in the heart of Souris.

Moira's eyes were alight with suspicion and disbelief as I led her to a cart for passengers, open topped with only two seats facing each other. Everyone else piled behind us into the other railcars, the little steam engine at the head—we'd stolen that too—began to huff and puff. Barely a moment before we took off, Maude and Isabella rushed to our car to join us, and off we went covering a kilometre in minutes.

Maude and Isabella talked on the other side of us about taking a stroll through town before meeting us at the tavern later. Maude completely at ease, leaning back in her seat to play with the hair of the woman who'd once infuriated her, eyes aglow in adoration as Isabella talked at length about her garden.

Other crew members were sitting all around us in the rail cars, their voices echoing off the cave walls, talking about their lives and loves. Families they hadn't seen in months, lovers on the bud of becoming something more, everyone looking forward to the inevitable party that'd be happening tonight.

I closed my eyes, letting myself relax, picking out Markus's voice in the car behind us. He was talking with Rodger about how his sister had just moved to Seven Peaks, becoming an apprentice on one of their great forges, while Rodger was complaining about his latest love affair.

I opened my eyes, staring over Maude and Isabella's shoulders to spy Charlotte and Jacine in the car ahead, Jacine with her nose in a book muttering about its inaccuracies, Charlotte's head leaning against her shoulder, snoring heavily, the noise from their throat so audible it somehow echoed in time with the chugging of the rail engine off the stone walls.

I looked around at my officers, in brief amazement that we'd held together as long as we had. Somehow, despite the odds. Pirate crews were *not* known for their stability.

And yet... Here we were.

My family.

But... I found myself jealous of them.

Each one of them had something in Souris. Each one of them had a partner, or a family, friends... And I... *didn't.*

The only connection I had here was mother, and the less I thought about her, the better.

Oh, to be sure, I had women who warmed my bed when I was here, but was my heart ever in it?

Letting out a sigh as I closed my eyes once more, I concentrated on the rush of air blowing past my face rustling my hair, before finally letting myself register the pressence I'd been suppressing since the moment I pulled Moira close on the ship.

I listened to her heart beat, the little *ba-thump* of excitement, of *wonder*, as she talked back and forth with Maude and Isabella. *Happy.* That's what it was. She was *happy.*

I'd brought her here, given her this, and… Why? Because I was *smitten?*

Was I that pathetically lonely?

I let my eyes wander her jaw-line, the colour of her hair catching the torch light, the smile of excitement on her face…

Maybe…

No.

The pump of her heart was all it was. The memory of her *taste.* The hunger swirling in the back of my mind as it always was, leaving me trying to fight off the urge to bite into that beautiful neck.

Letting out a little huff in the air, a cold dead smile on my face, I felt I could at least take solace that if I didn't have anything besides my revenge to keep my heart warm every night, that at least I provided the chance for everyone else to have something in Souris to call their own, the tiniest bit of home to come back to.

Now even for the daughter of my most hated enemy.

Even if dead women didn't get dreams… That was still good.

Leaving Moira in Jacine's care to get acquainted with the town, I set out to obey my responsibilities first and foremost.

Then I could join the fun.

I first visited Adam McCrosswick, Souris's Commander of the Watch. This was the main reason that Souris was *our* friendly port, because as long as Adam continued taking my bribes, the merchant lords in Varcna City didn't know what the fuck was happening in their sleepy little town.

Adam was more than ecstatic to see a chest full of silver from the tax ship we'd raided set on his desk.

Next, I stopped by Juliette's, the seamstress, where I made arrangements for repairs to my coat, and entertained her proposition for the possibility of a replacement. Quite possibly the fortieth time she'd made that proposition.

I *liked* this coat.

After, I ran into Moira exploring the town, after she'd somehow escaped Jacine. I took her to the castle forge, where she nearly danced in delight as Old Man Tom showed her the workshop we had built for him. He was just as happy as she was, excited to finally have an apprentice worthy of his skills, as he attempted to chase after her manic energy with his crutches as she wandered from piece to piece.

She was still giddy after we left to make our way to the tavern. "Can you believe he has a proper blast furnace? Out here? Where the heck did he get that from?" she asked, nearly vibrating with glee.

"Where do you think?" I raised a suggestive eyebrow, leading her up the hill to the center of town, street lamps lighting our way.

Her mouth opened in a silent "Oh" that nearly made me swoon on the spot. To hopefully *not* do that, I explained the story.

"Shipment off the coast of Hordalu," I extrapolated, looking for something to distract from that amazed look in her eyes. "Was bound for Rygfylki I think. Private order from Seven Peaks."

She brought a finger to tap at her chin in thought as she thought about what I'd said. "I doubt Jarl Isolde was pleased about that," She murmured, and she was right. We didn't take Norn ships often, as they were more trouble than they were worth.

"Of course not. The bounty for my head in Norlondia is about as high as it is in Kitaxia for a quarter of the ships lost."

She was silent for another moment, contemplative. "What about here in Varcna?" she asked.

I rolled my shoulders, letting a sigh escape me, patting her head. "Dear, we're not in Varcna. We're in *Port Sable*," I said, waving my other hand towards the tavern as we turned the corner. "And Port Sable, is *ours*."

She pushed away my hand in annoyance, making me laugh as I motioned for her to follow me into the tavern. The moment we were through the door, we were met by a wall of noise. A cheer that exploded from the packed room was enough to deafen, now that we were properly into the celebration. I made a dramatic bow to the revelers, which only elected a feedback loop of cheering.

The Tavern was a beautiful mix of stone and wood, looking downright cosy, yet somehow managing to fit nearly a hundred people in comfortably. A sturdy staircase on the far wall led to a gangway above that led even further to rooms for the night, a wide dancefloor occupied by countless round tables hosting crew with ale and heaps of food, the bar at the opposite wall a flurry of activity of servers going to and from the kitchens beyond.

Music filled the room from a small corner stage where a trio of bards sang shanties and protest songs, and the door was never closed for long, people coming and going at nearly all hours.

I weaved my way through the crowd, seeing my regular table by the fireplace rapidly vacated by crew and villagers who knew better, leaving only Maude, who didn't move from her seat.

She was radiating nervous energy, making her twitchy, her heart beating like a racehorse. Which was *very* unlike her.

As I sat down in my spot, feeling the pleasure of the roaring fire warming my back, Moira sat on the opposite side of the table. I narrowed my gaze at Maude.

"What's wrong?" I asked quietly, but near enough that she could hear me over the crowd.

"You noticed? Of course you noticed. You notice everything," she replied, taking a deep breath, looking at me with fear in her eyes. "I'm about to do something very stupid," She nearly whispered.

If *Maude* was about to do something stupid, may the Goddesses have mercy on us all.

At least I'd get to watch. I tilted my head at her, wondering what she could possibly mean. "Is it something you… want to do?" I asked.

She nodded, looking almost wild, like she was looking for an escape from this exact moment. "More than anything," she replied, her tone serious.

I tilted my head back and forth looking for—*aha*, before grabbing a tankard of ale off the tray of a passing barmaid, who gave me a dirty look for a brief moment before realizing who she was staring at, quickly skittering away from my smile and wink. I handed my stolen prize to Maude.

"For the stupidest of things you're determined to do anyway, liquid courage does wonders," I suggested. It absolutely wasn't at all, but it seemed like Maude just needed a push. Something to give her the excuse she was looking for.

She stared at the offered drink, looking like she was debating her taxes. I had seen Maude take a drink maybe a handful of times, and never in quantity, but she grabbed it and downed the whole thing in seconds, amazing even me.

"Okay," she said, rolling her shoulders, steeling herself for what she was about to do, before suddenly standing quickly enough to make the chair scrape.

"Here goes," she murmured, taking a deep breath. Then she marched over a few tables, to where Isabella, Jacine, and Rodger were chatting with a group of sailors from the gunnery crew along with a few locals. I noticed the cloth of green she had been sewing earlier, held tightly in her hand.

She tapped Isabella on the shoulder, making the whole table turn to stare. My eyes opened wide, wondering if this was going to go where I thought it was going. I quickly grabbed Moira's wrist to get her attention, but I'm quite sure she was already staring.

"Isabella of the Everwilds," Maude said quite formally, as more and more chairs scraped against the floor as several bodies turned in their seats to see what was going on. "You annoy me to no end, make me question my every choice, and sometimes leave me doubting my own sanity. But you also have added to my life in more ways than I can possibly count, push me to confirm rather than reinforce my own beliefs, and bring out the best version of me I can hope to imagine. I can no longer imagine what life would be like without you by my side."

Maude took a knee, lowering herself before Isabella, carefully unfolding the green cloth in her hands, showing the intricate design of a giant tree, and the sea intermingled in its roots, holding it up for Isabella to take or deny.

"Will you marry me?" Maude asked with all the reverence of someone at prayer.

Isabella looked speechless, the sound of her heart pounding in my head, even in this crowded space full of noise. The only thing louder was Maude's. She stood slowly, appearing to show grace despite the panic only I could hear in her heart. I felt Moira's hand tighten around mine.

Isabella lifted the cloth from her outstretched hands, examining its beauty. The tradition of a cloth for a proposal must have been from Isabella's homeland, but the melding of family crests was of the three nations. Maude had chosen herself as the sea, and Isabella as a great and mighty tree. The family unit would use that melded symbol from there on out on all matters, with each child adding their own symbol depending on their birth month and name.

My own parents had been a lynx and a wolf. On their marriage tapestry they both hunted endlessly, chasing each other over the surface of the moon in my own sigil.

Not that they knew my *actual* sigil. No one knew my birthdate.

Isabella's eyes welled up in tears, as she clutched the cloth close to her chest, leaning down to tip Maude's chin up towards her. "Of course I'll marry you, you silly, silly woman." And lifted her into the most passionate kiss I thought I'd ever see.

Wild cheers of happiness and congratulations sang up from the crowd, and I found myself standing with the rest of everyone present, screaming for joy.

But as the crowd simmered into a happy joy, the bards in the corner singing of true love, I found myself sulking into my seat. Again, jealous of that connection that they had been able to find in each other.

I knew I should've been happy. Two of my friends were getting married. I *was* happy.

So why am I so sad?

Markus joined me at the table after we made our congratulations, while Moira left with Jacine a moment after to float from table to table, making introductions, and *yes*, admitting to people she actually *was* royalty. I watched her open up to our world, and our world happily take her in.

Markus watched my stare with a broken smile.

"You know," Markus began, his words twisted in his mouth, like he really didn't want to say them. "As much as I hate myself for suggesting it, I think... she might actually be *good* for you."

I nearly spit out my drink, turning to stare at him with disbelief. "*Markus*," I managed to say in annoyance. He rolled his shoulders, sighing before he downed his own cup of ale, leaning back in his chair.

"She's not afraid to stand up to you," he said with a groan, stretching in his chair. "She's direct, angry, and has a hell of a temper."

I could only stare at him questioningly, wondering at his change of heart.

He finally noticed me staring, a smile spreading across his face. "What? Just because I don't like her, or *trust* her, doesn't mean I don't think you and her would hit it off in bed," he said with a shit-eating grin

I reached over, and did my best to pull my punch as I hit his shoulder, the sound of knuckles hitting his skin audibly as he rocked in his chair.

I wanted it to *hurt,* not to break his arm.

"Sweet merciful Dark Lady, Claire, what the hells was that for?" he screeched, rubbing the spot where I'd punched him.

I took another sip of my ale, staring him down. "Markus, you've been nothing but rude to her. I love you like a brother, but you're a Gods damned idiot when you're trying to be helpful sometimes," I muttered over the lip of my drink.

He laughed at that, settling back into his chair, attempting to punch me back playfully, but he was easily blocked. "Oh, hush woman. You know I care about you," he said in between jabs

A ghost of a smirk lifted the corner of my mouth. I couldn't stay angry at him. "I know," I replied.

A few minutes passed as our banter quieted down, turning instead to look over our crew, our families, in silent appreciation. As much as Markus enjoyed teasing me, we enjoyed each other's company, but I was distracted tonight. My eyes were on the lookout for the flash of red hair darting through the crowd.

I found myself surprised that Markus not only wasn't against the idea of me chasing her after all, but had thought about it, and now thought it was a *good* idea.

And that… left me feeling almost… *giddy*.

A scoff escaped me into my drink, as I shook my head at this feeling in my chest.

Smitten. Was I really smitten with Lady Ameritia's daughter?

I examined every feeling I had about Moira, like a fisherman examining his catch for rare finds. The memory of our duel, the confrontation in the cargo hold, her signing the Code, our interview when we'd first captured her...

And in every fucking minute of being in her presence...

An *excitement*. The want to eliminate the distance between us.

Might as well admit it.

"What do I even *do* Markus? She hates my guts," I whined, my gaze to the ceiling.

He snorted into his drink, setting it down to pick at dish of fried fish he'd ordered, smelling of oil and greese.

"Does she now?" he asked, sounding as if he was entertained by my statement.

I rolled my eyes, embarrassed that I was asking for romantic advice from my quartermaster.

Who'd made a point of never being with *anyone*.

"You're absolute shit at this kind of thing you know," I muttered, reaching for my drink.

His laugh was boisterous and happy as he clapped me on the

shoulder. "Yet people keep expecting me to have some sort of stupid wisdom, for 'being above it all'. I don't fucking know Claire. Either she likes you or she doesn't. Go figure it out," he told me, shaking his head.

And with that, he clapped my back once more, threw some coins on the table to pay for his meal, and fucked off, leaving me to my brooding.

To where I didn't know. I didn't care.

A part of me was desperate to shut down.

Smitten with a girl who wanted nothing to do with me.

Of fucking course I was.

I was *dead*. Perpetually hungry. A murderer.

A monster.

And monsters didn't get happy endings, last I checked.

I nearly didn't notice the flirting of one of the barmaids at first, too distracted in my downward spiral of depression and downing cup after cup of ale.

Just because I couldn't get drunk didn't mean I didn't appreciate making the effort.

But soon, it was unavoidable. The plunging neckline of the barmaid's dress as she put the.... eighth? Ninth? Ninth or tenth drink in front of me made me finally look up to recognize Sarah.

Sarah and I... over and over again found ourselves in the same bed when I was in port. Apparently tonight would be no different.

Desperate to feel *something,* I nursed my drink until she felt brave enough to whisper her invitation into my ear, and then tore out of my seat, near dragging her towards the stairs. Her giggles touched by the excitement I heard in her heart.

But the feeling of eyes burning into my back made me look over my shoulder at the crowd as we weaved through the tavern, seeing a flash of red hair and green eyes.

Moira's gaze following after me, an indiscernible look of... *disappointment* on her face.

I stopped walking, but Sarah didn't. She sauntered past me, then began pulling me the rest of the way up the stairs. I felt… conflicted as I let myself be led after Sarah, watching Moira get up in a huff, making big steps for the door outside.

Her last look of disappointment was all I could see as Sarah weaved us through drunken crew and into an unoccupied bedroom. She pulled me into it playfully, but forcefully, not unusual for us. She slammed the door, pushing me against the wall, her mouth moving pleasantly at my neck since she was too short to reach my lips. My hands rested motionless on her hips, as her mouth moved down my collarbone to my breasts, down in between them, and lower still.

Sarah started tugging at my pants, yet I heard myself whisper, "Stop." She didn't.

Running my hand through her hair, her soft breathy gasps against my lower abdomen pleasing, my thoughts were clouded with letting her finish whatever she was going to do next. But I couldn't get Moira's eyes out of my mind.

Those gods damned eyes.

I pulled Sarah's hair back lightly, pulling her face away from me. "Stop," I said more forcefully. I didn't want to hurt her, but it was clear to me now I was going through *something* and was in no place for fun.

She smiled mischievously in reply, pulling away from me to stand, before pulling off her dress entirely in one single stroke.

My mind emptied as I saw nothing but her bare skin, her dress flowing off her like water, before it pooled at her feet.

Now, there were a few things I couldn't say no to. Sarah's body was *absolutely* one of them. She sauntered backwards towards the bed, tugging my shirt to pull me forward. I let myself be pulled for two steps before I stopped solid.

Finding… *something* in the core of my soul that made me say the impossible.

"No," I said quietly, surprising even myself. I blinked rapidly, as if I had just surfaced for air from a deep dive below the waves.

What am I doing?

Sarah sat down on the bed, looking up at me strangely. "What's the matter with you? You pulled *me* here," she asked.

I couldn't stop myself looking her over as she leaned down onto the bed, as she traced a hand up her curves, taunting me with a welcoming finger.

Running a hand through my hair, I felt a growl escape my throat. "I'm sorry. I can't. Not tonight," I muttered before, just like that, I opened the door and slammed it behind me, leaving Sarah in the dark.

Before I could ask myself what the *fuck* I'd just done, I rushed down the stairs, weaving through the crowd to find Rodger drinking by the door.

"Did you see Moira?" I asked him quietly. He looked up at me, sadness in his eyes. I had to deal with whatever the fuck was going through my own heart right at the moment, and couldn't be bothered to help his. He nodded.

"Left a few minutes ago. Said she was goin' to the docks," he murmured sadly. I nodded, barely managing to get out a "Thanks" before I tore out through the entryway doors. Near running down the streets towards the woman that for some reason, I couldn't stop thinking about.

It didn't take long to find her. I could smell her in the subtle breeze of the air, a waft of forge fire and salt, wandering through the docks and onto the beach. In moments I was walking along the sand, sure that I was following her trail, and proven correct when I found her sitting quietly by her lonesome.

She was staring into the waves, with the crescent moon hanging quietly over the entrance to the harbour, throwing a pale shadow into the calm water.

I walked towards her slowly, not wanting to startle her, waiting for her to notice me. When she finally did, she did a double take.

"What are you doing here? I thought you'd be with… that pretty lady," Moira murmured through her surprise. "That… *really* pretty lady," she embellished, eyes falling to the sand, teeth biting at her lip.

Ignoring her question for a moment to *think*, I took off my sword belt, planting my scabbard into the sand and took off my hat before placing it gently on top of the hilt. Free of anything that might impede me, I let myself fall into the sand beside her.

Laying on my back, distinctly not looking at her, but at the ghost road of stars above us all. Trying to think of something to say.

Nothing came to me. No clever retort, no smug reply.

So, I just spoke from the heart.

"Were it any other night home, I might've stayed with her," I said. "But it's not. I'm here with you." Admitting that felt… Fuck. It felt like chewing rocks.

I could feel her gaze on my face, but I kept purposefully not looking at her, instead focused on the galaxy bright and beautiful above us.

"You were… so sad after the proposal. Why?" she asked, a stirring of limbs in the sand beside me, I could see her fingers pulling at each other out of the corner of my eye.

It made me sigh. One more thing she had noticed. She apparently could see right through whatever armour I used to shield myself from the rest of the crew.

"I've bedded more people in that room than I care to count," I replied, the tone in my own voice almost unrecognizable to me. "Yet the last person I felt anything close to what Maude and Isabella feel for each other died… Gods, it'll be almost seven years ago now?"

Moira twitched beside me. I wasn't sure why I was being so candid with her, admitting this freely.

Maybe I wanted to.

"Would you… tell me about them?" she asked, a touch of fear in the beat of her heart.

I gulped. I tried to picture her face, the last woman I actually *loved.* Guilt reared its ugly head as it always did when I tried to recall her. I remembered less and less each day.

With a sigh, my eyes seeing the mix of greens and purples mix in the sky above, I told Moira what I remembered. "Her name was Sadie Wroth. We signed onto the same vessel as young women in desperate need of work that wasn't the sex trade. She came from Trodera, I was from the Haxla slums. We met in the foremast mainstay after she grabbed my shirt to make sure I didn't fall off because I'd lost my footing. But she pulled too hard and we headbutted each other hard enough that I broke her nose with my forehead," I laughed, already feeling better about everything as Moira laughed too.

"She had a crooked nose forever after that," I continued. "I gave her my ale ration for two weeks to make up for it, until our water rations ran out and that was all I had to drink. She got docked pay for a week because she was such a lightweight that she was buzzed for our shifts. She taught me half the rope knots I know because she was so much better at it than I was." I hummed in happy memory remembering how she used those knots in our bunks as well. "She was an amazing lover, and I cherished every moment I had with her. But when our captain turned us pirate, during our third raid, she took a sword in the back."

A single intake of breath, my voice hovering on the edge of a sob. Suddenly I was thankful as my breathing stilled, that I didn't *have* to breathe.

"She died in my arms," I whispered, avoiding Moira's gaze. I didn't dare look at her. It took everything I had to not let myself cry. "Captaincy… Doesn't leave a whole lot of room for weakness. For vulnerability. So I've done my best to leave her behind." The sound of my voice ironing up was familiar, the choke of a sob dying in my throat as I smothered the grief. As I always did.

I expected Moira to comment, to push, to dig for more.

But she didn't say anything. I think she could tell that if she pushed any harder, I'd clam up.

"Thank you for telling me," she said quietly after a long silence, laying back in the sand beside me, staring up into the star filled sky. This far down the beach the light pollution was negligible.

We were quiet for some time, just listening to the waves, and the light wind through the palm trees behind us, the distant shouts and music of the town, with the glory of the night sky above us.

After a while, it was Moira who finally broke the silent peace we'd found ourselves in together. "I owe you a story, don't I?" she said quietly, making me chuckle as I remembered the duel.

"You do," I confirmed, fidgeting with a buckle on my waist while she was silent for a bit longer.

She looked to be debating this story, but it was a moment later before she took a big hearty breath and began talking.

"My parents have... connections. But part of that is that they must maintain... alliances. So, I was promised to someone when I was very young," she explained.

I nodded, stealing a glance at her. Her gaze was directed skyward, her eyes twinkling in the starlight.

"Ah the life of a princess," I murmured, and she choked out a ugly laugh before continuing.

"I pleaded with my parents, anything but that. It was the last thing I wanted, and I told them I wouldn't marry the person they picked out, or *anyone* they choose, willingly ever in my life. But they insisted. So, I ran away."

Her fingers dug into the sand as she spoke, some intense memory playing out in the tension of her body. I listened quietly, wondering where this story was going.

"I stole my father's fastest ship," she said, like she was planning a heist. "Told the crew we were on a mission for him. And sailed as far away as we could."

"Where did you go?" I asked, genuinely curious, but something my question was apparently funny as she answered with a laugh.

"Hanso," she said with a wicked smile. Now it was my turn to twitch. The Capital of Itha-ki was *not* close by any stretch of the imagination. It wasn't just on the other side of the Western Continent, it was on the far side of the *world*. Near about as far away from here as you could possibly go.

"The Western Continent is very far, my dear," I admitted quietly, pride in my voice that she'd made such a journey. She gave me a look at the pet name, something in that look that I found *oh* so cute.

"A year at sea felt much longer than I could've imagined. It's one thing to look at a map, but another actually going there," she admitted, something changed in her voice.

I smiled, knowing that feeling all too well. While I hadn't sailed beyond the seas of the Great Divide that separated the Three-Nations, I'd certainly grown to acknowledge the distance travelled versus the summary of a map.

"But I wasn't just going there to get away from my parents," she added quietly. "I had access to so much of their information networks. There was something in Hanso I wanted. *Needed*." She seethed that word. *Need*. It stirred something in my gut as our breathing matched the pulse of the waves.

"Did you find it?" I asked quietly, feeling her head nod in the sand beside me. What could she possibly need so much that she'd traveled to the far side of the world to get it?

"It cost so much. More than I could ever have imagined, but I got it. An Ithakian Priest, from some obscure sect in the Steppes outside the capital. A years long ritual blessed by the Goddess of Change."

She breathed out the culmination of her story, her most proud victory.

"It... changed me. Made me the woman I always saw myself as. *Finally,* I was me." She said it with so much *pride*, her words dripping with happiness. "And even when my parents agents eventually found me and dragged me kicking and screaming back to Haxla, they couldn't take that away from me. Much to their absolute fury." Her fists clenched as her voice hardened, an unbeatable determination in her tone.

I felt tension in my shoulders, my heart so happy for her. It was clear she'd sacrificed so much for this, but was beyond happy with the results.

"Despite all the hardship, my parents, and the fact I could never leave the prison they'd constructed… I've never wanted anything so badly again," she said softly as she leaned up from her laid down position to look at me with those perfect glistening green eyes staring into mine. My heart lurched in my chest at seeing her smile, the feeling of absolute *joy* on her face.

My hunger lay in the back of my throat, forgotten, as my fingers tingled with the need I suppressed to reach for her.

She stared at me, not answering for a quiet moment. Her gaze was as hungry as mine. I didn't stop her as she rolled over to half lay on top of me, her hand landing beside my head to hold her up just inches above my face, her hair trailing in soft lines to tickle my cheeks. "Until now," she whispered as she closed her eyes and lowered her lips onto mine.

CHAPTER EIGHTEEN

"On some far river under the world, a mountain castle sits high,
Where my love sits and waits for me, I go passing by.
Where my love sits and waits for me, as I go marching on,
For I'm a sailor on that silent river, and I'm far away from home."

—Prayer poem to the Veiled Lady, as spoken by Captain of the
Queen of Sardis, Tarrick Yondu

I reached up and ran my hand into her hair, pulling her into me, feeling her breath mixing with mine as our lips moved in time with the surge of the water meeting the shore. I could've spent eternity there in that moment, but she broke away much sooner than I expected, pushing herself roughly out of my embrace entirely to stand up in a rushed panic.

"Why did I do that? Oh my god I just *kissed* you," she murmured in an alarmed huff, hand covering her lips, looking from the sea and back to me like she was searching for a way out.

For a moment I was dumbstruck, whiplashed by first her enthusiasm, now surprised by her denial.

Eventually, my reaction settled on delighted amusement, and I chortled with pleasure, propping myself on my elbows, staring at her with a smile plastered on my face as she began pacing.

"No. No no *no.*" She turned to look at me, blushed, cursed, and began stomping down the beach away from me, muttering "No!"

Rolling my eyes, I stood slowly, wiping the sand out of my coat and hair as best I could, before grabbing my hat and sword, and chasing after her. She was still muttering to herself when I caught up with her, matching her lengthy stride.

"You didn't seem opposed to that at first," I said with a smirk, enjoying this far too much.

"You… I… We… No. We *can't*," she countered, still stomping up the beach towards the docks.

"And… why? Exactly?" I asked, still a hint of humour in my tone. I wasn't about to let her get out of this without an explanation. Especially when I'd spent *months* denying admitting my attraction to her.

She stopped, whirling and poked me in the chest, her eyes hard. "Because. You're *you*," she stated as if it was the most obvious thing in the world. "You're Claire *fucking* Vessia, Captain of the *Wraith*, bane of all of Kitaxia. And I'm..." she scrambled for the right words, while I motioned for her to continue.

She exasperatedly sighed, all that wild energy dying out in a single hushed breath, only to look at me with a defeat, with no answer because we both knew it already. She was a *princess.* She was my crew. She was nothing. She was everything. How to sum up so much complication in so few words?

That look of defeat in her eyes, mixed with longing... Only now did I realise that there was something serious about this to her. To her, it wasn't just a fling, not only a want to explore each other's bodies. I took off my hat to rustle my hand through my hair before putting it back on.

I would be a fool to overlook her feelings despite how it ached in my chest to hear her say 'No'.

I reached for her, taking her lightly by the shoulders, making sure to stare her in the eyes, putting meaning into my every word. "Moira." I felt her melt a bit in my hands, which made me want to *kiss* her that much more. Instead, I doubled my focus on my words. "I'm… the Captain. For the foreseeable future, I will be the Captain. I must maintain a level of separation from the crew. That's how this works. I can't show favouritism—"

She burst into hard laughter, that kind I'd rarely seen where something had finally got under all that armour she wore to keep out other people.

"Claire," she muttered between gasps of laughter, the first time she'd *really* said my name.

"It's not because you're Captain, or I am, or *was*, the princess," she muttered.

I was... confused. What else could it be about? She wiped away a tear, finally also realizing this was a serious moment, and that I *very much* did not understand what the problem was here.

"It's because you're a *terrible* person," she stated, as if it were the most well known fact in the universe.

It seemed once again, Moira knew exactly what to say to level me low.

Something must've shown how broken her words had left me, because she reached for my cheek with a pained expression, but after pausing mid-air, pulled back.

"Claire..." she said softly.

Again, my heart lurched in my chest as I lowered my hands from her, letting her escape my grasp. I didn't have to stand here and hear this. I turned to pull away, but she reached and grabbed a handful of my shirt, pulling me back.

I let myself be pulled, and felt her hands settle on my hips.

"Let me speak. Please," she asked.

I tilted my head upwards, annoyed and infuriated at her words, the whiplash worse than a snapped sail line from going from kissing to being called, for all intents and purposes, a monster.

But... she asked.

I brought my gaze low again to look her in the eyes, giving her the tiniest of nods.

She pursed her lips, clenched her jaw, as if scared at my reaction. Her hands tightened at my waist, but she took a breath and began to speak.

"You kill people. You've murdered more of my countrymen than I've *met*. You torture people, and you're so caught up in whatever has you so pissed off against Kitaxia, against my *mother*, you've never stopped to imagine what *peace* might look like."

She motioned her hand around the settlement, down the beach, and towards the cove where the *Wraith* sat docked, before settling it on my shoulder.

It felt... nice to be in her hands like this. Even if she hated me.

"You've built a *life* here. For your friends and family, but... You don't *enjoy* any of it. I've been watching you ever since we docked.

You're like an island of misery, unsatisfied unless you're actively about to cut someone open, putting you one step closer to mother."

I seethed in a breath through my teeth, but... couldn't deny her words.

I would rest when Ameritia was dead. *Then* I would know what peace was like.

But as her hand trailed down my shoulder... over my jacket collar... tracing my collarbone and up my neck... A mischievous glint in her emerald eyes, I was beginning to wonder.

"*But...*" she whispered, a smile on her face, eyes following the space she traced with her fingers.

That tone of her voice... I latched onto it like a drowning man grasping a life-raft.

"You care about your crew. You've built something *wonderful* here. You're considerate and kind and in command. There's a *warmth* in you that even I can't deny," she whispered, her hot breath on my neck, her nose a touch away from my chin.

If I could've blushed, I was quite sure I would be.

"But you're *dangerous*. It's sexy in its own right. You're... *it's so hard* to stay away from you." Her eyes couldn't help flickering towards mine, fluttering eyelashes and stolen glances. "And... as much as I *want* you... you have so much blood on your hands you might as well be swimming in it."

Aye, there was the barb in the sting. One more rebuttal to add onto the growing pile.

"And... I wonder if it'll be *my* blood you add to your collection when you realize that your war... is getting you nowhere." Her last words were hushed, her true fear finally spoken aloud. She was scared of me. Yet she bit her lip, looking at my neck like *she* wanted to bite into it.

I wanted to deny her. To shout her down and tell her in all the ways she was wrong. To vindicate myself and show her that I was just as human as anyone here. That her fears were unfounded.

But I would be lying.

How many times *today* had I thought about drinking her dry once again?

I breathed in deeply, unsure.

She all but admitted attraction to me, but had deep moral qualms about any relationship with me.

But her hands still held me close.

Moral questions or no, this doesn't have to be complicated.

"Then for now... I understand," I whispered, before I grabbed the back of her neck with one hand, her waist with the other, pulling her into a deep kiss.

A momentary tenseness took her, before she melted. Her arms slipped around my neck, fingers in my hair, little moans coming from her mouth. I pulled her tightly against me, feeling her squirm, and before I lost myself in her, I just as quickly let her go. Stepping out of the embrace and leaving her standing there gaping after me with lust in her eyes.

"Just something for you to think about," I said with a smirk as I walked my way back up the beach towards the tavern.

I heard her heartbeat, a *ba-thump-ba-thump-ba-thump* in my ear as the distance grew between us, just waiting for her to shout my name, follow after me, *anything*.

She didn't follow.

But *Gods*, I wished she had.

Souris harbour was an ocean of quiet this late in the night, save for the islands of noise here and there throughout the town. The tavern and the town square were the most boisterous, and easily avoided.

Because I needed quiet. I needed to *think*.

My heart ached at her denial of me. She certainly had her reasons. I couldn't tell her to just get over them, but a deep-seated part of me *very much* wanted her to just...

What *did* I want?

Why did I feel so... *much* for her?

She was...

She's so Gods damn pretty.

It should be so simple.

So why did it hurt?

I'd *finally* gotten what I'd been wanting for weeks now, if I was honest with myself, I thought I should be ecstatic. I had the beginnings of some off-again-on-again hate-based relationship with a girl I liked.

That's what I *wanted* wasn't it? That was *simple.* Kissing Ameritia's daughter, how could revenge get sweeter than that?

But fuck. That kiss.

I was rubbing my thumb over my lips in sweet memory, and didn't even see the runner nearly collide into me.

"Uh, Captain?"

I blinked my eyes, as if seeing the man appear out of nothing in front of me, taking a *bit* longer than I needed to recognize him. One of the settlement's outer watchmen, taking a few steps away from me with an odd look.

"Sorry. I was... distracted. What can I do for you?" I asked, my mind a haze of memory, for once my *own.*

The man nodded, handing over a document packet. "I've been looking for you, Captain. Commander McCrosswick said to pass this on as soon as possible, ma'am," he reported with almost professional military efficiency.

I eyed the man with trepidation, unsure why Adam hadn't passed this along when I was dropping off his cut of the loot earlier, but took the packet nonetheless.

For a human it would've been hard to see in this light, even with the streetlights, but my vision could read the words upon the page with ease.

It was several notes and reports of ship's passing through the James Straits, from one of Souris's outposts on the other side of the island. Depending on how ships left the straits and in what directions, the outpost could make reasonable guesses as to where ships were heading.

And this one had made a note of a Kitaxian warship convoy passing by, but had disappeared in a fog bank.

There wasn't a chance they were heading here, despite what I'd told Moira; this was sovereign Varcnan soil. Kitaxia would be six different kinds of idiotic to attack us here, even if they knew where we were, but as my memories went back to the Count's ship... and the coffin that was meant for me... I wouldn't put it past them.

It was even possible they were remnants of the High Seas Fleet, chasing us all the way from Norlondia.

I handed the document back to the runner, holding it as if it were a bomb. "Get the battery up and running. Charlotte has command. Get to it," I ordered. They would hate me for it, but it was better to be safe than sorry.

The runner nodded before taking off towards the Watch's headquarters to pass my orders down the line. Charlotte would hate me for it, but I'd prefer not to be caught with our pants down if that convoy was indeed on its way here.

Hoping that I was wrong but I'd done all I could.

I was back where I started, left once again with nothing but my bruised heart.

The night was still young, and now I was left to question what to do with it. I decided against returning to the tavern, where the noise and the inevitable questions waited. Instead, I strolled through the settlement, remarking on just how much it'd grown over the years, letting my mind drift towards thoughts of a pretty girl with red hair.

I wasn't sure where my feet were leading me as I stomped down the streets of Souris. I was too busy remembering Moira's face from every angle, what she looked like when she was sad, angry, and the sound of her laughter.

It should've been fucking simple. She was just a pretty face and one step closer to revenge. It didn't make sense to get such silly things as *emotions* involved with her.

I shuddered, unsure of what to make of this gooey feeling in my chest, the ache of needing to taste her lips again.

Even the hunger roiling in my throat seemed lessened with this unfamiliar feeling in my chest. I felt almost panicky, unsure.

I thumbed my mouth in worry and tried to remember the kiss. Her hands in my hair... not pushing me away, but pulling me closer…

turning the thought over and over in my head until I groaned into the night sky in frustration, my complaints echoing back from silent streets, still with no clear answer on what to do.

I walked past Juliette's tailor shop, the forge, even rounded the tavern once, seeing it still going strong with merry cheer.

But merry cheer wasn't what I wanted right then.

Souris wasn't large; you could walk all the streets in a couple hours. Despite being captain, I didn't have anywhere to go. I didn't own a house like others did. I usually just slept in one of the rooms above the tavern, or back in my cabin on the ship, there was no one other than my officers I considered safe enough to share a space with.

Maybe Moira was right about me. I'd not put down roots here at all.

But... there was one place I could go. One more place here that held a tiny piece of me.

I shuddered in slight disgust. But maybe... maybe it was worth trying.

Finding myself before a quiet cabin in the space where settlement met jungle, halfway up the hillside, stood the one place in Souris I avoided like the plague. Once upon a time, it'd been bare hill, but now a sizable home I'd built with my own savings stood on one of the best views of the harbour, just down the path from the battery.

My mother's house.

I mounted the steps to her patio, seeing the lights on inside despite the late hour. I gave the screen door a quiet knock, her main door not even closed, the screen door letting in the cooler night air, Mum's voice echoing out to my ears as she hummed an unfamiliar tune.

"Oh, what is it now. I told you watchmen I'm quite alright up here, I—Claire."

And just like that, her tone shifted from some simple joy to disappointment in a heartbeat.

This was a mistake.

"Mum. I'm sorry I'll—" I began to stammer out.

"You've come up the hill, at least come in for tea, silly girl." With that tone of voice, there was nothing I could do. Vampyri or no, she was still my mother.

I choked back a bite of remorse, nodding as she pushed open the screen door, waving me inside.

My adoptive mother looked, unsurprisingly, nothing like me. I was tall, she was short. I was lean, she had some weight on her. She was stooped over with advanced age, and I was still youthful. My hair was black, hers brown. Mine a mess of lengthy braids, hers styled with precision.

Although she had adopted me when she and Mother June were in their late fifties, Mum was well over eighty now.

And despite everything, she still hadn't forgiven me.

I stepped inside, quietly removing my boots, and brushed my feet on the doormat, followed by the removal of my hat to hang on a coat rack. A stickler for cleanliness and tradition, my mother.

She puttered into her small kitchen, and I wandered around, looking at the room I normally tried desperately to avoid. Pictures hung everywhere of Mother June and Mum before the purges. Their shop that they had in Hightown. Mother June's father smiling happily on their wedding day. And of course, the most controversial picture Mum still owned, the picture of Mother June before she was... well, herself, hanging in the place of honour above the fireplace.

Mother June hated that picture. I was almost certain she'd destroyed all the copies. Where Mum had dragged it out of, I had no idea. In her grief, she'd held on to every piece of Mother June she could.

Even the pieces Mother June had spent her life trying to cut out.

Nothing made me want to tear down that picture more.

"Alright, here's some tea," Mum said. "Now sit down and tell me why you're bothering me after years of not visiting me since you plopped me in this Gods forsaken port." She shuffled out of the kitchen, setting down a tray *just so* on the small table, where yet more pictures sat of her and Mother June happily living their lives before the purges.

It really was a mistake coming here.

I sat down at the table, waiting for her to pour the tea into tiny useless cups, as if she was still at court. Mum was the daughter of a merchant bordering on nobility, and never let me forget it.

Her face was grey and well-lined from years of disappointing frowns, but I remembered how Mother June had brought out the best in her. It was a shame that the best part of her died with my other parent.

"It's... good to see you, Mum," I said quietly, my hand wrapping around the teacup, more appreciating it for its warmth than taste. It certainly was no hot cocoa. This brew would be bitter.

Mum let out a scoff of disapproval, showing me that she didn't believe a word of my lies. "It is certainly a pleasure to see you as well Claire," she said in that feigned indifference she'd perfected over the years.

What am I doing here?

"Come on. Out with it. Why else did you bring me here?" she asked.

I reached up to stroke my hand through my hair, unsure. "Bringing you here was for the best. If the Kitaxians found out you raised me..." I began to explain. For the hundredth time.

"Then I'd be dead. So what? I'll be dead in a year or two anyway."

I reached out to take her hand, guilt eating at my insides. "Mum. You can't talk like that."

"Sure, I can. What else would happen? The Veiled Lady coming for me herself? Please." She pulled her hand out of mine, and sipped at her tea, angry blue eyes staring at me over the saucer.

"Mum, you were living in a shack on the street," I murmured, remembering the wreckage of boarded up driftwood and pieces of old salvage. "At least here you have a house."

She sniffed, which to my long-practised ears meant she was losing patience with me.

"At least back in Haxla I knew who was who. Here, I don't know anyone," she replied, looking at the walls like they were closing in on her.

Smuggling my mother out of Haxla had been no easy feat, but apparently giving her her own house in a town where she didn't have to beg for scraps wasn't enough for her. This argument would get me nowhere. I breathed in deeply, letting it out slowly, my hunger making my mouth feel parched.

I had never told her about what I was. She had thought I was dead with the rest of Kitaxia after my hanging. Hells, she was *there* in the square that day. She saw me die.

I was still half convinced that she thought to this day that I was an interloper. A monster wearing her daughter's face.

Maybe I was.

"What do you *want,* Claire?" she asked, setting her tea quietly with a clink as teacup met saucer. I twisted my vision away from her to look at the nearest picture of her and Mother June hanging over the table, some moment of them intertwined with each other, laughing with the harbour of Haxla in the background.

Gods. I wished more than anything Mother June was still alive.

"How did... what was... what was it like when you and Mother first met?" I asked quietly, my voice barely a whisper.

I could hear her heart skip a beat, felt the table shift as she stiffened in her seat.

"Found someone special?" she asked in reply, her tone suggesting more disbelief than wonder. Gods did I not want to answer her. but... I was this far in, I might as well go all the way.

I shrugged, bringing my gaze to my mothers, to her old and withered face. "Maybe," I admitted.

She knew about Sadie, the only person I ever really loved. She knew she died, not long before we were captured in the shipwreck. It was actually in the last letter I ever sent home.

But she also knew about Paul.

The man I was still *technically* married to.

The man who I was supposed to make happy enough that he would pay to have Mum move into some nice home in Midtown after the purges.

The man I left after two months of 'happy matrimony' to sign onto the very ship where I met Sadie.

The man who abused me for two months of hell. After I left him, I'd swore I would never let another man touch me again.

Mum was never happy about that decision. She thought I

should've toughed it out for both our sakes. I sent her every penny of my earnings on that ship, but it was never enough. Never as much as what marrying Paul meant to her.

Marrying Paul had meant getting something close to her old life. Out of the gutter and back to rubbing elbows with low nobility.

But she was my mother. She'd raised me when she literally had no obligation to. Adopted me, rescued me from dying as a babe. How could I not pay that back?

My insides flip-flopped with guilt as I'm sure we both remembered all of the baggage between us.

I took a sip of my own tea, only to tell myself to never take another sip of it. So *bitter*.

Mum sighed, hers sounding so much like my own. Some things you just got from your parents, adopted or not.

"Well, with your reputation, you could have anyone in half of the darn three nations," she said with some wry mirth. "From what I hear around town, you've already had half the women here." That mirth twisted into disappointment.

"*Mum*." I looked at her, horrified, almost certain I was blushing despite my inability.

She gave me a disapproving stare. "Don't act mortified if you're guilty as the Lady of Sins, Claire Vessia." She spat, raising a condescending finger.

I glared at her, wishing my mother wasn't so... difficult.

"Mum. I swear. If all you're going to do is insult me than—"

"You look at her as if she hung the moon," she interrupted, again. But the words didn't make sense.

"I'm sorry?" I asked, unsure of what she meant, only for Mum to sigh.

"Don't make me repeat myself Claire. It's rude. But if you must hear it again, I'm answering your question."

She shifted her weathered gaze from the tea tray to the photo hanging over the table. The expression shifting across her face was something I hadn't seen in years.

Longing.

"You know you're in love if you look at her as if she's hung the moon," she whispered.

Looking at her gaze towards the picture of Mother June, I breathed deeply, recalling my memory of seeing Moira crying on the beach. Her head between her hands as she looked out over the water, her hair cascading down her back like a fiery waterfall. Another memory of her laughing at one of Charlotte's jokes. Another of her hammering on the forge with concentration, unaware of me watching from the doorway.

Every single time, I couldn't stop thinking the same damn thought. *She's beautiful.*

"Fuck," I mumbled out, raising a hand to rub at my eyes.

"Claire! Language!" Mum snapped, reaching across the table to smack me upside the head.

"Ow! Mum!" I whined.

"Don't you 'Mum' me, with a mouth like that I should wash out your mouth with soap!" Her voice raised near to a yell, a shiver of fear running down my spine from the threat.

I rubbed at the back of my head with the briefest of smiles as I stared down the woman who thought me more disappointment than daughter.

My head didn't actually hurt, but that wasn't the point of it.

I could be a deadly *Vampyri* pirate captain, a terrifying monster personally responsible for the deaths of hundreds, but that didn't mean shit to my mother. Even if she somehow knew about me being a *Vampyri*, I'm not sure that would stop her from treating me like she did.

I sighed, setting down the tea that was beginning to cool despite the muggy air.

"Thank you. That's... actually very helpful," I admitted quietly. The expression on Mum's face twisted into surprise. Like she hadn't expected me to thank her. Which to be fair, surprised me just as much.

"You're welcome." She snorted a laugh. "If you're thanking me, now I know it must be serious," she said, smiling behind her tea.

CHAPTER NINETEEN

"Getting married in the Great Divide has been contentious ever since the purges. That's what it was all about. Kitaxia wanted a perfect breeding ground for new soldiers to fight off an invasion or brewing rebellion. It's sickening. They outlawed same-sex marriage and told the men that they owned their wives, and told the wives they were nothing without children… To them, anyone marrying who can't produce children is anathema to their plans."

"It's all about power. Give some to men to have over women, and they'll fight for it. Bastards."

— Overheard conversation between Jarlessa Isolde Viken and Jarlessa Olga Hordalund

I pulled at the coat's stiff collar, wanting to run my hand through my hair, but knew I wasn't allowed to. Once Juliette had stuffed me into the stiff formal wear, she had forced me to sit down for an *hour* to do my hair.

An hour. On *hair*. Who had the time?

And then on top of that, she had her partner Micheal come and put paints on my eyes, something I'd only seen highborn ladies like my mother did. I felt ridiculous.

But, when they finally showed my assembled picture in the mirror, everything in me tried to deny the image presented to me.

There was no way in any of the nine burning realms that that was *me*.

The outfit that Maude and Isabella had designed for me was a perfect cut of a naval officer's uniform, with a dark twist. It was black instead of blue, the rank insignia were red instead of gold, the cut just slightly different enough to be almost sinister looking, and the collar, while high around the sides of my throat, dipped in the front to show the hint of bosom. How it'd been made in just a few days was beyond me.

My hair was braided expertly, styled into the folds and weaves of highborn Norn women, while the paint on my eyes were dark in shade, highlighting the green from my irises, while making me look even paler than I already was.

I was *striking*.

I looked exactly like what I was. A captain. A pirate. A *Vampyri*.

"You've both done me a great service," I murmured through barely held back tears, much to Michael and Juliette's delight. We attempted a hug without smudging makeup or upsetting what must be the hundreds of pins in my hair. I left them with a courteous bow, and promised I wouldn't mess with my look for as long as I could manage.

Making my way out of their shop and to the wedding venue in the centre of Souris, I got a *lot* more stares than usual. Probably had something to do with looking as fancy as I did with an umbrella in the middle of the day.

Not being allowed my spectacles or hat, I had to do *something* to keep out of the sun.

Contrary to what everyone expected, they were not holding the wedding at Miss Cavendish's tavern. Oh, to be sure, the *after-party* would be held there, but the ceremony itself was in the main market square, where the docks met the town proper.

Isabella's faith from the eastern continent had some very specific rules about how one was married, and we made every effort to accommodate her. Digging up the centre of the market square to plant a tree was a *bit* of a hard sell. Nonetheless it had been done. The sapling now sat in a place of honour in the centre of Souris, where a little protective iron-wrought fence that Moira and Old Man Tom had put together guarded it diligently.

Not that I had seen Moira over the week. She was avoiding me like the plague.

I reached the border of the square with Juliette and Micheal running up behind me to their seats with a brief wave.

Finding Jacine pacing the border of the murmuring crowds at the edge of the seats, it was plain to see that she was muttering to herself. She looked up, confused, and then did a double take. "Cripes captain. I thought you were an admiral strolling down the street for a second." She looked me up and down with wide eyes. "You look really good. Like, *really* good," she murmured, waving a hand up and down my form, making me smirk in appreciation. Never did I ever think I could clean up *this* nice.

I caught myself *again* reaching to stroke a hand through my hair, forcing myself to stop, afraid I'd ruin my look with barely a glance. "Blame the soon-to-be brides. They picked out everything," I said with a laugh, wincing against the sun. It was difficult to see, everything glinting with painful light. But it was a sacrifice I was willing to make for the brides. Even if it meant taking an extra week on shore, putting me even further away from a proper meal. My hunger was *not* impressed.

Jacine rolled her eyes as she nodded. "Tell me about it." She motioned to her own dress, a deep green woven with intricate sea waves sewn along the bottom. She was the maid of honour, and it was the first time I think I'd ever seen her in a dress. While she had usually made no real effort to look extra feminine, today she glowed in it. It warmed my heart.

"You look good yourself, Jacine. You look happy," I commented, crossing my arms around my umbrella, keeping my hands from clenching my fingers into fists. The sun was bright and angry, and it beat down mercilessly.

I hated that even now, on what should've been one of the happiest days of my life, I could feel my eyes wandering Jacines neck, wrists, *hungry*. I couldn't just have a free day.

But Jacine's replying smile was, if anything, impossibly brighter than the sun. "Today two of my favourite people are getting married. To each other. And I'm the fucking maid of honour. Gods. No, I can't cry yet I can't ruin my paints." She wiped her hand back and forth over her face in a rush to put air on her face, making me laugh.

"Alright then," I said with a happy sigh, trying to hide the hunger simmering in my throat. "Let's go see them off." I looped an arm through hers and we walked into the crowds together with matching smiles.

Markus, the best man, was easy to track down. Standing stoic in his suit, he looked more like a guardsman for the little sapling that was serving as the altar than a member of the wedding party. He flashed a smile at us as we walked towards him. "Looking sharp, Captain," Markus said with a wink.

"Thanks," I replied quietly as the noise of the crowd was slowing down as everyone was beginning to find their seats, the appointed hour near.

Charlotte ran up the aisle towards us in a rush, a suit matching Markus. "Okay, Good. You're here, one less thing to worry about," they murmured, their gaze looking to-and-fro in a rough panic.

I knew that look.

"What's wrong?" I asked.

"Oh nothing," they replied. "Other than Rodger somehow being already heavy into his cups blubbering on the docks, everything's in place."

Everyone's expression fell in despair at their words, Markus groaning while Jacine winced.

"Is he able to make it?" Jacine asked, a hand on her heart.

Charlotte tossed their head back and forth before nodding. "He'll be here, but someone will have to hold him up I think."

Well, it *was* a wedding. Something was bound to blow up in our faces. This was tame so far.

Gracie joined us minutes later, still patting out splotches of sugar from her own teal dress. "I'm… I made it! Gods, I hope this is fast. I left Annabelle in the kitchens with about eight different pots to watch!" She spun in place, making her dress twirl, a light dusting of flour puffing out into the air around her.

We all laughed at Gracie's panic, assuring her everything was on time. She had been up in the tavern helping out her sister's kitchen staff putting on one hell of a reception feast.

We were still chattering around the iron fence as the last few people found their seats, and in the back, I saw the signal I had been waiting for.

"Ladies! Gentlemen! Honoured friends!" I shouted over the little bits of conversation still floating throughout the square, making everyone scatter to their positions. Markus, Charlotte, Jacine, and Gracie were in the wedding party, with me in the centre.

I still couldn't believe they'd asked me to officiate.

"It's time for the ceremony to commence."

As the last stragglers quieted their conversations and found their seats, Rodger staggered up the aisle, bleary eyed and blabbing about how happy he was for the couple, but after some reassurance, we finally decided he was sober enough to stand on his own.

Sucking in a breath for the misery I was about to put myself through for a moment, I shuttered the umbrella, hanging it off the sapling's fence. The sun immediately let me know I was unwelcome in its light, the feeling of sizzling skin skittering across my scalp.

I had minutes before it became a problem. An hour before it became *dangerous*. I gave the signal. Behind me, one of the bards—a quiet and soft-spoken friend of Maude's by the name of Lucina— rounded out the wedding party, began to play a tune on an instrument I had never heard of, let alone seen.

It was a strange thing. An enormous, bulbous wooden instrument that resembled a woman's curves. So large she had to straddle it from behind, one hand on the strings, and another on the bow—though for a bow, it didn't look like any weapon I'd ever seen. As she slid the bow across the strings, it began to hum in response.

I wasn't prepared for the music that came from the hollow of that thing, for it was beautiful—one of the most beautiful things I had ever heard. It was as sultry and deep as the waves of the sea.

As she started playing—beauty Norn skalds would've killed to hear—the brides had begun striding down the aisle towards us, hand in hand, in time with the music.

As they strode up from the docks, Maude and Isabella looked picturesque with the evening sun setting over the water behind them, their dresses matching in green and blue swirls. Maude held the cloth she had sewn in one hand, with her other holding Isabella's aloft, while in Isabella's other hand hung two small wooden bracelets.

The music swayed every soul in the square to teary eyes, blinking rapidly to not miss a moment. Their stride was confident in every step, finally standing before me and the assembled bridal party with the final note of music. Lucina stood and placed her instrument on her chair. I looked over to bow towards her in thanks, and she returned a cute curtsy before taking her place on Maude's side of the party.

I turned to Maude and Isabella, who were in near giggles looking up at me. "From the deepest parts of my heart, I thank all of you who join us on this day, to celebrate the union of two of our best and most cherished friends, Maude Winters, and Isabella of the Everwilds," I said, looking out at the crowd, my *family*. "In all my years of sailing the sea, never had I witnessed a love such as theirs. One that many would mischaracterize as disagreement or rivalry, but one I know, in fact, to be passionate."

That elected a few chuckles. They'd certainly fooled me for months. Months arguing back and forth at each other, then winding up in bed together the moment we hit port, then back to arguing.

I continued. "While methods to tackle problems, relationships, and solutions differ as much as the lands of their birth, I cannot describe the joy I have felt at seeing them understand the universal truth that our differences are what make us stronger, together."

A few nods throughout the crowd, the expressions on Isabella and Maude's face nearing tears. My pain wanted me to hurry this up, but I loved Maude and Isabella more.

"The sea calls out to each of us. But as we all know, the sea demands much, and we will always find ourselves in need of safe harbour, for the land to take us into her bosom for safety and reprieve." I looked down at the two smiling women. "Just like your union, it will be a balance, a push and pull, the never-ending struggle of the tides, the love affair between the sea and the land." I looked to the tree they had planted together behind me. "May you hold that balance not 'til the end of your days, but the end of all days."

I carried deep admiration for both of them, as I hoped I was getting across to the crowd with my speech… but the tiniest bit of me was wondering if anyone would make a similar speech at my own wedding.

If I ever had one.

I lifted my palm to Isabella. "Isabella of the Everwilds," I said quietly. "Do you, in body, spirit, and heart, swear upon the land of your birth, the lessons of your Teacher, in the deepest roots of the forest, and to all those gathered here, to hold, cherish, and love Maude Winters in all aspects of life, death, and the beyond, through all pain and joy, laughter and tears, victories and losses?"

She nodded. "I do."

"Then place your bonds of matrimony on her person, and know her as wife."

She took the wooden bracelets, sliding one onto Maude's wrist, its matching partner onto her own.

I turned to Maude. "Doctor Maude Winters." I usually forgot that Maude was actually legally a doctor till I had to use her title in any fashion. "Do you, in body, spirit, and heart, swear upon the land of your birth, the Gods above and below, in the eyes of the Lady of Promises, and all those gathered here to hold, cherish, and love Isabella of the Everwilds in all aspects of life, death, and the beyond, through all pain and joy, laughter and tears, victories and losses?"

She nodded. "I do."

"Then place your bonds of matrimony on her person, and know her as wife."

She grabbed the cloth in her free hand, placing it over the hands she still held with Isabella, over the wrists that held the bracelets, and squeezed it over their arms. I placed my own hands over all of it, before invoking the last line of the rite.

"By the power invested in me by the laws of the sea, the code upon which we have signed, and in my authority as your elected Captain, in witness and in friendship, I pronounce you married." And released my hands.

"Now fucking kiss already," I added, shouting to the crowd.

The kiss was passionate and heated as they lost themselves in each other. The cheer went out from every living soul in Souris, and echoed across every crevice of the harbour and settlement. Maude and Isabella giggled as the tears started to fall, and the two of them ran down the aisle to the docks flanked by well-wishers, where a longboat with a team of rowers were taking them to a private beach house down shore.

We followed them out and waved them out of the harbour as the sun dipped down below the horizon. With the lack of light, I felt my skin finally settle, a sigh of relief escaping me. "Now who's ready for a party?" I screamed to the crowd, and was met by a huge cheer.

As every person in Souris piled into Miss Cavendish's tavern, I couldn't help but remark to myself that a wedding reception wasn't too different from our regular parties when we landed in port. Only the food was nicer, the dance floor was extended, and everyone was dressed fancier.

Thankfully, my usual table wasn't one of the ones moved to make room for dancing couples. So, I found myself at my usual perch nursing a flagon of ale, wishing I could itch my scalp as it healed, watching the night unfold.

Rodger didn't take a spare moment to restart his deep dive into his cups once again, bursting into tears over anything and everything. The poor man. I silently thanked the Gods for Lucina and her kind heart, who apparently had taken it upon herself to spend most of the evening watching over him, guiding him from table to table, making sure he didn't hurt himself in his drunken stupor.

Charlotte was immediately holding court, racking up an absolute score of silver in a high stakes card game with several onlookers, and from the looks of their serious gaze at their opponents, they'd likely be there for the rest of the night.

Gracie, was helping out in the kitchens, talking animatedly with her sister whenever they so much as looked at each other, Gracie likely telling stories of our naval exploits while Miss Cavendish probably went on at length about dreary settlement life.

Somehow, this was entertaining to both of them.

Jacine was floating from dancer to dancer, showing off her long legs and sure stride, laughing with each new partner, and politely turning down all requests for 'further activities'. I'd never seen her take anyone to bed before, and I doubted tonight would be any different.

I was still here, in my isolated corner of the tavern, looking upon all I'd built like an outsider peering in.

In fact, if it wasn't for the clothes and the food, it was just like any other night. But it didn't *feel* like any other night.

Markus was sitting with me, also looking over the festivities with a drink in hand, and stroking his chin thoughtfully. "You haven't seen her, have you?" he asked quietly, leaning back so far in his chair that it creaked, his suit jacket unbuttoned and his collar loose. I shook my head. There was only one woman he could've meant.

"You have me figured out that easily, eh?" I murmured quietly, nursing my own drink.

He leaned towards me with a smirk. "Don't act like you haven't been looking for her since you sat down, Claire." Fucker. I was, but I was trying to not look that desperate.

I tossed my head back, looking into the ceiling, wishing to be anywhere but here, having this conversation. "So what if I have? Gods, Markus, am I that fucking pathetic?" I ran a hand down my face, pulling it off quickly, the sudden fear of Juliette manifesting out of nowhere to shame me for messing up my paints.

"Claire, you got it *bad,*" he said with a laugh. I fixed him with a glare that he was busy ignoring, leaning back in his chair, but I couldn't help but guide one of my boots underneath the leg of his chair and tip it back just enough to cause him to panic.

"Fucking nine burning realms, Claire!" he yelled out, waving his arms dramatically to get his balance back. "Trying to fucking kill me, I swear. Giving me a Gods damned heart attack."

We laughed it off, watching Jacine dance with yet another partner, Lucina hauling Rodger outside to either get him settled for the night or to puke out his plethora of drinks. Charlotte was winning yet another hand, the threats of violence and pulled knives at their table due any moment now.

And then there was me and Markus. Markus joyfully watched us all with a scientific curiosity, while I sat with a hole in my heart, longing for a girl who'd been avoiding me for a week.

She'll come around. This is nothing more than a simple fling, after all.

"Was she even at the ceremony?" I asked quietly, staring into my drink as he nodded in reply.

"Far back corner. You couldn't have seen," he replied, still smiling.

I sighed into my cup, tipping it back, wishing for just a moment that I could get properly drunk. I waved for another.

"Trouble in paradise?" Markus asked, elbowing me with an ugly smirk. "Could it be... that the royal bitch… turned *you* down?" he teased.

My face must've given it away, as a moment later laughter burst from his gullet.

I reached up, threatening to smack him, but it did nothing to stop him. Here I was, down in the dumps with hunger and misery, and here he was mocking me for it.

"Who would've thought! *Captain Claire Vessia*, after the one thing she can't have," he stated, raising his fists to defend himself from whatever assault he thought I was about to send his way, a knowing smirk behind them. "Royal puss—"

Oh no you fucking don't.

He wasn't expecting the sudden boot to the chair between his legs, as I kicked it back and to the floor. It took him with it, an ugly sounding '*oof*' as he splayed out with a laugh onto the floor.

"That'll teach you to refrain from commenting further on my love life, Mr. Clun," I threatened, turning back to my drink.

It was at that moment Jacine swept from the dancefloor to our table, a look of humoured disdain at Markus picking himself up off the floor, taking a seat opposite us.

"Gods. It's like mom and dad are fighting," she said quietly, and both of us turned to fix her with a glare so severe that she held up her hands apologetically, scooting backwards in her chair.

"Sorry! Sorry! Poor choice of words," she stammered out, her hands waving me off in apology. I let her get away with it, sighing, *again,* into what must've been my fifth or sixth drink. I wasn't counting.

She stared at the cup in my hand, her eyes trailing to the empties littering the table, a look of worry creeping onto her features.

"I forgot just how much you can put away..." she murmured quietly, just loud enough for both me and Markus to hear.

I shrugged, waving at the barmaids for another drink.

"I haven't fed in over a week. Maude and Isabella have been too busy wedding planning to 'collect' more. I'm a *touch* cranky" I admitted, pinching my fingers together in front of my face. I watched their expressions shift into further worry as the barmaid passed yet another cup into my waiting hand.

"I think I'm entitled." I said quietly, raising the cup to my lips, hunger wishing for *anything* but more ale.

"Hold on, not so fast. You don't just get to say 'love life' and move on," Markus said as he finally settled back down into his chair, a hitch in his voice from drink. "Do you love her?"

I nearly scoffed into my drink.

Love. Of course not. Smitten *at best*.

All I wanted was to bed her so I could claim ultimate revenge against Ameritia… Didn't I?

"How in all the hells could I love her, Markus? She's the *princess*," I spat.

He nodded, taking a sip from his somehow un-spilled drink on the table. "Agreed. That's a relief then," he muttered, gasping with satisfaction into his cup.

Jacine winced, and I felt...

What was this feeling?

Love? Of course not. It was one fucking kiss.

Two. Two actually. But that still doesn't change it. I'm just physically attracted to her. Nothing more.

Jacine had been about to say something, but her eyes snapped to surprise at the sound of the entryway door opening and closing, loud enough to be heard over the music and shouts of everyone nearby.

I followed everyone's gaze to the door, where Moira, striding towards our table in a dark blue shimmering dress, twinkling in the light like the night sky, the colour of the sea at night with her red hair pulled into a woven bun, her eyes shining like emeralds.

I felt my breath hitch in my throat, and more than one pair of eyes turned to follow her hungrily as she strode through the crowd towards my table.

"There you are," she said quietly, her hands on her hips.

As if I would be anywhere else.

"What did you do to Rodger?" she demanded of me, my eyebrows raising into my hairline. Oh Gods, what did he do now?

I leaned back in my chair, letting my gaze shift to Jacine, then to Markus, who probably didn't know any better than I did what this was about. We all exchanged worried glances, shakes of our heads, leaving me with no option but to look up at Moira, trying not to be distracted by just how beautiful she was.

Her hair, usually let loose, was tied up in a purposefully styled messy bun, a few strands of red hair framing her face. Her neck looked long and flushed, and *oh so inviting*.

But her hateful gaze told me she wasn't going to let me get close.

At least not yet.

"I have no idea. What's this about?" I asked.

"He was down at the docks, blubbering about how he didn't know what he was going to do to support his family now that he wasn't a part of the crew anymore. I'd assumed you kicked him out, but apparently…"

Ah.

I turned to Markus, suddenly relieved. "Do you want to tell her, or should I?" Markus shook his head, motioning towards Jacine, who was already beginning a long explanation of Rodger's complicated relationship with half the members of the crew and locals, leading him to drink heavily when said relationships exploded, making him believe that he'd have to leave the ship. Which left him feeling he should drink *more*, which left him believing he'd *already* left the ship, and was now destitute.

Moira nodded along with the explanation, until she finally heard its complete history.

"There's no need to panic yet, let him sleep off the drink and talk to the rest of us before we hold him to something so absolutely idiotic," Jacine summarized at the end of her spiel.

We all nodded at her summary. This was a story as old as time by now.

Moira's heart settled before she spoke. "Good," she replied. "That's good. I was worried something awful had happened," pulling at her fingers, breathing out a grateful sigh.

But I wasn't going to let this opportunity pass.

"Right now, you have bigger things to worry about," I said, a growing mischievous smile on my face as Moira's hands froze, and eyebrow raised. I could feel Markus's rolling eyes at me, as if to say *Really?* While Jacine looked *delighted*.

I raised my empty palm towards Moira, voicing the silent question in my eyes. "I'd be more worried about what I'm going to do if you turn down this offer to dance."

Jacine's throat made a noise between a snort and a laugh, while Moira's eyes challenged mine. There was a battle raging in her even over this small thing.

I could see the debate in her eyes, and hear it in her heart.

I prayed to every goddess who was listening that she would say yes.

A skip in her heart, but an icy smile on her face as she slipped her hand into mine, pulling me towards her ever so slightly, enough to bring me to my feet.

My drinks forgotten, hunger shoved aside, nothing mattered to me save for Moira as we walked hand in hand to the dancefloor, eyes locked onto each other.

It was just a dance. What was the harm in one little dance?

CHAPTER TWENTY

**— *Overheard conversation on the deck of Royal
Kitaxian Warship Vanguard***

Cheers echoed around the tavern as I let Moira pull me from my table to the dance floor, while the bards played a steady tune of some kind of waltz. I didn't consider myself an expert dancer by any means, but I knew enough to impress most of my partners.

As one of Moira's hands rested on my shoulder, the other reaching up to hold mine, I hugged the back of her waist tightly to me. It somehow felt like the moment of our duel, with the barest hint of fear in my gullet that I was in over my head.

As the first notes of the music played, I quickly found that I wasn't leading her, she was leading *me*. But as the song's familiarity played out, I eventually began to find my stride and match her bit by bit.

We whirled and dived, dodging other dancers like we were gliding on ice. With a shiver rising up my spine to the music, I dipped her low, watching her back arch beautifully in my grasp, a smile playing out as I pulled her back into my embrace.

"You know what you're doing… Barely," she breathed out, not

taking her eyes off of me. I held back my shrug, doing my best not to prove I was a horrid dancer.

"I admit I'm not as practiced in this kind of footwork," I muttered, feeling the hitch of a laugh in her, a slight rumble under my hand around her waist, the only real betrayal that she was enjoying this.

"What? Duelling and swordplay don't translate well, you think?" It was her turn to show off as she spun me out from her embrace, before reeling me back in in perfect time with the music. "I think it translates perfectly," she whispered with a smile, hands wandering my waist as the song's beat continued.

But as the song transitioned into a softer tempo, our steps slowed into a more intimate sway as a result.

"Have you… given it anymore thought?" I asked quietly, trying not to hear Markus's complaints in my mind from mere hours ago, certainly not recognizing the tone of softness in my voice. Gods, when *did* I get it this bad?

There was only one thing I could've meant.

Us.

She twitched, breathing shallowly for a moment as we twirled. She was silent for the rest of the song, each second, each *note*, feeling like something was stabbing me from the inside. My chest ached, and I wanted to reach in and scoop it out to be rid of this pain. Her silence was near insufferable.

"Is there... anything I can do? Or should I just... leave you be?" I asked quietly as the song came to an end. I prayed that maybe, just maybe, since we were still locked in an embrace, that it meant we were going for another song.

But... she began to move away... and then paused. She looked up at me, her hand reaching out to cup my face, her fingers ever so gentle, so *warm*, as she rubbed her thumb down my cheek, tracing my jaw, leaving a trail of longing in her wake.

"Claire. I'm sorry..." she whispered, her eyes tearing up. "But we can never be." Her words might as well have been a stake of Scarwood, stabbing into my heart with how much they burned.

I looked into those perfect green eyes, her flame-red hair framing her face, the splash of freckles thick across her nose and cheeks, seeming to give her a permanent blush. I looked for anything in those eyes that told me she was telling a lie.

And found none.

"I understand," I said quietly.

She held my face a moment longer, biting her lip before she removed her hands, leaving me standing alone on the dancefloor. I didn't move as I listened to every step of her feet out into the night, leaving the crowded tavern. Nearly every pair of eyes in the room thankfully looking anywhere but at me, purposefully avoiding seeing what just unfolded here.

Only Jacine and Markus, looking at me from my table with pity, were looking upon me as I realized that a heart that couldn't beat could indeed still break.

I didn't know how long I stood there, lost in the rejection. Eventually I realized my feet worked, and I forced myself to wander outside the tavern. I needed to get away from the mess of people, the noise, and all those warm bodies.

Stomping through the night, I clenched one hand in a pocket, the other grasping the hilt of my sword to silence its clink at my side. Hollowing myself of feeling, left with the only thing I couldn't remove completely, no matter how hard I tried.

My hunger.

It'd been too long since I fed. I had figured I could deal with it. I'd dealt with worse.

But now it simmered in the back of my throat, urging me to take advantage of my foul mood, pushing all sorts of impulsive thoughts into my mind.

I didn't remember making my way to the docks, sitting on the pier looking out over the waves as they lapped the shore underneath me… but that's where had ended up. With my legs swinging under me, just over the edge of the waves, I could hear Jacine's heartbeat down the beach. She had followed me, keeping an eye on me, the smoke from her pipe wafting in on the wind.

That worried me. She only had that pipe out when she was scared. But if she was smoking and watching me, that was even more worrying, because that meant right now she was scared for *me*.

Captain Claire Vessia, damned witch of the Wraith, laid low by Ameritia's daughter.

An ugly snarl escaped my throat. I couldn't figure out why and how this one woman had such a hold of me.

I had plenty of people who wanted me. Sarah. Charlotte and I had found ourselves in bed a few times. The dozen or so women around town whose names I couldn't be bothered to remember.

But never did I *love* someone.

I wasn't *capable* of it. Not anymore. I was a *monster*.

I was forged in the fires of Lady Ameritia's dungeons, tempered on the burning rope of the noose, simmered in the drowning waters of the ocean.

My *trauma* had forged me into a weapon pointed straight at the heart of Kitaxia. This was all I knew. That I would bring unspeakable violence upon those who had wronged me. *That* was my purpose in life.

I couldn't be *in love.*

But was it really because of Ameritia?

Why else does this feel so painful?

I tried to muster any explanation while I looked out over the water, a shifting mirror reflecting the moon and galaxy above. Maybe it was because it was a stumbling block in my revenge. That... it wouldn't be *perfect* unless I had her.

But I'd already *kissed* her... wasn't that enough? Did I really need *more*?

When I had Lady Ameritia finally under threat of my blade, couldn't I taunt her with that alone? Why would I need *Moira* for anything else?

What am I doing? Why am I trying to rationalize this? She doesn't want me. She hates me. That's that. End of story.

So where did that leave me? With nothing. No one.

All those feelings during Maude and Isabella's wedding, and their engagement... All of them coalesced within me now. Never would someone declare at my wedding how much they knew I'd always loved them, and that they loved me. Never would I be able to hold someone I cared for close and comfortable without worry. Never would I have someone who understood every facet of me.

I would walk the world alone, for the rest of my days.

Forever.

That was the kicker. *Vampyri* were immortal. I still wasn't sure I'd really accepted that. Isabella had been the one to tell me that little factoid. She was the only other person I'd met who'd known another one of my kind.

Apparently on the Eastern Continent we were more common. Her great-grandmother had helped build a home for a *Vampyri* who had been exiled from Draculesti to the Everwilds.

Isabella had grown up knowing that same man, and he hadn't aged a day.

I breathed out some deeply held breath, no longer caring about my paints and hair, reaching up to rub my eyes in frustration, pulling out my hair pins, one after the other.

My thoughts were a jumbled mess as my locks finally fell free of their complicated braids, a wild mane shadowing the edges of my vision, as I stared down into the moonlit water beneath my feet. My mind a tornado of images and considerations as a defeated sigh let out of some deep part of my soul.

How long could I keep this up? Still snapping at Kitaxia's heels with nothing but blood and vengeance to fuel me?

I never got the chance to answer that question as a gun cocked against the back of my head.

I had never noticed the heartbeat. I wasn't listening for it. And if I wasn't safe in Souris...

I raised my hands slowly into the air, the press of the barred shoved into the back of my neck to make the point.

"Get up," a gruff voice ordered. "You look fancy enough. Give me an answer and you'll live. Where can I find Vessia?"

I slowly got to my feet, hearing Jacine's panicked heartbeat from behind a pile of barrels nearby.

It seemed I'd be eating tonight after all.

"That's *Captain* Vessia to you," I said quietly before my leg shot out behind me and hit him solidly in the gut, an *'oof'* coming satisfyingly from his lungs as a result.

He held his shot as he staggered back, probably trying to make sure when he did fire the pistol, it'd count. I turned around just as he fired, his shot perfectly aimed at my heart. I tried to duck under it with my speed, and felt the bullet dig into my shoulder instead.

The pistol's explosion of fire rang out throughout the night, echoing off the surrounding buildings. I ignored the flash of pain as my arm went numb, and he stared in horror as I didn't even slow in my steps.

He screamed as I wrenched his head to the left in a sickening crunch, and tore my fangs into him, drinking deeply. The pistol shot pushed out my shoulder as it healed was instant relief, clinking as it hit the cobblestone just as my tongue got a taste of him.

A taste of the most important mission he'd ever been given. Determination to succeed, and the greed of one hell of a payout if he could find where someone lived —where *I* lived— orders passed on from a high-ranking scout officer on a beach not too far away...

I sorted through his memories, searching for the most immediate of details and—

Oh no.

Jacine had ducked as the shot rang out, probably afraid that it would hit her in some freak aim, but she ran out from her hiding spot towards me as I drained the rest of him. I dropped him like a sack once I'd had my fill, and Jacine made a disgusted noise.

"That is some of the grossest shit I've ever seen, Claire," she said quietly as I wiped my mouth and licked my fingers clean.

"Then you be the *Vampyri* bitch in charge of this mess," I muttered, attempting some step of dark humour as I kicked at my assailant's corpse.

My joke fell a bit flat as Jacine looked from the corpse to me, a weak smile on her face as she put a hand on my shoulder.

"No fucking thank you," she said with a smidgen of a laugh despite how serious her heart was pounding in my ear.

We wouldn't be alone for long, the sounds of a slew of watchmen mobilizing from their night stations, trying to find the source of the obvious gunfire echoed throughout the vicinity.

We both turned to the dead assailant, and I cursed as I looked his clothes over, hoping I was seeing something wrong in his blood memories. But his uniform confirmed it. "He was looking for me. But I think we have bigger problems," I spat.

I dragged him to a nearby streetlight, so she could see his outfit. Jacine gasped, hands flying to her mouth in shock, "What the fuck is a Kitaxian scout doing here?" she stammered out.

We never got to answer that question before all hell broke loose.

A brief twinkling of light out of the corner of my vision, illuminating three ships by the flashes of cannon. Another breath and the echoing sound of cannon fire sounded from just outside the bay.

I grabbed Jacine by the waist and dove for the ground as our world ceased to exist.

The buildings around us exploded into millions of pieces of rubble, debris of stone and wood shooting out in every direction. Throwing myself over Jacine to shield her with my body as best I could.

Something smashed into my shoulder, something *heavy*, causing me to cry out. As soon as the stone and debris settled around us, I breathed heavily as my skin knitted together against what had just torn into me, and *pushed*.

The thud of a large chunk of wall slid off me and Jacine onto the ground behind us, a cloud of dust and debris making us both cough.

And just as quickly as everything had exploded, silence reigned, the crinkling and groaning of rocks and wood the only sound scratching through the night.

"Are you hurt?" I breathed out, lifting myself off of Jacine, a slew of pebbles, dust, and ash falling off me as Jacine coughed out a shake of her head, grasping my outstretched hand to lift her to her feet.

"What in the nine burning realms was that?" Jacine asked, her voice shaken. I pointed out towards the bay, where just as I'd pointed, another illumination of cannon fire flashed the three ships out of the dark into existence, the sounds of the cannons staggered past us a second later.

"Down!" I screamed, grabbing Jacine into another crouch.

The sound of cannonballs sliced through the air above us, into a section of the settlement a few blocks up the hill. I pulled Jacine back to her feet, spitting a curse.

"It's the gods damned Kitaxians. They mean to end us," I muttered, watching an entire block of the town the volley of cannon had slammed into go up in flames.

"Oh my Gods..." Jacine murmured, tears in her eyes.

I pulled her face to mine, held her close to make sure she got every word of what I was about to say. "Jacine. I need you to go get everyone you can find. Anyone who can't fight, send them to the warehouses. Anyone who can, to the battery. Can you do that for me?"

She took a moment to breathe, and then nodded, her tears stained black by her face paints.

"Stay safe. That's an order," I demanded. "The moment you hear cannons, duck. Can you do that for me?" She nodded again, her teeth chattering, shock beginning to get to her. "Good. Go." My heart lurched as she stood shakily, before she rolled her shoulders and nodded.

Jacine took off at a sprint, coughing through growing smoke, just as another barrage began.

I didn't bother hitting the deck, instead breaking off to run up the hill, not giving a damn about bothering to hide my true *Vampyri* speed, crossing blocks in seconds.

My people were dying, and I would not hold back.

I raced past Juliette's and Michael's shop, now openly in flames, sprinted past the tavern, a mess of people rushing inside to get into the tunnels. I kept going, onto the well-worn path up to the secret defence we'd been building for years.

Charlotte's hidden surprise.

Thankfully I wasn't the only one on the path, and torches were already being lit up at the battery, cannons pulled back and loaded, one by one.

I reached the mouth of the battery to a slurry of activity, most of the watchmen and sailors manning the guns still in their wedding attire.

"Claire! Thank the fucking Gods, get on that cannon and start shooting!" Charlotte yelled out from behind a cannon the moment I stepped inside, pointing at one sitting without its crew. Charlotte's pockets were still full to bursting with silver from their winnings.

I nodded, and hauled the 18-pounder back myself, a few sailors stopping mid-stride to stare at a feat that usually took four men to do.

We had one good chance to really inflict some damage before we alerted the ships to our presence. We had to make it count.

More and more people flooded into the battery as the seconds ticked by, but it wasn't enough. Every minute was spent in lives. The few people streaming in were either drunk, wounded, or civilians looking for safety from the shelling. It was taking far too long to load every gun but eventually, we had every cannon loaded and aimed at our intended target, the easternmost ship.

"Ready..." Charlotte called out, every hand raised affirmation, the lit wicks hovering over their firing chambers.

"FIRE!" they screamed out.

A moment of singular silence, as dozens of wicks were lowered onto priming vents, a slew of sizzling before—

I lit my own firing line clear, as a forty-gun barrage echoed from the reinforced hill above Souris, cannonballs finally answering to the unmitigated battering the settlement had endured so far.

I dropped the firing wick beside my gun to lift a spyglass borrowed from Charlotte and watched the easternmost ship in anticipation, shrouded in the darkness, knowing the shot would take another second to travel that far.

And was rewarded when the ship splintered as cannonballs tore into it like tissue paper.

"Reload!" I screamed out as we readied another barrage.

The other two ships began to sail off, suddenly aware they were in range of a very dangerous counter-attack, firing their guns as they went. I doubt they expected such a massive battery guarding a tiny port, but we'd spent years preparing for exactly this moment. Not only were we in a perfect firing location to protect the settlement, but we were also heavily reinforced. The amount of punishment the battery could take would all but eliminate their ammunition and we'd likely still be able to counter-fire.

The question was how much of Souris would be left standing by then.

The two ships which were yet unbothered by our barrages began to move away, opening up the distance, but we'd done enough damage to the one we'd focused on to isolate it in place. Whatever we'd hit, it'd been important enough to keep them still.

We pumped another three volleys into it before it split in half, slowly sinking into the waves.

I smiled as I watched it sink into the shallows offshore, but grimaced once I eyed the other two ships. Now that they knew what they were dealing with, they would maintain their distance, but not stop shelling the town.

They'd only stop when they were sure most of us were dead.

CHAPTER TWENTY-ONE

"My experiments in testing Human and Vampyri combat capabilities might as well be comparing a bug to a bear. There is no comparison. While modern firearms seem to have shifted the balance of power slightly in favour of Humans, the undeniable facts are proven on the front lines of the never-ending wars in the north. It's quite simple math, the side with the Vampyri wins."

— From the journals of Valerie Du Bois, Scholar lord of Draculesti

"They're storming the beaches!" A man shouted from the entryway to the battery, collapsing to his hands and knees, crawling as his heart beat frantically.

The man's black frock coat was nearly unrecognizable. It marked him as one of Souris' watchmen under Adam's command, but it was soaked with bloodstains.

I almost threw the spyglass back at Charlotte, diving for the man, my knees biting into the dirt as his heart slowed with each thump.

"Captain..." he gasped out, reachin for me as I lifted him from the sand. "They're... everywhere," his words faded as all life left him, a slew of bullet holes in his back, bleeding into the dirt.

I cursed myself that I didn't know the man's name. He was dying to give us a warning instead of getting help, and *I didn't know his Gods damn name.*

"Charlotte," I muttered through gritted teeth, setting the man softly into the sand. "Don't stop firing. Not until the guns melt or you run out of ammunition," their face was a stoney mask on the other side of the dead man as cannons continued firing all around us.

I don't know what Charlotte saw in my gaze as I wiped the watchman's blood off my hands in the sand, doing everything I could not to lick my fingers, but nothing could've shocked me more than the seriousness of their salute.

"Yes, ma'am," Charlotte stated, holding their salute.

Gods, we were absolutely *fucked* if Charlotte was showing respect.

"Be about it, Charlotte," I ordered. We would need the unthinkable to get out of this mess alive.

They nodded at my command, turning on their heel as if they'd been practising drill all their life, and began bellowing more orders to the gun crews.

I jumped to the top of the battery's battlement, looking out over the chaos, trying to think of some last card to play.

Souris was no longer a port, it was a firestorm. Of the two surviving ships out in the harbour—I assumed Kitaxian warships because *who* else could it *possibly* be—only one was still firing into the settlement. The other one had shifted its focus to the battery, but we'd built it far too well built into the hillside for the assault to do much damage.

It'd be a gunnery duel of attrition. They'd fire a salvo into the town, we'd fire a salvo back, on and on it went until someone ran out of ammunition or got a lucky hit.

But that wouldn't stop their marines storming the town.

I could see the beginnings of building-to-building gunfights already, the flashes of musket fire tiny bright explosions to my improved vision. From here I could even see their longboat landing where they were erecting a defensive palisade just in case they got pushed back.

Getting to the *Wraith* wasn't an option. All the crew were scattered among the town, probably half of them probably as drunk— if not more—than our gunners up here.

We needed to group what fighters we could, as many as were still alive and functional, and push the Kitaxians back, while the battery hammered the other ships into hopefully retreating.

It was the best-worst plan I could think of.

I grimaced as I jumped down off the battlement, taking off at a sprint for the town, knowing that it was an absolutely shit plan, but it was all I had and we were out of options.

With my speed, I reached the first townhouse battle in seconds, where a group of harried defenders were holding the watchmen's headquarters against a company of Kitaxian marines. The marines were holed up in the buildings across the street, each taking potshots at each other with the occasional lobbed grenade.

It would've continued to be a pitched battle for hours yet, but the marines didn't have a *Vampyri* on their side.

Climbing up the ruins of a building next to one that the marines were in, I took a running jump, propelling myself through the air dramatically, crashed through one of the windows, and landed in a crowded room with a huff.

I looked up to see four uniformed Kitaxians all staring at me in abject shock, their rifles still halfway out the windows.

"Hello boys," I said with a grim smile before unsheathing my sword.

They made valiant attempts to turn their rifles towards me, but I had three of their throats slit before the fourth one managed it in time.

Shame he was a poor shot.

Ducking under his rifle with ease, I knocked it upwards with my blade before punching him in the face with its hilt.

He staggered backwards, dropping the rifle, leaving me with ample opportunity to tear into his throat with my teeth.

Drinking my fill of him, organizing his memories into something I could use, parsing his orders, the general invasion plan, *everything.*

With that knowledge now firmly mine, ambushing the rest of the attackers throughout the rest of the building was almost easy. I had the Watchman's headquarters relieved of attackers in minutes.

I stepped out of the house towards the embattled watchmen, two of them taking potshots that missed me by inches, scattering the stones at my feet.

"It's me!" I screamed at the building, as several curses lit up the night before the gate was opened. I didn't blame them for almost shooting me, but damn it, they could've at least had better aim.

"Captain?" someone screamed back.

"Who the fuck else!" I yelled back.

A cheer went up throughout the building as the gate was opened fully, and two watchmen waved me in.

"Thank the Gods, Captain. We feared the worst," one of them stated as I rushed inside the building.

"Tell me about it," I replied, just as more cannon fire sounded throughout the night. The crumbling telltale noise of a building collapsing somewhere nearby a few seconds after made everyone wince.

"Who's in charge? Where's McCrosswick?" I asked the watchman, but his face told me everything as it lowered to the floor.

The man gulped, like he was swallowing a musket ball. "Dead, ma'am," he replied.

I clasped him on the shoulder, squeezing it ever so slightly. "We'll make them pay," I said, meaning every word. I didn't particularly like McCrosswick, I knew him as a greedy and corrupt son-of-a-bitch, but he was well liked by his underlings. That was enough to make me sad at his passing.

"Claire!" Jacine's voice shouted from a doorway before the woman took a running jump into my arms. I snuck my free arm around her, twirling her in the air, thanking every Goddess I could name that she was okay.

"Jacine, am I ever glad to see you," I set her back down, as she greeted me with a smile.

Her grin was as bright as the morning dawn. "Just you wait, ma'am." She turned back to the room she had burst from, before yelling into the opening. "Hey, asshole!"

Rodger's head burst out through the door in alarmed confusion, before happy recognition overtook it all, a moment later coming out to scoop us both in a giant hug as he laughed.

But the hug was cut short by the sounds of cannon fire, far too close.

We rapidly broke apart, tensing in case we had to duck, but the barrage wasn't meant for us. Tension left my muscles reluctantly, I knew that wouldn't be the last volley of death.

"Have either of you seen anyone else?" I asked with panic in my voice as we separated, my sword hanging lightly in my hand, my other not leaving Jacine's shoulder.

They exchanged a look, waving me into the room. "Come on. We'll do a quick overview now that we're all not being actively shot at," Rodger murmured, showing us inside.

It looked to be the watchmen's briefing room, large maps posted to the wall of the local trade routes, but on the large centre table lay a map of the town, my eyes picking up the jist of it almost immediately.

"I just came from the battery," I said, pointing at the location on the map. "Charlotte's there working the guns, giving the ships something to think about. I'm hoping we'll sink one more of them, but that's unlikely now that they know it's there," I explained. "They'll stay out of range."

They both sighed with relief at hearing Charlotte's name, understandably so, but I motioned for them to spill the rest of what they knew.

"We're mostly holed up here in the guards headquarters, here at the tavern, and at the battery," Jacine said quietly, tapping a finger at the three locations.

"There's pitched battles in every corner of the town, but the docks are by far the worst of it," Rodger slurred, not having fought off his drinks yet, tapping at the docks. "It's a warzone."

"What about our people? What have you heard?" I asked.

Rodger wrinkled his moustache, but it was Jacine who spoke up. "Last I heard, Markus is in the tavern, trying to get people in the carts out to the warehouse and sailors back to the *Wraith*. Gracie and Miss Cavendish are there too. The wedding was a blessing in more ways than one." Her face looked ashen as she explained, but her eyes were focused on the map as she grasped her chin in thought. "Most of the townsfolk were at the tavern already and have been evacuated out through the tunnels."

"Maude and Isabella?" I asked. In a crisis like this… I didn't want to think about how many injured we were going to have.

Jacine let out a light laugh. "Ironically, they're the safest of the lot. They were at their little honeymoon beach house down shore. They've been alerted and are on their way to the warehouse to set up a field hospital." She tapped the hidden cove on the map.

I breathed through my teeth, terrified of the next question I was going to ask.

"My mother?" I asked, genuinely afraid of what I was about to hear.

Jacine waved off my worry. "She's fine. She was still at the tavern when the shots rang out, and was one of the first on the rails to the warehouse."

The chopped relief I felt that my friends were okay nearly made my knees give out from underneath me.

They were okay.

I let out a breath I didn't know I was holding, despite not needing to breathe. But there was one more to ask about. A girl in a blue dress and shocking red hair.

"Moira?" I asked. Again, they exchanged a look that suggested something.

"No one has seen her," Jacine murmured, her voice laced with sadness, as worry seeped into my bones. The tone of her voice, the looks they both shared...

I knew what they were thinking.

It was too convenient. That the Kitaxians not only would ambush us in the dead of night, but on the very night when most of the crew would be incapacitated? The wedding was planned in a fucking *week*. There was absolutely no way they could've timed it that perfectly without inside help.

But if Moira *had* betrayed us, I couldn't think of a way she could've gotten word back to Kitaxia. But the fact that she was missing right now was a bit more damning than I'd liked to admit.

The thought sat in the pit of my stomach like a stone, guilt warring with my heart.

I ran my hand through my hair, the fancy braids now thoroughly ruined from blood, ash, and gunpowder.

Later. We'll deal with it later. We won't know unless we find her.

First things first. My town was full of fucking Kitaxians.

"I'm going to the docks," I stated, my voice even, as if I was announcing I was going for a pleasant walk.

"Claire..." Jacine murmured, reaching out to me, but stopped after I fixed her with a glare.

"That's where you said the fighting was thickest right?" I asked, staring at Rodger, who nodded.

"That's the closest spot to their longboat landing. It's where they're funnelling marines in from," he replied.

I looked at the map, tracing the shortest line route from our current location to the docks.

I will find her. And then I'll know the truth of it.

"Stay here, hold the fort. Try and re-establish contact with the tavern if you think you can, but your safety is priority number one," I ordered. " If you think you can't hold here, fall back to the battery and reinforce Charlotte. Clear?"

Jacine nodded, moving towards the door, but Rodger stood where he was, his eyes still on the map.

"What are you after Claire? We've lost," Rodger stated, his voice full of sorrow.

Jacine paused in her tracks, both of us looking at Rodger with disappointment and shock.

I rounded the table, grabbed his shirt collar, twisting it in my fist so he had to face me, forcing him to look me in the eye. "Because I'm still here, and I will admit Kitaxia's won when the Veiled Lady comes for me her damn self."

The smell of alcohol still sat on his breath, and disappointed, disgusted, I shoved him away into a chair, baring my fangs. "And the Gods themselves won't be able to stop me from saving everyone."

Traitor or no, that included her.

I gave Jacine one last hug goodbye, making her promise to look after Rodger. I'd left him sitting in that same chair with an aura of defeat, and it took everything in me to not smack some more sense into him.

Leaving the Watchman's headquarters, I rushed down the streets, tearing into marines wherever I found them.

I singled out the officers for feeding, ripping into their memories for any sign of Moira, but wasn't having any luck so far. House after house, block after block, body after body.

Souris felt like it was twenty times its size.

Blocks I'd crossed with regularity in minutes took an hour to cross.

Each one had marines hiding in the damnedest places, places that I'd only be able to find by listening for their traitorous hearts. Fighting off invaders, stabbed, shot, then the cannons would fire, and *twice* on my way to the docks I found myself buried in rubble, having to rely on my ungodly strength to free myself.

It took forever, having received more wounds healed over in one night than I'd ever gotten over five years of sailing, but finally, I reached the docks, and realized the description Rodger had applied to it was if anything an understatement.

A warzone.

The Kitaxians had entrenched themselves in the sandy beach around their landing, not a few minutes walk from where me and Moira had lain in the sand, and dug in several defensive trenches surrounding it, three lines deep. From there, they had stormed on one front towards the town, on the other towards the docks.

I had largely liberated the town, going building by ruined building, and they were falling back into the trenches as our people were slowly grouping up.

We were winning the ground battle, albeit slowly.

From my position at the top of the last building before the beaches, a watchtower to plan my next move, I felt like some field marshal of old.

The closest of the surviving Kitaxian ships was beginning to burn in the night, one of Charlotte's cannons setting something on fire aboard, giving the trenchworks an ugly glow of flickering red light reaching into depths of shadowy black where men crouched, firing off rounds into the counterattack.

The burning ship was still firing back in defiance, but if its crew couldn't get those flames under control, it would eventually reach the magazine and the whole thing would go up.

I was debating just how to get around the trenches, maybe using one of their own longboats to get to the ship further out, storming the damn thing myself, when a door behind me slammed open.

I turned to see a panicked Kitaxian officer clutching a bleeding shoulder staggering into the room.

We blinked at each other in surprise before he began to raise a pistol as I leaped to jump him.

The shot rang out.

My world went black as my face exploded into pain.

Ba-dum. Ba-dum. Ba-dum. Ba-dum. Ba-dum. Ba-dum.

I didn't know how long I was unconscious.

I awoke to the sounds of shouts and gunshots, and to some of the worst hunger and pain I'd ever felt since awaking in this life. It took all I had just to stay conscious. I couldn't even open my eyes.

My ears rang, my face felt smothered in something, a skittering in every muscle, a seeping down my neck. It itched, it burned, it felt like there were cinders in my jaw. I dug my fingers into the floor, wood bending under the force of my grip, splinters digging into my skin, that was *nothing* on the fire still skittering all over my face, my scalp, my neck.

A pop in my ear, and then the noise and gunshots cleared into discernable voices. "Get on that shooter in the other window! No, you idiot, not that one, THAT one!" A voice I didn't recognize, ordering another. Another shot echoed, this time sounding much closer. I forced myself to speak, just to prove to myself that I could, but what came out of my mouth gurgled in my throat as I choked on it.

I rolled myself over in the sticky wet mess I was in, to cough out whatever was in my throat.

As I spat it out, my broken breathing getting better with each breath, I finally forced myself to open my eyes and see that the wet mess I had woken up in wasn't water.

It was blood. *My blood.*

And something more solid that I didn't want to speculate on.

"What in God's glorious name? Is she *alive*?" Another voice sounded in horrified disbelief.

The voices were meaningless. Everything hurt. And I was *starving*.

I folded my body to sit on my feet and knees, touching my face gently. *Healed.* Thank the Gods it was night. I'd *healed.*

"God have mercy," one of the voices said with terror as I leaned down again to cough out more blood covered mess, some of it chunkier than blood could possibly be, finally looking up at the officer who'd shot me and another marine that'd joined him.

"You shot me in the face," I muttered in quiet amazement. "You shot *me*—in the fucking Gods damned *face*," I said again, growing anger and fury pairing with the horrid hunger at what healing such a wound had cost.

How the fuck I'd lived, I had no idea. I laughed there in the dark for a brief moment, feeling like the weight of a ship had been pressed onto my face, as I slowly stood, first one foot, then the other.

The other marine suddenly decided to take his chances with the window, jumping through it and screaming in terror to avoid whatever damnation I was about to visit on him.

Smart move.

The officer who'd shot me, however, looked to be too scared to dream up such a solution. I took a few paces towards him on shaky legs, but he was frozen stiff with shock. Not that I blamed him, seeing a dead woman walking. He didn't even bother defending himself as I grabbed him by the collar, lifted him clean off his feet, and tore my teeth into his throat.

The taste of his blood was all but ignored as I focused more on drinking to fill the void healing had created than for any purpose of mind. A series of brief images flashing through my mind as I drank, all shoved aside without a care.

I was *hungry.* Starving. He was nothing but an appetizer. There would be more out on the streets—

An image of red hair flashed through my mind's eye.

Moira.

My eyes flashed open, hunger pushing me to absolute *fury* as I locked on the memory. They'd dragged her to the longboat landing, taking her to one of the ships. I impatiently ripped his throat out in a bloody mess with my fangs, his body falling to the floor. My fingers clawed across the window frame, wood groaning as my nails dug into it, as my gaze looked over the battlefield and onto the landing and its surrounding trenches.

A single thought of focus as I gasped out a still warm breath, swallowing the last of the officer's blood, the smell of gunpowder and rubble in the air.

They'd taken her.

CHAPTER TWENTY-TWO

"My latest experiment destroyed most of the lab last night before having to be put down. As such, future experiments will only proceed with the utmost safety precautions in place when testing the limits of Vampyri physical strength. The problem, as always with Vampyri, lies in our ability to control. At some point, overwhelmed with blood and injury, the hunger pushes even the eldest of us to slip into bloodrage. That is to be avoided at all costs."

— From the journals of Valerie Du Bois, Scholar lord of Draculesti

I picked up my discarded sword from the floor, tonguing over my fangs as I hopped through the same window the marine had jumped out of a moment before. A rush of air flew past me, before I landed as silently as a cat beside his broken body.

He groaned in pain, clutching his shattered legs as I stomped away. I didn't even know if he noticed me. I certainly didn't care, because my attention was locked on the first line of trenches in the sandy dunes.

I walked towards them with a quiet fury, blood still dripping down my chin, my sword in my hand looking like it was painted red with how much life it'd tasted this day.

As I closed the distance, one boot in front of the other, finally one of the marines saw me.

I did not change course. I did not run.

At least not until the first musket shot bit into my fucking shoulder.

A hiss escaped my mouth as I stopped my advance for all but a moment, pain forcing me to pause and search for the shooter. The light of the moon and the fire of the Kitaxian warship was enough. Three of them, all lining up for another volley of fire, all at *me*.

They'd taken her.

A growl became an ungodly roar as I charged them.

The bites of pain in my shoulder, my chest, my stomach, and my leg told me I had been shot. *Many* times.

But they were nothing. Pain was nothing. Nothing could stop me.

They had Moira, and she was *mine*. Never would the Kitaxians hold anything of mine ever again. I crossed no man's land in a rush, dropping into the first line of trenches, chopping the head clean off one of the marines as I fell into the defence works.

The second man didn't even see me until my teeth were in his neck. The third screamed and panicked a shot off. The bite of a bullet in my arm did nothing to stop me as I snapped his neck.

Finally, I recognized the markings of another officer, his blade out, but I parried it away in two moves to grab him by the neck.

"Where is she?" I compelled into his eyes with every bit of my will, leaving that as the only question in his head. I needed to find her. I *had* to find her. Nothing else mattered.

"Who?" he choked out, the breath rapidly escaping his lungs as my fingers dug into the flesh of his neck, blood pooling from my claws puncturing his throat.

"Moira. Red hair. Tall. Captured. Where?" I demanded, my words a knife I was carving into his soul, let alone my claws in his neck.

He writhed, trying to get free, but the compulsion overwhelmed him, forcing him to answer. "She was captured. Taken to the landing..." he managed to sputter out.

I ripped his throat out, leaving him bleeding in the dirt as I jumped out of the trench to rush the next line.

A shot to my neck finally forced me to take a knee. *Ba-dum.* My skin suddenly felt like it was on fire. *Ba-dum.* The sounds of little clinks of metal hitting the stony beach all around me. *Ba-dum.* The healing was growing the void of hunger in my stomach, even in the middle of the night. *Ba-dum.* The hunger... *Gods,* the hunger. *Ba-dum.* I stood, again running for the line, tearing into the soldiers with wild abandon. *Ba-dum, ba-dum, ba-dum.* As my heartbeat quickened, I found myself moving faster, stronger, impossibly fast through the lines, slashing through limbs, blades, and iron with ease.

Badumbadumbadum.

I didn't even remember rushing the final line before the boats. My mouth was a bloody mess as I screeched some inhumane sound from my throat. One body after another after another, all the while screaming the one driving thought pushing me onward:

"WHERE. IS. SHE?"

The last man in the trenches, some officer of rank confirmed to my wild-eyed compulsion that she had been taken to the ships with a handful of other prisoners. That she was important, wanted by the King.

I bled him dry, tossing his corpse to the mud. I didn't even bother with the longboat, instead sheathing my sword and diving into the sea.

The shock of the water finally made me realize that I couldn't recall most of what I had just done. My hunger was still raging in my chest, despite having gorged myself on Kitaxian blood, but I had to get to her first. I had to get her back.

My ragged breath silenced as I cut through the water, and my heart slowed to its usual quiet stillness.s

I swam towards the nearest great hulk before me, quite alike the *Wraith* in shape. It should have been a near exact layout. They were ships of the same class, but the orange glow of the fires aboard suggested it didn't have long left before *something* exploded into a catastrophic firestorm that really shouldn't.

I ducked beneath the waves as I closed in, going underneath the vessel with ease. I found the familiar-yet-foreign ship's ladder on the other side, and ducked into an open gunport, smoke rising from the fire inside.

Ironic. This wasn't unlike how we'd stolen the *Wraith* so many years ago. If I had a silver for every time it had happened to me, I'd only have two silver, but it was still weird that it had happened twice.

I snuck as quickly as I could through the boiling decks, most of the sailors and marines passing me by entirely, not giving a single care to one sea-drenched woman when flames were licking at every corner of the ship. While I was going down to the brig down in the depths of the ship, everyone else seemed to be going upwards to the weather deck, trying to get off before the fire reached the magazine.

That didn't stop me from cutting down every single one I could get my hands on, devouring as many as I could to fill the void in my unending hunger.

In brief flickering moments of flame in between bloody feedings, the bowels of the ship eventually opened before me. A place that somehow no flames had reached just yet, yet ironically enough, water had. Some of Charlotte's shots from the battery had done more than just start a fire.

I sloshed my way through the flooding deck, making my way through the doors that separated the cargo hold and brig…

And found it empty.

She isn't here.

I kicked in the cell door with a yell, the metal indenting in an ugly groan before I made my way back upwards into the smoke-filled gun deck, crew actively jumping out of the gunports.

It wouldn't be long now. The fire was climbing deck to deck, reaching ever more important pieces of the ship. Tinier explosions could already be heard every few seconds as it reached ammo lockers from several locations.

I didn't give a damn for the fucking fire, focused on climbing further up onto the weather deck, sails just now beginning to lighting up in flames. Running to barge through the captain's door, I couldn't help the slightest feeling of deja-vu from its carved designs matching the doors back on the *Wraith*.

The room was as shattered as it was empty. Broken glass covering the floor, papers scattered everywhere, a hole in the wall where a cannonball had ruptured clean through the wall, littering shrapnel everywhere. Three bodies near where the damage was worse, bleeding out… but one beating heart hid somewhere in the room.

They were easy to find. I just had to follow the trail of blood.

Hiding in the corner, a piece of wood sticking into his guts, slowly leaching the life out of him, the epaulettes on his shoulder marked him as a lieutenant.

A brief protest. His cries of denial at his doom were ash on the wind, easily denied. He tasted of nothing but burning flesh. A disgusting flavour. Sometimes the memory of dying was all that was left in the blood.

But his blood memories showed me a better prize. The boat carrying Moira had initially made its way here, but then made for the other ship after the fire broke out.

She wasn't here.

I growled, rage and hunger pushing me to pick him up and throw him out the glass panes and into the sea, not even bothering to finish him off. Storming back out onto the weather deck, the smoking wreck of the ship groaned under me.

The other ship was still sitting there, undamaged, just off the fore, no longer spitting out marines to assault Souris, but now taking survivors on board.

Making ready to leave.

And they had Moira.

"Fuck!" I cursed, kicking a smoldering pile of rope across the deck. I paced, unsure of what to do—but the smoldering pile of rope showed me a possibility I hadn't considered. I watched with fascination as the sheet of sail right above it shifted forward from the smoke wafting off the rope, an idea forming in my mind.

I turned to look at the ship off the fore, almost dead ahead of us. I could almost draw a straight line from bowsprit just in front of me to the other ship's aft.

Right where it should be. It *was* a standard line of battle after all.

Maybe I could make it prove to be their undoing.

I lashed the helm as best as I could with what little undamaged rope I could scrummage up, and then set about the most difficult part of my insane plan.

The anchor.

The chain was too thick for me to break, Vampyri strength or no, and I didn't know how long I actually had before the fire reached the magazine. It could be minutes or it could be seconds.

And to raise the anchor would take *hours*, time I just simply didn't have.

So I resolved myself to do the only thing I could think of.

Brute force.

I wrapped my arms around the bottom of the capstan that housed the anchor chain, and heaved with every piece of might I could scrounge. The wood groaned in protest. I screamed in fury as if the fucking thing was a representation of all of Kitaxia.

Where my arms met against the outer surface of the capstan, suddenly collapsed inwards, my grip crushing around the coil of chains at its core, and I lifted with every muscle in my body screaming in protest.

Ba-dum, ba-dum, ba-dum, ba-dum.

With my heart providing the last bit of strength I needed, I lifted the anchor chain, capstan—all of it—free of the vessel, and tossed it over the side in a final yell of defiance. The last of the anchor chain trailed after it, taking out some of the side of the ship under me with the force of its weight.

I nearly lost my balance as the entire ship lurched, suddenly free of the heaviest item aboard, nothing holding it in place. I grabbed the nearest flaming piece of debris, and lit the piles of rope I'd placed under the masts, each pile lighting up in glorious fire.

Not that they'd needed the extra effort. One was already lit by the time I got there.

But the effect was instantaneous. Free of an anchor, the smoke from the flames billowed up the masts, and into the burning sails, fueling an upwards draft that was just enough to make the entire ship begin to move forward. Slowly at first, but quicker every second as it cut through the water.

Straight towards the last Kitaxian vessel.

I stumbled across the rapidly shifting deck, the wood protesting the supports crackling into flame underneath my feet. I got myself to the bowsprit, and hung on for dear life.

The other ship grew in view, as shouts and screams of the improvised fire ship lurching rapidly towards the other instilled terror into every man aboard.

There were only two places Moira could be on board that ship, either in the brig, or the captain's quarters, and if I timed this right...

The momentum of the ship was still gaining speed and momentum, putting the very tip of the bowsprit just in range of the glass panes of the captain's cabin.

I'd only get one shot at this...

I backed down a few steps, the flaming fury of the ship at my back, and took off at a sprint to make a running jump, the tip of my boot pushing me off the last step of the bowsprit. My body was weightless in the air, the force of my jump timed *perfectly* as I arched to crash through the captain's windows.

I landed neatly among the crash of glass and shattered gasps, drawing my sword and scavenged pistol as I stood. The sight that greeted me was enough to make me see red. Four officers and the captain. Moira *chained* to a fucking chair, a hasty looking bandage job under her ribs.

Pistols were raised and aimed, but not only did I have surprise on my side, I had *speed*.

I shot first, dropping one of the officers instantly as the musket ball got him in the corner of his mouth, taking out his jaw. Ducked as three shots went out the window behind me, just before the ships finally crushed together, buckling the entire deck underneath us.

Using the momentum of the ship buckling forward to my advantage, I rushed to slice the throat of the closet officer with the tip of my blade, before pushing past him to the third.

I ran him through, pushing myself close to him, shifting him around rapidly to use his body as a shield. The captain and last officer fired their pistols a half second later, the man I'd stabbed crying out as he died, absorbing shots meant for me.

I grabbed the second pistol from his waist, aimed, and shot the last officer in the head before throwing the body off my blade.

One to go. It was just me, the captain, and Moira. The captain drew his blade, putting up a ready defence, but I didn't care.

I walked forward, his inevitable doom, as he stabbed at me in blind panic. I moved to deflect it, more angry than purposeful, but he'd been counting on it. Had I been careful or composed, I could've dodged or cut away or a million other responses.

But I hadn't. My gaze was on the girl chained to the fucking chair.

His blade pierced my shoulder, and I was *done* with the pretentious thought that I needed a sword to kill him. I shoved forward, grabbing the captain by his ugly scrabble of hair, and sank my teeth into his neck as his sword pierced ever further into me.

He tasted of nothing but bitter disappointment and *disgust* at Moira.

I drank my fill of him, feeling him writhe in pain as I made it *hurt*. If I wanted to, I could drink a man over *hours* and have him thank me for it. But this man, I drank in less than a minute, my feeding violently ripping his veins asunder. He screamed as he died in my arms, doing almost nothing to satisfy the void in my gut.

Drained to almost nothing, he fell to his knees, drowning in what little blood he had left, before falling onto his back, dead before his head hit the deck.

I rolled my shoulders and head, trying to get the feeling of *vileness* out of my system, grabbing the sword in my shoulder and pulling it free.

In an instant, it healed over, and for the first time since I'd jumped into the water, I breathed.

I turned to find Moira pulling at her bonds, trying to get away from me.

Which made me realise I was a stupid fucking idiot.

She had just seen me feed. *In front of her*.

If she didn't know before, she certainly fucking knew now.

But that was a thought for later. I needed to get her to safety first and foremost. Sheathing my sword, I grabbed the manacles on her ankles, ripping them off her with ease, the metal bending to my fingers. I did the same with the ones on her wrists.

She began to push backwards as her limbs were freed, but I reached for her. "Moira," I said quietly, kneeling before her, holding her face in my hands, my thumbs brushing over her cheeks. "You're alive," I whispered, feeling the sob in my throat.

She nodded, pain crossing her face, as her fear simmered down into recognition. She hadn't recognized me. That was all.

The bandages around her midriff were still *heavily* seeping. I needed to get her to Maude and Isabella. *Now.*

"I'm going to get you out of here," I said, my voice a promise of iron.

She nodded wordlessly, faint. I snaked an arm under her back and under her legs, and carefully lifted her into my arms.

As much as I wanted to be, I didn't have time to be as careful, especially with such precious cargo in my arms. I spared one glance towards the fireship outside the window, its weather deck now completely collapsed inwards, flames over every inch of it spewing several feet into the sky, impaled on the aft of the ship I was standing on.

It would go up any second.

Dashing for the door, a boot to its frame sent it tumbling down the weather deck. It wasn't the time to care about another soul on board.

I had Moira, and I had to get her to safety.

I jumped clean over the railing, and into the water below, not letting go of my prize despite her scream.

The light harbour waves swallowed us. I kicked as hard as I could for the surface and shore, holding Moira's head above the waves, with no care for my own.

We made it in minutes thanks to my speed.

Finally getting sand underneath my boots, a hearty sigh escaping my lungs as my feet stepped forward towards shore. "You're okay?" I asked as I lifted her above the waves, her body shivering in my arms.

"Hurts," she barely mumbled out, clutching at her waist. I nodded, taking one last look at the ships in the harbour over my shoulder.

Just as they exploded.

The fireship went up first as the flames finally touched the magazine, a spew of fire and igniting gunpowder shooting out directly skyward. A scream of hissing flames echoed throughout the night as a miniature sun eclipsed from inside its hold.

The force of the burning bulk's explosion forced tons of water away for a half second, before it all rushed back in, ripping the aft off the other ship as it pulled the other vessel down, letting water rush into the other hold.

But also raining fire from the other ship.

Some tiny little spark must have wormed its way into the other ship's magazine as well, as it too buckled from unmitigated force of its entire store of gunpowder erupted into flame and fury, fire spiraling out its gunports in dances of light.

A fire reaching the magazine was every captain's worst nightmare, and this was proof aplenty.

Both ships succumbed to the explosive flames, masts decoupling with their respective decks, crashing into the sea, as both hulks slowly began sinking into the water, the cries of drowning and burning men echoing through the night.

I spared them no pity.

Lifting Moira in my arms, I gave one last glance to the damned ships before I took off at a tireless run through the settlement.

I didn't know what state the tavern was in, but Maude and Isabella were at the warehouses beside the *Wraith*. Rather than risk time trying to speed towards the tavern, I sprinted towards the general shortest route to our hidden dock.

On our way we passed all manner of folks running to and from, some following our same route towards the warehouses, others barely touched by the fighting, civilians wandering about trying to figure out if the fighting had stopped.

Others were shell shocked, wandering crewmen who still held their weapons in hand, looking for a threat from every corner.

Part of my thoughts argued for me to stop and take charge, but my mind was distracted by the burden in my arms.

She'd lost consciousness somewhere between the border of the town and the jungle dividing it and the warehouses, making me curse and push my inhuman speed faster.

The jungle opened up to the secret dock, crowded with people rapidly getting out of my way as I ran into the crowded warehouse, screaming, "MAUDE! ISABELLA!"

Several heads turned to me, staring in open mouthed shock. But blessed Maude stepped out of a screened area, still in her wedding dress with a blood-soiled apron tied over it, looking at my panicked and wild eyes with icy concern, her hands thick with gore.

She waved me over, and I trotted over to her dividing screen where a body was being removed from an operating table, her gaze as worn as I felt.

Taking one look at Moira in my arms, she grimaced. "Follow me," Maude said sternly as I did as she asked. She led me to a fresh cot, not yet bloodied by another occupant. "Set her down here, gently," she ordered.

Nodding meekly, I bit my lip in worry. I couldn't lose Moira now, not after all this.

I lowered Moira as kindly and softly as I could, as Maude pulled a wheeled tray holding some tools closer to her reach.

"Your dressing?" she asked, pointing at the bandages around Moira's still bleeding wound. My hunger reared its head as I watched her begin to cut away the bandages.

I shook my head. "She was captured. Taken to the frigate. I—I just got her out," I stammered, somehow breathless despite not needing to breathe.

Her eyebrows raised. "That explains the state of you then, at least," she murmured exasperatedly, wiping her brow, where a splotch of blood marred her forehead. What could she possibly have meant by that?

I stared at her in confusion.

"Claire. You're a bloody fucking mess," she added, before her attention shifted back to Moira.

I lifted my hand, and really *looked* at it for the first time in a few hours. I was soaked, a mix of dried salt from the sea still dripping from my fingers, gunpowder caked under my nails, mixed with blood and sand. My skin was death-pale, pockmarked by blood and ash coating nearly everywhere I looked. I reached up and touched my face, feeling more grit of the same.

"Oh." No wonder everyone was staring at me.

"Go clean up," Maude ordered. "You're more at risk of contaminating her and the rest of the patients than anything else right now. You can come right back."

Even if I wanted to, Maude's command was inviolable, her gaze locked on Moira's laboured breathing with such intensity. She didn't even have to finish her explanation before I rushed away. If it was for Moira's safety, right at that moment, I would move mountains.

I stepped out of the warehouse, looking for some way to clean myself up in a bit of a focused daze. I'd walked by the well on the other side of the paved path separating the docks and warehouses almost three times before I registered it. It was the one the *Wraith* used for taking on water.

Beginning to systematically take buckets of water, I stopped to scrub off every inch of my body. I took off my coat—the fancy looking admiral's cut that Julliette had spent Gods knew how long making—grimacing as I realized that not only was it a lost cause, it was a shredded mess.

In fact, *everything* was. Pants, shirt, coat, everything was more shreds of fabric than anything recognizable.

How the fuck am I not in several little pieces?

With a need for clothes, I snuck aboard the *Wraith*, quietly slipping into my quarters for a fresh set.

Where my usual outfit was sitting, unmarred, freshly cleaned on my bunk.

I stared at my jacket, hat, and spectacles, like a woman comparing herself to a stranger. Seeing the pieces of the image of *Captain Claire Vessia* left me briefly wondering who they belonged to, as if somehow, that *wasn't* me.

I reached for my jacket, feeling its thick coarse fabric, —prickly almost— as the terrified faces of those I'd killed today replayed in my mind's eye, their dying memories swirling in my thoughts.

I collapsed down onto my bed, beside my clothes, my fingers wandering to my wide-brim hat, pulling it onto my lap. How many did *Captain Claire Vessia* kill *just* tonight? How many did I lose? All to save a woman I didn't even know I could trust?

Moira could've been the *source* of this attack, and I'd let my emotions get the better of me, pushing all else away once I saw she'd been taken. How many more lives could I've saved had I been more *tactical* about this?

A tiny droplet of red, splashed onto the pale skin on the back of my hand, and I stared at it in confusion, before another joined it.

Another, and another.

A choking sob building in my throat that I worked to suppress, as I reached up to touch a finger to my cheek, and found myself crying.

Tears of blood, for all the blood I'd spilt, all the lives I'd lost, all the souls I'd murdered.

I clutched my hat to my chest, lightly, afraid that I'd ruin it, as grief tried to have its way with me. Forcing me to confront the memory of the lives I'd taken, the lives I'd spent tonight, all to save the life of one woman. How many would we find out we'd lost when the sun rose over Souris?

Five years I'd worn the persona of *Captain Claire Vessia*. Five years I'd led this crew and this settlement. Five years I thought I was building something better outside of Kitaxia.

For five *Gods damned years*, I thought I was saving people I cared about, while carving out my revenge with every ship captain I ended.

All I had to show for it was blood.

There has to be a better way.

Wiping away my bloody tears, I shoved the thoughts from my mind, finished changing, and headed straight back down to the warehouse.

Where Moira lay unmoving, breathing shallowly.

Isabella had joined Maude, the pair of them carefully removing the last of the sticky red bandages on her stomach. "Did you see what did this to her?" Isabella asked, seeing my approach. "It looks to be shallower than I'd expect."

The final bandage was removed, leaving me to grimace. Even now, having just had my fill of battle and blood, hunger reared its ugly head. But I managed to force it down and look as asked, I had seen enough wounds to know it well enough.

"Sword blade." I answered. "Looks to be a panicked or surprised cut from whoever she was fighting." Huh. It made me wonder why they hadn't run her through, with a cut like that they'd have the opportunity. And she *was* an expert dualist. For someone to get a hit like that on her, they'd have to have swarmed her. It was almost like they thought they were coming for a rescue, not a kidnapping.

And then the reason for it all smacked me in the face with the force of a cannonball, my mouth hanging open in shock as I stood there and stared at the woman I'd cut so many down to save.

"They didn't think she'd fight." I murmured. "She didn't betray us." a hand raising slowly to my mouth.

The vindictive voice of hunger swirling in the back of my mind took the opportunity to say the one thing that could hurt the most as I looked at the woman trying not to die in front of me.

No… I saw the chains holding her down. Moira had nothing to do with this. The only person who got my people killed was me. They died because I couldn't protect them.

I'm *the source of the attack.*

She really was ours. Never theirs.

She was *mine.*

Isabella let out an annoyed sigh, as if to suggest —*of course, you idiot*— as she readied a poultice of some sort while Maude looked to be poking in her guts. I paced around them, like I was some judge of their work, or looking to guard Moira from the spectre of the Veiled Lady herself.

She looked pale, far too pale, her breathing far too shallow.

"Her intestine is somehow not damaged as far as I can tell…" Maude murmured, squinting into the wound. "But she's lost too much blood. I can patch her up, but it'll be touch and go for a bit." I bit my lip, crossing my arms as I tried to smother the building worry in my gut.

Trying to not let her words affect me, managing only a brief nod.

"I'll stay with her," I whispered, continuing to pace. Maude didn't argue or say I should be anywhere else, like I probably should've been. I could've been tabling losses, pushing the advantage, giving orders.

Should should should. So many shoulds.

But instead of doing anything I should've done, anything *Captain Claire Vessia* should be doing, once Isabella vacated her seat to tend to others in worse condition, I swooped in to take her place, reaching out to hold Moira's hand. It felt light in my grasp, and cold.

Cold. To *me.*

I rubbed my thumb into her palm as Maude started stitching up the mess of her stomach.

Hunger roiled in my gut, pain in my jaw, and my crew and family laid dead or dying around me. With nothing to be done but sit here and wait to see if I would lose Moira so soon after I pulled her into my life, I leaned down to put her freezing hand to my lips as I mouthed a prayer to the Goddess of Fortune into her skin.

I needed her to bless Moira, since today she had obviously turned from *me.*

CHAPTER TWENTY-THREE

*"Lord Admiral, I'm afraid to say that the Squadron is
now officially overdue."*

*"They'll turn up. Three of our best ships? Nearly three thousand of our
best men in uniform? With the element of surprise? I'll admit Vessia is
a good Captain, but her winning this fight is an impossibility. They're
probably just combing the settlement for our 'prisoner'. Trust me
Commander, they'll turn up."*

*"Lord Admiral, I'm just saying. I think we should be prepared. Vessia
sending three-thousand of our best to the bottom of the Great Divide
would sure as hell stir up the Church again."*

**—An update on the 57th Squadron to Randall Givens, Lord
Admiral of the Royal Kitaxian Navy, given by his
Chief of Staff, Commander Leplanche**

"Ma'am?" the voice at my door stated. "Markus and Rodger are here."

I nodded in the dark, giving Moira's hand a little squeeze, before lifting myself up from my bedside where she was sleeping soundlessly. I'd dragged my chair from my desk to my bunk, and had been watching over my charge like a silent, cold, stone-faced gargoyle.

Beds were currently at a premium, and so I'd given Moira mine. Her heart was slow and rhythmic, but getting stronger by the day.

Walking to my cabin doors, I thanked the sailor who'd given me the news, and he returned a brief salute. He wasn't one I recognized. One of the new faces we'd taken on to make up for our losses.

Our *substantial* losses.

Stepping out into the light of day, the sun bled through the cloud cover seemingly to specifically smite me. My skin itched painfully, a feeling of burning flesh skittering over my exposed arms as I closed the door lightly behind me, walking across the busy weather deck to where Markus and Rodger were just climbing aboard. I clasped Rodger's hand with a grim smile that he didn't return.

A look like that told me I was about to get news I wouldn't like.

That's what these past three days had been full of.

Letting go of his hand, I looked from him to Markus, moving to greet my quartermaster as well, but instead he only stared at me with hollow eyes, shrugging me aside to slink off towards his cabin.

"Markus?" I called out, now *very* worried about whatever news they had to deliver.

But Markus didn't answer, or even turn to face me. He just kept walking towards the officer's quarters, opening the door and disappearing inside.

I turned back to Rodger, who was staring at his shoes, a look of pure misery on his face.

"Claire," he said, his voice barely audible. He very obviously didn't want to say what he was about to say. After a moment, only once I'd clasped his shoulder, did he finally let out a shaky breath and nodded to himself. "We have the final counts... and... they found his parents."

I closed my eyes briefly in agony, suddenly understanding Markus's expression.

Oh, by all the Gods, no.

"Both of them?" I asked, staring after the still open door to the officer's quarters.

"His... sister is in Seven Peaks. That's all he has left." He let out another shuddered breath, holding his elbows as if to stop himself falling apart. "A cannonball hit their house. They died in the collapse."

I held a hand to my face, unable to believe the loss. I'd *only met them* recently. Two more faces that I'd never see again, memories full of smiles and laughter at unsubtle hints towards Markus that he should be chasing a relationship with *me*. The fact that hear their voices again felt like I'd swallowed lead, a weight in my gut.

And that wasn't even the worst of the news.

"How many?" I asked, not moving my hand from my face, moving it to cover my mouth as I stared into the deck.

Rodger gulped once more, his own eyes closing.

"Fifty-six of the regular crew, eighty of the watchmen. Of the civilians... more than two hundred."

The anger, paired with the hunger, roared in my chest.

Ameritia will pay.

It was time to end this.

I *had* to end this.

"There's one more thing," Rodger said, quietly interrupting my brooding thoughts of blood-soaked revenge.

He reached into his coat pocket to hand a bloodstained letter towards me. "This was on one of the commanders on the beach." He didn't elaborate what was written there, or what had been done with the man, but I took it as if it held poison, fighting the temptation to rip it into pieces.

"Thank you. Get the others. Meeting in half an hour in the warehouse," I commanded.

"Aye ma'am," he replied with a nod, marching off back down the gangplank.

I breathed in an aggravated sigh as sailors worked around me to stock the *Wraith* with as much as we could manage.

They didn't know where we were going, nor did we really have a destination. Our one safe harbour lay in ruins.

Where *could* we go?

I walked back into my quarters, the relief of darkness a silent relaxation in the set of my shoulders, sitting by Moira's bedside. Her soft breathing was my only real comfort these last few days.

Looking over her, with her bandaged chest, covers pulled up to her chin, red hair a waterfall over my pillows... My hunger swirled in my stomach, my jaw ached. She was *vulnerable*, and the monster in me knew it. I could drain her dry right this instant.

But.

I... liked her. She was pretty, smart, and deviously funny. She wanted to be free of Kitaxia just as much as I did. And... I had promised.

She signed the Code. She was *mine*. I wouldn't so easily toss her aside for hunger.

Forcing myself to restrain the beast in my head, I sighed as I leaned back into my chair and opened the crinkled letter, the damn thing seemingly a step away from collapsing into pieces from salt and blood. Yet somehow, it was still legible.

Barely.

To Admiral Stevenson of the 57th squadron,

From the desk of Lady Ameritia August, Heir apparent to the Kingdom of Kitaxia and wife of the Lord of the Admiralty:

Your orders are as follows: Sail to the James Strait in south-eastern Varcna, and head for the waters off the port of Souris, where the crown has learned that the dread pirate Claire Vessia makes berth with her crew. The locals are apparently sympathetic to her cause, and are Varcnan citizens, but head them no special quarter.

You are to burn Souris to the ground, and penetrate Vessia's deepest defences.

You are no doubt wondering why a Kitaxian naval squadron is being sent to storm Varcnan lands, and although your questions of the crown would be hardly permitted, I will mitigate some of your concerns.

Vessia has captured my son, Prince Nicholas. You, as a personal friend of the royal family, are one of the few in the kingdom aware of his 'condition' and therefore able to recognize him. He is of extreme import to the crown, Vessia has likely hidden him away in some confined corner of the settlement.

Once she and her crew are dead, you will search high and low for him. Once you've recovered him, or his body in case of his demise, you are to return him to Haxla with all haste.

Do not disappoint in this task, and there shall be great reward upon your return. Included are detailed descriptions of Vessia's ship and crew, of which updated bounties have been posted in every city in the three nations of the Great Divide. If you bring forth Vessia alive by some miracle of the true God above us all, I will include her bounty on top of your reward.

Godspeed Admiral.
Lady Ameritia

I read the letter with disgust, tossing it to the floor.

All of this blood, for what? She didn't even care if Moira was brought back *alive*. I counted the dead in my head, imagining their faces. All that had died in this private war between me and Ameritia.

In a single day, Lady Ameritia had ordered as many people murdered as I had killed over nearly five years.

And those were just the ones I *knew* about.

I cupped my face into my hands, almost sick with disgust and grief. So many dead for nothing but hate.

It had to stop.

I had to find a way to *end it*, or we'd just be endlessly trading lives for all eternity.

Lifting my head from my hands to stare at Moira, her words suddenly so poignant. Her little speech I thought were naive and ill-thought. I'd been so focused on the blood, on the wreckage I could cause Kitaxian shipping... I didn't ever try to think of how to just... *end* things.

What would it take for peace?
I could end it. Once and for all.
I just have to be lucky.

I thought... maybe I had an answer. It would be a long shot, I was still so unsure, but if I succeeded... I let myself imagine it as I leaned back in my chair, and just tried to breathe through my exhaustion.

A world in which maybe, just *maybe*, I could rest. My revenge sated, with no oppressor threatening to rule over us with an iron fist, no one to threaten the lives of the poor, the innocent, and the *different*.

It was a dream, an *ideal*.

Dream or not, I hungered for it.

Imagining it, I fell asleep far too quickly.

As they always were, the dreams were waiting for me.

The chains, holding my body awkwardly to the wall. The laughing guard throwing his boot into my stomach. Lady Ameritia staring with a knowing smirk, pointing her bloodied needle at me from beyond the cell doors while the guard pulled my hair back painfully. All the while the noose tightened around my neck. The drop of the floor underneath me making the rope go taught, and as I choked back the air in my throat as the jeering of a thousand peasants watched me die.

I startled awake.

Long practised at this by now, I didn't rush myself. I didn't suddenly push to my feet in an effort to get away from my dreams. I didn't make a noise. But I rubbed at my eyes and a shuddered breath escaped my throat as I tried not to sob.

"I think that's the first time I've ever seen you be still for more than five minutes, let alone sleep," a weak voice sounded in the dark.

A voice I'd been aching to hear for three days.

I pulled my hands away from my eyes in surprise to see Moira, awake, looking at me with concern, a low light from some disheveled curtain behind my desk giving her just enough light to see. I leaned forward, reaching to take her hand with a smile, but stopped myself, remembering she wanted nothing to do with me.

"You're awake," I said, hearing the relief in my own voice. She nodded, smiling right back at me. I began to stand, to get out of her hair, and to get the doctors. "I'll get Maude. I'll be—"

"Sit your ass down, Captain," she demanded.

I stopped mid-rise, and did as I was told, letting my body settle back into the comfort of the chair. I folded my hands into each other in between my legs, learning forward towards her.

Those damn eyes of hers welling up with tears, making the green in them all the more crystalized.

"You came back for me," she stuttered, almost crying, her voice breaking.

"Of course I did," I replied, but she lightly shook her head, reaching out towards my folded hands. I opened them for her to grasp.

"No one's ever come back for me before," she said with a weak smile, squeezing my hand lightly. I gently replied in kind, afraid I'd break her.

A moment where we did nothing but quietly look into each other's eyes passed, her looking to form some words or request.

That I would wait eternity for.

"Don't… say anything. Just sit with me please," she finally asked. "I'm… not the greatest I've ever felt. And you make me happy. For some stupid reason," she muttered, shaking her head in frustration.

Afraid I'd break this moment between us, I didn't dare say a word, didn't dare move.

But she was planning on shattering it anyway. "I'm going to lay here and feel terrible and enjoy your company," she began to say in a huff. "At least until I'm on my feet again. Upon which I'm going to go back to trying to stop remembering that you exist."

I winced.

I didn't say anything. She hadn't asked me to. I sat there and held her hand as her eyes closed and her breathing settled, but she kept her hand in mine. I kept it there, holding as still as I could until she fell back asleep, her quiet breaths more even, her heart stronger every waking moment.

That comment at the end or no, I thanked every Goddess I could name that she would live.

She could hate me all she wanted, but as long as she *lived*, I would be happy.

But she wouldn't stay sleeping for long, and she obviously needed Maude or Isabella to look her over. Plus, I had a meeting with the officers here any minute now, if I hadn't missed it already.

I filled a mug full of water from my canteen, set it on the bedside counter, and left a quick scribbled note.

*Back shortly. Meeting to plan next moves. Drink and rest up.
— Claire*

I set it under the mug, and gave one last glance towards the woman in my bed.

I couldn't help pushing one stray strand of hair free of her face, letting a cool finger slide down her cheek. She let out an exhausted sigh at the interruption, murmuring in her sleep.

Knowing she was going to be alright lifted a weight from my shoulders I hadn't known was there to begin with. I left her in my cabin, setting out towards the warehouse.

Our secret dock had, for all intents and purposes, become a refugee camp.

It'd been three days since the siege. All attackers that had been found alive had been interrogated and shot, all of them stating the same inevitable truth.

Kitaxia knew where we were. They would send more ships. Some of the higher ups in ranks that I hadn't personally slaughtered in my blood rage had stated that there was even a payoff to the merchant princes of Varcna City to blame the destruction of the port entirely on *me*.

That didn't go well to keeping them alive.

We were out of options. We had no idea *when* more ships would come, but they *would* come.

The question was, did we abandon Souris? Or stay and defend it?

If we did the former, the next question was where did we go? And no one had a good answer. If we did the latter, the question was more dire. Because then it was the morbid calculus of asking ourselves how long we could hold out.

Kitaxia had an entire navy to throw at us. We had *one* good ship, a coastal defence battery, some friendly merchants with ships of their own, maybe a smattering of a handful of other pirates who *might* help. But if we stayed, we'd be pinned down, never able to pirate on the open seas again.

It'd be a slow and painful death.

I had a different plan.

The docks and warehouses were a mess of bodies and supplies, turned from storage into a temporary field hospital and emergency housing.

Cots lined nearly every spare space, a holding area for two hundred wounded, while tents lined outside were crammed full of the displaced from Souris.

We really wouldn't have the final body count for quite some time yet, not until we'd dug out the last of our dead from the rubble.

The smell of the dying permeated the docks, blood in every corner, my hunger harder to control by the second. Smothering the urge to tear and gorge myself on the cries of the wounded was a never-ending war in my mind for control.

I breathed through my teeth, always staring straight ahead while trying to avoid the smell, as I made my way into the warehouse's side office. Everyone but Charlotte was waiting patiently. They had decided to sleep in the battery with a full complement, just in case more ships showed up.

Maude and Isabella were also missing, but one of them promised to be here for this despite the fact they were too busy saving lives. Most of their dire cases were over by now.

Jacine and Rodger were talking animatedly by the window. Rodger seemed to have gotten over his hangover after the opposing ships were sunk, throwing himself into whatever task assigned to him with guilt-motivated ferocity. Jacine had been helping Maude and Isabella, making splints, setting bones, even improvised amputations. We were that desperate.

She was a carpenter, and a carpenter knew saws.

Markus… was a shell of a man. Sitting in the middle of the room before the desk, looking at nothing and everything, a thousand-yard stare boring into the carpeted floor.

Guilt reared its ugly head as I wondered if I could've done

something to save his parents. *Anything* to relieve him of this pain.

But there was nothing I could do. I couldn't protect my own people. Some monster I was.

I was only good at taking life.

And I had one more life to take.

I cleared my throat to announce my arrival, everyone save Markus looked up to nod towards me.

"Glad you all made it," I said with a weak smile. "Now, as soon as one of—ah, here she is." I stepped out of the way of the door.

Maude dashed around me, talking as she marched. "Let's make it quick, I have a billion things to do please," she muttered, taking the office chair behind the desk. I'd been intending to take it, but she looked ready to fall over in exhaustion, her eyes sullen and red-rimmed. I didn't find myself wanting to rob her of the only rest she'd get.

"Alright. Quickly then." I nodded, putting my hands on my hips as I silently paced, wondering how I'd sell this, examining each face in the room that was waiting for whatever I'd call this meeting for to be said already.

Just get it over with.

It only ends with her.

"I want to go to Haxla, and kill the royal family," I stated, already cursing the words the moment I said them.

My voice seemed to hang in the air, hovering like fog, making the air thick to breathe as each heart hammered in turn.

Even Markus raised his head from the floor to stare at me with widened eyes.

Good. He's still in there.

"I'm in. So is Isabella I assume," Maude muttered, standing up from the chair with a groan. "Now if you'll excuse me, I have lives to save before we all go throw ours away," she said, her tone almost polite, leaving just as quickly as she stormed in.

Leaving me in my own state of shock.

"I uh... huh," I mumbled out, running a hand through my hair in surprise. "I wasn't expecting her to agree to that."

Jacine let out a brief laugh at the same time, before Rodger spoke up. "I know the palace like no one else here. You're doomed to fail without me... I'm in," he admitted quietly, stroking his moustache.

"Me too. Where the *Wraith* goes, I go," Jacine said, her laughter morphing into the first warm smile I'd seen on her in days, tapping at her chest in reassurance.

"Markus?" I asked quietly, turning to my last officer, my oldest friend.

He breathed out a sigh so long and shuddered, I nearly jumped in fright. It was the most life I'd seen out of him in days.

"Can you give me and the captain a moment please?" he whispered, just loud enough for us to hear, his voice hoarse.

"Of course. Come on," Jacine replied in kind. She grabbed Rodger by the wrist and dragged him out the door, and closing it behind them.

Leaving me and Markus alone in the quiet room.

The silence became somehow absolute, despite the office being the centre of so much chaos. Just outside the door, people screamed in pain, Maude and Isabella saved lives, Rodger and Jacine beginning to coordinate cargo for some ridiculous notion of a last hurrah.

My frantic energy wanted to pace, my hunger wanted to rip into Markus's throat, and my anger wanted to scream at him to join me.

I held it all in check, electing to sit on the desk before him, leaning down to meet his eye-level.

"The truth is Claire, I'm not in the best state of mind right now. I'm... hurting," he quietly admitted. He breathed in a sigh, looking out the office window to the broken bodies beyond. "I'm not sure throwing everything we have left at one final roll of the dice is the best idea... But now that... that..." He sobbed through his tears, ugly intakes of breath. "I don't know. Now that they're dead... I can't tell you no. I want the bastards to pay as much as anyone." He choked out, his cries reaching every corner of the room before he looked up at me.

I forced my throat to swallow, nodding as I ground my teeth together.

"I understand," I said quietly.

"My family is dead. I have to go north and tell my sister." He motioned vaguely in the direction of Norlondia. "And now you're telling me that you want to go into the belly of the beast, headquarters of the fleet, and assassinate the royals? The ones who did this—" he motioned towards me, up and down. I knew what he meant. "—to you? After all this time? Why? Why *now*?"

I clenched the wood of the desk, grinding my teeth, forcing my fangs to hold where they were. I didn't know that I could explain.

"Because it's all I have left, Markus," I admitted. "I'm out of moves. They won't stop, *she* won't stop, until all of us are dead, and I'm..." My throat closed for just a moment, remembering once again the iron coffin on the Count's ship. It made me reach for my throat, the rope burn still fresh in my mind, the sensation playing on my skin even now.

The memory of the noose was never too far away.

There was only one way this was going to play out.

"I'm telling you this, and only you," I let go of the desk, rubbing at my thighs in worry, wondering exactly how this would go over with him.

"We're not going to Haxla. *I'm* going to Haxla," I stated.

He squinted his eyes in confusion at my explanation, just for a moment, before they widened in understanding.

"You're dropping me off so I can do it myself, and then either she's dead, or you're going to never see me again," I stated, now that the words were in the air, a feeling of assuredness settling over me.

Markus's mouth slowly gaped open as his eyes welled up, his expression shifting from fury to fear and back again.

"No. Absolutely not," he demanded, rising from his chair in an angry rush. "That is the most idiotic thing I've ever heard come from your mouth." He paced around his chair, beginning to rant. "And I've heard *a lot* of stupid shit out of your mouth. But this takes the cake. You think you're just going to waltz in there and kill her? Claire, no. Just, no. We'll think of something else. We're not done yet, we can find another port—"

"She won't stop Markus," I interrupted, shaking my head as I locked my gaze at my boots, pushing my hair out of my face. The quiet pleading in my voice that finally broke him.

He stopped his pacing, shaking his own head, as the tears continued down his cheek. He grasped the back of his chair, leaning onto it to hold himself up.

"Claire... We just lost so much. *I* just lost so much. Don't ask us to lose you too," he whispered, just barely biting back a full breakdown.

My heart broke for him. For the crew. For everything we built here.

It was over. My grand scheme of life outside of Kitaxia, biting at the heels of the empire.

But it didn't have to end. Not if I ended Ameritia first.

I hopped off the desk, pushing the chair to the side and wrapped my arms around Markus's broad chest, hugging him tightly.

I hated that as I placed my head against his chest, even now in this charged moment with his heart thumping in my ear, that my hunger *roared*.

"Markus... I love you like a brother," I whispered. "But I need to do this. Not just for me, but for all of us. If I win... then things might *actually* change. *Kitaxia* might change. This is how I keep you all safe *for good*. And... I need your help to do it."

His arms crept around me, as if unsure at this moment of affection.

"Please, help me," I pleaded.

I could hear his lungs expand with a sigh, his heartbeat in my chest that even now, I had to clench my teeth to keep from screaming and ripping into him.

"Claire... You're my sister, my comrade in arms, and my best friend. I think you're a stupid fucking idiot, but because you asked... I'll help you. What do you need?"

CHAPTER TWENTY-FOUR

"Hunger. On one hand, feeding as a Vampyri is a strangely intimate experience, a relationship between predator and prey. Testing has proven that unless the Vampyri in question is focused on dealing harm, the Human subject finds it a pleasurable experience. But to entertain a thought of this scientist being philosophical for a moment, the hunger of Vampyri presents an interesting challenge for society. We take, and take, and take, our hunger driving us to take everything there is to take, and provide nothing in return to our ecosystems. Nothing for our prey to thrive. This scientist wonders if Vampyri are truly symbiotic to Humans, or simply a virus designed by one of the Thousand Goddesses to wipe out humanity."

— From the journals of Valerie Du Bois, Scholar lord of Draculesti

I was starving.

We'd set sail, heading straight for Haxla, but I wasn't sure if I would last that long.

I hadn't fed in days. *Weeks.*

Maude and Isabella had put their foot down, with a third of the crew dead, half the remaining crew wounded, there would be limited blood available, if any.

First it was the anger, the *crankiness.* How annoyed I was by every little thing. How bad I thought it was then, ha. If only I'd known.

Then it was the sickness. Weak limbs, old wounds aching, my hair turning grey.

I was down to one vial a week. A single little vial of barely anything, more wetting my taste than anything resembling an actual *meal.*

Now it was the *madness.*

My throat was maddeningly dry, my thirst unquenchable, food and water made me sick, and my eyes... had long turned to red, no trace of green within them.

I didn't dare take my glasses off outside of my cabin.

It was the same, day in, day out. Pacing a tight circle around my cabin, sure to wear down the floorboards into dust, maddeningly rubbing my jaw and throat as it ached, my fangs refusing to recede. It was if my muscles refused to obey any longer, now the monster was incapable of hiding.

But I mandated no change of course. While we had plenty enough rations to see us through this venture, We were in no state to do a proper boarding, and I would risk no more lives until this was *done*.

I would rather starve myself than have us lose one more person to Kitaxia.

But Gods, was that a challenge.

I didn't dare look in my mirror, afraid of what new detail I would discover about this cursed existence.

Never had I been so hungry, not even since the very beginning, with Harold.

His face haunted me. Looming in the shadows like a cruel taunt in every dark shadow of my cabin. If I could kill him, my saviour from the sea, why not kill some poor crewman?

We could continue to sail with one mysterious death, couldn't we? I could—No.

I cursed, pacing even more, looking for anything, *anything* to distract myself.

But we wouldn't be in Haxla for days yet.

I chewed on my finger, circling my cabin in as wide an arc as possible, worry and stress eating at me from the inside. My fangs prickled the skin of my finger, and I nearly fainted at the taste of my own blood, instantly dropping to all fours, coughing as if to puke.

Thank the Gods I was alone in my cabin again. Moira had vacated my bunk without a word the day Maude had given her the all-clear to return to work. It had left me as broken hearted as when she'd left me on the dancefloor, but I could've lived with that. As long as she was alive. But if she had to see this…

"Damn it... Damn it all to hells..." I raised my shaky hand to my face, licking the spot my fangs had nicked clean, feeling the skin seal.

For whatever reason, the taste of my own blood was anathema. It made me immediately and deliberately ill, and I took steps to avoid it. Yet another rule of my life.

But I needed something. *Anything*, to get my mind off of my hunger. *Maybe... maybe there's a hidden store!*

Maude was smart like that, maybe she hid some away just in case...

I shook my head free of the pipe dream. I'd asked her, *several times* already, and she didn't need me bothering her for what I was sure was the ninetieth time since we left Souris.

I'd been fighting off intrusive thoughts for days now, twisting my every perception into suspicion and betrayal hiding in every corner.

'That crewman is hiding a Scarwood stake, better drain him and sift through his memories just to be sure!' 'Gracie was hiding blood in her flask!' 'Maude kept a secret vault of vials!'

It never ended.

Letting my body fall to my side onto the floor, I shook my head, trying to free my thoughts of secrets laying just out of reach, rocking back and forth, holding my knees, running a hand through my hair.

But... what if... Maude is hiding it... all for herself!

I growled, stopping all movement, my mind a mess of fog. There was no way that was possible. Maude wasn't a *Vampyri*. Why would she hoard blood?

But the hunger wasn't interested in listening to reason.

I had my coat, hat, and spectacles on before I brought my mind to a skittering halt.

Claire. Get a hold of yourself.

I ground my teeth, my fangs making it slightly awkward in my mouth, but since I was dressed... I held my lips firmly closed, and walked out into the evening air, silently thankful it wasn't daytime.

If I'd thought the daylight had been bad before, it was downright malicious when I was this hungry. My eyes had felt like they were burning out of their sockets being out in the light, my skin actively boiling, smoking even just from the ambient sun. The very idea of that cursed orb in the sky enough to make me seethe in the dark.

I told myself I was just going in for a 'chat' with Maude, in hopes that some new solution would present itself.

The logical part of my mind knew better. Or what was left of it at least.

My hunger was harder to control with every step. I dared not breathe, least I smell some crewmate and lose control.

I strode below decks, eyes locked forward, not acknowledging a soul, and all but swooped into the surgery bay.

"Claire. What are you doing here?" Maude's voice of impatience carried through the surgeon's office before I'd even passed the flap separating it from the passageway. She sat at her desk, looking over at me as if to dare me to demand something of her.

"I'm... I'm just..." I stuttered, doing my best to hide my fangs with pursed lips.

Maude sighed, taking off her glasses, rubbing at her eyes, before tossing them onto her desk. "I can't, Claire. I can't justify it, and I've given you all I can without risking the crew's own health. Including *me*." She smirked, letting her hand fall from her face to close her eyes sleepily. She'd given me more of *her* blood than anyone else's. I could see the faintness in her eyes, her pale skin.

"You can't get blood from a stone," she murmured.

It was the way she'd said it, as if it was a funny quip. That I was so hungry that it was *funny*.

I slammed my hand onto the doorframe, my fingers digging into the wood as if it were mere putty. "Then get more, damn it!" I screamed into the office, my breaths heavy and laboured with how hard I was trying to hold myself back from jumping her then and there.

She staggered out of her chair, backing into the wall, staring at me with newfound fear and terror.

Yes, be afraid, for your life. You're next.

But... that was *Maude*. One of my oldest friends.

I couldn't *eat* Maude.

I turned my head away in a rush, needing to get away from her now, before I did something I'd regret.

"Claire?" Maude's voice stammered out in a panic, before I ran away from the surgeon's office, back towards my cave of solitude.

At least there I wouldn't be tempted to murder my own crew.

I rushed past several panicked faces and stammered questions, but didn't give a single reply. My mind focused to the point of getting back to my cabin, because if I wavered from that point, I would kill someone.

Slamming the doors closed behind me, I finally let myself breathe, alone in the quiet of my room, my thoughts a raging tempest of terror and hunger.

"FUCK!" I screamed, flipping my map table over storming over to my desk ready to toss it through the windows.

Only to stop dead as a statue as a knock sounded on my door.

I paused, heaving in a breath, ready to tear into the person who walked in my door, my fangs fully bared in anticipation.

I waited.

It was Maude with the vials. She had to have seen how bad I was, and changed her mind. It has to be her!

Maybe, just maybe, I could take those, and fight the urge to tear into her long enough for the vials of blood to settle some of the hunger. And hopefully not kill her.

The growl that escaped my throat terrified me as the door opened.

Because the next person to walk into my quarters wasn't Maude with dreamed up vials.

"Captain?" Moira's unsure voice said, the door closing behind her quietly as she stepped into the darkness.

I whirled around, jaws open wide in a roar, the last of my humanity lost as I charged her.

She wasn't afraid. She looked *resigned.*

The hunger drove me forward. I didn't want to hurt her, I didn't. But I craved her. *Needed* to taste her. My hunger would not be denied its violence. I stopped short of tackling her to the floor, but the force of my momentum slammed her back against the doors.

Not so much holding her aloft, but instead pinning her against the door, a guttural growl escaped my throat. An inhuman noise of terror.

But her heart betrayed no fear.

Pulling herself taut against me, she tilted her head to the side, giving me easy access as her hand reached around and into my hair and pushed me into her neck.

As my fangs bit into her, she held onto me tightly… and I *drank*.

The taste of her... her flavour of sorrowful song… that same flavour I'd nearly dreamt about since I'd first tasted it months ago.

The taste of the love of her people, the shame of her god, and the twists of secrets in secrets. She tasted of the hatred of her parents, her family, and the craving for anything but what she was born to do. It was a sweet and mournful song, and it was music to me.

I drank all of her fears and worries, her loves and joys, and just as I started to taste the deepest pits of what she thought of *me*... it hit me that I had taken far too much from her.

"Claire…" she whispered weakly, tugging on my hair lightly. "That's enough. Please. You're hurting me."

Hunger rolled in my gut, demanding *more*.

She's a princess. Drain her dry and forever remove the stain of Kitaxia from—

No.

Hunger would not get the best of Claire Vessia this day.

I pulled back from her neck, licking the droplets of blood from the wounds my teeth had made, deliberately slowly, and I felt her shudder underneath my tongue. I went to step back, her blood trailing from my chin, but it rapidly became apparent that I had indeed taken too much.

Barely able to stand, she began to fall.

Shit.

I caught her up in my arms as she collapsed against the door, suddenly worried I'd hospitalized her *again*.

She let out a light sigh, despite her heart suddenly needing to work *extra* hard in her chest. I placed her gently in my bunk, which made her laugh darkly.

"How is it, despite trying to avoid you, this is the second time I've ended up in your bed?" she demanded sheepishly, her tone betraying an light-headedness.

I couldn't help my laugh matching hers. "You're as dangerous as you are delicious," I said quietly, repeating the words I had spoken over our duel.

Stepping away from the bedside, touching a finger to trap her blood trailing out of my mouth, sucking it dry. My hunger, *thank the Gods*, was so much better.

I was still ravenous. It would take far more than just a paltry feeding to satisfy the eternal test against my willpower, but she'd bought me some fucking *sanity* for the moment.

She watched me with some discernible hunger of her own, but there was no surprise there.

"Do you need Maude?" I asked. I'd taken so much that a part of me was worried I'd done some permanent injury. But her heart was strong, and there was a smile on her face, but I was still having trouble *thinking* past how fucking delicious she tasted.

She shook her head, trying to raise herself out of bed.

Oh no. Not just after I'd nearly killed her.

Again.

"Lay. Down," I ordered, putting a hand to her shoulder. There was no way in the nine burning realms that she was getting up when she could barely walk.

She stopped, and fell back into the blankets. Probably remembering that my bunk was a lot cozier than her own.

Rolling my eyes at her determination to escape my cabin despite the second near-death experience she'd had in recent memory, I walked over to grab a chair from the fallen mess of my map table, dragging it back to my bedside.

What in the nine burning realms she was doing here, *now*, was beyond me.

I fell back into the chair, leaning forward over the bed frame, resting my head on my folded hands. Swallowing the last tastes of her, I felt my sour mood and hunger slowly settle ever more.

Enough for me to have a lucid conversation.

"You knew," I said quietly, not in the form of a question. That much was obvious with how she had practically invited me to feast on her.

She nodded. "I knew for a while. Since that moment you stole a bit of my ale. Right after the storm on that second day." That was… *earlier* than I thought she would've figured it out.

I remembered the moment she mentioned. When I had taken off my spectacles to scare some sense into her.

She'd seen the red in my eyes.

I breathed in and out, letting out a pained laugh. "Maude figured it out in a similar way," I admitted quietly.

She pulled my sheets up to her chin, clutching them in her fist, some mix of revulsion and desire mixing on her face as she looked me over.

"I'm sorry," I said quietly, my eyes turning down to the floor in guilt. "I've been… pushing myself. I hadn't fed since—"

"Since the battle with the captain," she interrupted.

"So, you did see that," I murmured in idiotic self-defeat.

"Claire, how the fuck could I not? You pulled a *sword out of your chest*. It was right in front of me," she replied exasperatedly.

I shrugged, unsure what to say. She hadn't brought it up afterwards. I'd assumed it was just one more thing lost in the thick of battle.

A sigh, a look shared between us. She demurred, her face adopting worry.

When did I let her start calling me 'Claire'?

"But if you hadn't fed since then…" she all but whispered, clenching the sheets tightly. "I'm surprised I'm not a corpse right now."

I raised an eyebrow and said the only thing I could've. "You asked me to stop."

Her face silently morphed into shock, mouth hanging open. "You… what? How?" she asked, voice full of disbelief.

Shaking my head, I admitted probably the worst kept secret on this entire ship. "I'd never willingly hurt you, Moira. Never. Even at my worst."

Her eyes narrowed at me, as if I had lied.

"I assumed you were feeding on someone, or multiple crew. But no one's showing the signs. How do you do it?"

I tilted my head at her questioningly, before realizing she would know *a lot* about *Vampyri* feeding habits from her mother.

What *were* the signs of constant feeding?

"Answer the question," she demanded when I didn't immediately answer her. A determination in her gaze that was inviolable.

I wanted to scoff at her, ask her a million different things about what she knew…

But something told me that everything she thought of me would depend on my answer.

"Maude and Isabella know," I explained. "They get a vial from each of the crew once a year for 'medical purposes.' I take a vial a day usually, feed enough on prizes to buy a free week. It helps offshoot the days of the year we don't have covered. But with the battle..."

Her eyes widened in surprise, as if she couldn't believe what she was hearing. "Huh."

Quietly, she absorbed this information. I could almost hear the cranks turning in her head, only to be drowned out by the silent thrum of waves against the hull outside, the whistle of wind against the windows.

She looked pale, paler than Maude had been, giving *me* a run for my money. I didn't know if it was because of her complexion, or from my feeding, or both.

"Are you *sure* you don't need Maude?" I asked.

She nodded, sinking deep into my blankets. "I'll be okay. The room is spinning profusely, and I'm light headed as all hell, and I think I might faint if I stand," she said in slurred speech.

"Maybe I should—" I began to say before she interrupted me, waving off my concern.

"Maude will be here soon anyway. She sent me up here."

That surprised me. "... Why?" I asked.

She shrugged, nuzzling my pillow. "Because. She said you were in a bit of a craze. Needed someone to talk you down from doing something stupid. I knew you hadn't fed in a while, and figured you had hit a breaking point." She smiled as she said the next bit. "Wanted to see what you'd do with me."

Now it was *my* turn to be surprised. I laughed, sitting back in my chair, shaking my head profusely. She had tempted death. "And? Did

I live up to expectations?"

She stuck her tongue out at me, making me laugh even more. But after my laugh had quieted, she...

Looked at me.

Really looked at me. Eyes glistening with what I was almost certain was adoration.

"You keep on surprising me, Claire Vessia," she said quietly.

That caught me. I didn't even have a chance to respond as she rolled over, seemingly to end the conversation, slowly falling asleep in my bed.

Leaving me with nothing but the sound of the ship breaking through the waves, the muffled thumps of crew above and below, and her quiet breathing. It wasn't minutes before her heart slowed to that pace of rest I knew so well from her recovery.

I grabbed a spare blanket, and threw it gently over her body.

She was quiet, her heart slow but steady, and I found myself in amazement of her. She knew I was bloodthirsty, dangerous, all but certain to kill her, and yet strode in here like she had a death wish.

She had stared her death, *me*, in the face, and I had blinked first.

Oh Gods. I'm in deep for her.

I... I'm pretty sure I'm in love with her.

That feeling settled into my gut, with a warmth and comfort that was all-consuming, seeming to dilute the very hunger in the back of my throat and for a moment, just a singular glorious moment while I looked at her sleeping soundly in the bed I often despised...

I lived without worry.

After briefly showing Maude that I didn't leave Moira a bloodless corpse like she had expected, I thought I should take my time quietly using the first clear thoughts I'd had in weeks to plan an assassination on Lady Ameritia.

But then I had a better idea.

Moira slept through the entire next day, and into the following evening, awakening to see me lighting candles, a yawn escaping her. "That was the best sleep I've ever gotten on this ship," she said, stretching her arms over her head, the *crick-crack* of her shoulders audible from my bed. "Why do you get the best bed on the ship? You don't even use it," she mumbled sleepily, running her hand over the sheets.

I froze mid-lighting the last of the candles, staring at her with a raised eyebrow from the dining table, silently inviting her to think more about what she had just said.

She gulped, slipping out of the covers I had thrown over her. "Right. Sore subject. Anyway, I'm sure there's a million work orders waiting for—"

"Get over here, Moira," I commanded in the tone I reserved for captaining.

She stopped dead halfway to the door.

I pulled out one of the chairs to my mapping table. It'd been set back upwards, but it was cleared of maps this night. It's original purpose as a dining table in use once again.

Laid out across the table was the finest dining we had on board. The original silverware that I had never used once, a hidden bottle of wine from the back of a cabinet I'd ignored for months, stew, veggies, and even the remnants of some rabbit that was hunted right before we left Souris.

Gracie had been ecstatic when I'd asked her for this miniature feast.

"Sit," I said quietly, pointing down at the chair in my hands, severely enough that it was an order. Yet she looked about ready to bolt. "Doctor Winter's orders," I added, making her grumble, but she walked over to sit in the offered chair. Once she'd sat down, I pushed her into the table with an over gracious bow.

"Oh, so chivalrous Captain," she said, sarcasm bleeding through her voice. But her eyes opened wide as I popped the cork off the wine, and poured into the silver goblet.

"Where in the blazes did you get a Varcnan Chateau 1632?" she asked with amazement, eyes locked on the label.

I chuckled darkly, pouring my own cup. "Pirate," I whispered.

"Fair point. It's just I haven't seen this vintage since I was a teenager. Mother was dying to get her hands on one for ages." She sipped at it and let out a quiet moan of pleasure while I sat down at her right.

"Tell me about her, if you want," I asked, hoping for any conversation I could get with her.

Even if it was about my immortal enemy.

She eyed me warily over the cup of her goblet. But after taking a bite of the rabbit, her face melted into a bit of bliss, and finally gave me a little of herself.

"She's a very… spiteful woman," she murmured around her food. I wanted to snort at her statement of fact. That I was *here* was ample evidence of that.

"She hates everyone, save her favourites. I'm pretty sure she doesn't even like father, despite me existing. She's exact, taxing, and precise, but she also likes… I don't know how to describe it. Fascinating people and things? If you somehow impress or surprise her, you'll be the apple of her eye for a bit. She likes to see what people will do when given the opportunity."

I nodded along, delighted that she was sharing anything at all with me, learning about a bit of Ameritia I'd never thought to see.

"What about your father?" I asked, swirling my wine in its goblet. It was… *fine*. But I wished I could've had it spiked with something… stronger.

She shrugged, digging into her plate of food while I barely sipped at my drink. My hunger still simmered, and I didn't have to pretend to like food for her. Still didn't stop me stealing a bit from her plate every so often, which earned me a glare in mid-explanation.

"He's… the exact opposite of mother. Stern in that military sense. Thinks the world can be solved if only he has enough ships and soldiers. Crunches numbers and calculations and not much else," she chuckled. "They must be absolutely livid that I didn't come home. I almost want to be a fly on the wall when they learned I disappeared off that ship."

An odd thought poked into my brain. "Funny you mention that. Hang on." I extracted myself from the dining table, drawing open a drawer in my desk, and reached for the letter from the washed-up admiral Rodger had given me. I sat back down and passed it to her. "This was found on one of the commanding officers of the attack," I said quietly, watching her take it up and begin to read.

She paled with every word. Her eyes panicked, avoiding mine. "What's your bounty up to now? She mentioned it."

I smirked. "Before the battle where I got *you*, it was twenty-five thousand." I said quietly. "The notice that was attached to this letter said a hundred thousand pieces of silver."

She paled even further. Any whiter and I'd swear she would be a ghost. It made me chuckle as I held my hand out for the letter. Not everyone was worth more than small islands.

She glanced over it once again, before placing it in my hand gently, as if it were a scorpion. I put it back into its place and settled back into my chair, where she was pouring a hearty second cup, downing half of it near instantly. I grabbed the edge of the goblet, slowly pulling it away from her face.

"Easy. You're still a bit hazy from blood loss. That's going to hit you like an iceberg," I warned.

She shook her head, almost regretfully putting her goblet down.

I barely heard her quiet murmur. "I just didn't think mother and father cared about me that much to justify such a thing."

I was surprised at her words.

"Only mother would be vindictive enough to go to Grandfather about me running the fuck away from home. *Again.*"

I considered her. Here was the girl who looked like how her blood tasted. Trying her damn best to get away from her family, her old world, her gilded cage.

And I would not let her go. She was *mine.*

"Well," I said, my tone evening out through a cleared throat to disguise my blush. "Regardless. As long as I'm alive, no one will drag you back there." That was my promise to her, and I intended to keep it.

She looked up at me with curiosity. "You're saying that just because you want in my pants," she said with a snort.

But I didn't laugh or even chuckle as I leaned forward. "I mean it. You signed the Code. You're one of us till death or release," I said quietly, reaching out to rest my hand on her cheek, cupping her chin. She didn't stop me. "And I don't plan on releasing you. Ever," I murmured, pulling her ever so close, to lean forward and kiss her. A chaste kiss, a second of her lips on mine. But *Gods*. The taste of wine on her lips as she gave a breathy gasp against my mouth. It took everything I had to pull away from her back into my chair.

She reached out towards me, but only my hand stayed in place, still cupping her cheek. She kissed the palm of my hand, her eyes hungry for more.

But there was something I needed to say, because this had gone on for too long.

"I will ask this once. You've been reluctant towards my advances, and I've pushed every boundary you had. I'm sorry for that and it ends tonight. If you say no, I will stop all of this. No questions asked, no more advances, no more flirting." I held a baited breath, suddenly the most scared I'd ever been in my life. I'd thought of her as *mine* ever since the battle. But she wasn't mine. She was *hers*. "With all that said… do you want me?"

I watched the very real fight in her eyes. She bit lightly into my hand. I tried to hold my expression as neutral as possible as I waited for eternity to pass while she deliberated.

The candles on the silver stands glowed quietly. The waves gently rocked the ship, the barest taps of rain beginning to beat against the windows. The muffled footsteps of crew above our heads on the quarterdeck. But loudest of all, her heart beating in her chest.

She sighed away from my hand, taking her goblet and downing the rest of her wine.

Once it was down her throat, she chucked the empty goblet over her shoulder, the thing clattering against the deck as I eyed her with a questioning glance and a raised eyebrow. Standing suddenly, she wrenched my chair out from the table in a huff, straddled onto my lap with a leg on either side, and pressed her lips onto mine in a breathy sigh.

That was answer enough.

Her hips ground against mine as I grabbed them and pulled her more tightly on top of me, smiling into her lips, a moan escaping her mouth. "That seemed——" I started in between breathy kisses. "A very enthusiastic——" Her hands wandering my neck, leaving a trail of warmth in their wake. "——answer." I wanted to eliminate any space between us, this was a taste of her I'd been wanting since the moment I met her, if I was being honest with myself.

She tore her mouth away from mine to mutter the one thing I'd been dying to hear before bringing her lips back to mine. "Shut up and fuck me, Captain," she demanded.

Growling, I slid my hands down her back and under her legs, lifting her with ease. Standing up from my chair, pushing the table clear with a brief free hand, the clutter of silverware tumbling across the table and onto the floor. Before I finally set her roughly onto it, her legs wrapping around my waist as I leaned down on top of her.

She tugged my shirt over my head with ease, and as I let it flow off me, before standing up straight to let her get a view, while my hand wandered over her top.

Reaching for me, I could see her eyes wandering over my topless frame. I laughed as I moved away from her grasp, instead reaching for her boots, tugging them away with ease, then moved to her pants.

She seized up for a moment, her heartbeat staggered from excitement into fear, confusing me briefly as to why. I paused for all but a breath, but continued once she nodded at me.

Grabbing the waist of her pants and pulling them down, her fear melted away. I ran my hand up her shirt, her searching hand grasping my wrist to hold onto as I began kissing her lower abdomen, sneaking under her thigh and up under her waist to push her up into my kisses as I went slowly lower, and lower still towards her centre.

Her hitched breathing made me smile as I bit her lightly here and there, not with my fangs, but little teasing bites, making her flinch with every tiny nip.

Fangs were for later.

Finally, ever so slowly, ever so teasingly, I kissed the very top of her centre, a little bushel of well trimmed red hair tickling my lips. I lifted her right foot to sit on the table, opening her wide, while I adjusted her left thigh to rest on my shoulder.

I kissed the inside of her thighs, running my tongue everywhere but where she needed it to be, finally enough to make her mutter, "Get *on* with it already."

I breathed onto her, making her shudder.

"Get on with it already *what*?" I tsked. She wasn't in control here.

Her entire body twitched as she froze, clearly frustrated that I was going to make her say it. She sucked in a frustrated breath, her abdomen flexing in *need*.

I leaned away, resting my head on her thigh, smiling all the while. "I'm waiting," I whispered, my tone perfectly even.

I could wait here, looking up at her as she writhed against me, for all my days. In this *perfect* moment.

Finally, her body relaxed against me as she relented. "Get on with it already, *Captain*."

I nodded, kissing her thigh, letting my tongue roll across it from bottom to top. "Close. But not quite," I whispered, my breath raising goosebumps around her most intimate of areas. Teasing her was just simply a *delight* that I intended to make as long as possible.

She propped up on her elbows to stare at me, eyes aflame.

"You're insufferable," she muttered as I laughed, tracing a finger around her centre, its muscles already contracting in response.

"You're insufferable, *what*?" I countered, watching her bit her lip and clench her hands. Gods, was she beautiful.

The noise she let out was aggravated, but perfect. "You're insufferable, *Captain*. Now will you get on with it, *please*?" Her voice caught in a pleading and heated breath, making me chuckle. *Delicious.* Every word of it.

"There's a good girl," I said quietly to her as I began in earnest.

CHAPTER TWENTY-FIVE

— Captain of the Queen of Sardis, Tarrick Yondu

She smelled of the forge, of sweat and smoke, of determination and patience.

She was perfect.

Her quiet breathing on top of me with her head tucked under my chin made me sigh happily, enjoying the feeling of her skin on mine, the odd flush of warmth I felt as my body leeching heat off of her.

I gazed around the cabin, thinking… that it somehow felt more alive with her in it. Gods, I must have it *really* bad if I was trying to be poetic about this moment.

That I had this one steady beating heart, the loudest noise in my cabin, no, my *world*.

Snuggling my face into her hair, I breathed in her smell. Moira's own breath was quieting as she passed into slumber. Tired and blissfully relaxed, I couldn't help joining her in my exhaustion.

But the dreams were waiting for me. As they always were.

Maybe it had something to do with how easy I fell asleep with Moira in my arms. That I wasn't as mentally guarded as I usually was. Maybe it was just the feeling of comfort of having her there.

But this time, the chains on my limbs felt as real as my own skin. The hands of the guards felt as intrusive as that very first night. The laughter of Ameritia felt near enough to be whispered in my ear. The tightness of the noose that robbed me of breath, and I so very needed to breathe.

I shot out of bed, grasping at the blankets less than an hour into our rest, gasping for air in a bright panic.

"Claire. Claire. It's okay. You're okay."

Moira.

I was beyond terror, beyond fear, I was *scared.* Her hands wormed into mine, and I grasped onto her wrists in panic.

"You're okay Claire. You're okay. Claire, look at me. Look at the walls. Your sword on the rack beside you. The light peeking in through the curtains. You know where you are. You're on the ship. You're not back there."

My breath was stuck in my chest, my eyes following towards the things she pointed out. It took so much effort, but finally I was able to push a breath through my panicked throat, and slowly, I felt my gasping start to calm down.

"That's it. That's it. Claire. Look at me. Look," Moira pleaded, and I did. Her eyes were so Gods damned pretty, her expression full of worry. "I won't let anything happen to you. You're okay. You're okay." She thumbed shapes into the palms of my hands as she murmured quietly, and I felt myself slip back down into the covers, her hand on the side of my head. "That's it. Good. Go back to sleep. I'll be here. Watching over you. I promise."

As I listened to her voice, I held it like a candle to my heart, a light in my very dark life.

And I slept. And the dreams were not waiting for me.

A thumping at my door a moment later awoke me yet again, forcing me to let out a long yawn as I looked out my window at the rising sun. Moira's arm was draped over my waist, her face snuggled into my neck. The knocking came once again, and I grumbled that I still must not have slept more than another hour. If it wasn't dreams waking me up, it was the crew.

I extricated myself from Moira's limbs carefully, trying not to wake her, while amazed at feeling flush with her warmth. It was an unfamiliar sensation. To be *warm*, after years of cold. I grabbed my jacket, throwing it over my naked body, holding it taught, and opened the door quietly.

"There you are. No one's seen you in a while, and we should be seeing—" Jacine started rambling off before she stopped mid-sentence, staring at me as I was rubbing at my eye.

"Wait. Were you actually sleeping? *Actually,* actually?" she asked, her tone full of surprise. Something about her expression told me I should be worried, but I was still processing being awake, my head felt unfamiliar. *Fuzzy* almost.

I yawned, and she looked even more alarmed somehow.

"Barely," I replied. "But I'm up now. Might as well be useful. I thought you were busy with the grappling hooks?"

Jacine stared at me open-mouthed, looking dumbfounded. "Claire. I finished those hours ago," she stuttered out, disbelief in her voice.

Hours ago?

My hand paused mid stroke through my hair, noticeably messy as what she had just said hit me. I looked again at the sun rising over the horizon. The *wrong* horizon. It wasn't rising. It was *setting*.

I had slept. A full day.

I looked down at my hands in shock, feeling so much lighter. As if a weight that'd been chained to my feet had been finally freed.

I turned from where I stood in the doorway to look at Moira, who still asleep, clutching my pillow as a replacement.

Gods above and below, I really do love her.

Jacine stepped forward just enough to peer around the door, saw Moira's sleeping frame, and jumped back in surprise with a squeak.

"I uh. Sorry. I shouldn't have peaked," she murmured, face beat red but a very much *delighted* expression crinkling in her eyes.

I shrugged. "I imagine if you tell anyone, she'll probably kill you. Or make *me* kill you." I laughed, feeling *so good*. Better than I had in months. No, *years.*

I didn't have time to really process how happy my body was before Jacine suddenly wrapped her arms around me, hugging me tightly. Her grasp dislodged my unsure grip on my jacket, nearly making it fall off.

"I'm happy for you," she said quietly, holding me ever so tightly, before disentangling her arms from my shoulders, giving me space to pull my jacket more securely around my naked frame.

"I'll give you a bit and talk to you when you're not still half asleep," she said with a laugh.

She all but pushed me back into the cabin, and I closed the door with a small wave, before I turned to crawl back into bed wrapping my arms once more around Moira.

She mumbled awake, barely coherent. "Who wuz?" her sleepy voice murmured into my breast.

"Jacine. She said hi," I murmured, planting a kiss on her cheek.

That woke her up. Her head shot up to look at me, rapidly trying to blink away sleep. "You told her?" she stammered out to my shrug.

"She saw. Didn't mean to." I kissed her on the top of the forehead as she grumbled.

"Thank you. For last night," I said quietly. Her eyes glazed over as she tried to remember what I was talking about, the *aha* moment eventually coming as she let me pull the covers over us once more.

"S' fine," she mumbled. "You needed help. So I helped." She laid her head back down on my chest in a content sigh as I ran my hand through her hair, scratching the back of her neck lightly.

I used my other hand to lightly run my nails over her back, leaving goosebumps in their wake, her breathing slowly coming to time with how they trailed up and down.

I wished we could've stayed like that forever. Because sooner than I'd like, the ship's bell dinged, and crew muttering began echoing through the walls.

Just a little more time. Please.

But the shouts increased, the bell rang again, and again, and *again*. A moment later and a pounding sounded against the door; a summoning. I had to extract myself from bed.

Our time was up.
We were here.

I stood on the forecastle as the great island of Kitaxia grew in the distance. It'd been more than five years since I'd seen her, but I'd recognize its shape anywhere, the glowing castle towers and city lights even visible from here.

Haxla.

"Alright folks. Stick to the plan." I shouted, pointing out towards a Southeasterly direction. My familiarity with Haxla was such that I didn't even need a map to know its shape.

The cove was picked out as our anchorage for a multitude of reasons. It was isolated, off the patrol routes of the navy, and close enough that the city was within a day or two of walking.

For humans.

But I also chose it because it was special to me. Memories of improvised vacations there when I was still small, as it was quieter and harder to reach than others nearby the city, and therefore more likely to be empty in the dead of winter.

Winter was dreary and cold in this part of the world, and I didn't count on anyone seeing us there.

Not that'd we'd be there for long.

Somehow it felt like it'd been a lonely trip. Weeks at sea without a single vessel on the horizon between Varcna and Kitaxia. It felt like the Goddess of Fortune was paving the way for me, now that my luck had run out. Part of me wished for some excitement on what I was sure to be my last voyage, especially for a *meal* for Gods sake, but no, that wasn't to be.

But... I had one last night with Moira, and I wouldn't trade that for the world.

I tried to push her out of my mind, despite the warmth in my heart... and the guilt in my stomach at what I was about to do.

This is the only way she stays safe.

Not just her. All *of them.*

I owe her that.

The *Wraith* glided into the cove as if it was made for it, and the anchor was dropped. I gathered everyone to plan our next moves, lying through my teeth about scouting missions, how long everything was going to take, all the while sharing a quiet look with Markus, and doing my damn best to not look at Moira.

And then time seemed to evaporate on me.

Night changed to day, and Moira dragged me once more to bed. Delighted with every second I could get with her, every moan, every breath, every little *taste* I got of her. I did my best to savour every second, for I was quite sure, it was all I was ever going to have.

I wanted nothing but to fall asleep in her arms. That *peace* that she'd finally brought me, was… *Everything.*

But in order to protect my crew, protect *her*, I had to sacrifice it.

It took so much to stay awake with her warmth bleeding into me, not letting myself drift off into peaceful oblivion that only she brought. Waiting, staring at nothing, until just after sunset, crawling out of bed like some shameful lover. After she'd fallen asleep, my every muscle protesting the betrayal I was committing, I laid my coat on the pillow.

It broke my heart as she snuggled into it.

Gods. Please. Don't make me do this.

But there was nothing. None of the thousand and one goddesses descended into my cabin to save me from sacrificing this happiness. As always, these past five years, it would have to be me to push through the change I wanted in the world.

I leaned down, gently, and kissed Moira's forehead. The softness of warmth seeping into my lips the last I'd ever have of her. Pulling away, I could feel the bloody tears welling up in my eyes, but I blinked them away, shoving it all down, down, down. Threw my hat and spectacles onto the desk, and quietly extracted myself to the weather deck, hand over my mouth to silence the sobs in my throat.

Markus was the only one on deck waiting for me, carrying an

armload of weapons, and everyone else sent below.

I couldn't stop looking at different parts of the ship while I was walking towards him, pushing Moira out of my mind. Would this be the last time I saw that sail? Run my hand along this railing? Trace the shape of that odd dent from that duel years ago in the mainmast?

My fingers traced the wood grain of the vessel I'd made my own, my home on the waves. If I failed… I was going to miss this ship. Almost as much as I was going to miss Moira, the crew, and… *hot cocoa.*

I sighed longingly, imagining a different life as I stepped towards him, grasping his outstretched hand with a grim smile.

Markus looked like he had a million and one things he wanted to say. But he couldn't stop me. Not now.

"Mr. Clun," I mumbled through my smile, somehow sounding like I hadn't just been a step away from breaking, a slight touch of gallows humour in my voice.

Markus nodded glumly, awkwardly crossing his arms over the pile of weapons he was holding in some manner of disapproval after he pulled his hand from mine. "I still don't like this, Claire. I don't like this one bit."

It changed nothing. I shrugged, silently holding out my hand for the weapons he carried.

He sighed aggravatedly, finally offering the first belt of throwing knives, and I set about strapping it around my waist to add to my sword-belt.

"This is the only way you all stay safe," I said as I tugged on the straps, making sure everything was secure. "Who knows," I joked. "Maybe it'll all go swimmingly and I'll be back before sunrise."

Markus snorted in reply, passing me the next belt with several grenades attached to it.

I breathed a sigh of shuddered relief, somehow calm despite everything. There was nothing to do, but *this*. My course charted, my path set.

It'd end with Ameritia. It had to.

My heart was another story. It was back in my cabin shattered into a million pieces, but at last, once I'd done this, Moira would have nothing to fear.

She'd be safe. Free from the clutches of her mother, forever more.

Markus and the rest of the crew free to sail the seas, find some other little town to bribe into the new Port Sable, pirating to their hearts content without fear of the navy coming to wipe them out of existence.

But to give them that opportunity, I had to kill my maker.

Braiding my mess of hair as tightly as I could, I strapped the last belt of knives to my chest and stepped up to the railing, grasping a handful of rigging. I ran my thumb around it longingly, wishing I could have just one more moment with my ship. My home.

At least she would be in good hands.

"Markus, it's been an honour. The ship is yours." My voice was stern, commanding, somehow hiding the brokenness of my heart as I stared into the water over the side. "If I'm not back in forty-eight hours, get the hell out of here. Go... somewhere. I'm sure you'll figure it out."

Markus gave me a crisp salute. "Ma'am," he stated, his voice clear as a bell. Seeing that filled me with pride, and a touch of comfort. At least I was leaving everyone in good hands.

I hope.

I turned my head to give him one final nod, the rope in my hand one final squeeze, and dove off the side.

The crash of water was cool on my skin, leaving me mourning the warmth Moira's body had left in my skin. It brought back so many memories of swimming under the sea.

But today… the one I could recall was the moment I woke up in this life. My body being tossed into the waves without a care after I was hanged.

Maybe if I was lucky, I'd be able to return the favour to Lady Ameritia.

I cut through the water with ease, the waves of the cove negligible with my strength, and in minutes I was stomping through the chop and up the beach.

I didn't dare look back, immediately taking off at a run for the capital.

If I saw the *Wraith* sitting in the cove behind me, I wasn't sure I would be able to summon the strength to do this again.

Quickly, the rolling hills of the cove and its surrounding countryside turned into rotting farmland, growing less and less desolate the closer I got to the spires growing in the distance.

There were only so many hours of night to sneak into Haxla, and provided everything went to plan, I had to somehow find a single woman in the entirety of the palace, if not all of Haxla.

If I was still searching by morning, I wasn't sure my body and mind could take it. I was only running on my brief feeding with Moira, and I was still ridiculously *hungry.*

And as much as I hated the beast that was Kitaxia, no innocent civilian deserved the wrath of my hunger.

And that was *if* I wasn't spotted by the guards doing something idiotic as scaling the walls.

Running at speed towards the city's outermost gate, I stopped to examine the defences, but calling it 'defences' was maybe rather charitable. Only a single guard awaited me. Compelling him to let me pass and forgetting he ever saw me was as easy as breathing.

Thankfully, the Gods seemed to be looking out for me tonight.

I thought about feeding from the isolated guard, but didn't want a single drop of evidence of me being here in this accursed city until Ameritia felt my blade cutting off her fucking head.

I passed into and through the city as quietly as I could. The outer slums that I knew well from my youth, all shacks and lean-tos against faded storm coloured-buildings that looked as though the slightest breeze would collapse them, the occasional remains of some poor soul near death huddled up against the cold.

The smell was horrendous, a permanent miasma of desperation, sweat, and rot.

It permeated the air, until I stepped into the mid city, where the merchants and artisans lived in my memory but now… it looked much different. Nothing was like how I remembered it.

Gone were the bakeries, cobblers, and weavers. Now churches dominated the skyline, dormitories of piety filling out the rest of the spaces. Gone were the smells of industry and the desperate, now incense burned through the air, doing a shit job at covering the smell of the lower city. The entire city had been transformed over the last five years.

So amazed was I by the spires reaching into the sky, I almost didn't see the posters at eye level.

And once I did, I couldn't believe what I saw.

The posters on the church walls, on the entrance of every dormitory, were of *me*.

Or at least *alluding* to me.

I tore one off a church door, reading it in detail.

Beware the pirate menace!

Only in God may we find solace from the death of Kitaxia's noble sons!

Every day at sun's zenith bend your head in prayer, devoting your faith to the Royal Kitaxian Navy and its efforts to destroy the vile unbelievers at sea.

And below those letters, printed in red, was quite possibly the crudest sketch of me and my ship I'd ever seen, on an ocean of blood. They'd drawn a vile cackle on my blood-smeared face, my crew replaced by laughing skeletons at my command, and the ocean around the *Wraith* full of bodies floating in the waves.

My legend, it seemed, was alive and well in Haxla. If a bit… *macabre.*

I briefly stood there in wonder, in front of a Kitaxian church in the city that had destroyed me, about what my legend would look like after tonight.

After I'd murdered the crown princess. *Ameritia.*

Would the people see me as a liberator? Or as an agent of chaos? Some demon from their faith?

Did I care?

No.

Tonight, it was about ending the cycle of violence between me and Ameritia. Nothing else. Kitaxia would live on in whatever damn form it wanted after, as long as that *woman* was dead before the sun rose. My grudge was with *her,* and once she was dead, me and my crew would pluck at Kitaxia's corpse for as long as we could.

Let them build their churches. Whatever helped them sleep at night.

I let the paper fall to the cobblestone, crushing it under my boot, and made my way towards the palace.

The palace gates had me feeling slightly suspicious.

One guard at the outer city gate was one thing. Only having *two* guards at the gates to the palace seemed just unfathomable.

Years I had spent thinking through my revenge, paying off palace informants, waiting for the opportune moment to strike, but held back for fear of the impossibility of it.

I thought there would be a small *army* in between me and the palace. Any direct assault was doomed to failure. I didn't even think I'd get this far *tonight*.

But here I was. Before the palace gates without a soul even knowing I was in the city.

It was *too* easy.

A few paces down the palace wall, stabbing my daggers into the weak mortar and brick with my Vampyri strength, and in minutes I was over the wall with none-the-wiser. Much sooner than I thought I'd be able to, I found myself stalking the palace grounds, every instinct in my head screaming at me to get away from here. Tall towers of brick and marble surrounded me, casting long shadows of absolute darkness that put the black of night to shame. The servant houses outside the main castle tower putting even the mansions of the Upper City to shame in size, but lacking… an ornamentation. Everything looked simple, spartan. No paints, no colours, no flowers, just dreary grey and black, everywhere I looked.

It was *too fucking easy.*

Guards were few and far between, but slowly… something felt… *off*. The palace was engulfed in a scent. Not the miasma of the lower city, nor the incense of the upper city.

A smell of wines and perfume, of old blood and vials, of memories and chains.

The very walls reeked of it, putting me on edge, my shoulders hitched up in alarm at every shadow as I delved deeper and deeper into the palace grounds.

My guts roiled as the feeling that she was just around the next corner skittered across my nerves.

Against my baser instincts, I knew I had to follow that feeling to its source.

An open window just barely above ground level led me into the main castle tower, a room full of polished wood and drapes dyed a deep blue, with well-made paintings of famous naval engagements upon the walls, giving the inside of the palace the first real hint at ornamentation. A minister's office of some sort from the looks of it.

But following the stench of Ameritia out into the hall led not up into the royal apartments and into further finery like I expected… but down.

A passageway where the rich oak walls with art and finery turned into hard uncompromising stone and an iron barred door, left ajar.

She was down there, I was certain of it. I stepped down into the depths below ground, the stones set into the walls reminding me far too much of the dungeon cell I languished in before my hanging.

Bringing back memories I cared not to remember.

Despite my alarm and anxiety, I took solace knowing nothing could find me. My quiet footfalls were soundless, I held no light to show my way, nor did I need one. No one had seen me enter the city.

But yet I still felt as if my every move was watched.

I slinked into what appeared to be a cellar, huge wine casks dominating the walls, before going down yet another set of stairs, hidden behind some pile of crates covered in the cobwebs of years.

Another cellar, another staircase shrouded in darkness and hidden away.

Further and further down into the depths of the castle, the stench grew more and more as I went further and further into the depths of the castle. But it was becoming apparent I was stepping into the one place I'd hoped to avoid.

The dungeons.

The smell of her was powerful enough to make me wince. That rose scented perfume I remembered her reeking of was everywhere. It seeped like blood from the walls. Yet not to be deterred, I snuck as quietly as I could lower still, as cells began to line the walls.

The feeling of something inside me began to direct my path. My choices about which winding route through the cells becoming almost known to me. Like something was singing in my blood to show me the way.

I should've turned back. I should've never left the ship. I should've stayed in bed with Moira, and sailed to the far side of the world. But it felt like it was calling me.

That to turn back now was impossible. It made me feel sick to my stomach.

I followed that instinct to a single door in a far-flung corner, I didn't want to think of how many stories down, where the first light I saw in hours burned in the crack underneath the door.

It felt like opening that door was the beginning of the end. But I had to know.

Opening the door as quietly as I could, the jangle of chains inside alerted me to someone aware of my presence.

A quiet voice murmured into the darkness as I stepped inside the dungeon, growing unease settling into my gut as I saw a single torch flickering down the hall, the click of quiet sure steps echoing against the stones.

I drew my blade as quietly as I could.

"My lady, please, take all you need..." the voice murmured, almost pathetic in its mewling.

I gulped, my mouth watering, as a new aroma bit into the overpowering stench of Ameritia.

Blood. Someone was bleeding.

I rounded the last corner and felt my heart jump into my throat.

A young man, chained to the wall, exactly like I'd been so long ago, unsteadily swaying back and forth as if in a dream. And there, latched onto his arm with a vial and a needle, was the very person I'd come to kill.

Lady Ameritia, smiling at me sweetly.

Five years hadn't touched her. Still tall, proud, and regal. An expensive dress worth as much as the *Wraith*. A heavy furred coat, the softest thing I'd ever seen.

Looking at me over her shoulder with a vile grin and sharp blue eyes.

"Ah, and the prodigal childe returns. I was wondering when you'd show up."

I'd forgotten her accent, her rancid words, and her beauty. She turned her attention from me to the young man, withdrawing her needle to pull his hand to his elbow to staunch the flow of blood, and corking her little vial.

"My lady?" the man murmured, reaching against his chains for her. She looked back at him nonchalantly, waving her hand away at him.

"*That's enough. Sleep now,*" she murmured, in that *tone*. It felt so strange to hear now that I recognised it for what it was.

And in an instant, the man leaned back against the wall, sliding down as much as his chains allowed, and was out.

My guts flip-flopped in horror as I realised, she was doing the exact same thing to him that she'd done to me. *Again.* Some condemned man, here to be bled to death until she was done with him. Was she going to turn him as she did me? Or was I just special?

Regardless, it stopped *now*. I raised the point of my blade towards her, holding back the multitude of curses I'd darken her name with.

My maker.

But she seemed to be unbothered with me. Unthreatened, despite me advancing with blade in hand.

"Oh, come now Captain," she almost poetically murmured. "You're not that pathetic. Or is the legend of *Claire Vessia* all just bluster?"

She wasn't even *looking at me,* her gaze locked on the vial in her hand. It made me so damn angry, seeing her. A vicious boiling in the pit of my stomach, clench and grinding teeth, a growl in my throat. I clenched the sword in my hand, stepping ever so closer, yet, with a bite of fear in my gut.

She may scare me, but I'm not the same woman I was five years ago.

I was the best duelist on the Great Divide. I was *Claire Vessia,* bane of Kitaxia. And I was not leaving here without ending her.

"You took everything from me. My life, the sun, my *soul,*" I spat towards her, the point of my blade closing to her throat inch by inch.

She sighed, still not even bothering to look at me as she eyed the vial of blood from the young man, twisting it this way and that in the tiny sliver of torchlight from the single flame set into the wall. "And I gave you so much in return, my childe, my *Captain.*"

She pocketed the vial, finally turning to stare at me as my blade's point began to dig into the flesh of her neck.

Yet she stood there, unbothered. A wide smile on her face. "The dreaded pirate Claire Vessia," she whispered, her voice smooth and low as the tide. "My creation. You did everything you were meant to do *perfectly.* If only you'd played your part to the end, you would've been welcome in our new world."

Everything I was meant to do?

I felt my stomach churn in terror and confusion. But my blade was at her throat, the tiniest wellspring of blood trickling down it. I could end this. Remove her head and be done with it, and then get back on the seas with my family.

But what had she meant?

I tensed as I watched the plotting in her eyes. One swing, that would be all it would take. One swing that would separate head from neck.

But I had to know. I had so many questions. "What do you mean? What was I 'supposed' to do?" I asked. "Why did you turn me?" My voice hardened to fury.

Her expression didn't shift a muscle, still that wide, terrifying smile as she raised two fingers to tap on the blade at her neck. I grimaced, pulling it back ever so slightly, stepping forward instead to let it rest on her shoulder. "Explain," I demanded.

Her face noticeably twitched in revulsion, but she nodded.

"I was like you once. Trapped." Her honeyed words insinuating that we were *similar* nearly made me chop her head off then and there. "I was forced into a marriage I wanted nothing to do with. And then, a man from a far away country came with an offer. He would give me immortality. The chance to outlive my husband and rule Kitaxia *alone* in the new world we would build. In exchange I prepared Kitaxia for his people's arrival."

My eyes narrowed as she tilted her head slightly sideways. "And you, my darling creation, have helped that cause tenfold..." she mumbled, *happily.*

I'd *helped* her?

"You better start making sense now." I shoved myself forward, closing the remaining distance between us, pushing my blade even more into her throat. One cut away from the end.

She tilted her head back and laughed, not giving a care in the world to the blade digging into her neck. "I needed Kitaxia destabilized, bleeding resources, and its people pushed further and further into the arms of the church," she all but sang. "And you played your part of the demon to be feared with such style and grace. Gods woman, they made *plays* about you." She laughed, and *laughed*, and I wanted nothing more than to silence it.

She raised her fingers to run along my sword point, dragging them along its length towards me, and I felt myself shudder in fear as her eyes locked onto mine.

"A *demon* on the seas, killing noble Kitaxia's sons. An easy scapegoat for a failing economy. Nobles fattened on greed while the commoner finds solace in the church, knowing they will be rewarded if they just *obey*. This is what they wanted."

Gods. She had said *Gods. Plural.*

Ameritia, Crown Princess of the holy kingdom of Kitaxia… didn't believe in the church she *created.*

Why?

I didn't get time to debate the question, as she suddenly grabbed the base of my blade between bleeding fingers, a wicked smile on her face.

"But then you fucked it all up," she spat, her teeth elongated in her mouth, and finally, the image of Lady Ameritia was shattered.

The woman in my memory, gone.

This was the monster that had taunted my nightmares all these years. The Vampyri, *my maker*, staring at me with fanged teeth, gasping as she tightened her grip on my sword, its point beginning to dig into her shoulder.

"You shouldn't have stolen from *me,* captain," she said longingly, like a lover as she licked a fang. And then she did the last thing I expected.

She shoved my sword into and *through* her shoulder, tugging me forward.

She seemed to barely notice it, and I only made my situation worse as my instincts conflicted. The *Vampyri* in me wanted to run. The swordsman in me wanted my fucking sword back.

Any day of the week, a weapon was better than none, and the swordsman won out. I held on tightly as she pulled the blade in further, and so I tried to raise a knee to her gut to pull it free.

I was so focused on the threat of being disarmed and fighting the screaming of every muscle of my body trying to get my blade away, that I didn't notice the true threat until it was too late.

She reached around with her free hand, grabbed the back of my neck, and shoved me in closer to her.

Closer to her, and her *teeth.*

They latched onto my shoulder, making me cry out in pain. Two twin icicles of lightning digging into my flesh.

But that was just the beginning of it.

I'd drained many fools over the years, and knew the feeling intimately. I could make a bite feel like the most normal thing in the world, or as pleasurable as the most sensual kiss.

Or I could make it hurt. *Bad.*

Ameritia didn't seem too intent on making me comfortable as she devoured me.

I cried out in anguish as I finally let my blade go, letting it stay stuck in her shoulder, and tried to wrench myself free of her as every inch of my skin felt aflame. A draining feeling of losing every bit of energy I had made my protests feel weak and half hearted. A subtle painful tug, the point of my gravity shifting upwards as she drained me, limbs feeling heavy and useless. The pain of her teeth growing with every passing moment, the sound of her throat gulping down my blood somehow horrifically sticking out in the mess of my struggle.

Fuck.

I grasped at her hair, her shoulders, trying to push or pull myself free, but her fangs were stuck in me and not to be dislodged.

In mere moments I felt blackness creep at the corners of my vision. She was going to kill me. *Again.*

My limbs felt like they'd been weighed with cannonballs, my feeble attempts to free myself growing sluggish, before falling to hang at my side as deadweight. I didn't need to breathe, but my gasps of pain quieted, and everything began to feel numb.

And just when I thought I would die yet again, the dark threatening to swallow me whole… she detached from my shoulder, a wild moan echoing from her mouth, and dropped me to the floor.

I fell in a heap as everything began to fade.

"No… no, Captain. You're not going to die just yet. You have sins to answer for." Her words were the last thing I heard before my sword clattered to the floor beside me. I tried to reach for it, but couldn't see it.

I couldn't see anything.

My eyes fluttered open, and my hunger awoke with me, a fierce growl growing in my gut.

Ravenous. Starving. *Hunger.*

Blood. I need Blood.

A guttural noise of need escaped from my mouth as I went to raise my foot to the floor, but it was held fast in some binding, and as I tugged my hands, I realized that was the case for all my limbs.

I needed… Gods. It was impossible to think.

Blood. Where?

Think.

I shook my head as I looked to my extremities. My ankles were bolted to the floor, with my wrists attached to chains pulling them to the corners of the ceiling, forcing me into a permanent kneel.

Fuck.

A clutch of laughter dragged my eyes from my bonds to where Lady Ameritia sat a few paces away in a fancy high-backed chair. Beside her was a table covered in instruments I could only guess at the purpose of, while she smiled as if pleased with an experiment she had just confirmed the results.

I tested my bonds once more, finding no give I could exploit. I glared at her, not giving her a single word, but unable to stop breathing heavily, in *need* of sustenance.

She held my stare for a moment, before reaching over to the table to grab a vial of a dark coloured liquid. My nostrils flared as I realized what she held in her hand.

"Good, you are in there. Answer me, and maybe I'll feed you before we behead you and throw your body to the flames," she said as if I was over for tea. "That was our deal before, so long ago. Wasn't it?"

I seethed at her practiced laughter, low and sullen.

She leaned forward, not making a sound other than the rustle of fabric of her dress. The quiet of the stonework room was absolute. I had no idea where we were. Someplace different than where we were before.

This felt… *lower*. Dark and dead. Almost cavernous. Only one torch, shadows that even my eyes had a hard time seeing through at every other point of the room.

And the *smell*, everything reeked of blood.

Ameritia tapped the vile of blood against her chin thoughtfully, considering me carefully with her pale blue eyes. My breath shallow as I cried, openly, unable to take my eyes off the vial in her hand.

I need it. I need it. I need it. I need it—

"We shall begin, firstly, by you answering for your most heinous grievance, captain." She said it with a severe tone, leaning forward into the torchlight. "Where is my son?" Her hand shot out quicker than I could realize, tilting my chin upwards. "Where is Nicholas?" She almost spit the question in fury, angrier than I'd ever seen her.

I eyed her, remembering the day we stormed the convoy clearly. The day I met Moira.

"We never found him." I hated to misgender her like that, but if it led her off Moira's trail… "He dove from the ship. Made for shore," I murmured quietly. Hoping the quick lie would satisfy her.

Her eyebrow raised before she burst out laughing.

That laugh. I'd seen it before. But not on her face.

"How very glib, Captain, but do not lie to me." She tsked, waving a single finger back and forth, while her nails dug into my chin, still pulling me forward. "We know you took him."

There's nothing for it. If I'm going to die, then I'm going to Gods damn earn it.

I'd been living on borrowed time. Maybe I was always fated to be here, die at her hands. Because twice now, here I was, with Lady Ameritia fucking with me hours before my appointed death.

And I was tired of playing by her rules.

I felt it bubbling up in me before I could stop it, laughter at the ridiculousness of it, and I couldn't stop once I had started. Ameritia looked at me curiously as I cackled.

All our 'deal' had done, so many years ago, had let me slaughter hundreds of Kitaxian sailors.

All for nothing.

I'd failed to kill her, but that didn't mean I had to entertain her.

I laughed, and laughed, and laughed. And when I couldn't laugh anymore, I wanted to cry, but I wouldn't give her the satisfaction.

"Did you… get that out of your system?" Ameritia asked, barely held fury in her voice. I looked away from the vial to her hard eyes.

"Oh, it's just too fucking funny." I said quietly, tilting my head as mockingly as I could in my bonds. "I know exactly what I did with your *daughter.*"

Ameritia's face contorted into pale unabashed wrath as I gendered Moira correctly.

"Because she's been uh, working *under* me," I said with a wink.

Finally, the mask cracked, as she hissed at me with fangs fully bared, a moment of the true visage of the Vampyri she was. Well, before her hand slammed into the side of my face with the force of a landslide.

I nearly lost consciousness again from the pain of her claws raking across my face.

The points of her fingers dragged across my face, leaving trails of burning pain from my temple acoss to my chin, and just as quickly knitting together but not before a splash of blood hit the floor. "You insolent, ridiculous, monstrous, vile, you, you, you—" she raged as she rose for another strike.

The taste of my own blood in my mouth making me groan in both pain and hunger, the feeling of sickness bubbling up in my gut that I barely managed to keep down.

She paused, moving instead to right herself and smooth her dress, her fangs retracting neatly. She looked anywhere but me as the full revelation sunk into me.

I'm going to die. So be it. But please, at least let my family live.

I couldn't guarantee their safety, but maybe the Gods could. The navy would continue to hunt them under Ameritia's direction.

I'd failed. *Miserably* in fact.

But for now, at least I'd kept them out of her grip.

All I had left was hoping Ameritia choked one me while she devoured me whole.

She looked at me with disgust, and I couldn't stop giggling at her despite the hunger in the back of my throat twisting it into a pained growl.

"So, you've let him indulge in these… *fantasies* while he was on your ship? Ugh. Of course you have," she said with a dismissive wave as I shrugged, or as much as I could in my chains.

"It wasn't a fantasy, you stuck up sod. She's completely a woman." I said with quiet cheer in my voice, glaring up at her with my best snear before I spat blood at her feet. "And I do mean *everywhere.*"

That memory of Moira writhing in pleasure under me with my fingers in her and fangs in her neck… I'd hold onto that *dearly* as I died.

Ameritia looked at me with no emotion, instead eyeing the blood dripping down my chin from the cut she had made with a hunger I recognized all too well.

"I think after you die, I'll track down that Ithakian priest, and feed him his own intestines until he tells me how to turn him back," she said, with such severity that I'd have been surprised if she hadn't tried already.

I wanted to laugh, but I didn't think I had any more in me. By just being herself, Moira had accomplished more to hurt Ameritia than I probably ever could, and I loved her ever the more for it. I tried to take some solace in the fact that she was with some of the best people I knew, and out of Ameritia's reach.

"You'll never find her," I whispered quietly through a pained smile. I would have to die believing that to be true. It was the only way I could think of to die well.

She was too quick for my starved gaze to follow. A second later something sharp burst into my ribs, just under my breast, and out through my back. I gasped out in surprised breathlessness, as I was suddenly staring into the ice blue eyes of Ameritia, inches away from my face.

"You know what's so interesting about our kind, my childe?" she murmured quietly into my ear, fangs poking out over her lips as she twisted whatever she had stabbed me with, making me yell out in agony. "We don't die."

A blade maybe, stuck in under my ribs, rubbing against bone, through a lung if I were to hazard a guess through my pain, considering I couldn't draw a breath. A dripping sensation onto my thigh, a flow over my stomach that could only have been blood.

Fuck

She stood up, the thing left stuck into my ribs and began to pace back and forth in front of me as my vision had shifted into red, leaving me to grimace against the thing that'd been impaled into me, unable to remove it, unable to speak.

"But oh, don't get me wrong, we can certainly be killed." Her eyes wandered down to where my blood was dripping down my gut. "Under very specific circumstances." She disappeared, her voice suddenly coming from behind me, a whisper in my ear. "Beheading and fire are usually the most common tactics. A Scarwood stake through our hearts paralyses us. A rose placed upon us while we sleep means we will not wake. There's even some scholars in Itha-ki who think they know a way to reverse our condition altogether. Not to mention the Undying King of Draculesti. Only the Gods know what he does."

She leaned down again to caress my cheek, a wistful sigh escaping her as my world focused on the thing in my gut, a growing pool of blood at my feet.

"I can keep you here. Tortured. Bleeding. Never feed you again." She traced the shape of my jaw, as I panicked through my breathless gasps, trying to wrench my hands free to tug this accursed thing out of my stomach. "And you would never die. For eternity you could suffer here for what you've done to me. But sadly, my father, in his idiocy, has declared your capture to the populace."

My entire body erupted into pain as I finally got out a scream, upwards into the high stone ceiling, wrenching against my bonds. A second and she was gone again, her fingers disappearing from my face, and the blade, *a fucking spear*, ripped out of my chest.

Ameritia tsked at my scream, hefting the spear already thick with my blood in her hand. I could feel the wound in my chest slowly beginning to knit back together, but I could see the look in her eyes.

It would be open again.

I would be *covered* in open wounds soon enough.

"I have three days before you reach the executioner's axe to try and make you tell me where you've taken my son," she said quietly, lowering the blade to my chest, its point resting just under my collarbone, her smile monstrous with fangs fully bared. "Let us make the most of it, shall we?"

CHAPTER TWENTY-SIX

Moira

❝It's been three days; we should've left yesterday!" Markus screamed, his voice barely audible over the din of everyone else's yelling. It was hard to exist in this space without Claire, but now it was impossible. I watched the officers' argument in the space reserved for it, while everyone also knew it was the space I'd reserved for my grief, none of them willing to order me out.

I was a part of this, but separate. An outsider looking in.

"She's our captain!" Rodger screamed back, slamming a fist onto the desk in-between them. "She would've come for any one of us! If it was you up in there, you *know* she'd be storming the battlements!"

Markus was technically the captain now, and he stood behind Claire's desk, his hands braced on the wood. Her chair sat empty beside him,… At least he wasn't in her seat. Not yet. It sat empty beside him, its void of space looming in all of our hearts.

"We owe it to her. She's done everything for us," Jacine added her yell to the debate. To even hear her husky voice yelling at anything was rare enough.

"Yet she's also put us in this impossible situation. How can you not see that?" Markus countered.

"I, in case you didn't notice, would be blaming the Kitaxians for that," Rodger stated, crossing his arms, but Markus rolled his eyes.

"Says the Kitaxian," Markus replied with disgust. "You've probably been waiting to turn her in for years."

Rodger put a hand on his blade, moving to draw it. "How fucking dare you? I ought to—"

"ENOUGH!" Maude screamed, slamming both her hands onto her end of the desk, the other side of Claire's chair.

Everyone shut up for half a second, and nothing but the waves echoed through the hull as I lovingly stroked my hair, feeling its strands, the curls. Looking at the shine in the candlelight. Over and over and over. Years I'd longed for hair like this.

My heart breaking all over again as I held my hair in one hand, Claire's jacket in the other.

I tightened my grip around Claire's jacket, smelling the last bits of her that I could, the well-used fabric smelling of sea salt, driftwood smoke, apple ale, and the smallest tinge of dried blood.

I breathed it in, and wondered if I was strong enough to do what I needed to.

What only *I* could do.

"We're still here, because we can't make a decision," Maude admitted quietly. "So. Let's put it to basics. Option one. We try to rescue Claire." She flicked up a finger, making a list in her mind. So very like her. "This will likely go very badly." She grimaced, before flicking up another finger. "Option two, we run, try to find a new life either pirating or going merchant."

"Fuck if I know anyone onboard this ship willing to do that without Claire at the helm," Charlotte muttered from the corner of the room, flipping a knife over and over in their hand.

"You can say that again," Jacine said quietly from where she stood near Maude, arms folded.

"Markus," Rodger said somberly, letting go of the hilt of his sword, pleading with our quartermaster. "You haven't called a vote to leave."

Markus's face twisted at Rodger's words, his expression telling me all I needed to know.

We were going to attempt a rescue.

Markus hadn't ordered the ship to leave. He was acting captain, and he hadn't... *captained.*

"Put it to a vote," Maude ordered, knocking a knuckle onto the desk. "All in favour of a rescue?"

She raised her hand, followed quickly by Rodger and Jacine. Charlotte grabbed their knife out of the air, sheathing it, before raising their hand as well. All eyes rested on Markus, who begrudgingly raised his as well.

"Then it's settled. We're going after her," Maude stated. It was done. We were going after her.

I breathed out a sigh of relief, clutching the jacket ever tighter. At least now I wouldn't have to convince them.

"Now, *how* do we rescue her? Rodger, any ideas?" Maude asked clearly, folding her hands together as if he held all the answers in the world and she was a dedicated student.

But Rodger wouldn't have the answers. He'd not been a guard since I was a child. He didn't even have a moustache back then.

I remembered.

"There's plenty of passages in the palace," he admitted, stroking his moustache. "The problem is getting in to use them in the first place." He motioned with the other hand in the air as he spoke. "Our scouts came back saying there were dozens of guards at the outer city gates, not letting a soul inside. It'll be a tough nut to crack."

I let out a shuddered breath, standing up from the bed I'd been curled up in, setting the jacket back onto the pillow. Running my hands over it one last time, feeling it's coarse fabric, extra thick to keep out the sun.

How dare you leave me here.

If Claire only knew the lengths I would go to get her back... That I'd do even *this.*

My steps rang out against the deck, somehow loud, audible, *shattering.* Just the small space from Claire's bunk, to where Charlotte sat, once again tossing their knife.

"I can get us in," I said quietly, holding my hand out for the knife.

"I'm sorry?" Maude asked quietly from the desk, a touch of disbelief in her voice.

"I can get us in," I repeated, more loudly for everyone in the room to hear.

The room grew quiet, just the sounds of creaking wood as the ship rocked in the waves. Charlotte stared at me with a look of confusion as they stopped tossing the knife.

"Please?" I asked, the beginning of tears in my eyes, suspicion growing in theirs as they slowly put the knife in my hand.

It felt so light in my hand, yet it weighed heavy with dread.

I don't want to do this.

I must.

Reaching behind my head, I grabbed a fistful of my hair, and raised the knife to it.

A multitude of gasps shattered the silence of the room, cries out in protest as they began to understand.

I hesitated for all of a second, feeling my face twist up into a grimace as I began to tear up more, and then forced the knife through my hair before I lost my nerve.

I breathed yet another shaky breath, not really thinking that it was my hair I was hacking away in a rush. The sound of knife slicing through my hair felt like I was cutting through my soul, but if I stopped now, I wouldn't be able to start again.

Ever since I left Haxla on the trip for my arranged marriage, the same trip that had seen me abducted by Claire and her gang of pirates, I'd finally been able to grow it out further than ever before. The waves of suntanned auburn hair that my entire life, I'd wanted nothing but to grow out, fell in bunches onto the deck, something in me wilting as I watched them fall. Because again, it was mother, *always mother*, forcing me to cut it and shove me back into my dead-self. My dead name. My dead *gender*.

Cut. Cut. Cut. Cut. Cutcutcutcutcut.

And then, there wasn't anything left to cut anymore.

There was only one face I could meet. Only one person who could understand completely. I rased my gaze to Jacine, my best friend, my *sister*, and saw her tears for me. Her mouth covered by her hands, deep brown eyes crying freely in shock.

I wanted more than anything to break, here and now, melt onto the floor and grasp every strand of my hair and *mourn*. But there was so much to do. If I stopped, I would break. I breathed heavily as I addressed the next step in my plan.

"Rodger, I'll need to borrow some clothes," I murmured through pained breath. I couldn't bring myself to look anyone else in the eyes, afraid of what I'd see there.

Disappointment. Disgust. Confusion. Those I was familiar with. But not Jacine. Never Jacine..

"You're closer to my build than Markus," I explained, a panicked air rushing out at my every word.

"I'll... go get you what you need Moira," Rodger stated quietly, turning to leave the room at once.

I handed the knife back to Charlotte, and they took it gently from my hand, as if I was handing them my heart, before they stood slowly and opened their arms with a thin smile.

I settled myself into them, and they wrapped their arms around me ever so kindly, as if I was made of glass, and just as quickly, let me go but held onto my hands, holding me like an anchor in a rough storm.

"I need your help, I—"

They squeezed mine in turn, interrupting me as they shook their head. "Anything for you, babe," they said with a sweet smile.

A weak laugh escaped me, a choked laugh, before I nodded, wiped my eyes, and turned from them to face the rest of the group with my plan.

"Rodger is the other obvious choice to come with me. He was a guard and knows the palace. We need two more men. Charlotte could pass for one. No women allowed throughout the palace grounds, not without chaperones." My words were chopped, brief, *pained*.

But there were only a few people I could trust to bring along with me. "Markus?" I asked.

He might not like me. But I trusted him.

He stood from his chair, turning to look out the windows behind Claire's chair.

"No," he muttered, as everyone stared at his back with unbelieving anger. He'd been fighting *everything* since Claire failed to turn up. Moving, looking for her, votes…

He was broken. Just like me. I didn't think either of us could function in a world without Claire.

I sighed, my emotions raw as I stated where that would leave me. "Then either come up with something better, or you might as well shoot me, right here, right now."

Every eye whirled around to face me, Markus included.

I didn't add a single word. My point was made.

I would not live in a world where the woman who loved me for *me* was left to die at the hands of a woman who'd done all she could to smother who I was. I'd rather die.

Markus stared into my tear-stained eyes for what felt like an eternity, before he finally nodded. "Fine. I'll go."

Tension left my shoulders, only to re-tense a moment later as I realized that meant we were going through with this. "Thank you."

Everyone began mulling out of the cabin, until only Jacine was left with me, as I finally let myself stare down at my hair on the floor.

Only Jacine could really know how much pain I was putting myself through with this.

"Moira, Gods above and below, I'm so, so sorry," she said quietly, wrapping her arms around me as I finally broke, sobbing as I collapsed into her arms.

"Hail, declare yourself!" The lead guard stated, holding up a hand to block our approach. More than twenty guardsmen stood ready to inspect any interloper with force. Too many for me and my impromptu honour guard to handle.

I expected to have to bribe maybe one or two gate guards on the outer palace walls, the outer city gates to not even be *manned*.

Not for the outer city gate to be a small castle unto itself.

Striding forward with a quiet confidence that had been honed in years of stepping around mother without showing my fear, I pulled out my best casual smirk to come out and play at the man demanding our names.

An act. It was just an act. I'm just pretending, like I always did before. I'm not that person anymore, I never was.

I kept repeating that phrase in my mind as Charlotte, Markus, and Rodger's gazes prickled the back of my neck

I coughed, trying to force my voice deeper than I'd used it in months. "You doubt my person?" I asked, unable to bring myself to deadname myself as well. The very thought nearly put me to tears.

The guard squinted in suspicion. But it wasn't him who put two and two together.

"Your... your *highness*?" another guard stammered out, eyes seemingly bugging out of his helmet.

The moment he said the words, every soul manning the gate froze, and I felt the intense examination of two dozen pairs of eyes.

I had to give the one that *did* recognise me credit. I looked very different.

Between the months of Maude and Isabella's medicine, which had done *wonders*, and what the priest from Itha-ki had accomplished, it had taken quite a bit of effort to make me look like my old self. Jacine, Maude, and Charlotte had spent hours trying different paints, clothes, and all sorts of methods, but I still looked more than a bit feminine.

"One and the same," I stated with a fake-ass smile, lying through my teeth.

I was *never* that man.

The guard who recognised me elbowed the other and saluted. A few more seconds of awkwardness followed as no one seemed to be able to deny the fact that it was the '*Prince' of Kitaxia*, here in the flesh before the city gates.

"I'm so sorry I didn't recognize you, your highness! You look... not quite yourself," the first guard said before he bowed his head at his fellow's elbowing.

I rested a hand on the pommel of my sword, hoping I looked impatient, trying to avoid looking down at my bound breasts, or for the descending red curls that should be blocking my vision.

"Well, yes, a year at sea captured by pirates will do that to you. I have these fine men to thank for my rescue, thank god." Every word a needle jabbed into the back of my throat, but I had to. *I had to.* I did my best to adopt a flippant attitude, top tier royal bullshit. "I'm taking them to my grandfather to request a handsome reward. Now, if you would please?"

I motioned towards the gate, hoping to get my point across. The guard stammered before nodding, then bowing, then nodding again. It seemed he hadn't gotten a lesson in royal protocol. He turned to shout at the gate controllers on the wall above a moment later.

"Open the gate for the prince! You, you, and you, escort him to the palace!" He shouted, pointing at several men in armour with pikes and pistols, then to me.

It took everything I had not to correct him. To choose the path of least resistance.

It hurt, that fucking word. '*Him.*' I hated it. It felt like I'd been dipped in slime, looking like I did, being called such. A skittering feeling of vile disgust, a cloak of misery that I couldn't untie, its neck cord strangling me. It made me feel ill, my heart battering in my chest, a growing panic.

I was a *girl,* damn it.

Charlotte leaned in to suddenly whisper in my ear. "If you kicked his ass topless, think he'd get the message?" I had to bite down hard on my lip to stop from laughing at their words. I turned to look at them, flashing them a grin.

They gave me a sly wink, hand in their coat pockets, ready to draw the grenades I knew were there. All I had to do was say the word.

At least I had some reaffirming friends on this hellish rescue. Charlotte looked more at home with masculinity than I ever did, but still, I could tell they were also having struggles with hiding so much of themselves. It was in the shuffling of their feet, like they couldn't keep still. A restlessness.

I reached for them, giving their wrist a squeeze in thanks. In reassurance. We'd get through this together.

The gate crawled open as the rest of the guards moved into an honour salute, and the lead guard stepped aside. The newest guards to my entourage fell into step with my fellow crew, and off through the city we marched.

Through the lower city, mother's grand experiment in action.

The poor, the destitute, and the desperate. The sick, the broken, and the *dying*.

All would be saved, all would be forgiven, if you just found your way into a church. There would be food, there would be shelter, there would be community.

Providing you adhered to the church rules. The *Kingdom*'s rules.

Women were to be mothers, silent and obedient. Men were to be soldiers, to fight for kingdom and god.

The guards escorting me alongside Charlotte, Rodger, and Markus stared straight ahead, their armour stamped with not only the lion of my family's house, the symbol of the kingdom, but the bloody red hand of the Church of the King Undying.

That was a new addition since I'd left, and I didn't like it one bit. God asked much of Kitaxia, and despite both our roles in this country, I didn't consider myself devout. Mother on the other hand… Even being raised by her, I didn't know what she believed. Regardless, she was just doing her best to help it along. Why, though?

We made our way through the lower city, into the upper levels full of the churches and dormitories of people who'd accepted the faith, pleading themselves to kingdom and god. I dared not look at the people, for if I did, I would lose myself to anger.

"What in the *fuuuuuuck*," Charlotte's curse under their breath made me feel a *little* better that I wasn't losing my mind. "It's like it's one big cult," they mumbled under their breath.

"Now you see why I left," Rodger stated, even though he was alarmed himself.

He left before this had *really* started.

But finally, the palace gates stood before us. If the outer city gate was well-manned, this was a *fortress.* Easily a hundred or more guards stood ready and looking to kill on command, each holding a blade, a pike, or a rifle, all at their posts with determined professionalism.

"Declaring the prince, Nicholas August. Make way!" one of the guards escorting me shouted.

My jaw clenched, my fingers dug into my palms, my entire body *burned.*

Fuck them. Fuck *all of them.*

I wasn't *him.* I wasn't that name, I wasn't, wasn't, *wasn't.*

But lo, the point of the exercise was done.

The guards moved away. The gate opened. A hundred souls saluted for me, ready to die on their swords if I so much as suggested it.

Idiots.

I stomped through the gates, without another word, my little entourage in lockstep behind me until we passed the invisible barrier where the guards would not step, and they stayed on the other side of the gate as it began to close.

Leaving me, Markus, Charlotte, and Rodger on the path towards the towering castle before us.

No commoners were allowed on the palace grounds unless specifically invited.

The gates clanged closed, and I led my little party forward towards the great doorway where a footman stood still as a statue, nodding.

"Your highness. Welcome home," he stated, his eyes cast downward professionally.

With a sigh, I felt the ghost of an old life wash over me. Countless memories of greeting the footmen politely before going back up to my rooms to cry or get ready for some royal bullshit event.

I wouldn't have it.

"Where's my mother?" I asked. I wouldn't spend one extra second in this accursed place than I had to.

"Your highness, your princess mother is in a foul mood, and declared the lower levels of the castle off limits. Be on your guard," the footman replied.

Telling me without 'telling me'. Like they always did. Palace staff worked around mother's… *habits.* It was the only way to not wake up one evening with teeth in your neck.

"Dungeons then. Thank you. That'll be all," I stated, waving off the footman, and immediately wandering not inside the palace, but *around*, through the outer grounds.

I left the footman standing at the door, my entourage following after me confusedly. I felt a million questions at my back that waited until we were out of earshot.

"Holy shit that worked?" Markus stammered out behind me, making me stare at him over my shoulder. It seemed he didn't believe that I could deliver on my promise.

Rolling my eyes, I bit down on the pure anger that wanted to cuss him out. It wasn't time for 'I told you so's. Not yet.

But Markus wasn't seeming to let this go.

"Just... you, that was the perfect chance to—"

I groaned, rubbing a hand over my face, not giving a damn about the damn paints disguising me anymore. "Markus, if you say one more word, I will cut off one of your fingers, I swear to the Gods," I muttered, turning around to point a delicate finger into his chest.

He snapped back his retort, seeing how much I was not enjoying this line of questioning, and nodded.

"Good." I turned back around, leading them to where I thought the side entrance to the lower levels was. "I thought it was just... ah. Here."

I led our party to a quiet turret arching into the sky, heading towards where the turret met the wall, flattening where it should've curved. I poked a few bricks, missing the one I needed, getting it on the fifth try, the hidden passageway clicking open as the bricks attached to the door swung inward.

I waved them all inside, closing the door behind us.

"So, plan?" Rodger whispered as I once more took the lead down the stairway.

"Hope we don't run into guards, nobles, or my mother. Especially my mother," I muttered, raising a finger to my lips to silence them as I drew my blade.

Anyone past here would be an enemy.

It was quite possible that Mother's 'declaration' limiting who was allowed in the lower levels meant there'd be fewer guards down here.

But I didn't think I'd be that lucky.

We searched for hours, yet the halls were empty. Nothing frequented these halls but Kitaxia's long dead.

Or soon to be dead.

The dungeons below the palace were huge and sprawling, yet I knew my mother's favourite places to keep her 'projects'. But one workshop after the other turned up emptier than the previous one.

But then we found something more freshly disturbed.

One cell, separated from all the rest. I knew it as the place mother kept the most recently condemned to death. This one, unlike all the others, still had the tinge of torch-smoke in the air.

Someone had been here recently.

Inside lay a man who'd been dead for maybe a day or two. Bled dry like one of Claire's worst victims, and the rot had set in quickly as a result. Patches of bones poked out of his skin, already clean of fluids.

But there was something on the floor in front of his cell that shouldn't have been there.

Claire's sword, covered in long-dried blood.

Only hers had that intricate basket design that I obsessed over, the metal-smithing downright drool-worthy. That sword was *beautiful*, unique, and just frankly astonishing to see her use. To see it here, in this dark and depressing place felt like disturbing a tomb.

"What in the Goddesses' names is *that* doing here," Rodger whispered from behind me as I knelt beside it, picking it up as if it were a long-lost babe. I would *not* leave this sword behind. Not in this accursed place.

With a careful finesse, I held it close, no matter the bloodstains. I gave out a teary laugh as I nuzzled the sword's handle, making

Charlotte pat me on the back.

Claire was here. And mother had her.

Which meant...

"Fuck," I mumbled, sheathing my blade and taking Claire's up in its place. She would absolutely want it back.

I'd made an obvious misstep. Claire was a *Vampyri*, which meant mother would need a *Vampyri* prison. And there was only one place in all of Haxla for such a prisoner.

We need to go into the Vault.

I silently cursed mother and the whole damn royal family, myself included, for the existence of such a place.

The Vault was from the time of the Blue King, first ruler of Kitaxia. My ancestor.

Legend said he had to fight against a coven of witches in order to claim the land Haxla was founded on, but discovered their lifespans were tied to his own. Neither the witches nor the king could die while the other lived.

And so he had captured them and created the Vault in which to bury them in the deepest pit he could find. His hopes for immortality were quashed though when his son betrayed the witches in a plot to overthrow the Blue King, by filling the Vault with fire, burning them alive.

And it was in that same Vault that mother hid her most important toys and experiments, reinforcing the very walls with chains strong enough to hold even the strongest of prisoners.

It was so deep below the stones of the palace that the light of day could never touch it.

That was where Claire would be.

Now sure of where to go, I led them down into the depths of the dungeons, where no living soul dared to go, down past rusted stairs and levels of disuse serving no purpose other than a passageway from above to below.

I'd only been down in the Vault once, where mother had tried to instill in me... the necessary 'iron will' for ruling Kitaxia one day. She had put a knife in my hand and told me I wasn't leaving the vault until I slit a captured man's throat.

Three days later, he was dead of starvation and I wasn't too far behind and mother admitted defeat. Not that she ever meant the throne to go past her.

I grimaced as memory after memory of palace life surfaced in my mind, and I reached up to tangle my fingers in my hair in comfort, only to stop and feel a wave of sadness bounding around inside my chest at what wasn't there.

I couldn't stop now. The die was cast, and everyone was counting on me. If I made a single misstep... we'd be lost down here for hours.

No one had disturbed these levels other than to go to the Vault in generations.

We each held a torch, making our way ever downward as echoes of... *something* began to reach into our ears from below.

"Any idea what that is?" Rodger asked in a whisper, to which I shushed him immediately. Mother's hearing was legendary throughout the palace. But she'd likely already heard us.

The noises of ghastly wails made me feel all but certain that we were on the right path.

Finally, the orange glow of torches glowed in the chambers ahead of us, betraying the Vault's location, as the staircase that had felt never-ending, finally ended.

The corridor widened and before us stood the great door to the Vault, now long ago rusted into uselessness, ajar just enough for two men to step into it shoulder to shoulder. The seal of a great lion on its front long faded away... but even now our family took it as their symbol. It hung on every Kitaxian banner from warships to castles.

I hadn't been down here in so long... I shuddered at the memory from a lifetime ago.

We stepped ever so closer to the great door just as a scream echoed from inside, and it took everything I had to hold in place. I finally recognised the wailing.

Claire.

Her scream died into a quiet sob, her voice mingled with another, the mumbling details lost in the echoing against the stone walls.

I motioned the others forward as they all drew their blades. I doubted it'd be enough against mother, but I could hope that luck was on our side.

We stepped through the Vault door, into the bright well-lit room beyond, and made our first intrusion into one of the realms of the hells.

Claire was nowhere in sight, but what greeted us made all of us gag in disgust.

An orange glow flicking from the few lights set into the walls illuminated a simple desk. It sat in the centre of the room with a plain looking chair, a few sheets of paper, a writing quill, along with several tools of science, and a few vials of blood. Behind, lay an archway to some darkened room where the screams must be coming from.

But shoved into the corners of the room lay countless bodies in pieces, stripped of clothing, all disposed of with malice into ugly piles, left to rot. Blood seeped silently from newer ones, others stank of rot, showing bones reaching out of the maggots. Where the blood was still fresh, it pooled towards a great drain sitting in front of the desk in the centre of the room.

The stench was unimaginable.

Another scream echoed from the room beyond, past the piles of rot, and we stepped quietly past the desk, trying to avoid the sticky pools of coagulated blood soaking the stony floor.

Stepping closer towards the room beyond the small archway, our torches bringing new light into the room, where a figure stood with her back to us.

A laugh in the blackness as our torches made the light claw further into the dark, and I recognised the shape of mother standing with a small knife. Another table stood nearby with an arched chair, yet this one grander than the last with a plethora of bloodied instruments between us.

And beyond her, another shape taking form in the dark, kneeling before her with outstretched arms...

Claire.

Every muscle in my body ached to go to her. Free her from the chains that tied her arms to the corners of the ceiling and the bolts tying her legs to the floor. She was bleeding all over, no shirt covering her.

Her body was a broken mess of open wounds, some healed, some not, some actively knitting together, her eyes, staring at us with remorseless hunger, pupils dyed red.

"Claire..." I couldn't help her name escaping from my lips, as mother's shoulders rolled back in a silent laugh.

"Ahhh. There he is. My *son*." Her voice echoed off the walls, hitting me from all directions.

I winced at the misgendering, finally shifting my gaze from Claire towards my mother.

Mother looked like me. Or I looked like her. A pale reflection of each other. One bright and alive, the other dead yet still standing, glaring at me with her icy blue stare.

Gods did I ever hate that I looked like her.

At least I was taller, broader in the shoulders. I'd hoped that I'd looke even more different after a year apart. She certainly looked the exact same. I wasn't sure if I should laugh or puke.

She was my age when she'd turned cold... Into a *Vampyri*.

"Now both of my children have returned to me. Both failures in their own right. How depressing," she said with a smile, walking ever so gracefully towards me, her arms outstretched as if welcoming me into an icy hug.

"And who are these fine gentlemen you've brought? Don't tell me you've brought me a snack, my boy," she said with that accent from another world. I still don't know where she'd gotten it from, it was nothing like the Kitaxian one.

I shook my head, my cheeks heating with shame at every remark.

"They rescued me, mother. I was hoping for—"

"Don't lie to me, boy. I hate it when you lie," she interrupted, twirling the knife she had in hand between her fingers.

Fuck.

I looked from her to Markus, to Charlotte, and finally to Rodger. They barely masked the terror they must be feeling. Mother had that effect on most people.

But it was now or never.

I gave them the briefest of nods, before going in for a stab with

Claire's sword.

The point of her beautiful blade weighed so heavy in my hand, but my jab was short, quick, and *perfect*. I was the best duelist in the palace.

But my skill was nothing when compared to mother.

But I also *knew* that.

Because as expected, she disappeared, too fast for the human eye to track. I predicted that she would likely jump behind me in ambush, so I twirled in a corrected swing...

Only to slash air. Because she hadn't gone for me.

She'd gone for Charlotte.

She appeared behind them, one hand reaching from behind to cover their face. They reached up to try and pry her fingers off, a muffled scream echoing from behind mother's hand.

"Enough of this, my son," Mother demanded. "You will stand down, and order these buffoons to drop their blades. Maybe then I'll make their deaths quick. Otherwise..."

"Mother wait—" I screamed, but she wasn't listening. She never listened, but Gods I wished she would this once.

She reached around with her free hand, and plucked out Charlotte's eye as if picking a fruit from an evening walk, throwing it to the floor with a smirk and a roll of her eyes, as if to say 'oops!'

I was certain Charlotte's scream would haunt my nightmares for the rest of my life. It echoed off the walls, as it reared up into such a high pitch, before gurgling down into a sob.

All the fear I felt in my gut at seeing mother shifted to rage, as I tightened my grip around the handle of Claire's sword.

I had a plan, but it didn't involve anyone getting *hurt*.

"Moira!" Claire screamed out, sagging against her bonds behind me. I knew I shouldn't let my eyes off of my mother, but I wasn't ever in my right mind where Claire was concerned. I spun around on the spot to look at her.

"R-r-r-run!" she screeched, her mouth hanging open, fangs on display.

Even now, she looked at me with a terrifying hunger, licking her lips and running her tongue over her fangs as she told us to flee.

Charlotte had already lost an eye, and Claire was hurt. My plan was becoming harder to put into motion by the second.

I had one chance. I tightened my grip around her sword... breathed out, and dropped it to the floor.

"Fine! FINE!" I pleaded, shifting back around to face my mother, but she was gone. Disappeared.

Charlotte lay gasping on the floor, blood trailing in between their fingers as they grasped at their face. Rodger and Markus stared at me in disbelief. "Please," I begged both of them. Rodger looked ready to spit an angry rant at me, but followed suit.

Markus held his ground.

I tilted my head just enough away so that my right eye was out of where I thought mother might be, and gave him the tiniest of winks.

I had one shot to make it count, and I couldn't let any of them get hurt. It was now or never.

I trusted him, but sometimes I wonder if he trusted me.

He stilled for a moment, was sure he was going through everything I was too. Surprising me, he finally dropped his blade.

"Alright mother. Please. Don't hurt them," I murmured to the empty room, stepping forward, holding out my arms.

We'd done this more times than I could count.

We'd fight, scream at each other, she'd threaten to kill me, and then I'd admit defeat, we'd hug it out like nothing was wrong, and I agreed to put on the costume of masculinity once more until it became too unbearable for the millionth time.

Rinse, repeat.

"That's a good lad," she muttered, before appearing out of the darkness behind Rodger, kicking his leg out from underneath him, its snap making me want to cry as I realised that it sounded far too much like the snapping of ship lumber. Rodger yelled out as he collapsed to the floor, and the squeak Markus made was heartbreaking.

Rodger was on the ground, holding his leg, Charlotte the same, clutching their face.

Markus, staring from the monster that was apparently my mother, to me, and back, probably wondering if he was next.

Mother stepped forward past him, ignoring him completely, as if she was in a court dance.

Before she wrapped her arms around my shoulders awkwardly, letting out a sigh like she *missed* me.

We'd never fit together well, me and mother. I tried to remember how it felt to have her arms around me like when I was little.

When she'd sang me to sleep, told me stories about legendary pirates from ages past... But even now, I remembered that she'd never been that person. More than once she'd just assumed she had, told me she did. Tried to make me remember that way, but it was Dad who sang me to sleep, told me stories.

Even before she had turned, I was nothing more than a bother to her. I was a tool, a plaything, to be taken out and used as necessary, and then promptly put back into the cupboard where I belonged.

I was *hers.* She never listened to me, never really cared, and worst of all, never apologized.

That would require her realising she'd done me wrong.

And now here she was once again. Taking my love, my family, and my friends, because I was *hers.*

But no more.

Her cheek was cold to the touch where it met my face, and I tried not to shudder. It was so much like Claire's... but Claire sought out heat like a man dying of hypothermia. She always had a hint of it on her person. A warm drink in hand, a plethora of blankets, standing near a fire...

There was always some warmth to Claire.

I doubted the nine burning realms themselves could warm mother up.

She pulled back slowly from our awkward embrace, Markus now trying to do his best to take care of Rodger and Charlotte, while I stared death in the face.

Mother kept her hands on my shoulders as she pulled just enough away.

Just enough.

"There you are," she murmured. "I'm so glad you've seen sense and returned to us." Her nose just a few inches from mine, looking satisfied with herself. "Now, as soon as I deal with your troublesome... *partner* and her miscreants, we shall see about getting you back to Seven Peaks. You've always wanted to see the Forge cities, haven't you?"

Her grin was wide, and unlike Claire, she went above and beyond hiding her *Vampyri* features.

Fifteen years, and I could count how many times I'd seen red in her eyes and fangs over her canines on one hand.

But if anyone was the monster in this room, it was her.

And I would end her.

I'd let my hands go dead at my sides rather than hug her, and as she pulled away, my hand drifted up my back, and into the under-layer of my jacket, where I'd gone out of my way to put the one thing I knew would hurt mother.

The Scarwood stake. The same one mother had likely put in the Count's hands, meant for Claire.

Claire had given it to Jacine to throw overboard, and I'd stolen it. It took some quick woodcarving to swap it with another piece of similar looking wood.

As far as Claire and Jacine were concerned, it had been thrown overboard.

I was still worried about needing to possibly fight off Claire at the time, and thought there was no better option than Scarwood. *Vampyri* were near impossible to kill without one.

I pulled it out of my jacket, shoving it up under mother's ribs. Into her heart. I couldn't deny the feeling of cruel satisfaction. Justice for a life lived with a genocidal monster.

She screamed briefly as the smell of burning flesh met my nose, and tried to pull away from my arms as the stake bit into her core, and then just as quickly, her scream silenced.

She collapsed backward into an ugly pile on the floor, still as the dead, the stake sizzling in her chest. Paralyzed.

Not breathing, her body was too still. The illusion of life was gone entirely from her person. She really did look dead.

"M-m-m-Moira..." Claire whispered behind me. I turned away

from my mother to stare at the woman I loved, taking a half step towards her before she roared and snapped her jaws towards me, held back by her chains.

My heart lept in my chest as I jumped backwards, nearly tripping over mother's body, and Claire's face twisted into guilt.

Even as she licked her lips.

"I-I-I'm sorry," she stuttered, face twisting back and forth between pure adoring *hunger* and an ugly grimace as she fought it.

She motioned her head towards the others behind me.

"Get them—" her voice rumbled with a growl towards us

I shifted from where I stood, looking at our master-at-arms and gunner, breathing quickly on the bloody floor, Markus fashioning a splint from torn fabric and pieces of blood-strewn tools. Charlotte sat up, wrapping some torn shirt around their face.

She's telling me to get us out of here.

"Not without you," I whispered, leaning down to grab mother's wrists.

"Moira—"

"Shut up, Claire," I demanded, leaning down to drag mother closer and closer, her body surprisingly light.

To kill her, once and for all, I'd need to behead her, throw the head and body into separate fires, all with the stake still in her heart to keep her paralyzed.

Or at least, that's what I *thought*. Mother hadn't exactly been forthright about her secrets in killing her, and there were only so many books I could read in stolen hours when I thought she wasn't looking.

Regardless, I needed to kill her. And Claire needed blood. A *lot* of blood.

I could take care of the rest later. Right now, I needed to help Claire. I stopped just out of Claire's reach with mother's body, Claire arching forward in her bonds towards me. I had to make sure to keep the stake in my mother's ribs otherwise she'd wake up.

Because we would *not* get a second chance.

"Shut up, and *eat*," I ordered, lifting mother's wrist to Claire's mouth.

It took everything in me to not look at Mother, so I instead looked at Claire's face.

I didn't know if *Vampyri* could drink each other's blood, but we didn't exactly have a lot of options. The dead bodies in the previous room looked multiple days old, and I knew *Vampyri* needed fresh blood.

Claire had all but a second of defiance with mother's offered wrist before hunger won out. With animalistic need, she bit down messily onto mother's wrist and drank.

And then it was like a light had turned on behind her deep red eyes. They *glowed*.

She drank, and drank, and drank... And I could tell *something* was happening. I didn't know what, but if it settled her hunger, then I would be happy.

With only the sounds of Rodger's heavy breathing, Charlotte and Markus muttering to each other about transportation, and the sound of wet swallowing from Claire's throat... her eyes slowly, ever so slowly, began to turn a pale shade of green.

She finally spat out mother's wrist, and I all but shoved mother off of me.

"Claire?" I murmured, unsure. My hand shakily reached out to her cheek.

And then she smiled, that agonizing smirk on her face that she only made for me, and I knew she was back.

"Moira," she whispered, and I threw my arms around her, lowered my face into her neck and sobbed as the tears began to fall.

"Claire... I'm here."

EPILOGUE

Claire

I sat on the forecastle railing, the dip and bob of the *Wraith* cutting through the waves soothing as we cut south-by-southwest, back towards Souris.

I wasn't sure of what to feel. I was still half convinced this wasn't a dream. If it was, at least it wasn't one of the horrid ones Moira had to nurse me through.

But I knew better.

Sitting there, watching the sunrise over the port horizon, feeling the morning rays begin to burn into my skin, finally I got the familiar reminder that I really was here. The pain sizzling across me light bit into any exposed area it could, reminded me that I was back aboard my ship.

Not back *there*.

The survival urge in my gut pushed me to get into the shade, to throw my coat over my shoulders, *anything* to get out of the blasted sun…

But I forced myself to stay. Sitting on the railing, looking at the dawn.

Our star was pitiless, but the pain was… welcome. Its burning warmth told me I was alive, reminded me I wasn't in the dark cold cells of Ameritia's clutches.

The light became almost blinding, but I ignored it. Its heat became intrusive, but I stomached it. It was determined to wipe me off the face of the planet, but it would not be rid of me.

Not that easily.

If I could survive Ameritia's cuts, I could survive a little fucking *sunshine*.

So many thoughts tossed about in my head like ships in a storm.

What had Ameritia *meant*? How tangled was this web that I'd been working inside of? Whose purpose was I *really* serving?

And what would happen now that she was dead?

All these *questions* that none of us had answers for. Ameritia had taken the answers to her grave.

For she left no writing, no evidence, not even a hint of her plans. We combed through the royal apartments after, and found *nothing*.

Less than nothing.

Only the chambers of a woman long dead, and the corpse of the king.

I snorted at that revelation. Kitaxia was waking up this morning to the fact that their entire royal family was dead or missing. Years I'd talked rebellion, but the king had been dead for longer than *I* had.

Nothing but a skeleton in his bed with a crown. Ameritia had been pulling the strings for years.

But then… what had she meant? That her father had announced my capture to the people? The King sure as fuck hadn't, he was *dead*.

Regardless, we had no answers, and were as aimless as the Kitaxians.

We weren't holding out hope that there were still survivors mulling about in Souris, but we figured it was better than any other option we had for now. At least there we could stock up on water and food for the long haul... to wherever we ended up.

Whatever was decided, we'd at least go together. There were plenty of other ports that could be made into the new 'Port Sable' so to speak.

And staring directly into the sun, I thought that maybe, just maybe, it was time to think bigger. Moira was right all that time ago. I'd been so focused on revenge, I hadn't been thinking of the big picture.

Pirate port? *Ha.* No, that was small-time thinking.

'Port Sable' as it was, was nothing but a port where the moment we became inconvenient, the powers that be would come for us.

While Ameritia had her tools cutting me to pieces, I thought about all the power she had. All the power a single woman possessed because a nation invested her with it.

If I'd been in her position... I'd have done it differently. I'd have done it right.

Vampyri or no… the idea of a nation, a united people... There was something there. I mean, arguably, if I could craft a 'nation' of pirates on the *Wraith*, and make it fair and equitable to all… What would a full on *pirate republic* look like?

Now *that* was an idea.

The sun was starting to win this little battle I had picked between us, yet I still found myself smiling despite the pain, excited for the future. That I had a loose idea of… *something* I wanted to build. But there was a threat to that idea, some greater power at work that Ameritia had answered to.

Ameritia. What a fucking bitch.

I still didn't really understand what had happened when I drank her blood. It felt like drinking raw *power.* I was stronger now, faster. Even my hunger was a lesser force in my throat.

I could stand here in the sun and *not* seethe in as *much* pain.

Still hurt like hell though.

But the days I spent in that room haunted me still, despite the culmination of my revenge.

Oh, the absolute satisfaction of cutting off her fucking head. Moira was happy to pass that part off, which was completely understandable. Besides, we had needed to get Charlotte and Rodger back to the ship as soon as possible.

The smell had been the worst part. Of Ameritia's corpse in the flames... It was not likely to leave my memory anytime soon.

In hopes of turning my mind back to reality, I refocused on the morning sun, testing my newfound willpower as far as it could go. Its light simmering on my skin, making the hunger rumble in the back of my throat, pushing me to move somewhere, *anywhere,* that wasn't the brightness of the unyielding day.

"Claire! What in the Goddesses' names are you doing!" Moira's voice shouted from across the weather deck, over the hustle and bustle of the crew. I turned to spy her over my shoulder, standing in the doorway to my—now *our* cabin, her hand on her hip.

I sighed in humble happiness. She was *safe*. She'd come for me. And now no one would ever come for her again.

I was so fucking glad that everyone was okay, relatively speaking.

Rodger and Charlotte had taken their injuries in stride, Rodger remarking that he thought he'd 'look quite dashing with a cane' and Charlotte cackling as they explained that they 'still had one good eye to shoot fuckers with'.

And Markus was staying on 'until something better came along'.

Still, I wish they hadn't had to make such sacrifices, just for me.

Moira's short hair was another such sacrifice, and I could only imagine how it pained her. Gods how she'd cried once back on board, like I'd never heard her cry before.

Hours in my arms, crying for such a small thing that obviously meant so much to her.

That she had sacrificed it for *me* did not go unnoticed. I would cross any ocean, face any trial, strike down any foe for my love.

She hadn't believed I would accept her as *her*, and I had to tell her in a million different ways that hair or no hair, she was not only a woman to me, but the woman I wanted more than anything else.

I imagined that it would take us both ages to come to terms with what we'd had to go through for each other. But we had just that, all the time in the world with each other.

And that's all I wanted. All I needed and more.

I stood up from the forecastle, dropping down to the weather deck, and sauntered towards my cabin, letting myself be swallowed up in its comforting darkness and into the embrace of the woman I loved.

Several leagues north of the *Wraith*, on the cold shores of the Norlondia, and within its grandest city-state, stood a woman.

She was a giant of a woman, tall even by Norn standards, and while decorated in the finery of someone born of wealth, she had not inherited any of it. For her face told the story of a battle-hardened woman, covered in scars and scratches, some decades old. It suggested of her a warrior's life, and this is what she saw herself as first and foremost.

A warrior.

But, second to that, she saw herself as a leader of her people. A uniter. A banner for her people to flock to for the betterment of their country.

If only, to her at least, they wouldn't be so damn *idiotic*.

For she may be a warrior and a leader, but she had the one thing most of the other leaders of her people did not.

Cunning.

And because of this very trait, she was, as she almost always was, staring at a map.

Facing her from this map was the ultimate question of her people, the question every Norn who ever dared call themself Jarl has ever asked.

How to unite Norlondia?

Fourteen Jarldoms remained, of which hers—the Jarldom of Viken—was by far the largest. Through no small effort of the woman in question. By blade, by conquest, and by treaty, in a single lifetime she'd taken Viken from one above average forge-city with a harbour, to nine forge cities and enough territory to begin drawing the concern of Kitaxia and Varcna. She'd expanded Seven Peak's trade and reach across the Great Divide and had embassies around the world.

Itha-Ki and Draculesti, both powers on the Western and Eastern Continents respectively, knew the name Seven Peaks, and desired the goods she had mandated to be produced.

She thought of herself as unstoppable, that *surely* the other Jarldoms would fall in line and bend the knee to her eventually. Could they not *see* the amazing things she was doing for their people?

But Gods above and below, they were clinging to power like screaming children clinging to their toys before bed.

She clicked her tongue, wondering about the several different diplomatic plays she had working. There was the Councillor in Varcna that showed promise, the expedition north with the Sea-people's confederation, and—of course, she laughed as she remembered that whole disaster with the Kitaxian king's grandson.

Vessia. The pirate. Opportunistic crow.

She snorted, her eyes wandering the map as if she could spy her ship from here like the Goddess of Skies.

Five years Vessia had been pillaging the trade lanes, almost exclusively targeting Kitaxian shipping like she had a grudge to settle. If the rumours were true, that they really had hung her back in the day and she'd somehow lived… Maybe she did.

But still, it was no skin off the Jarl's back that Vessia had kidnapped the pious fool's noble scion.

She had other irons in the fire.

She began to wonder about the possibility of a false flag operation among the Jarldoms in the north-east before a knock came on her door, disturbing her thoughts.

"Enter," her booming voice commanded, echoing off the stone-walls surrounding her office.

One of the unbloodied nobles rushed in, breathless.

"Jarlessa, there's news from Varcna. This just came in from a ship in the harbour." He bowed his head ever so slightly, before shoving a note on top of the map in front of her.

With an annoyed sigh, she took it in her calloused and scared hands, reading it briefly.

"Oh. Well," she said, surprised. The words she'd just read were impossible to her. "Kitaxia's attacked Varcna?" she murmured, confusedly. It was unexpected. Kitaxia was a power focused *inward*. Control. It was all about control with Kitaxia. The only times it struck *outward* was to control its own population in some way. Why start a war?

"That's the *official* report, but please read on, Jarlessa," the noble stated, almost excitedly.

She did so, and was yet again surprised, her mouth hanging open as the letter imparted its revelations unto her.

"You're joking. Souris as Vessia's port—No. Actually, yes. That makes perfect sense."

The facts turned in her head, like she was examining a coin by flipping it over and over and over. And then it coalesced. Everything, clicking into place.

Vessia had the king's grandson.

And Kitaxia knew where Vessia was. Likely the whole time.

Those rotten bastards.

"What was the result of the battle?" she asked, her eyes searching the map for the far south-eastern corner of Varcna, Souris so far south it was almost off the map.

"Vessia sank all the attacking ships, but the settlement was destroyed. A pyrrhic victory I'm afraid."

Jarlessa Isolde Viken smiled.

A desperate pirate, and a royal prince, she could use that.

"Perfect. I need a fast ship, and someone important enough to send a message to Vessia that is believable, that we don't mind dying on us if she decides to kill them anyway."

She stared at her map, grinning for the first time she could remember.

Finally, the opportunity she'd been waiting for.

Now, not only Norlondia was at play.

The entire Great Divide could be hers, if she played her cards right.

Reviews are critical for the success of indie books.
Please consider leaving an honest review of this book
and any other you read via whichever review platforms
you use. You'll make a lot of indie authors very happy.

If you want the latest news about upcoming books by
Leslie Allen, join the mailing list at leslieallen.com

ACKNOWLEDGEMENTS

In the years since I decided I was going to publish this work, I always knew what I was going to put into this section. I'd dreamed of it, as I think most writers do. The people I'd thank, the multitudes of appreciation of those who got me to the point where I felt safe and comfortable enough to write, and gave me the tools and knowledge to put this book in as many hands as possible. Yet now that it comes time to it, I'm speechless. Years of effort to get to this moment, and I'm struggling to put it all into words. But I'm going to try my best.

To my wife… Gods. What can I say? You've been with me every step of the way from the very moment I decided to start writing again, supporting me the way only you know how. You've given me space, freedom, and safety to explore my creative side. Supported me with love and caring that I didn't know existed or deserved, and allowed me to feel safe being a bit silly for the first time in my life. I've said I love you a million million times, and I'll say it a million million more. I love you with every fibre of my being, and I love that you love me. Even if I'm a clothes pirate.

To Cat; Dearest, without you, none of this would've happened. You've given me not only the tools to see this through, but also the love and care that make me feel like I can stand tall and proud with my work. We fit together so well, and if it's been a delight getting to know you, it's been a wonder getting to love you, a blessing getting to adore you. I will always thank the Fates that they eventually threw us together, despite years of near misses, and I'll remember standing in the tide chasing hermit crabs with you for the rest of my days.

To Dad; I wouldn't be the woman I am today if it wasn't for you, and I'm so so proud to be your daughter. Through thick and thin, we've gotten through the best and worst of life, and if it wasn't for you and Karen shoving a book in my hands and telling me I was grounded if I didn't finish it, I wouldn't have the love of literature I'd have today. (Redwall, for those curious as to which book) I'm so thankful that of everything, you taught me how to be kind. I love you, and can't wait for you to come home.

To Mummsy and David, Thank you for making space for me in your lives, and the kindness you've given me. You made being an out of place east coaster on the west coast a delight, and I hold the memory of watching the lightning with you from the shores of Cape Breton dearly.

To Potato, you know what you did. (I love you)

To my beta readers and editors, but especially Lilian Zenzi, thank you. The insights you gave to this book helped me realise the worst and best of it, and made me find the hope in my own writing. You showed me that I had something special that deserved its place in the world, and I'm so thankful for what you've shared with me.

To Walker, Allie, and Tabby, Thank you for entertaining my rants about publishing, my never ending pushes to read everything I've ever written, and my general complaints about society as we know it. I can't wait to see you all again, and hope that the Fates are treating you kindly despite your places across the world. May we meet again soon.

And of course, thank you, dear reader. For taking the chance on a newbie indie author, on gay vampire pirates (I mean, that is a hells of a sell, I don't blame you) and getting far enough to read this in the first place.

Protect Trans kids, progress is not linear, and you are the most dangerous thing in the woods.

Till next time,

Leslie

GLOSSARY

While not every book needs a glossary, for folks unfamiliar with naval terminology this book might be challenging to understand without some knowledge of how ships work. Let this basic glossary help you get ship-shape.

Aft - To the rear of the ship.

Binnacle - The closed glass housing that holds the ship's compass and more delicate navigational equipment.

Brig - A heavy merchant ship, usually at least the size of a warship, but with no weaponry, using that space for cargo.

Broadside - When a ship appears lengthways to give the maximum possible number of guns ample firing angles.

Captain - The executive officer of a ship. Often regarded as the end of the law on a vessel.

Fore - To the forward end of the ship.

Forecastle - The raised platform on the front of the ship.

Foremast - The forwardmost mast.

Frigate - A ship designed for a good balance of firepower and manoeuvrability, typically having one large and continuous gun-deck.

Galley - The ship's kitchen.

Gundeck - A deck dedicated to hosting the ship's cannons.

Hull - The body of the ship.

Magazine - The closed off storeroom of gunpowder aboard a ship.

Mainmast - The centre mast, typically the strongest, widest, and tallest.

Mizzenmast - The rearmost mast.

Man-O'War - Any ship designed specifically for battle.

Mast - A tall upright post, spar, or structure, holding up the sails of a ship.

Master-at-arms - The ship's officer in charge of weaponry, and also something akin to a law officer aboard a ship.

Port - Left side of the ship.

Quarter deck - The raised deck on the rear end of the ship. Typically where officers and the Captain stand.

Quartermaster - The ship's executive officer, or second in command. Typically the crew's elected representative to counter the executive authority of the Captain.

Rigging - The ropes, pulleys, and knots that support the masts and sails.

Schooner - A speedy type of vessel, some of the fastest sail ships ever designed. Typically used for fishing, cargo, and even racing.

Sloop - A ship designed specifically for speed and manoeuvrability, lightly armed. Can sometimes also be called a 'Sloop-of-war.'

"Spanker" - The rearmost sail, often mounted to look like a giant leaf from the rear of the ship. National flags, and pirate flags, are often flown from this point.

Spar - The long poles of wood that hold the sails, attached to the mast.

Starboard - Right side of the ship.

"Tops" - The raised platforms built around the masts high up in the rigging.

Two-Decker - A ship with at least two dedicated gun decks. A large, heavy ship meant for taking and receiving punishment. These can have several dozen cannons.

Weather deck - The deck in which is exposed to outer elements on at least two sides. Typically the first deck of a ship that's outdoors.

ABOUT THE AUTHOR

Leslie Allen is a librarian, sailor, astronomer, and has travelled the world. Yet she somehow found herself back home in small town Nova Scotia.

She is often simultaneously plotting her next tattoo while sipping white hot chocolate and plotting the downfall of her characters. She devours stories in every medium she can find, but her favourites are movies and video games, and being eternally frustrated that they never go far enough.

Sails of Black and Blood: The Revenge of Captain Vessia is her first book.

Find her on Twitter, Tumblr, and Bluesky via linktr.ee/leslieiswriting
Or visit her website, leslieallen.com